"So you remember..." Jake breathed, his lips warm against her hair.

"Why shouldn't I?" Lani protested, electrically aware of his hands at her waist as they danced to the seductive rhythm. "And have you told my mother of that little encounter, or are you saving it for some more intimate occasion?"

His grip tightened. "Why shouldn't I tell Clare we've met before? As I recall it, you were quite provocative then. Not at all the passionless puritan you've grown up to be!"

"You—you—you're despicable!" she choked. Then suddenly her opposition crumbled. He was right. It was her own unwilling attraction to him that was driving her to these lengths. "Please—" she whispered, blind to everything but that she must get away before she betrayed herself.

"Don't," he said, moving his hand to cradle the back of her head, and the room swam as he rested his cheek against her quivering temple.

It was madness. But for now, no one else was aware of what was happening. They were alone on an island of needs and feelings and bonemelting closeness, and when his fingers spread possessively along the curve of her spine, she knew she was incapable of resisting him....

ANNE MATHER WILD CONCERTO

W🌐RLDWIDE

TORONTO • NEW YORK • LONDON • PARIS
AMSTERDAM • STOCKHOLM • HAMBURG
ATHENS • MILAN • TOKYO • SYDNEY

Published July 1984

First printing October 1983

ISBN 0-373-97009-9

CHAPTER ONE

LANI ST. JOHN was fourteen years old when she first saw Jake Pendragon.

She was holidaying with her parents. It was one of the few occasions when her mother and father were able to get away together, and instead of flying off to some exotic destination, they had driven south and west, into Cornwall.

Lani could never remember a time when holidaying with her parents had not proved something of an emotional ordeal. They were both so different, the one so volatile, the other unwilling to compromise on the smallest detail, and out of their normal environment, they generally fought like cat and dog.

Theirs had been an unlikely combination at best. Clare, Lani's mother, was a soprano with an international reputation, while her father was a solicitor, dry and prosaic. Lani had never been able to understand the swift and passionate infatuation that had brought them together, and more than fourteen years on, their marriage was shaky in the extreme.

This holiday, Lani learned in later years, had been a last-ditch attempt to patch up their differences, to iron over the cracks in their relationship and try to recapture the magic they had lost. It hadn't worked. As soon as

her mother had discovered that one of the reasons her
father had brought them to Cornwall was to enable
him to visit a wealthy client, she had taken off back to
London, leaving Lani to pacify her father as best she
could.

Mount's Bay, even in April, was not the warmest
place in the world, and Lani's first sight of Tremorna
Point was with an iron gray sea leaping greedily about
the headland and an icy wind rattling the windows of
Mrs. Worth's castle.

Of course it wasn't really a castle. It only looked that
way to Lani's imaginative eyes, but sitting beside her
father in the car they had had to hire that morning—
her mother had taken their car—she knew a sudden
uplift to her spirits. Even her father glanced her way in
mutual understanding, the morose expression he had
worn since her mother's departure vanishing beneath a
smile of shared conspiracy.

The Worth residence stood on Tremorna Point, apparently oblivious to the elements. It had a sloping
gabled roof, with scalloped crenellations that gave it its
medieval appearance, and narrow shuttered windows
below overhanging eaves. It was not a particularly attractive building. Its stone-built facade gave it a rather
grim appearance—an impression that was heightened
by the reflected light from a wild and stormy sea.

When her father brought the hired car to a halt below the steps that led up to the pillared front porch,
Lani thrust open her door and got out without waiting
for his permission. Curiosity, and her vivid imagination, were already painting pictures of the occupants of
the house, and she half expected some dour man-

servant to open the door and bid them enter in deep sepulchral tones.

The reality proved to be very different. In fact, the door did open as Roger St. John was getting out of the car to join his daughter, but Lani didn't think the young man who emerged could be anyone's butler. Butlers didn't wear collarless sweatshirts and tight-fitting jeans that made her own designer cords look quite respectable; nor did they have untidy dark hair that needed cutting, or adopt that air of amused condescension when they found someone staring at them. Her own cheeks turned quite pink when he returned her appraising stare, and she was glad when her father came between them and went to meet the young man.

"Mrs. Worth is expecting me," he said, giving Lani time to recover herself. "My name's St. John. Roger St. John. Mrs. Worth's solicitor."

"Oh, yes. Mr. St. John." The young man held out his hand and Lani's father shook it. "The old lady did say something about a solicitor. I remember now. Won't you come in? I'll let her know you're here."

Turning, he went back into the house, and Lani's father beckoned for her to join him. "Come on," he said, "stop daydreaming. At least it sounds as if I'm going to get to see her."

Lani hurried to catch up with him, and as his arm came across her shoulders, she said perplexedly, "Have you tried to see Mrs. Worth before?"

"Oh, yes." Roger St. John nodded. "Several times. Unfortunately, Mrs. Worth can afford to be elusive, and I'm afraid she doesn't have a great deal of interest in the handling of her estate."

"Is she very rich?" asked Lani, as they passed beneath a carved lintel and entered a gloomy carpeted hall. Her father smiled.

"Very rich," he agreed, looking speculatively around him. "You wouldn't think it to look at this place, but I can assure you, our client does not have to worry about providing for her old age."

Lani glanced about with interest. The hall was not particularly wide at this point, but it seemed to broaden beyond the curve of the stairs, and she could see potted plants and hanging creepers, as if that latter half of the hall formed some kind of conservatory. To left and right of them four darkly paneled doors, two on each side, apparently gave access to the living rooms of the house, but all of them were closed, and Lani wondered where the young man had gone.

Her curiosity was satisfied a few moments later when he appeared on the balcony at the top of the stairs and invited her father to come up. "The old lady is waiting for you, Mr. St. John," he said, although his lips twisted as he said it, as if his words were not exactly the truth. However, Lani's father was only too eager to grasp any opportunity, and bidding her to accompany him, he started up the staircase.

The stairs began just beyond the second door on the left-hand side of the hall. They mounted three steps before taking a right turn, then ran the rest of the way up the side of the hall. At the top of the stairs a long landing, railed above the arch of the hall below, gave onto a long corridor with several doors and passages leading from it, and Lani realized the hall below had been deceptive. The house was much bigger than it had appeared downstairs, and she colored in embarrassment when she realized the young man was observing her evident bemusement.

"It's this way," he said laconically, leading them down the corridor to a door that lay at the far end. Lani had scarcely time to register the scarred and shabby paintwork before he had thrust open the door with a flourish and ushered them into the room. "Mr. St. John, old lady," he announced with deliberate irreverence, and the old woman propped against the pillows of the huge bed that dominated the room regarded him with obvious hostility.

"I told you, Jake—" she began, only to break off abruptly as Lani followed her father into the room. "What's this?" she cried, her lips curling in distaste. "Jake, who is this child? Get her out of my bedroom at once. You know I don't allow children in my room."

Lani thought the old woman looked a little like a witch, curled there in the middle of the big bed, screaming vituperatively at the young man, who seemed less than perturbed by her utterances. She decided she didn't like Mrs. Worth any more than Mrs. Worth liked her, and she didn't like her bedroom, either, crammed as it was with lots of little tables and chairs and overstuffed sofas that smelled of decay.

"I'm afraid Lani is my daughter, Mrs. Worth," Roger St. John was explaining rather awkwardly. "Her mother... well, Lani has been left in my care, and naturally I couldn't leave her at the hotel."

"Your domestic arrangements are no concern of mine, Mr. St. John," the old woman declared harshly, and the young man smiled as he made to leave them.

"Where are you going?" Her sharp eyes had caught his movement and her words arrested him. "I didn't give you permission to leave us. Kindly come in and close the door while I'm talking. It's drafty."

He sighed then, his hand on the doorknob, but made no effort to do as she had bidden. "No time, old lady," he said, his dark gaze narrowed and indolent. "So nice to meet you, Mr. St. John—Lani." His mouth quirked. "I'll ask Hannah to come and show your visitors out later."

"You'll do no such thing!" The old woman was trembling with rage. "I haven't finished speaking to you, Jake. Where are you going? What are you going to do? I won't have my nerves shredded like this just because you have some crazy idea—"

"Later, old lady." The young man's eyes flickered broodingly over her visitors. "You know where I'll be. We can talk later—"

"All right, then take the child with you," the old woman commanded shrilly. "I'll not have a child in the room while I have a confidential conversation. Take her with you; entertain her!"

"Oh, but—" began Roger St. John doubtfully, only to have his words overridden by the young man's anger.

"I'm not a baby-sitter, old lady," he averred, turning toward the door, but this time Lani's gasp of indignation caused him to hesitate.

"I don't need anyone to take charge of me, daddy," she exclaimed, facing her father with burning cheeks. "If...if Mrs. Worth has no objections, I'll go for a walk along the cliffs. I could do with some fresh air. It's rather...stuffy in here."

"Are you sure?" murmured her father anxiously, and Lani nodded her head vigorously.

"I'm sure," she declared, avoiding the young man's faintly admiring eyes. "I'll only walk a short way. Then I'll wait for you in the car."

Mrs. Worth snorted. "There's no need for you to wait in the car, girl. Hannah—my housekeeper, don't you know—she'll give you a glass of lemonade in the kitchen, if you ask her nicely."

"I don't want a glass of lemonade, thank you," said Lani stiffly, and sensed rather than heard the young man's muffled amusement. "I'll see you later, daddy. Don't hurry. I'll be quite all right."

She passed the young man in the corridor, and he inclined his head in mocking salute as he closed Mrs. Worth's bedroom door behind her and followed her down the stairs. But Lani was determined to ignore him after the way he had spoken to her, and she was taken by surprise when he stepped in front of her before she could open the front door.

"Bravo," he remarked lazily, and although she wanted to treat him frigidly, like the heroines did in all the novels that were smuggled into the school dorm during term, she couldn't prevent her lips from twitching when his broke into a grin.

"Well," she said, by way of justification, "she's a horrible old woman! Shouting like that and ordering people about. I don't know why you put up with it. Do you work for her or something?"

"Or something," agreed the young man, opening the door. "She's my grandmother. Only don't tell her I've told you. It's not something either of us is very proud of."

Lani stepped into the chilly air outside, shivering in spite of the warm red corded anorak she was wearing over her sweater. She wondered how...Jake, if that was his name, could stand to be without a jacket, but in all honesty, he didn't appear to feel the cold.

They descended the steps together, and suddenly Lani wished she had not been so vehement in her bid for independence. She liked talking to him. She liked his dry humor. And when he started across the expanse of salt-sprayed turf that was all that separated the house from the edge of the cliff, she asked him where he was going.

"Home," he answered her shortly, pushing his hands into the pockets of his jeans, and Lani's green eyes widened.

"Don't you live here?"

"At the house? No. My home is down there." He pointed toward the cliffs. "Out of sight of the road."

Lani followed him to the edge of the cliff and peered over rather nervously. A path, practically overgrown with weeds and marsh grass, wound its way down the cliff face and disappeared. But jutting out from the rocks she could see the wooden slats of what appeared to be a precariously placed veranda, and she turned to look at him.

"That's your house?"

"The Sea House, yes."

"The Sea House," Lani repeated. "What a lovely name for a house. May I see it?"

Jake regarded her quizzically. "I thought you wanted to go for a walk."

"I wanted to get out of that room," exclaimed Lani

crossly. "Besides, you and your grandmother spoke as if I was a child. I'm not a child. I'm almost fifteen!"

"And I'm twenty-three," Jake retorted dryly. "I admit you're a little too old to need a baby-sitter, but you're definitely too young to be seen going home with me!"

Lani sighed. "That's silly. You're not a sex maniac, are you?"

"It's not something I talk about," remarked Jake with a mocking grin, but Lani was frustrated.

"Really," she persisted persuasively, "what harm can it do? I only want to see the house."

"I think not," said Jake flatly, pushing back his hair with a rather impatient gesture. "Look, I'm sorry if I offended you earlier, but I'm not used to dealing with embryo feminists. Put it down to experience." He grimaced. "Now, I've got some work to do. Goodbye."

Lani would not be put off that easily. "What kind of work?" she asked, as he started down the cliff path. "I thought you said you worked for your grandmother. What do you do? Look after the house for her?"

"Among other things," he agreed, glancing back over his shoulder. "Enjoy your walk. It's been nice meeting you, Lani."

"It's been nice meeting you, too," murmured Lani grudgingly, watching until he disappeared from sight. Suddenly, all the excitement had gone out of the day, and she hunched her shoulders broodingly as she turned to look up at the windows of Mrs. Worth's house.

How could the woman treat her grandson like that, she wondered, scuffing her canvas shoe against the turf. She really was an objectionable old witch, and if she was Jake she wouldn't have put up with her shouting for another minute.

He really had been rather nice, she reflected, allowing his dark image to blot out the rather ugly lines of Mrs. Worth's mansion. Tall, lean and attractive, with that very dark complexion Cornishmen sometimes have. He didn't look at all like his grandmother, whose appearance had not endeared her to Lani in the first place, and remembering his lazy eyes and mocking smile, she wished she had not jumped so quickly to defend herself. Until then, she had thought her father epitomized everything she should look for in a member of the opposite sex, but Jake was nothing like Roger St. John. Her father was always so particular about his appearance, but he didn't look as if he'd been poured into his clothes. He was handsome, too, but his skin didn't look as if he had spent the past six months in the Bahamas, nor when he moved did he have that curious feline grace that gave Lani a peculiar feeling in the pit of her stomach. It was an odd analogy, but although Jake was almost exactly her father's opposite, Lani found him the most attractive man she had ever met.

Abandoning these thoughts, she turned to look down the cliff path again. The jutting veranda was still visible, and she sighed rather impatiently at the realization she would probably never know what his house was like. And why shouldn't she, she asked herself defensively. There was no law that said which way she should take her walk.

Telling herself she was only doing this so she would have something exciting to tell her friends when she went back to school after the Easter holidays, Lani took a cautious step down the steeply sloping path. The only other occasion she had had anything exciting to report was when her cousin Robin, who was two years her senior, had kissed her under the mistletoe at Christmas, and that had been so revolting she had had the greatest difficulty in convincing her best friend, Libby Forster, that she had actually enjoyed it. Robin's boyish lips had been so wet and sloppy, and his breath hadn't been particularly pleasant, either. Lani had been glad when her father appeared and broke them up, even if she had told Libby she had been furious.

Beneath her, the sea was splintering against the headland, the surf leaving traces of foam on the rocks. It was unnerving to imagine what could happen if she missed her footing, and halfway down she was tempted to climb back up again. She hoped her father wouldn't come looking for her. She doubted he would approve of this escapade, but she was committed to go on, if for no other reason than that the idea of turning around on the path was almost as terrifying.

The house was there below her now, and every now and then on the wind she heard the sound of music. Jake must have turned up his stereo to compensate for the noise of the ocean, she thought, scrambling down the last few feet. Whatever he was doing, obviously he liked an accompaniment, and she knew a moment's compunction that he might think she was prying.

The house itself was an amazing feat of engineering. Someone had blasted a shelf in the cliff face, and the building had been erected under the overhang. Two-storied, it nestled on its shelf as if it had always been there, the wooden veranda Lani had glimpsed from above jutting out on a cantilevered framework that was embedded deep in the rock below. The view from the veranda must be magnificent, she thought admiringly, brought to a dead end by a flight of steps that led up to a side door. But obviously, this was as far as she could go, unless she chose to disobey Jake.

The music was clearly audible now, the plaintive sound of one of Chopin's sonatas, she decided, having studied musical appreciation for two years. She was surprised. She would have expected Jake to like the kind of modern music she enjoyed, but there was no accounting for tastes.

The music stopped abruptly a few seconds later, the discordant sound of someone bringing his hands down hard on the keys making the strangely poignant melody come to an end. Lani was surprised, as much by the angry disruption of the piece as by its sudden cessation. It wasn't a recording at all.

Curiosity getting the better of her, and glad she was wearing soft-soled shoes, Lani cautiously mounted the steps to the veranda. She didn't attempt to knock at the door. She knew if what she suspected was true, she would be even less welcome right now. Instead, she tiptoed around the curve of the building and peeped hastily through the first window she came to.

"What the hell do you think you're doing?"

She was almost scared out of her wits by the angry voice that accosted her, and unable to remember anything she had seen, she turned to face her irate captor. He had shed the sweatshirt now, and in a short-sleeved cotton body shirt, he looked even more attractive. But his expression was not attractive—it was almost ugly—

and Lani expelled her breath anxiously, not sure how to handle this.

"I was walking," she offered hurriedly. "I heard... music."

"So you came to spy on me?"

"No."

"What else would you call it?"

"I was curious, that's all," exclaimed Lani, recovering a little from her fright. "I'm sorry. I didn't know the path was private. I... I thought it might lead somewhere."

"It does. Here," he declared flatly.

"I meant somewhere else," retorted Lani, straightening her shoulders.

"So what are you doing on my veranda?"

She shrugged, realizing there was no point in lying to him. "I'm sure you know why," she murmured. "I heard how the piece ended. I wanted to see if it was really you playing."

"It was." He lifted one hand to massage the muscles at the back of his neck. "So now you know." He shrugged. "Oh, what the hell! You might as well come in. I was just about to make myself some coffee. Do you want a cup?"

Lani let her breath out with a gulp. "I'd love one," she said, and after a moment's hesitation, he indicated that she should precede him around the side of the building and in through the door she had seen earlier.

She found herself in the room she had glimpsed briefly through the window, and she was surprised to discover that although it was quite comfortably furnished, there was no carpet on the floor. Instead, the floor was wood, and despite being worn in places, it still gleamed with the patina of age.

Dominating the room was the piano she had heard him playing as she'd descended the cliff path. It was a polished baby grand, and she wondered briefly how it had ever been transported down the cliff. Right now it was strewn with sheets of the lined manuscript used by a musician when composing or arranging a piece of music. But Lani didn't pay these much attention. She was too interested in examining the rest of the room and its long narrow windows that overlooked the stormy ocean.

"I'll get the coffee," said Jake, crossing the room to another door that apparently led to the kitchen and stairs. "Sit down. Make yourself comfortable. I won't be long."

Lani seated herself on one of the two chintz-covered sofas that faced one another across the hearth. A log fire was smoldering in the grate, the only kind of heating she could see, and she held her hands out toward its warmth, looking about her eagerly.

Apart from the piano, there were books in the shelves by the fireplace, and a drop-leaf table was pushed into one corner. There were several chairs and a small cabinet, and a stereo deck with a pair of speakers fastened to the walls. There was no television that she could see. Everything had a practical use, as if it was necessary to conserve space, and it seemed odd that he should be living here alone when his grandmother had so many unused rooms up at her house.

He came back carrying two earthenware mugs of coffee, and she took one gratefully, smiling her thanks.

"I didn't expect this," she murmured as he seated himself opposite her.

His mouth twisted as he countered wryly, "What did you expect?"

Lani colored. It was an annoying habit, one she hoped she would grow out of, but now she tried to hide her embarrassment by changing the subject. "Was the piece you were playing by Chopin? I've been doing some musical appreciation at school, and I recognized the style."

Jake spread his legs apart, cradling his cup between his hands. "What else do you do at school?" he inquired without answering her question. His dark eyes appraised her. "Let me guess—you like art and drama."

Lani resented his mocking tone. "As a matter of fact, I enjoy maths and English best," she said defensively and not altogether truthfully. "And sports. I love swimming."

"Really?" Jake regarded her intently. "Well, yes, I guess you are tall for your age. What do you plan to do when you grow up?"

"I *am* grown up," retorted Lani shortly. "If I lived in any other country but England, I'd be old enough to get married. That's hardly childish, is it?"

"Okay." His lips twitched. "What do you plan to do when you leave school, then? What do your parents want you to do? Follow in your father's footsteps?"

"Perhaps." Lani was growing tired of this kind of questioning. "Tell me about your work, Mr. Worth. Are you a professional pianist? Ought I to have heard of you?"

"Pendragon," he said flatly, momentarily confusing her. "My name's Jake Pendragon. My mother was the old lady's daughter."

"Oh!" Lani sipped her coffee. "That's unusual, isn't it? Pendragon. It sounds sort of . . . Arthurian. Is it?"

Jake gave her a wry look. "You ask a lot of questions."

"So do you." Lani was indignant. "And you must admit it is rather mysterious, you living down here alone, and your grandmother having that big old house to herself."

Jake lay back against the cushions, allowing the mug to rest on his flat stomach. "There's no mystery," he declared carelessly. "The Sea House belonged to my mother. When my grandfather died, he left it to her. Now that she's dead, too, it's mine."

Lani frowned. "I see. But when your grandmother dies—"

"—her money goes to charity, or at least, I hope it does," responded Jake with alacrity. "She doesn't really approve of me, any more than she approved of my father." He paused. "My mother married without her parents' consent, you see, and the old lady's never forgiven her—or me—for going against her wishes."

"The mean old thing!" Lani was sympathetic.

"No sweat." Jake shrugged. "I don't want her money. I guess that bugs her, too."

"But you like living here?"

"Yes."

"And you do spend some time with your grandmother."

"Why not? She's a lonely old woman."

Lani shook her head. "I wouldn't."

"Oh, I think you would." Jake regarded her quizzically. "Old people are like children. They like to be humored."

Lani glanced at him between her lashes. "I suppose you think you're humoring me."

"How could I? You told me you weren't a child."

Lani was about to make some indignant retort, when she caught the humorous glint in his eyes and smiled instead. "Do you think I'm very precocious?"

"I think it's time you were leaving," replied Jake briefly, pushing himself up and finishing the coffee in his cup. "Come on, I'll walk you to the door."

"Oh, must I?" Lani was disappointed.

"I think you must," affirmed Jake, getting to his feet and offering her his hand. "If your father finishes his discussion with the old lady and comes looking for you...."

"So what?" Lani shrugged as she took his hand and allowed him to pull her to her feet. Close to him as she was, she was able to look up into his eyes, and she took full advantage of her moment of intimacy. "I'm not doing anything wrong, am I?"

"Aren't you?"

For a moment he didn't move away, and her slim young frame brushed tautly against the hard strength of his body. It was as if there was an electric current between them, a sudden absence of air that left her feeling shaky and breathless. She could feel the heat of his body, smell the clean male scent of his skin, and she sensed the sudden tension that put a barrier between them.

"No," she got out breathily at last, realizing how in-experienced she was, and he turned abruptly away.

"No," he agreed, his mouth compressing grimly. "But I wouldn't advise you to try that trick on anyone else."

"What trick?" Lani feigned ignorance. "I don't know what you're talking about."

"I think you do," retorted Jake, walking toward the door. "Have you got all your belongings?"

"Oh. . .yes." Lani glanced about her unhappily. "I didn't bring anything. Only myself."

"Hmm."

Jake inclined his head indifferently and, swinging open the door, he stood aside to allow her to precede him through it. The chilliness of the air gave Lani a reason for the shiver that feathered down her spine, and she stepped out onto the veranda feeling cold and miserable.

"Goodbye," she murmured, turning to face him, and Jake inclined his head in a silent acknowledgment. "I—you're not—mad at me, are you?"

"Mad at you?" Jake made a sound of impatience. "Go away, Lani. You're much too young to care one way or the other."

"I'm not, I'm not." Lani caught her lower lip between her teeth. "Mr. Pendragon: *Jake*! Please, don't be angry. I just wanted you to realize I'm not a child, that's all."

"You're much too provocative for me to treat you any other way," responded Jake harshly. "But don't worry. I won't tell your father, if that's what you're afraid of."

"I'm not afraid. . ." began Lani, and then broke off with a sigh of resignation. "Oh, well, I'd better go, hadn't I? I'm not going to convince you of anything standing here, am I?"

"No." Jake was adamant. "Can you make it? To the top, I mean?"

"I guess so." Lani nodded, and then, as he was about to turn away, she added, "If. . . if daddy has to come here again, would you let me come back?"

"I don't think that's likely."

"No." Lani was honest. "But. . . would you?"

There was a moment when Jake regarded her with faintly impatient eyes, and then his features relaxed. "I don't think I could trust myself," he remarked mockingly, causing the hot color to flood Lani's cheeks once more, and with an angry compression of her lips, she turned away. But it was humiliation that caused the unwelcome brush of tears against her cheeks, and the realization that to him she was still just a child.

CHAPTER TWO

LANI'S PARENTS WERE DIVORCED the following year.

The upheaval in the family had a disastrous effect on Lani's O levels, and her examination results were so poor that her father withdrew her from the boarding school she had been attending and sent her to a finishing school near Berne.

This idea didn't work out either, however. Lani was unhappy in a foreign country, and although she quite enjoyed exercising her French, her interest in social and economic skills was negligible. She pleaded to come home, to take her mother's place in their now empty house in Kensington, and after suffering her tears for more than six months, her father gave in.

For a time, this seemed a satisfactory solution. Lani practiced the skills she had acquired by choosing menus when her father was obliged to entertain clients and by acting as his hostess on these occasions. A blossoming teenage daughter was always an asset when the conversation began to falter, and it was generally agreed how like her father she was and how lucky he was to have such a charming companion.

The occasions that Lani saw her mother grew less frequent. When the divorce was first instituted, she spent most Sundays with Clare at the luxurious apartment she had leased off Belgrave Square. But since the separation Clare's career had flourished, and without any family commitments, she was able to accept longer and more demanding engagements. She had been invited to Glyndebourne the previous summer, and her success there had prompted a long tour of Europe, playing many of the most prestigious operatic roles. Her absence had lent a certain detachment to her relationship with her daughter, and when she returned to London, Lani sensed the distance swelling between them. Besides, she was fast approaching an age when her mother would prefer not to remember she had a daughter, and it was impossible not to associate this with gossip she read about Clare and various of her leading men.

Nevertheless, it was her mother's evident independence that finally forced Lani into making a decision about her own career. She had drifted for long enough, and while her father was quite content to see her filling her days with entertainment and shopping, she was beginning to find it boring. She was seventeen and she wanted to do something with her life.

In spite of what she had told that arrogant young man she had met at Mrs. Worth's house almost two years ago, she had enjoyed art at school, and although she knew she had no ability to either sing or act, drawing was something she had always found relaxing. With her father's endorsement, she enrolled that autumn at a college of further education, taking creative art and design as her prime subjects.

Lani enjoyed the experience of being involved with other people again. She had forgotten what it was like to have to run for the bus in the mornings, of gulping down her breakfast while it was still dark and returning home in the evenings feeling tired but content. She liked the course and her fellow students, all of whom were young and enthusiastic and eager to succeed.

It helped, too, to ease the hurt she sometimes felt in knowing that her mother seldom made any contact with her these days. Since the divorce was finalized, they seemed to have drifted farther and farther apart, and when she read about Clare Austin—her mother had always used her professional name—in the gossip columns, she found it hard to associate herself with the sought-after and successful woman her mother had become.

Only on birthdays and at Christmas did Clare make an effort to remember her daughter. Lavish gifts arrived, tied in expensive wrapping paper: delicate lingerie and exotic perfumes; a bracelet, inset with diamonds; a leather coat, soft and supple to the touch. Lani knew her father did not like these offerings, seeing them as Clare's way of salving her conscience for her neglect of her daughter, and in all honesty, Lani too would have preferred a more personal gift. But rather than promote any more bitterness between them, she pretended to enthuse over each item, only showing more enthusiasm for whatever her father had bought.

Lani found it was easier at college not to mention her mother's identity. As Roger St. John's daughter, she was just one of the crowd, and she preferred the anonymity. Only her closest friends learned of the relationship, and their usual comment was that they would never have guessed — that Lani was nothing like her.

Sometimes Lani reflected that their desire to re-assure her was not entirely complimentary. She knew she did not look a lot like her mother, but as Clare Austin was considered a very beautiful woman, it was not something of which she should be proud. Her pale skin and unruly auburn hair were nothing like her mother's pink and gold beauty. Only her eyes, with their curiously green translucence, gave any distinction to Lani's otherwise ordinary features. She was attractive, she supposed, if one liked tall girls with rather more flesh on their bones than was entirely fashionable, but compared to Clare Austin's slender elegance, she felt gauche and lacking in grace.

Toward the end of Lani's second year at college, she accidentally discovered she had an ability for telling children's stories. Her cousin Robin, whose kisses so long ago had caused her such revulsion, was now married and struggling to raise a family in north London. Sarah, his wife, had upset all their plans by producing twins within a year of their marriage, and once they were old enough to be left with a surrogate aunt, Lani had offered to baby-sit.

She found she loved it. The two-year-old boys took to their new "aunt" with great enthusiasm, so much so that before long, Lani was having difficulty in getting them to bed. The only way she persuaded them to stay between the sheets was by telling them stories, and soon she found herself making up tales about giants and gnomes and dragons and a witch whose spells kept going wrong. Her imagination knew no bounds, and in the weeks that followed, it seemed a natural progression to produce her sketch pad and illustrate her narrative, making the twins laugh with her humorous use of caricature and clever interpretation.

It was Robin himself who suggested she should do something with her inventiveness. Coming home earlier than usual one evening to find Lani fast asleep across her drawing pad, he had gazed in amazement at the lifelike sketches jumping out at him from the page, and although Lani had belittled her ability, he had been adamant.

"You've got real talent for this, can't you see?" he exclaimed, startling Sarah by his vehemence. "Lani, maybe your mother's artistic talent has been handed on to you in this form. For goodness' sake, don't knock it! You could sell these, I'm sure of it."

Lani grimaced, gathering her pads and pencils together. "Anyone can draw," she stated, putting her belongings into the canvas satchel she carried on her shoulder. "These things don't amount to much, honestly. You should listen to what Mr. Harris says about my lack of style."

"I don't give a damn what this Mr. Harris says," declared Robin fiercely. "No tutor is going to give his student credit for having this kind of talent. It's like—it's like comparing pop music to the kind of thing your mother sings. It appeals to the masses. But what's wrong with that? The masses are the people! Not the elite few!"

"Oh, Robin—" Lani gave Sarah a helpless look, and the other girl smiled.

"Take no notice, Lani," she advised her dryly.

"Robin thinks everyone is desperate to make money. It comes of having to struggle to make ends meet for the past four years."

"Well, why not?" Robin was impatient. "It's obvious Lani's taking this course at college to enable her to make a career for herself. Why shouldn't it be in this? Hell—she could write the books and illustrate them. You know how crazy our two are about her stories."

"Well...."

Lani could tell that Sarah was loath to admit she didn't think Lani's stories were very original, so she said it herself. "Do you have any idea how many people tell stories to their kids?" she asked Robin. "I'm flattered you feel that way, but really, let's not get carried away by this."

Robin heaved a frustrated sigh. "What's the matter, Lani? Are you afraid to try? Are you afraid you'll fail? Has your mother's success destroyed every scrap of belief in yourself?"

"*Robin!* That's a foul thing to suggest!"

Sarah was appalled, but Lani weathered his contempt. "Perhaps you're right," she admitted ruefully. "It isn't easy being Clare Austin's daughter. Perhaps I am afraid to know the truth."

"Oh, hell, Lani...." Robin looked discomfited now, and his wife cast him a reproving look.

"Well?" she demanded. "Are you satisfied? Now that you've made Lani humble herself, can we let this subject drop?"

Robin thrust his hands into his trouser pockets. "I'm sorry, Lani," he muttered, lifting his shoulders. "You know me: I always do the wrong thing."

"It's okay, honestly." Lani felt slightly embarrassed herself. She hadn't taken his remarks to heart half as much as Sarah imagined, and actually she felt sorry for him now, anticipating the argument that would ensue once he had taken her home.

In the car on the way to Lani's home in Pelham Court, she managed to keep off the subject, but as they circled the fenced-off square of grass and poplar trees that formed an island in the middle of the small cul-de-sac, Robin asked if he might borrow her drawings to show to a friend of his.

"I really would appreciate it, Lani," he said, making her refusal that much harder to voice, and with a helpless shake of her head, she gave in.

"Who is this friend?" she asked suspiciously, as she handed the sketch pad over, and Robin grinned.

"Just a friend," he replied, with some gratification. "See you next week. Sleep tight."

In fact, Lani forgot all about the drawings during the next few days. It was nearing the end of term, and she had plenty to do preparing her portfolio for the yearly assessment. Also, her father had developed a rather worrying cough, after being caught in a seasonal rainstorm, and she was kept busy making sure he did as the doctor had advised and remained in bed. Roger St. John was not a good patient. She constantly found he'd been using the phone when she was out of the room, keeping in touch with his office and the work load that seemed to have increased since Lani was no longer dependent upon him for companionship.

It was almost a week later that Robin got in touch with her again. Lani was surprised to hear from him.

She was planning to baby-sit for him and Sarah the following evening, and her first thought was that they had changed their plans. But Robin soon disillusioned her on this score, explaining that his call had nothing to do with their arrangement and that his real reason for ringing was because he wanted her to meet a colleague of his at lunch the following day.

"Tell me," he went on, "do you have any of that stuff of yours written down? The stories you tell Tom and Edward, I mean," he added. "If so, could you bring it along?"

Lani sighed. "What are you up to, Robin?"

"Are you really interested?"

"Of course I'm interested." Lani could feel a flutter in the pit of her stomach. "Who is this friend of yours you want me to meet? And why does he want to meet me?"

"Can't you guess?" Robin sounded smug. "He's an agent, of course. His name's Miles Rossiter."

"Oh, Robin." Lani glanced helplessly around the paneled walls, glad that her father was in bed for once and couldn't hear her here in the hall. "How does an architect get involved with an agent?"

"We went to school together," replied Robin airily, "and he's very interested in your drawings. He says if the standard of writing is anything like the standard of drawing, you may have a real chance of success."

"But Robin—"

"Have you? Any of your stories written down, I mean?"

Lani hesitated. "One or two."

"Terrific. Bring them along. One o'clock at the Mermaid. Don't be late."

IN THE MONTHS THAT FOLLOWED, Lani had every reason to be grateful to Robin. Her first book, *Matilda, the Butterfingered Witch*, was published the following spring, and its success led to another and another. By the time her course at college was completed, she had produced her fourth story about Matilda, and she had offers to expand her characters into a weekly picture strip for a children's magazine. Her biggest break-through came six months later, when the first set of three books was sold to a publisher in the United States. If the books proved successful with their wider audience, Lani knew she could consider herself totally independent.

Her association with Miles Rossiter was one of the bonuses from her involvement in writing. From the beginning he proved to be a good friend, and she knew she owed a lot to him, too, for his encouragement. At first, producing illustrations for something she had written seemed the height of conceit; and left to herself she might never have had the courage to go on. But Miles and Robin had had such faith in her, she had felt obliged to at least give them the benefit of the doubt, and the outcome more than justified their belief.

Her father was thrilled, she knew, although she suspected he would have preferred her to have a more conventional occupation. Writing was an artistic profession, and he had had enough of the artistic temperament in his life. However, Lani made sure she never indulged in any fits of temperament when he was around, and indeed she seldom experienced the kind of irritability her mother had often displayed.

Clare seemed delighted by her daughter's success.

The day Lani's first book was published, she sent an enormous bouquet of flowers and a bottle of champagne to toast Lani's future, adding she was sorry she could not be with her, but she was presently on tour in South Africa and would not be returning to England until the following year.

Lani didn't mind. She had the feeling her father was happier when Clare was out of the country. The constant dribble of gossip about her mother was wearing for both of them, and Roger St. John did not find it easy to accept that his ex-wife was associating with men other than himself. Much of what was written was probably exaggerated, Lani thought, but she knew her father, who was normally such a rational man, believed every word. He seemed to have aged a great deal in the years since the divorce, and Lani felt the strain of his disillusion. When Clare was away, however, the columnists had other fish to bait, and Lani had realized there was no truer saying than *out of sight, out of mind*.

Nevertheless, toward the end of Lani's course at the art college, news began to filter back from the United States that Clare Austin was being seen frequently in the company of a young concert pianist. Lani heard about it secondhand from Sarah, and she imagined how galling it would be for her father if Clare and the young American returned to London together. Until now, Clare's escorts had all been of a respectable age, but at forty-two, Clare had apparently found herself an admirer twelve years her junior.

"You can't blame her," declared Sarah, watching the anxious mixture of emotions crossing Lani's face. "I mean, it's not as if she looks her age, does she?

If I look like that when I'm forty-two, it will be a miracle!"

"And me," murmured Lani dryly, touching the tumbled weight of hair that refused to adhere to any formal style. "Oh, but Sarah, can you imagine how daddy is going to feel if she brings him back to England with her?"

Sarah shrugged her shoulders and moved to a more comfortable position on the couch. With another baby due in a matter of weeks, she felt too complacent to offer any real objections.

"It is more than five years since the divorce," she reminded Lani reasonably. Then, with more animation, she added, "Anyway, she's bound to want to see you when she does come home, so you'll probably get to meet him. Now that you've become so successful, she'll want to show you off."

"I doubt it." Lani grimaced. "I remind her of her age. I don't think even Matilda's success can overcome that obstacle."

Sarah looked sympathetic. "How long is it since you have seen her?"

"In the flesh?" Lani frowned. "It must be nearly two years. Yes, it was about a year after I started at college. We had a drink together after a concert."

"A drink?" Sarah shook her head. "Is that all?"

"It was at her apartment," declared Lani defensively, but she knew what Sarah was thinking. She had thought the same when she arrived at her mother's exclusive penthouse in Avenue Mews and discovered she was expected to take her place among a crowd of Clare's admirers.

"Oh, well—" Realizing Lani would prefer to change the subject, Sarah swung her feet to the floor. "It's time I went to collect the terrible twins. Goodness knows how I'll cope when the new baby arrives. If it wasn't for Robin's mother—"

She broke off abruptly, realizing how inappropriate her words must sound to the other girl, but Lani merely smiled. "I'll go and get the twins," she said, reaching for her sweater. "You make some tea. You know how much I enjoy showing off the new car."

LANI HERSELF was in the United States when her mother returned to London. She arrived unexpectedly one dull November day, and Lani heard about it from her father when she telephoned him from her hotel in New York.

"It was on the evening news," Roger St. John declared tautly, revealing the bitterness he still felt whenever he spoke of his ex-wife. "She flew in with this latest man of hers—the pianist. He's apparently got a concert at the Albert Hall, and she's here to support him."

"Oh, daddy!" Lani sighed, wishing she was there to comfort him. "I don't know why you let her upset you so. There have been men before. I expect there'll be others. Just try and put thoughts of her out of your—"

"She says she's going to marry this one," her father interrupted her harshly. "She says she's really in love this time." He snorted impatiently. "What she really means is that the years are slipping away, and she's not getting any younger!"

"Oh, daddy," said Lani again, feeling the helplessness that distance evoked. But her father was not finished.

"You realize this. . . pianist is almost twenty years younger than she is, don't you?" he grated. "Twenty years! My God, she's old enough to be his mother!"

"I — I heard that it was twelve years," admitted Lani unhappily. "But what does it matter, daddy? It's her life —"

"*Pendragon,*" snapped her father, ignoring her. "What kind of a name is that? Another gimmick to attract people's attention, I suppose. Classical music for the masses, and a handsome concert pianist to bring in —"

"Pendragon?" Lani had heard little beyond her father's first words. "Did you say Pendragon?"

"Yes. That's his name. Pendragon. I thought you knew."

Lani shifted back on the soft velour cushion of the couch, catching her breath with difficulty. Pendragon, she was saying to herself disbelievingly. *Jake* Pendragon. Oh, it couldn't be!

"Are you still there, Lani?"

Her father's voice sounded anxious now, and Lani hastened to reassure him. "Yes. Yes," she said faintly, "I'm still here. I'm sorry. What were you saying?"

"I thought you knew about this young man," exclaimed her father peevishly. "I can't believe you haven't read about them. The papers have been full of it."

Lani, who had spent the summer avoiding reading reports about her mother in case she inadvertently blurted something about her to her father, now shook her head. "It was Sarah," she confessed honestly. "Sarah told me. But she didn't mention the man's name."

"Huh." Her father sounded put out. "Well, I should have thought you'd have had some interest in the man who is reputedly going to become your stepfather. My God! The idea's obscene! Your mother must be out of her mind."

Lani couldn't argue with him right then. The possibility that her mother's new boyfriend was the arrogant young pianist she had met all those years ago in Cornwall needed some consideration. She was annoyed to find that her palms were moist and she was decidedly shivery. It was the cold, she told herself fiercely, promising to turn up the heat the minute her father rang off. But nothing could alter the fact that she had received a shock.

"Enough about her," said her father suddenly, to her immense relief. "You haven't told me what you've been doing. Did you see Lyn Vincent? What did he say?"

"Oh, yes." Lani expelled her breath cautiously. "I saw him. We had lunch together, as a matter of fact. He's going to do the books almost exactly as they were. He says he's rushing the first one out to meet the Christmas market."

"That's great news." Her father endeavored to infuse an element of enthusiasm into his voice. "So when will you be home?"

"The day after tomorrow, I hope." Lani heard the sigh of relief her father gave, and hurried on, "Lyn wants me to come in to the office tomorrow to discuss one or two modifications they've made in the dialogue, so children here can understand more easily. But I should be back by Thursday."

"I'll look forward to it." Her father was vehement. "Do look after yourself, darling. You're all I've got."

Even though she turned up the heat after her father's call, Lani could not rid herself of the chill that persisted long after she went to bed. Lying in the isolated luxury of the king-size four-poster, she could not dismiss the possibility that her mother's Pendragon was *her* Pendragon. The name was simply too unusual, and the fact that they both played piano was too great a coincidence to ignore. But how could it be? The man she had known had lived in Cornwall, at the Sea House. The man her mother was involved with was reputed to be an American. She must be wrong. She must!

She sighed. Not that she had any reason to regard Jake Pendragon as her property, in any case. She hardly knew him. Just because she had exaggerated their encounter for the benefit of the girls at school did not mean she should start believing her own stories. Nevertheless, she had spent several sleepless nights in the dormitory, composing letters to him that were never sent, and for a time she had believed she was in love with him.

The upheaval in her family life had changed all that. Her parents' divorce had driven a wedge between fact and fantasy, and by the time she returned from Switzerland, she had lost her desire for romantic entanglements. Her father was alone and lonely and he needed her. Her own personal feelings no longer seemed important.

Of course eventually she had found friends of her own, male as well as female. She knew without conceit that men liked her, that she was popular. She was not beautiful, as her mother was beautiful, but that didn't bother her. She had no shortage of admirers, and she genuinely believed it was her personality that attracted them. She completely overlooked the fact that an abundance of red gold hair, combined with clear green eyes and a flawless complexion, had their own particular charm; and the long-legged litheness of her body more than balanced the voluptuous fullness of her figure.

Lani arrived at Heathrow on Thursday evening. A light drizzle was falling as she emerged from the aircraft, and she was relieved when her father detached himself from the crowd of waiting relatives and came to meet her. He looked older, she thought anxiously, even though it was less than a week since she'd gone away. She guessed her mother's return to England had proved a terrific strain.

"Did you have a good trip?" he asked, after their initial greetings were over and he was helping her into his sleek Daimler. "The weather's been appalling since you went away. It hardly seems possible it's still seven weeks until Christmas."

"The trip was okay," Lani replied, as they joined the M4 into London. "As a matter of fact, it was raining in New York, too, when I left." She grimaced. "We should be grateful it's not snowing."

"Hmm." Roger St. John was concentrating on his

driving. "I suppose you're right. In any event, your mother looks lovely and brown. I gather she's spent the past three weeks in Antigua."

Lani sighed. Her mother already! Couldn't her father think about anything else?

"You've seen her?" she ventured cautiously, and he nodded.

"Last night," he agreed. "On the box. She was being interviewed by that fellow who has that twice-weekly chat-show."

"Oh, I see." Lani relaxed a little. "You mean Chris Faulds. What a pity I wasn't here. Did she handle it well?"

"As you might expect," replied her father dourly. "Your mother was always able to handle interviews. She looked positively radiant. Whatever that chap's doing for her, it evidently suits her."

Lani winced. "He was with her?"

"Pendragon?" Roger St. John used the name contemptuously. "No. He wasn't with her. I don't suppose he was invited. Who is he, when all's said and done? Nobody's ever heard of him."

Lani moistened her lips. "I wouldn't say that."

Her father's hands clamped on the steering wheel. "Well anyway, Clare was alone. She looked . . . magnificent."

Lani bent her head, wishing her father would stop thinking about her mother. It could so easily become an obsession with him; Lani knew that better than anyone. It resurrected her fears that her mother's career was tearing him apart, and she wished he would be more willing to meet someone else. But Roger St.

John wasn't interested in other women, and his ex-wife's affairs filled him with disgust.

Lani slept late the next morning. The telephone eventually got her out of bed at noon. Blinking sleepily at Mrs. Evans when she came to wake her, Lani did a double take when she saw the time, and the elderly housekeeper made a soothing gesture as her employer's daughter sprang swiftly out of bed.

"It's only Mr. Rossiter," she declared, as Lani hastily pulled her kimono about her. "He did say not to wake you, but I thought you might like to be up."

"You were right." Lani cast a brief glance at her reflection in the dressing-table mirror as she swept her hair back with a careless hand. "My God! I look awful. Why didn't you wake me sooner? I intended to start work again today."

"Your father said to let you sleep," replied Mrs. Evans comfortably, following the girl down the stairs. "And I agreed with him. Besides, Friday's not a day to start anything. Wait until Monday. That will give me time to tidy the studio—"

"I'll tidy the studio, thank you, Mrs. Evans," said Lani firmly, picking up the receiver in the hall. "Hello, Miles. I'm sorry I've had to keep you waiting."

"Lani." The way he said her name was indicative of the affection he felt toward her. "Hey, I've missed you. How did you like New York?"

"It was...different," she admitted honestly. "The people were very friendly, and they made me feel very welcome."

"But you're not sorry to be home?"

"You should have come with me," she declared frankly. "New York is no place for a woman alone."

"I wish I had," exclaimed Miles with enthusiasm. "I can think of nothing I'd have liked better. It was just impossible for me to get away this week."

"I know." Lani forgave him. "Is that why you rang? To apologize?"

"No. I rang to invite you out to lunch, but it seems like you're not going to be able to make it, so how about dinner instead?" Miles replied at once. "We could eat at the Mermaid. Or at my place, if you'd rather."

Miles lived in a service apartment in a modern block near Hyde Park, but so far Lani had evaded any invitations there. It wasn't that she didn't like Miles, she did, and she was quite prepared to accept that in time their relationship might well expand in that direction. But for now, she preferred to keep it within certain limits, and they did not include eating at India Mews.

"I can't this evening, Miles," she said with regret, relieved that at least her excuses were genuine. "I mean—it was quite late last evening when I got home, and daddy—well, I know he'll be expecting me to have dinner at home this evening."

"Your father is a selfish old man!" remarked Miles succinctly. "For God's sake, Lani, I haven't seen you for a week, either. Don't I deserve any consideration?"

"Of course you do." Lani was not offended by his candor. "Maybe tomorrow—"

"Evening?" he asked suspiciously, and Lani gave a soft laugh.

"If you like."

"Where, and at what time?"

"You can pick me up here, if you like," offered Lani, after a moment's hesitation. "Then we can decide where we're going to eat."

"Are you sure?" Miles knew her father did not really approve of anyone connected with the artistic side of his daughter's life, and although the two men had met, they were not exactly the best of friends.

"Yes, I'm sure," declared Lani emphatically. Perhaps it would help her father get his own life into perspective if she stopped protecting him all the time. "Come about seven, hmm? I'll be ready."

"And I'll be waiting," Miles assured her huskily. "See you."

Lani was in the shower when the telephone rang again. This time she heard it, but deciding whoever it was could wait, she allowed Mrs. Evans to take the call. It could be Sarah, she reflected. Robin's and Sarah's baby girl was being christened on Sunday, and Lani was to be her godmother. Sarah could be phoning up to check that she was back. Turning off the tap, Lani reached for the towel.

"Lani! Lani, can you hear me?"

Mrs. Evans's anxious voice brought a quiver of apprehension to Lani's stomach, and wrapping herself in a towel, she stepped out of the shower and went to open the bathroom door. "Is something wrong, Mrs. Evans?" she asked, her long hair dripping onto the carpet. "Who was on the phone? Daddy?"

"It's not your father on the phone, Lani," exclaimed Mrs. Evans reprovingly, her expression eloquent enough. "It's your mother. It's Mrs. St. John. Do you want to speak to her?"

Lani's stomach took a downward plunge. "My mother?" she echoed faintly. It seemed years since Clare had last contacted her. "I—why, yes. Yes, I suppose so. Will you ask her to wait a moment, while I put on some clothes?"

In the event, Lani paused only long enough to wind her hair up in a dry towel and pull on the silk kimono, before descending the stairs once again. Curiosity and the sickening tightness of her nerves were forcing her to hurry when common sense was telling her to take her time. She was slightly out of breath when she picked up the receiver, and she could hear her heart pounding as she said unsteadily, "Mother?"

"Clare," came her mother's crisp tones, familiar even after all this time. "Call me Clare, darling. Everyone does. How are you? How's your father? It's so long since we've seen one another."

"You and daddy?" Lani was briefly confused, and Clare uttered a sound of impatience.

"No. You and I, goose," she exclaimed shortly. "It's time we got together. That's why I'm ringing. I want you to come to dinner tomorrow evening. Say about half-past seven?"

"Tomorrow evening?" Lani's thumbnail probed anxiously at her teeth.

"Yes, tomorrow evening," agreed Clare pleasantly. "You know where I live, don't you? It's still the same apartment."

Lani panicked suddenly. "I can't," she said quickly.

"I—I already have a date. I—I'm sorry, mother. Could we make it some other time?"

"Lani." Clare sounded hurt now. "Lani, do you mean to tell me you're going to put some pimply youth before your own mother?"

"Miles is not a pimply youth, mother," Lani exclaimed defensively, but she felt guilty just the same. After all, it was almost two years since she had seen Clare, and being invited to share a meal with her was not so much to ask.

"Miles?" Clare was saying now. "Miles who? Do I know him?"

"I don't think so. He's my agent," explained Lani uncomfortably. "I—how are you, mother? I missed your appearance on television the other evening, unfortunately."

There was a pregnant silence for a few moments, and then Clare resumed their conversation, her voice distinctly cooler now. "I assume your father knows I'm back in the country, doesn't he?" she inquired, without answering Lani's question. "Are you sure he's not behind this sudden reluctance to see me?"

"No!" Lani's denial was vehement. "It's just—well, I've been away, too, and. . .and I have commitments."

"To an agent?" Clare's tone was scathing. "Lani, you disappoint me, you really do. I always thought we understood one another. Now it appears you've allowed your father's feelings to poison your mind against me."

"That's not true." Lani raised her eyes heavenward for a moment, and then after a momentary hesitation she gave in. "All right," she said tautly. "All right, I'll come." Better to get it over with, she told herself without conviction. Miles would understand. If she explained how inadequate her mother always made her feel. . . .

"Oh, good." Clare's satisfaction now was almost tangible. "So we'll say seven-thirty, shall we?"

"If you like." Lani was apathetic, but as usual, once she had got her way, Clare was prepared to be magnanimous.

"I'll make it up to you, darling," she declared warmly. "Now that I'm back in England, we can meet more often, go shopping together sometimes. You're growing up. We're more like sisters than mother and daughter, aren't we? Don't you think that's a good idea? We should be friends."

"Mother, I am grown up," said Lani flatly. "I'm over twenty you know."

"Isn't that what I've been saying?" Clare was characteristically obtuse, only listening to those parts of Lani's conversation that agreed with her. "Until tomorrow evening then. I'll be looking forward to it. Wear something pretty. I want to show you off."

It wasn't until Lani was halfway upstairs again that the full import of her mother's last statement struck home. Clare wanted to show her off! *To whom*, she wondered apprehensively. And more important, *for what purpose?*

Sinking down onto a carpeted stair, Lani pressed the tips of her fingers against her lips. She had been a fool, a complete fool! She should have asked her mother if they were dining alone, and if not, she should have stuck to her refusal. As it was, she had no way of knowing what her mother had planned, and the probability that Clare's latest conquest might be there was more than an even chance. She took a deep breath and surveyed her options: she could either go to dinner at her mother's as planned, or she could ring her back and make some other excuse. But what excuse? What could she possibly say that would convince Clare she was not allowing her father to influence her? The last thing she wanted was for her mother to start blaming her father for her lack of cooperation.

Sighing, Lani got to her feet again and continued upstairs. There was nothing for it; she would have to go, she decided unhappily. But the prospect of telling both her father and Miles was not one she was looking forward to.

CHAPTER THREE

LANI DROVE HERSELF to her mother's apartment in Avenue Mews. Her father had suggested rather testily that she ought to take a taxi, but having her own transport made Lani feel more independent. At least if she had her own car, she could leave when she felt like it, she thought defensively, refusing to admit how much she needed that reassurance.

Her father had accepted the news that she was dining with her mother with unconcealed rancor. "It's your life, I suppose," he declared, giving every impression that he thought the contrary, and Lani had to try to persuade him that she wasn't looking forward to it either. "Then why are you going?" Roger St. John countered brusquely. "After the way she has neglected you lately, I should have thought you'd have more pride. Or perhaps you're eager to meet your prospective stepfather. I imagine Clare will want your endorsement of her latest piece of folly."

"It's nothing like that, daddy," Lani had protested unhappily. "Honestly, I'm only going because it's so long since I've seen her. She is my mother, after all. I do have an obligation—"

"Clare forfeited any obligation when she walked out on you, Lani," her father retorted forcefully. "She's an unnatural mother. Why else do you suppose I got custody? She didn't care about you then. She doesn't care about you now. She only wants to associate herself with your success."

"Oh, daddy, I don't think that's very likely," Lani exclaimed. "Success is not something Clare has any shortage of, is it?"

"Clare?" Her father frowned. "You called her Clare."

"She asked me to," admitted Lani unwillingly, and her father drew in his breath impatiently.

"She would," he declared, his lips twisting contemptuously. "I fear your mother does not want to admit her age."

Miles was disappointed when Lani telephoned him with her apologies. "So when do I get to see you then?" he demanded, after she had explained her position. "How about Sunday? We could drive down to the coast."

"I'm sorry. I'm going to my cousin's baby's christening on Sunday," said Lani regretfully. "How about lunch on Monday? The Mermaid at one o'clock."

"I knew that dinner engagement was achieved too easily," muttered Miles gloomily. "Your mother doesn't want a third for dinner, does she? She didn't ask you to bring a friend?"

"I'm afraid not." Lani welcomed his wry humor. "Is Monday okay? Or do you want a rain check?"

"No, Monday is fine," advised Miles. "The Mermaid at one. Be there."

Avenue Mews was near Buckingham Palace Gardens, a cul-de-sac opening off Belgrave Square, where the exclusive block of apartments was guarded day and night by security men. Lani had to have her name checked and endorsed before she was allowed to enter the lift, and her face was a little red as she stepped inside. The last time she had come to see her mother, she had been one of a party of people, all on their way up to the penthouse floor, and she had not had to prove her identity to a suspicious-eyed commissionaire.

Her heart racing now, she looked down uneasily at the clothes she was wearing. She had had no idea how formal this affair was going to be, but mindful of her mother's suggestion that she wear something *pretty*, she had chosen one of the simplest outfits in her wardrobe. Her dark brown velvet suit went well with a cream silk shirt, whose wide sleeves complemented the severely cut lines of the waistcoat, and as it was a cold evening, she was wearing a camel jacket. She was not a "pretty" person, she told herself determinedly, as the metal cylinder propelled her upward. She was just a serious-minded working girl, and if Clare didn't like what she was wearing, then it was too bad.

Lani heard the sound of music and laughter long before she reached Clare's door, and her heart sank. So it was to be a dinner party, after all. Not the intimate little get-together Clare had first implied. She wondered why she had been invited. Clare had never cared to do so in the past. She could only assume her mother had been one short for dinner, and she had been the final resort.

Ignoring the feeling of bitterness this realization aroused, Lani forced herself to ring the bell set to one side of the double paneled doors. A maid opened the door to her, more flushed than Lani, and ushered her inside without too much ceremony. Lani recognized her from the last time she'd been there, and she was relieved when the woman used her name.

"Go right in, Miss St. John," she advised with a harassed smile. "Miss Austin is waiting for you."

The blue and gold luxury of her mother's drawing room was a stage where Clare held court. A molded ceiling, walls hung with blue and gold damask, alabaster pillars that framed the mirrors with which Clare liked to surround herself—it was every bit as dramatic as a scene from an Italian opera, and it took quite an effort for Lani to step into the room. Her mouth was dry, and she was conscious of being the cynosure of several pairs of eyes as she hovered in the doorway. Her mother, surrounded as usual by a group of admirers, hadn't seen her, and it was left to Elwyn Hughes, Clare's manager, to rescue Lani from the spotlight.

"Lani," he said, getting up from a couch and coming toward her. "My dear, I hardly recognized you. You're quite a young lady now."

Lani proffered a polite smile. She was used to Clare's associates treating her like a schoolgirl. Nevertheless, it took more of an effort this evening, with the knowledge of why she was here scraping like a knife across the sharp edge of her nerves.

"I believe you've become a writer since I saw you last," Elwyn went on, cupping her elbow in his hand and leading her across the room to where her mother was standing. "How clever of you! It must be quite a thrill, actually seeing your work in print."

"They're only children's books." Lani drew an uneven breath. "But yes, I do find the work interesting."

"I'm sure you do." Elwyn had gained his objective. Expertly insinuating himself and his companion into the group surrounding Clare, he said, "Your little girl is here, Clare. Aren't you going to say hello?"

Clare Austin turned almost too eagerly, Lani thought, and the smile that enveloped the famous Austin features seemed as artificial as the setting for their meeting. Lani had the distinct impression that Clare wanted her here no more than she wanted to be here, and she knew an almost irresistible impulse to turn tail and run.

"Lani!" Clare's greeting was so warm and friendly that for a moment the girl thought she had been mistaken. But then she realized Clare was acting. She was playing the part of the loving relative to perfection, and Lani was expected to follow her lead.

"Mother." For the life of her Lani could not have said "Clare" at that moment, and although her smile wavered a little, Clare held out her arms invitingly.

"Darling," she exclaimed, reaching out to enfold her daughter in her grasp. Lani was forced to return her embrace with every appearance of sharing her affection.

"I was just saying how Lani had changed," Elwyn remarked, perhaps perceiving that she was suddenly looking rather strained. Addressing Lani again, he went on, "It must be nearly three years since you came to see Clare at Covent Garden. I remember it was a performance of *La Bohème*. You came around to the dressing room afterward."

"What a memory you have, Elwyn." Clare's words did not sound complimentary, and he gave Lani a wry glance as her mother went on. "But you're late, Lani. I was beginning to think you weren't coming."

"Am I?" Lani's tongue moistened her lips as she cast a surreptitious glance about her. "I'm sorry. You'll have to blame your doorman. He seemed to think I might be a gate-crasher."

"That sounds like Craddock," remarked a rather languid young man, standing on Clare's left. "He takes his work very seriously. One would almost think he faced would-be intruders every day."

"Craddock does a good job," asserted Clare shortly, clearly not enamored of this particular young man, and casting another hurried look about her, Lani was relieved to find that the man she had expected to see was nowhere in evidence. She must have been wrong, she thought, breathing a little more easily, and she responded a little more enthusiastically as her mother began to make introductions.

None of the people she was introduced to was Jake Pendragon. Of the fifteen or twenty people in the room, she met no one with a name even resembling his, but in spite of the glass of champagne in her hand, she could not banish the dryness in her throat. Where was he? Surely it was inconceivable, after all the rumors, that he not be here. And yet he wasn't. Lani's disappointment was as shattering as her relief.

"So—the little goose has turned into a swan," remarked Clare dispassionately, when they briefly found themselves alone. "You've changed, Lani. You're not as self-conscious as you used to be. I don't know that I like it."

"Perhaps you mean I'm not so gullible anymore," murmured Lani carefully, and Clare's expression sharpened. "Why did you invite me here this evening, mother? Did you need me to make up the numbers?"

Clare's laugh covered any embarrassment her daughter's words might have caused, but her lips were thin when she responded. "You're very astute, Lani, but that's not why I invited you here. I wanted you to come. I am your mother, after all, and besides, I wanted to talk to you."

"To talk to me?" Lani was surprised. She and Clare had seldom talked, even in the old days, and it had been her father she had always turned to in times of trouble. "What about?"

"Well, darling, it's not that...simple," exclaimed Clare, schooling her impatience. "It's so long since we talked together. I don't feel that we're...in touch, if you know what I mean."

"I'm sorry." Lani found it difficult to feel any sympathy for her mother's predicament. "I—" she paused a moment, and then rushed on hurriedly "—I suppose it has to do with this man you brought back from America."

Clare's carefully penciled brows arched. "I didn't bring him back from America, darling," she exclaimed tersely, but Lani guessed, nevertheless, that she was right. "He's quite capable of looking after himself, believe me. However, you are correct to assume that it is my personal life I want to discuss."

"Oh, really, mother—" Lani turned her head away

tensely, wishing desperately she had never agreed to come, and by looking away, she was the first to see the new arrival standing silently in the open doorway. Tall, lean, dark-skinned—he was not so different, actually, from the way he had looked six years ago, except that his clothes were more expensive, his hair less unruly, his face harder and more cynical than Lani remembered. Or would she remember such a thing, she asked herself uneasily. She had been a child, a teenager, unable to distinguish between sarcasm and irony.

But she was not a child now, she was a woman, and the intensity of her gaze seemed to direct his eyes to hers. She had not expected recognition; she had not anticipated that he would remember the inquisitive teenager who had invaded the privacy of his home. And she was surprised when the tawny eyes narrowed and a troubled frown drew a line from his forehead to his nose. For what seemed an age but could only have been a few seconds, they stared at one another across the heads of the other people in the room, and then someone else noticed him, and his attention was distracted.

"Lani, are you listening—my God! *Jake!*"

Her mother, whose fingers had been squeezing her forearm only moments before, suddenly saw the newcomer too. Her hands fell from Lani's arm, and without a word of explanation, she left her daughter and made her way across the room to Jake Pendragon's side. The rest of her guests fell back to allow her progress, and Lani had an unwelcome and unwanted sight of what happened next. Not caring that their meeting was being observed by everyone else in the room, Clare flung herself into his arms, and as Lani watched dry mouthed, she kissed him full on the lips.

"Didn't you know?" The low-voiced question caused Lani to glance quickly at the man beside her, and she met Elwyn Hughes's sympathetic gaze blankly. "There's been so much publicity about them, I felt sure you must have seen it," he added compassionately. "Though I know for a fact Clare didn't expect Jake to be here tonight."

"She didn't?"

Lani voiced the words through parched lips, and Elwyn shook his head. "He was supposed to be in Cornwall, or some such place. He has relatives down there, I believe. In any event, Clare didn't anticipate him returning before tomorrow or Monday."

"I see." Lani took a hasty mouthful of champagne to try to ease the constriction in her throat, but it was useless. *Dear God,* she prayed, *don't let him remember me,* please! She couldn't bear to think of her mother's amusement if he chose to regale Clare with the details of her humiliation at his hands.

"Are you all right?"

Elwyn was looking at Lani anxiously now, and although she was grateful for his consideration, the last thing she wanted was to attract any attention to herself.

"I'm fine, honestly," she assured him, looking down into her glass. "I — er — I expect you're kept pretty busy, with — er — with Clare's engagements."

"Some." Elwyn shrugged. "She's giving a charity performance at the Royal Opera House next Thursday, but primarily she's here for more personal reasons."

"Oh . . . yes?"

Lani managed a casual note of inquiry, but inside she was sick with panic. She had to get out of here, she thought, but she knew she couldn't, and hoping against hope that Clare would forget all about her, she turned so she could no longer see either her mother or the man with her.

"Yes." Elwyn seemed to understand that she would prefer him to go on talking. "I know she wanted to see both you and your father. She's very proud of you, you know, though I have to say she might not have been so pleased if you had succeeded in her field, if you know what I mean."

He chuckled, and Lani forced a faint smile.

"And, of course, there's Jake's concert at the Albert," he continued flatly. "She wouldn't miss that."

Lani nodded. "He—he's a pianist, isn't he?"

Elwyn smiled. "He's a genius, Lani, only don't tell him I said so. Clare found him playing the piano, believe it or not, in some nightclub in San Diego."

Lani took a deep breath. "A nightclub?"

"That's right. I guess it was better than starving. Just because you're good doesn't necessarily mean you'll succeed."

She stared at him. "But—you said he was a genius!"

"Lani, Pendragon's a realist. He knew the chances of him making it big as a concert pianist without backing were slim. He took the only job that was offered to him."

Lani was loath to ask questions, but she found herself doing so. "In this. . club?"

"That's right."

"I see." Lani swallowed hard. "And. . . and Clare, of course, recognized his genius."

Elwyn sighed. "Look, kid, I know this must be pretty tough for you to take, but it wasn't exactly like that. I mean—well, your mother's still a beautiful woman. She needs a man around. Lord knows, I'd be that man if she'd have me, but she doesn't want me. She wants him, Pendragon, and whatever else he is, he's certainly a man."

Lani put down her empty glass. "Does she love him?"

"Well, she's crazy about him, if that's what you mean," remarked Elwyn dryly. "And he makes her happy. If that's what it takes, who are we to judge?"

Lani shook her head. "It's nothing to do with me, of course."

"Isn't it? If Jake marries your mother, he'll be your stepfather, won't he?"

Lani tried to focus on the lights of London, visible through the undrawn blinds at the windows. "They're planning on getting married?" she asked stiffly, and Elwyn shrugged.

"It's what she wants. It's what she's determined to have. And if Jake wants his name in lights at Carnegie Hall, then I guess he may find he wants it, too."

The appearance of a maid to announce that dinner was served prevented any further conversation, and Lani was relieved to see that her mother and Jake Pendragon had disappeared. Perhaps he was leaving she thought. Perhaps it had only been a fleeting visit. But her stomach plunged unpleasantly when she entered the dining room to find he was standing at the head of the table beside her mother.

Unlike the other guests, he was not wearing a tuxedo, but the bronze leather jacket he was wearing over dark suede pants did not look out of place. Lani reflected that his brooding good looks did not need a more formal outline. He was relaxed and indolent, completely at home with these people, whose income alone set them apart from him, and she found herself resenting his self-assurance and the aura of influence that surrounded him.

Clare was evidently instructing the maid to lay another place beside her own at the long table, and sickened by what she was witnessing, Lani was glad when Elwyn led her to a seat at the opposite end. "I'll join you in a second," he said, waiting for the other women to be seated, and Lani concentrated on the table in an effort to restore her composure.

She had to admit it was a beautifully set table, with transparent Minton china, fine Waterford crystal, glittering sterling silver, with stiffly folded napkins, and a centerpiece of fragile white orchids and scarlet rose mallow. Scarlet candles burned in gleaming silver sconces, and a single red rose at each woman's place enhanced the romantic atmosphere.

There was a moment's delay before everyone was seated. Clare and her handsome pianist seemed to be having a slight argument. But eventually it was settled, and everyone sat down. With the serving of the meal, Lani felt she could relax at last, and it was disconcerting to lift her head and find Jake Pendragon's eyes upon her once again. She looked away immediately, but not before she had glimpsed that faint look of inquiry in their depths. The slight smile that curved his lips went unanswered, as she deliberately ladled soup that was too hot into her mouth.

"I expect Clare will introduce you later," Elwyn said at her elbow, intercepting the hurried averting of her eyes and making the wrong assumption. "As I said earlier, I don't think your mother wanted the two of you to meet this evening. I think she felt it might be easier if she broke the news to you first."

Lani shook her head. "It really doesn't matter," she assured him tautly, refusing to respond to his conciliatory tone. "I doubt that anything my mother does can have any effect on me. We're little more than strangers, Mr. Hughes. I never realized that so clearly until tonight."

To her relief, Elwyn stopped talking after that, and the young man on her right introduced himself. It was he who had come to her defense over the matter of the security guard, and although her mother had told her his name earlier, she was glad when he reminded her of it.

"Somers," he said, "Paul Somers. And you're Clare's daughter, aren't you?" He grinned. "Somehow, I don't think our prima donna is too enamored of that fact."

Lani looked at him, intrigued in spite of herself, and he gave a rueful grin. "Well, you *are* a little older than she had led us to believe, you know. And taller, too. Quite a young Amazon, in fact."

Lani controlled her color with difficulty. "Are you a singer too, Mr. Somers?" she inquired pointedly, and he laughed.

"I'm afraid not. I scrape a fiddle for a living," he confessed, adding humorously, "Do I look like a tenor or a baritone with these lungs?"

He was very thin, and Lani found herself smiling.

"I'm sure you could do anything you wanted," she responded lightly, he inclined his head in mock gratitude.

"You're very kind, but I don't have the temperament for it," he assured her. "You should hear the rows that go on in rehearsal. Or perhaps you shouldn't. It would destroy your illusions forever."

Lani put down her spoon. "Is my mother temperamental?" she asked, and Paul glanced at her wryly.

"Don't you know?"

"I'm afraid not. Since — since she and my father divorced, I haven't seen much of her."

Paul nodded. "I see." He gave her a whimsical look. "Well, let's say your mother is not as bad as some."

Lani bent her head. "Have you known her long?"

"Your mother? For the last five years, I guess."

"Do you travel with her?"

"Occasionally. When the whole company is invited on tour. We went to South Africa last year, or was it the year before?" He shook his head. "She's just returned from the States, but I suppose you know that."

"Yes." Lani gave a brief smile to the waitress, who came to remove her soup plate, and saw to her dismay that Jake Pendragon was watching her again. Forcing her eyes away, she fumbled with her napkin, and was somewhat disconcerted when Paul said, "Have you met him?"

"Met whom?" Lani forced herself to meet Paul's gaze, but she knew he knew she was being evasive.

"Pendragon," he said, flicking a glance to the other end of the table. "Our diva's latest protégé. I saw you looking at him. I guess he's not what you expected, is he?"

"I wasn't—" Lani broke off, realizing that to deny she had been looking at Jake Pendragon was to put too great an emphasis upon it. "That is—no. No, I haven't met him yet." She paused. "I—I suppose you have."

"Oh, sure." Paul turned aside to help himself to several lean slices of veal from the tray being offered to him. "Jake's okay. He's got real talent."

"But not enough to make it on his own," murmured Lani tautly, taking only one small piece of the meat, and Paul shook his head.

"Now I wonder where you got that piece of garbage from," he remarked softly, looking pointedly at Elwyn Hughes, who was happily unaware of his regard. "Look, love, we're none of us perfect. We have to take our chances with what we have. If you see what I mean."

Lani looked down at her plate. "Oh, yes," she said. "I see," and Paul sighed.

"Have some more wine," he said, filling her fluted glass. "If Clare doesn't introduce you, I will. I want you to know he's not the bastard you seem to think him."

In the event, neither Clare nor Paul introduced Lani and Jake. When dinner was over Clare announced that coffee and liqueurs would be served in the drawing room, and in the throng of guests making their way through the double doors out of the dining room, Lani suddenly found Jake beside her. It was a heart-stopping moment when she felt his shoulder brush against hers, and when he turned to look at her, she wished the floor would open up and swallow her. She glanced around swiftly, but she couldn't see Paul Somers or Elwyn Hughes, and she thought how typical it was that this should happen when she was most vulnerable.

"Hi."

Jake's softly spoken greeting forced her to be polite, and schooling her nervous features she offered him a stiff half smile. "Hello," she responded formally.

Wishing the people ahead of them would move a little faster, she broke out in a cold sweat when he added, "Don't I know you?"

He didn't remember!

As her startled gaze met his, she saw that although he had seen something familiar in her features, he had no idea who she was. She pressed her damp palms to her sides as she made the perfect rejoinder.

"I—I'm Clare's daughter, Mr. Pendragon," she said. "Some people say I look a little like my mother!" Although most people said quite the contrary, Lani didn't care. It was imperative he should think that, and surging ahead, she put as much space between them as she could.

There was nowhere to sit down in the drawing room. After looking rather frantically about her, Lani went to stand by the long windows. As soon as coffee had been served she would leave, she thought determinedly, and then caught her breath anew as a second reflection joined hers in the darkened glass.

"Look, I'm sorry I didn't recognize you," he said, his mouth twisting attractively, and Lani's nerves tightened again. "I knew Clare had a daughter, but she— well, I guess I assumed you'd be just a schoolgirl. I apologize. Do you forgive me?"

Lani had to look at him then, her green eyes darting anxiously up at his dark face. Unlike most of the men of her acquaintance, he was a couple of inches taller than she was, even in her high heels, and she remembered how fragile Clare had looked beside him. He was not heavily built, but he was muscular, and if he had been indulged since he came under her mother's influence, it didn't show in the lean powerful lines of his body. But thinking of his body brought other images to mind, not least those of him with Clare, and Lani felt her stomach contract with something like revulsion when she pictured them together.

"Well?" he said softly, and she felt as if someone was rubbing sandpaper over her skin. "Am I forgiven? I guess you thought I was being either extremely rude or extremely fresh at dinner. But your face intrigued me."

"It's not important."

Lani said the words hastily, suddenly realizing that their conversation was being observed by more than a dozen pairs of eyes. Where was her mother, she wondered uneasily. She had the feeling Clare would not approve of this liaison, and she wished they were not so conspicuously placed by the window.

"Isn't it?" Jake was saying now. "I rather thought it was." His mouth curved dryly. "It seems obvious that something is bothering you, and if it's not that, what can it be?"

The tawny eyes were disturbingly intent, the thickness of his lashes hardly concealing their catlike scrutiny, and Lani felt the warm color sweep up her throat and into her face. "I don't know what you mean, Mr. Pendragon," she asserted stiffly, imagining how her embarrassment might look to other people, and as she prayed for deliverance, it came in the silk-clad person of her mother.

Clare appeared in the doorway, giving every impression of having been searching for something—or someone—and having found it in the least likely place. She crossed the room toward her daughter and Jake, with antagonism exuding from every pore, and Lani knew that her earlier apprehension had not been misplaced.

"So there you are," Clare said tightly, and Lani had no illusions as to which of them she was addressing. "I've been looking everywhere for you."

"Oh?" Jake turned to her with what Lani had to admit was admirable panache. "Well—where else would I be but here, making myself agreeable to your guests?"

"My *guests*!" Clare cast a scathing glance at Lani.

"Your daughter then," affirmed Jake, without emphasis. "You didn't tell me she was here."

"I was going to." Clare took a deep calming breath. "Get me a coffee, will you, Lani? Just ask Ethel and she'll—"

"*Lani?*"

Jake's harsh interjection overrode her request, but the girl didn't wait to see if he had connected the two coincidences. With a feeling of impending disaster she left them, crossing to where the maid who had admitted her was dispensing coffee from a trolley. After asking her to take a cup to her mother, Lani walked slowly but purposefully to the door and, collecting her coat from the hall, she let herself out of the apartment.

CHAPTER FOUR

LANI AWAKENED EARLY the next morning, unusually early considering how late it had been before she had fallen asleep. She lay there realizing she had no desire to get out of bed. It would be so much safer to stay in her room, she reflected miserably, anticipating the reprimand that was bound to come. She closed her eyes tightly as if to shut out the demands of the outside world. If that outside world was bounded by the liaison between her mother and Jake Pendragon, it was no less hostile for that, and she dreaded the prospect of facing up to her cowardice.

What must her mother's guests have thought of her last night, she agonized. What must her mother have thought when she walked out? What must Jake Pendragon have made of her childish behavior? It had been a reckless irresponsible impulse that had sent her fleeing from the party, and she was quite prepared to admit that Clare had every reason to be furious with her.

Rolling onto her stomach, she rested her elbows on the pillows and propped her chin in her hands. Lying to her father had been just as bad. But when she had returned home to find him waiting for her, she had not had the heart to admit the truth, even to him. How could she have told him she had already met her mother's lover before last night? How could she have explained her desire to escape? How could she have confessed that seeing them together had filled her with repugnance — not just because Clare was her mother, but because of the feelings Jake Pendragon aroused in her!

So she had lied to him. She had said she'd had an interesting evening and that Clare had been pleased to see her. She had not mentioned Jake, or the fact that he had arrived unexpectedly at the party; she had confined her story to descriptions of the apartment and the food, and how well her mother was looking. When her father commented that she was home earlier than he had expected, she had admitted to having a headache — which was no lie by then — and although her father was very sympathetic and insisted she go straight to bed, Lani had had the feeling he was not displeased that she had evidently found the affair rather taxing.

Expelling her breath with a sigh, Lani pushed herself up and out of bed. It was Sunday, she realized belatedly. Sarah and Robin were expecting her at their house for lunch, and afterward she was to be godmother at the christening. Although she wasn't really in the mood to be sociable, at least she would get out of the house, she thought gratefully, crossing the bedroom into her bathroom.

Her father was having breakfast in the morning room when Lani went downstairs, taking his time as he scanned the Sunday papers. He looked up in surprise when his daughter came in, already dressed to go out, and his eyes flicked over her fine tweed pantsuit appraisingly and alighted on the dark green velvet cap with its swinging tassel in her hand.

"Going somewhere?" he inquired, his brows drawing together as he spoke, and Lani subsided into the chair opposite him before replying.

"It's the christening today," she said, reaching for the coffeepot. "Robin and Sarah's baby, remember? I'm to be godmother."

"Dressed like that?" queried her father disparagingly. "What time did you tell them you'd be there? Ten o'clock?"

"No. About noon, actually," admitted Lani self-consciously. "But—well, I thought I might leave a little early."

"A little early?" Her father snorted. "It's barely nine o'clock. It doesn't take three hours to get to Chalfont."

"I know it doesn't." Lani stirred sugar into her coffee. "But it's such a nice morning, I thought I might make a detour. I want to do some preliminary sketches for the new book."

"Are you sure you haven't arranged to see your mother again?" inquired her father dourly, looking at her over the top of his newspaper. "Is that what this is really about?"

"No!" But Lani's color was high nevertheless. "Really, I've got no plans to see Clare again." She paused and then went on determinedly, "After last night, I doubt if she'll want to see me."

"Last night?" Her father frowned, folding his newspaper and laying it aside. "What happened last night? I thought you enjoyed yourself."

"I—well I did, I suppose," murmured Lani unhappily. "But—well, when dinner was over I left."

"I know. You told me." Her father looked perplexed, and Lani sighed.

"No, you don't understand," she said. "I left without telling Clare I was leaving. Oh—don't ask me why. I just didn't want to stay any longer."

Roger St. John leaned toward her. "Was *he* there? The pianist?" Lani nodded. "Did your mother introduce you?"

"In a manner of speaking." Lani had no desire to get involved with that. "Oh, I suppose I didn't feel comfortable, that's all. I wanted you to know, in case... well, in case she rings today."

"I see." Her father studied her thoughtfully. "And is that why you're making an early start this morning? Because you're afraid of what your mother may say to you?"

"Not afraid exactly." Lani sipped her coffee. "I'd just rather not speak to her at all."

"Hmm." He shook his head. "You know, Lani, I find it hard to believe you're telling me everything. Something happened last night, didn't it? Something you saw... or overheard. Can't you tell me what it was? I am your father, my dear, and I happen to care about you very much."

"Oh, daddy!" Lani avoided his eyes. "Nothing happened, honestly. I—I suppose I was...jealous. When—when Jake Pendragon appeared, she had no time for anyone else. I guess that was it."

"And I suppose she told you they're going to get married, didn't she?" exclaimed her father bitterly. "There's no fool like an old fool, so they say."

"Daddy, Clare's not old," said Lani flatly. "She

doesn't look a day over thirty. But please, let's talk about something else, can we? I'm a little . . . sick of the whole affair."

The telephone rang as Lani was on the point of leaving the house. She was actually in the hall, pulling on her leather driving gloves, when its shrill sound split the silence, and realizing her father was out of doors tending the plants in his greenhouse, she waited with some trepidation for Mrs. Evans to answer it. But either that lady knew Lani had not yet left, or she too was tied up with something else, because no one appeared. Lani wondered who was trying to reach them. It could be Clare, but it could also be any one of a dozen other people, and realizing it might even be Robin or Sarah phoning to change the arrangements, Lani reluctantly gave in. Picking up the receiver, she said, "Hello."

She nearly dropped it again when a low masculine voice said, "Lani? It's Jake Pendragon. I'd like to see you sometime today. Is that possible?"

"No! No, I'm afraid it's not." Lani was briefly tempted to hang up but then added, "I'm sorry, I'm just going out. Goodb—"

"Wait!" The word was uttered with rather more emphasis than his previous statement had been. "Lani, don't hang up. If we can't meet today, it will have to be tomorrow. I'll try to fit it in between—"

"Don't bother." Lani took an unsteady breath. "If Clare's asked you to ring me—"

"Dammit, Clare has nothing to do with this," he retorted, his voice rough with impatience. "No doubt she'll be contacting you herself later today, but right now this has to do with you and me. Only that. Now, can we meet?"

"I'm afraid not." In spite of herself, Lani's voice was annoyingly tremulous. "I—I'll be tied up all day. It was nice of you to phone, Mr. Pendragon—"

"It was not nice at all," he snapped, his temper threading. "Lani—"

"Goodbye, Mr. Pendragon," she said firmly, and without giving him another opportunity to speak, she rang off.

She stood for several minutes in the hall after she had replaced the receiver, feeling too shaken to move. But when the phone began to ring again, she snatched up her bag and her portfolio and quickly put herself beyond temptation. As she backed her Capri out of the garage, she could still hear the phone's persistent peal, but nothing could have persuaded her to turn back.

ON MONDAY LANI MET MILES for lunch at the Mermaid as planned and basked in the welcome glow of his uncomplicated admiration. "You're looking great," he said, after they were seated at a cozy table for two. "A bit tired perhaps, but that's only to be expected. Coping with jet lag can be really exhausting."

"Yes." Lani wondered what Miles would say if she told him it wasn't jet lag that was giving her sleepless nights. Her father had told her Clare had rung while she was at Robin's and Sarah's the previous day, and what with that and Jake Pendragon's phone call, Lani was finding it hard to relax.

"So, how was the dinner party?" inquired Miles, after they had successfully dealt with Lani's business trip to New York. "Was it worth standing me up for?"

"No." Lani's grimace was ironic. "As a matter of fact, I'd much rather have had dinner with you. But it *is* some time since Clare's been in England—"

"—and you felt obliged to play the dutiful daughter."

"Something like that." Lani's fingers were nervously twisting the stem of her wineglass as she spoke. "Let's not talk about Clare. I get enough of that from daddy."

Miles frowned, his eyes on her slim fingers. "I get the feeling it wasn't a great success," he remarked, and Lani met his gaze briefly.

"It wasn't," she agreed. "It was all rather a bore, really. I much prefer to mix with people who are not so...artificial."

Miles looked as though he would have liked to question her further, but Lani's expression was discouraging. Instead he asked about the christening, and she was able to tell him unreservedly that she had enjoyed herself very much.

"The baby's a darling," she exclaimed enthusiastically. "They've named her Helen, after Sarah's mother." She smiled reminiscently. "The twins were a little jealous of all the attention she was getting, of course, but that's only to be expected."

Miles regarded her warmly. "You sound as if you're envious," he said, and Lani smiled.

"Perhaps I am. Though not of the married state," she added firmly, just in case Miles was becoming serious. "I don't think marriage is such a good idea for someone like me. I—I'm too independent."

"What you mean is, your parents' divorce has made you scared to make a commitment," he declared. "You'd make an ideal wife and mother. Believe me, you're not a bit like Clare Austin."

Lani sighed. "How would you know, Miles? You've never met my mother."

"No, but I've read plenty about her," replied Miles staunchly. "But as you say, let's not talk about her. Tell me about the new book. Did you do those preliminary sketches yet? I think it's a good idea to introduce a new character. Have you got any idea what you're going to call it?"

The remainder of the meal was taken up with discussing Lani's work, much to her relief, and when they emerged from the restaurant into the chilly atmosphere of the November day, she was not disposed to linger.

"I'll ring you," she said, wrapping the folds of her cape around her. "Give me a few days to get something down on paper, and I'll be in touch."

"Okay." Miles regarded her resignedly. "But don't take too long, will you? I'd like to see you again before Christmas."

Lani smiled and looked away, her long hair lifting in the cold wind. Then, seeing her bus approaching along Piccadilly, she waved goodbye, and holding her velvet cap in place, she ran to catch it.

The bus dropped her at the junction of Finchley Road and Glendower Street, and she walked quickly along the side road that led to Pelham Court. She was glad she was wearing a pantsuit and not a skirt as the wind whistled around her booted ankles, and she was looking forward to getting home and settling in front of her easel. She was fortunate in being able to work at home, she thought, recalling her father with affection. He had had one of the four bedrooms converted into a

studio for her; its long windows, which overlooked the
walled garden at the back of the house, and the square
skylight provided ample light for both her writing and
her drawing.

She became aware of the car cruising beside her only
seconds before she reached Pelham Court, and her
head whipped around swiftly as the vehicle came to a
halt. It was quiet in Glendower Street at this hour of
the afternoon, and although she was not particularly
nervous of being out alone, there had been a spate of
muggings lately, which had aroused a lot of concern.
But the car was not the kind a thief might use, she saw
at once. It was a dark green Porsche, low and sleek and
expensive, and the man getting out from behind the
wheel was disturbingly familiar.

Realizing that attack was probably the best method
of defense, Lani gave him her most haughty look. "Are
you following me?" she exclaimed, her arms holding
the cape around her, giving her a defensive appearance. But Jake Pendragon did not seem to notice as he
sauntered round the car.

He was wearing black today, a fine-grained corded
jacket and matching pants, his pale lilac-colored shirt
providing the only lighter touch. He didn't appear to
feel the cold as she did, although that might have been
due in part to the black waistcoat, half-buttoned
beneath his jacket, and the wind played riot with his
hair, depositing thick dark strands across his forehead.

Dear God, thought Lani, hugging her bag against
her like a shield. What was he doing here? What did he
want? Did Clare know he was haunting her like this, or
had he kept his unwelcome interest to himself?

"I've been waiting for you," he said then, watching her with a level, catlike appraisal. "You look cold. Do you want to get in the car? Or would you rather we spoke here, where anyone can eavesdrop on our conversation?"

"I—I don't see that we have anything to say to one another," declared Lani, after a moment. "How did you know where I was? How did you know I'd be coming back at this time?"

"When I phoned earlier, your housekeeper told me you were out. I didn't believe her at first, but then she said you'd probably be back later this afternoon, and I decided that she'd hardly tell me that if you had told her to put me off."

"You rang," choked Lani. "You rang my home again?" She stared at him resentfully. "Did...did you tell Mrs. Evans who you were?"

"Oh, sure, I told her I was John Smith," replied Jake sardonically. "Don't worry. I didn't tell her my name was Pendragon. I guessed, after the publicity there's been, that my name isn't exactly the flavor of the month with your father."

Lani stiffened her shoulders. "How dare you?" she exclaimed. "How dare you come here, pestering me! Have you no decency? Have you no shame? We have nothing to say to one another, Mr. Pendragon. Please, let me pass."

"Not yet." Jake's hand was against the wall at one side of her, preventing her from getting past him, and when she moved to evade him, he stepped into her path. "Look, cool down, will you?" he said, his impatience quickening at her resistance. "I don't have to explain my actions to you. What I choose to do with my life is my affair. But, you...well, I wanted you to know that I had no idea Clare was your mother."

"Why should you have?" Lani's voice was cold and unyielding. "And what does it matter anyway? We hardly know one another."

"But we *do* know one another, don't we?" Jake persisted roughly. "When I saw you on Saturday night, I knew there was something familiar about you. Then when Clare called you Lani—" He sighed. "Was that why you walked out?"

"You flatter yourself!"

Lani moved to get past him again, but this time Jake's hand on her shoulder, a lean long-fingered hand, prevented her. "I don't flatter myself at all," he snapped, the tawny eyes glittering dangerously. "But if you persist in behaving like a spoiled child, I may begin to think you are jealous, after all."

Lani caught her breath. "You're hurting me."

"I can hurt you a hell of a lot more than this," he told her grimly. "Oh, for Christ's sake—" he let her go abruptly "—I don't know why I bothered coming here. It's obvious you're not prepared to behave reasonably. Go on. Go home. I'm sorry I detained you."

Lani was trembling as she moved past him, conscious of his eyes watching her until she turned the corner into Pelham Court. Then, as she hurried across the small square, she heard the powerful roar of the Porsche's engine, and seconds later the draft of its passing sent the leaves scattering in her path.

CLARE RANG AGAIN that evening, and this time Lani had no excuse not to speak to her. Leaving her father at the dinner table, she went out into the hall to take the call, closing the dining-room door behind her as a precautionary measure.

"Well! So you finally deign to come to the phone, do you?" Clare's first words were disparaging. "Just what the hell did you think you were playing at the other evening? Have you any idea of the embarrassment you caused?"

"I'm sorry, mother—"

"Sorry? Sorry? You haven't even had the decency to ring and make your apologies. You wait until I get in touch with you, and then pretend that you care how I feel!"

"I do care, mother." Lani caught her lower lip between her teeth for a moment. "It. . . it was an unforgivable thing to do, and I am sorry. Put it down to the fact that I felt—well, out of place there. I was on my own. I didn't know anyone. And I just. . . ran away, I guess."

"You knew Elwyn. You knew Paul Somers. Or at least, he told me he had been chatting with you. And Jake spoke to you. Wasn't that enough?"

"Oh, I suppose so." Lani's knees felt decidedly unsteady, hearing her mother speak Jake's name. "It was a silly thing to do. I admit it. I'm sure none of your friends blamed you for my foolishness."

"Hmm." Clare sounded unconvinced, but she had mellowed slightly. Presently she said, "I realize what was wrong, you know," causing Lani's legs to give out altogether, so that she sank down weakly onto the chest her grandfather had brought home from Africa.

"You do?"

"Of course." Clare made a sound of impatience. "It was meeting Jake, wasn't it? Realizing that your father and I are completely washed up. It upset you. I was afraid it might. But you're not a child now, Lani, you're an adult, and you have to face up to these things."

"Mother—"

"No. Let me finish." Clare was determined to have her say. "It was precipitate, I know. I had planned to talk to you about...well, about Jake, but his turning up like that really threw me. He had gone down to Cornwall. His grandmother still lives there, and I hadn't expected him back until Sunday. Well, as you know, he arrived, and I'm afraid I neglected everyone after that."

"There's really no need to tell me this," said Lani faintly, feeling sick, but Clare ignored her.

"Anyway," she went on, "now that you've met, it does make things easier. I want you and him to be friends, Lani. I mean—it's important to me that the two people I care about most should get along together. I know your father probably won't agree, but you mustn't let his influence spoil our relationship. And to that end, I want you to join my guests at the Royal Albert Hall on Thursday evening. Jake is giving his recital, and afterward, we're all going to have supper at Mancini's."

CHAPTER FIVE

THE HUGE CONCERT HALL was hushed and still as the wistful melody that had continually threaded its way through Rachmaninoff's second concerto drew to its final crescendo, and Lani, motionless in her seat, felt as if every bone in her body had turned to water. It was so beautiful, so moving, so passionately performed, that she felt as if she was hearing it for the first time. The romantic lyricism of the composer's work, the vein of melancholy that made the piece so haunting, seemed to have touched a responsive chord inside her, and the resentment and apprehension she had felt at the start of the evening had given way to a sensuous languor. Jake's playing had done that, his skill and sensitivity, the brilliant command he had of the instrument, drawing every nuance of emotion from the keyboard. The applause started the second the final note died away, and it was deafening. Lani, aware that her mother had risen to her feet beside her and was clapping louder than anyone, knew she should be applauding too, but she was still too bemused to take part. With a feeling half of impatience, she felt the dampness of a tear against her cheek, and impatiently brushing the unwanted betrayal aside, she rose abruptly to join in the ovation.

Fortunately, Clare was not aware of her right then,

and Lani was able to look down at Jake, taking his bow, without observation. In formal evening clothes he looked more attractive than ever, and she wondered how many of the young girls there had come for the music and how many merely to see him. He had the lean hungry appeal of a pop star, she thought, despising herself for being seduced by his talent, and she was glad he could not possibly see her among so many avid faces.

Taking her seat again as the young virtuoso left the platform, Lani faced her mother's challenging expression. "Well?" said Clare impatiently. "What did you think? Isn't he magnificent? Don't you envy him his talent?"

Lani had a few moments to gather her composure as other members of Clare's party interjected their own comments. "He certainly can play that instrument," commented Celia Nevill, one of Clare's American friends. "Those hands—don't they absolutely draw blood from the music! I shall never shake hands with him again without thinking about that."

"I don't suppose Clare thinks about his playing when he has his hands on her," drawled Celia's husband suggestively, and then said, "Pardon me!" in an aggrieved tone when his wife grimaced pointedly in Lani's direction.

Clare ignored them both, waiting irritably for her daughter's reaction, and summoning a note of indifference, Lani agreed that he was good.

"Good! Good! What kind of a word is that?" Clare demanded furiously. "He's fantastic! Brilliant! He's been compared to some of the most famous pianists that have ever lived, and you say he's *good*! Don't you have any conception? Don't you have any feeling for the music at all? For heaven's sake, Lani, I expected better of you. Can't you recognize genius when you hear it?"

Lani's face was scarlet, but she managed to control her feelings. If she were to tell her mother exactly how much Jake's playing had affected her, she would be betraying both her father and herself. And in any case, Clare only wanted confirmation that she was right.

"He is brilliant," she admitted quietly. "The audience has demonstrated that. You could have heard a pin drop while he was playing, and I should think the critics will find it difficult to fault his performance."

"I agree." Elwyn Hughes, who had been silent up to this point, leaned across to smile at Lani. "My guess is he's going to be swamped with offers after this. You're not going to see much of him, Clare, if he gets taken up by the media."

Clare's red lips thinned slightly. "Oh, I shouldn't worry about that, Elwyn. I'll make sure he always has time for me. After all, I discovered him. And I'm not about to let him forget it."

The remainder of the performance was an anticlimax for Lani. Jake returned to play three Rachmaninoff preludes, but they did not have the depth or passion of the concerto, and although he performed with style and elegance, she was all too conscious of Clare beside her, basking in his reflected glory.

After the recital was over, Lani was obliged to accompany Elwyn and the rest of Clare's party to the restaurant, where they were to have a celebratory supper. Clare slipped away after the performance to visit Jake in his dressing room, and Lani's nerves were tight as she got into the back of Elwyn's Rover for the short drive to Mancini's.

"Your mother won't be long," he assured her, catching sight of her white face in the rearview mirror, and Lani forced a faint smile, wishing desperately that she didn't have to go.

Mancini's was a large ostentatious restaurant, whose clientele was drawn primarily from those employed in the arts. It occupied the basement of a building in Knightsbridge, and as they descended the steps, Lani could smell the aromas of good food, good tobacco and expensive perfume. She had never been there before, and she looked about her rather apprehensively as the doorman helped her remove her cape. Then Elwyn linked his arm with hers and led her across the room to their table.

Because a small combo was playing in one corner, people tended to speak loudly to make themselves heard, and at this hour of the evening, a haze of blue smoke hung over the tables. One or two couples gyrated on the small dance floor, set at a lower level than the restaurant itself, and the atmosphere was hardly conducive to relieving the slight throbbing Lani had developed in her temples.

The table was set for eight: Lani and Elwyn, the Nevills, and two other guests of her mother's that Lani had known for a number of years. Elwyn got everybody seated and then asked what she would like to drink, and although she sensed his displeasure, Lani refused to have anything alcoholic. "I—I have to work tomorrow," she explained, not wanting to admit to having a headache, and Elwyn expelled his breath somewhat impatiently before asking what the others would like.

There were dishes of pâté on the table, and while they waited for Clare and Jake to join them, Elwyn accepted a finger of toast from the napkin the waiter proffered and spread it thickly with the rich paste. "Come on," he said to Lani. "Have some. There's nothing alcoholic about this." But Lani made a polite refusal. In all honesty she had no appetite at all, and she was not looking forward to the supper ahead.

Her mother arrived about twenty minutes later, Jake having shed his tailcoat for a soft velvet dinner jacket, whose wine red fabric complemented his dark good looks. Contrary to Lani's expectations, however, he did not appear to be in the same state of euphoria as her mother. Instead, he looked drained and rather tired, as if the emotion of the concerto had exhausted him. She had been dreading meeting him again after the way they had parted four days ago, but Jake scarcely looked at her. He accepted the group's congratulations without comment before flinging himself into the chair at the opposite end of the table, and it was left to Clare to summon the headwaiter and order the best champagne.

"We must have a toast," she said, vividly confident as she took the chair next to him. "You were a success, darling. You excelled yourself. Come along, stop looking so moody. I won't have you spoiling this night of all nights."

"You have a toast," declared Jake flatly, summoning another waiter. "Scotch," he said, when the man appeared. "With ice. A large one. Thank you."

Lani saw the way her mother's mouth tightened at this deliberate flouting of her arrangements, but evidently she was prepared to forgive him, for the momentary impatience was soon erased. With supreme panache, she took her champagne when it came and toasted him anyway, and Jake's brooding expression gave way to a reluctant acknowledgment.

"You were wonderful," exclaimed Celia Nevill, leaning across the table to touch his hand. "We all envy you, Jake. It must be so satisfying to know you've given a perfect performance." ·

"It wasn't a perfect performance," replied Jake shortly, loosening the top button of his shirt and pulling his tie free. "I messed up the adagio, and I finished the second movement ahead of the orchestra. There was nothing very satisfying about that!"

"You're being hypercritical," said Clare testily. "No one else will have noticed."

"I beg to differ," retorted Jake, the air of brooding malevolence returning to his expression, and Lani saw her mother give a restless sigh.

"Jake, even Malcolm Seymour complimented you upon your performance," she exclaimed. "And believe me, he doesn't do that for every struggling artist."

"Oh, thank you, Clare." Jake spoke the words succinctly, his mouth twisting with sudden irony. "It's so nice of you to remind me that I am just a struggling artist. That puts everything into perspective, doesn't it?"

He lifted his hand and attracted the waiter's attention again, and when the man came, he gave him a dazzling smile. "Another double, maestro, please," he ordered, with devastating aplomb, and Lani looked away in hot embarrassment when Clare's blue eyes filled with tears.

"You really are a beast, Jake," Clare choked, pulling a handkerchief out of her bag to dab her eyes, and Elwyn made a big thing of pouring everyone more champagne to cover the unpleasant silence. Even Lani had been obliged to accept some of the champagne to toast Jake's success, and she was glad of the glass now to hide her consternation.

Supper was served soon afterward, a mouth watering repast of smoked salmon and caviar, slices of chicken cooked in wine and cream, and a concoction of fruit and spun sugar that was flavored with white rum. It was a rich meal, seeming the more so by the lateness of the hour, and Lani noticed inconsequently that Jake ate no more than she did.

However, he did seem to recover his spirits as the meal progressed, and she decided rather caustically that the amount of alcohol he had drunk was probably responsible. Not that it had any visible effect on him, only in the way it removed the lines of dissatisfaction from his face, and made his temperament less volatile. He spoke quite amiably with Elwyn and the Nevills, reviewing his performance objectively with Clare and Maggie Pringle, her private secretary, and it was left to Adrian Dante to make Lani feel not left out.

Adrian was Clare's accompanist on those occasions when she gave a solo performance. As he had been around since before the divorce, Lani felt quite at ease with him. But her headache was not getting any better, and when Jake and her mother got up to dance, she mentioned the fact to Maggie.

"Oh, that's a shame," declared the older woman sympathetically, patting Lani's sleeve with purple tipped fingers. At least as old as her mother, Maggie did not have Clare's age-defying vitality, and at this hour of the night, her heavily made-up features looked haggard and ugly.

What am I doing here, thought Lani suddenly, looking about her with desperate eyes. It was obvious that Maggie's sympathy did not extend to suggesting she leave, and while Lani had been prepared to stay for supper, there was no earthly reason now why she should remain. Clare had not yet given her permission to depart. Until she did, Lani felt obliged to sit there, a part, yet not a part, of this celebration.

Her eyes turned irresistibly toward the dance floor. Jake and her mother had been joined there by several other couples, and the small area was crowded. As she watched, Clare lifted her hand to cup Jake's cheek. Lani looked away abruptly before he could turn his mouth against her mother's caressing palm.

When they returned to the table, she barely looked at them. Clare, noticing her daughter's preoccupation, beckoned her. "Come and join us, Lani," she exclaimed, her hand resting possessively on Jake's sleeve, and although she was loath to do so, Lani had very little choice in the matter.

"So," said her mother, after Clark Nevill had moved obligingly along the table, "Lani thought your performance was superb, didn't you, darling?"

Lani moistened her dry lips. "Oh—yes," she murmured, aware of those curiously colored eyes narrowed upon her. "I'm sure you've had a great success. Everyone seemed...delighted."

"Better than finishing on a discord, hmm?" Jake remarked, dryly, and Lani's color deepened at the deliberate insinuation.

"What do you mean?" Clare frowned, and Jake withdrew his arm from beneath her fingers to swallow the remainder of the Scotch in his glass.

"I guess I'm getting moronic," he said carelessly, setting the glass down again, and Lani shifted uneasily beneath his challenging stare.

"Come and dance with me, Clare." As usual, Elwyn defused the situation, drawing her out of her seat imperatively, causing her to glance up at him half-protestingly.

"I don't want to dance," she exclaimed, but her denial was halfhearted, and chivying her along, Elwyn led her down to the dance floor.

Left with Jake, Lani did not know where to look or what to say, and after viewing her evident embarrassment for several unnerving minutes, he laid a hand on her wrist.

"Let's join them, shall we?" he inquired, in a low taut voice, and twisting her wrist almost ruthlessly behind her, he drew her up out of her seat.

Short of creating a scene, she had to go with him, but once on the circular dance floor, she freed her wrist determinedly. However, it only served to make it easier for him to put his arms around her, and her hands pressed futilely against the ruffled silk of his dress shirt as he drew her swiftly toward him.

"I don't want to dance with you," she hissed in a low tone, meeting his enigmatic gaze with angry resentment. "Why are you doing this? You don't want to dance with me, either. And why did you try to embarrass me just now by talking about your treatment of Chopin?"

"So you remember," he commented, his hands resting with deceptive lightness at her waist, and as they were obliged to move to the seductive rhythm of the music or be trampled underfoot, Lani shook her head impatiently as she followed his lead.

"Why shouldn't I remember?" she protested, avoiding his eyes and focusing on the ivory fall of lace at his throat. "You were quite rude, as I recall." She paused. "Have you told Clare about that little encounter, or are you saving it for some more intimate occasion?"

His hands clutched her waist with sudden violence at her scathing words, and Lani was glad she was not wearing a low-cut gown. The cream silk jersey, with its loose cowl neckline and elbow-length sleeves, had seemed a suitable compromise between day and evening wear, and she was grateful now for its protection as his fingers bit into her flesh.

"Why should I tell Clare we've met before?" he demanded harshly, and Lani winced as his bruising hold brought her painfully close to the taut muscles of his thighs. "As I recall it, you were quite provocative. Not at all like the passionless puritan you've grown up to be!"

Lani caught her breath in stunned indignation, but Jake's expression was unrepentant. She stared at him furiously, willing him to retract his insulting statement, but as she did so, she could feel the disturbing pressure of sinew and bone assaulting her flesh, and her blood quickened unwillingly as awareness flared between them. He was too close, she thought unsteadily. She was much too conscious of the heat of his body, of the warmth of his breath, and the musky male scent he was exuding as he continued to use all his strength to overcome her resistance. Around them, the other dancers moved in undisturbed formation, totally unaware of the silent conflict that was ensuing. But Lani, troubled by her own vulnerability, sought any weapon she could as she struggled to prevail.

"You—you—you're despicable!" she choked, falling back on the only retort left to her, and Jake shook his head.

"No, I'm not," he contradicted her evenly, his eyes diminishing her defiance. "But right now isn't the time to debate this, is it, and unless you want your mother to overhear us, I suggest you pull yourself together."

"Me? Pull myself together?"

Lani practically squeaked the words, but then, all of a sudden, her opposition crumbled. He was right, she thought dully. She was treating him unfairly. It was her own unwilling attraction to him that was driving her to these lengths, and with a feeling of desperation she gave up the unequal battle.

Jake's hold on her gentled as she stopped resisting him, but the abrupt reversal of their roles brought her closer still. The sudden pressure of her face against the fine silk covering his chest made her intensely aware of the controlled power beneath that soft exterior, and before she could draw back, she felt the shudder of emotion that swept through him at this unexpected intimacy. His hands, which had previously caused her so much pain, now slid unresistingly over her hips, and with a feeling compounded of guilt and disbelief, she felt herself drawn close to him in such a way she could feel the sudden stirring maleness of his body against hers. There was no way he could remain ignorant of his own sexual arousal, and Lani's startled gaze turned to his in undisguised confusion.

"Please—" she breathed, blind to everything but the fact that she must get away from him before she betrayed herself, but Jake's fingers silenced her shocked outburst.

"Don't," he said, removing his hand from her mouth to cradle the back of her head, and the room swam as he rested his cheek against her temple.

It was madness, she knew. As they moved languorously around the dance floor, she knew she would regret this the minute she came to her senses. But for now, no one else was aware of what was happening. They were alone on an island composed of needs and feelings and bone-melting closeness, and when his fingers spread possessively along the curve of her spine, she knew she was incapable of resisting him.

The eventual cessation of the music achieved what she had not. When the group stopped playing and the lights, which had been lowered for dancing, were raised again, Jake had no choice but to step back from her, and Lani couldn't bear to look at him as a wave of shame swept over her.

"Come on," he said huskily, holding out his hand to

escort her back to their table, but now Lani found the will to shake her head.

"No," she said chokingly, "no, I can't!" and would have left him then had not Jake's agile reflexes prevented her from doing so.

"Yes," he told her steadily, "yes, you can," and while her eyes darted despairingly around the room, he added, "I won't embarrass you anymore, I promise."

What Lani might have replied to this statement was forestalled by her mother's intervention, Clare's blue eyes moving with a certain amount of wariness from Jake's to her daughter's. "Well, well," she said, and Lani knew her mother had immediately noticed her flushed face. "How kind of you to dance with Lani, darling. I didn't even know you were on the floor."

"No." Jake bit off the word flatly and gestured toward the dining section of the restaurant. "Well, shall we sit down? I think the band is leaving for its break."

"If you don't mind, I'll leave now, moth—Clare," said Lani stiltedly, knowing there was no way she could go back and sit down as if nothing had happened. The headache, which had briefly eased while they were dancing, had returned with greater intensity, and she longed for her home and her bed and a darkened room.

"Leave?"

Clare looked at her as if she couldn't believe what she was hearing, and Lani nodded. "I—I have got a bit of a headache," she admitted unsteadily. "Don't bother to break up the party. I can easily get a taxi."

"I'll take you," said Jake, astounding both Lani and

her mother, but after her initial reaction, Clare refused to hear of it.

"You can't," she exclaimed. "Darling, this is your party."

As Lani endeavored to assure her mother she could manage perfectly well alone, Elwyn once again came to the rescue. "I'll take Lani home," he said. "It's not much of a detour for me, and like her, I've got the beginnings of a headache, Clare. You and Jake go on with the party. I'm sure Maggie and Adrian, and the Nevills for that matter, are quite prepared to make a night of it."

"I'm not," said Jake, ignoring Clare's cry of protest. "Look, I've got eight hours of work ahead of me tomorrow. I suggest we all call it a night. If the others want to stay, let them. I, for one, need to get some sleep."

Lani left Mancini's with Elwyn a few minutes later, leaving her mother making her excuses to the rest of the party. Jake was still in the restaurant, waiting impatiently for Clare to finish her apologies, and as Lani got into the car, she felt a sense of gratitude that Elwyn had offered to take her. No matter how tempting the idea of Jake taking her home had been, she knew she should steer clear of him in future. He was dangerous—and unprincipled, she told herself severely—and she closed her mind to the thought that he might have been as shocked by what had happened as she was.

Even so, she couldn't stop thinking about him, and she was relieved to find her father had already retired for the night and was not waiting when she got home to demand an account of the evening's events. She was too distrait, too preoccupied with her thoughts, to give him an objective rendering of Jake's performance or a description of what came after. Maybe tomorrow she would feel more capable of doing so; maybe by tomorrow she would have got things into perspective again. But for now, as she shed the fine silk jersey gown and replaced it with a pair of white silk pajamas, she forced herself to remember that Jake had taken her mother home this evening, that she had every reason to believe he would spend the night at her mother's apartment — he might even be staying there for all she knew — and that the interlude on the dance floor had been inspired by nothing more than an overindulgence in alcohol.

CHAPTER SIX

LANI AWAKENED THE NEXT MORNING with an overwhelming feeling of depression. She felt dull and lethargic and in no mood to get up and start working, as she had told Elwyn Hughes she was going to do. It was only when her father came to tell her he was leaving that she realized it was later than she had imagined. It was such a dark and dismal morning beyond her window curtains, she had believed it was much earlier, and she struggled up on her pillows apologetically when he came to stand beside her bed.

"I'm leaving now, Lani," he said, looking down at her with a distinctly anxious frown. "Are you all right? You look very pale." His lips tightened. "Have you got a hangover?"

"No." Lani was indignant. "All I drank was two glasses of champagne. I just feel out of sorts, that's all. I suppose it's because I had a late night."

"I heard you come in," affirmed Roger St. John dryly. "After midnight, wasn't it? I assume the recital didn't last so long."

"We went to Mancini's for supper," explained Lani uncomfortably. "There . . . there were eight of us. It was supposed to be a sort of celebration."

"I see." Her father inclined his head, and watching his controlled expression, Lani wished her mother had not forced her into this position. But Clare was adept at getting her own way, and Lani knew that if she had refused to see her, Clare was perfectly capable of coming to Pelham Court and accusing her ex-husband of poisoning their daughter's mind. Lani had known she could not risk that happening. Her father's peace of mind was a frail thing at best, and so long as Clare remained in England, she had to try to keep them apart.

"I'm sorry I didn't join you for breakfast," she murmured now, changing the subject, but her father was not quite ready to leave it alone.

"And did you enjoy it?" he asked. "The concert, I mean. Is this man—Pendragon—any good?"

"Oh, yes." Lani's tongue circled her upper lip with some uncertainty. "He—er—he was quite good, actually. Elwyn seems to think he'll be very successful."

"Ah." Her father nodded his head, and she felt a helpless sense of protectiveness toward him. It might have been easier if she could have said Jake had been a flop. That way her father could have consoled himself with the thought that Clare had allowed her emotions to cloud her judgment.

"Will you be in to dinner?" Lani asked now, wanting to reassure him and not knowing how, and Roger St. John made an evident effort to gather himself.

"No," he said crisply. "I'm having dinner at the club with old Harrison. I promised him a game of chess several weeks ago, and he's pinned me down to this evening." He paused. "Have you got any plans? When are you seeing your mother again?"

"Oh...I don't know." Lani didn't want to talk about herself. "I've got to knuckle down to some work today. I promised Miles I'd have some preliminary sketches to discuss with him in a few days."

"I see." Her father moved toward the door. "Well, I must go. Good luck with your sketching. Don't work too hard, will you?"

In fact, Lani found it impossible to work at all. Later that morning, perched on a high stool in front of her drawing board, her mind remained stubbornly blank, and for the first time in her life, her imagination was stagnant. The day before she had made some initial drawings of the apprentice Matilda was going to employ, a character who was to form the basis of a new series of books she planned, but this morning even those drawings looked amateurish. No one, but no one, child or adult, would be convinced of his authenticity, she told herself contemptuously, and tore the sheet in pieces and scattered them on the floor.

The sound of the telephone was all she needed to destroy her concentration. It shrilled loudly from the hall below, and the piece of charcoal she was holding snapped between her fingers. *Oh, God,* she prayed, *please don't let it be Clare again,* and started abominably when Mrs. Evans hammered on her door.

"It's for you," she declared, opening the door a crack and putting her head around. "Mr. Rossiter. I told him you were in. Did I do right?"

"Oh—" Lani's relief was palpable. "Oh, yes. Yes. I'll

speak to him. Thank you, Mrs. Evans. I'll come at once."

Miles was reassuringly familiar, his casual tone filled with justifiable indignation. "Don't tell me you haven't got those sketches ready for me to see yet," he exclaimed. "It's almost a week since I've seen you. What have you been doing?"

"It's four days, and I'm afraid I've run into some complications," replied Lani ruefully. "I'm sorry, Miles. I am doing my best, really. But—well, circumstances have contrived to make working rather difficult."

"Circumstances?" Miles sounded skeptical. "What kind of circumstances? Oh, don't tell me; it's your mother, you've been seeing her again."

"As a matter of fact, I have." Lani sighed. "You'll have to give me more time, Miles. Actually, I was in the studio when you rang."

"I suppose you went to this recital last night," declared Miles shortly. "Pendragon's debut, as they're calling it. From what I hear, he's been playing the piano for a number of years. I wouldn't exactly call him an infant prodigy!"

Lani hesitated. "I—I did go to the recital, yes. And he was good."

"Oh, yes, I know." Miles snorted. "I expect you've seen the pictures of him and your mother in the papers this morning. Looking at them, I'm not surprised you're finding it difficult to concentrate."

Lani's throat felt dry. "Pictures?" she got out at last. "What pictures?"

"Of your mother and Jake Pendragon," retorted

Miles impatiently. "After the concert was over. Where were you when all the camera bulbs were snapping?"

At Mancini's, thought Lani silently, realizing now why her mother had sent them on ahead. "I—er—we all went out for supper afterward," she replied evasively. "Are the pictures good? Daddy takes the newspaper to work, and I've not had a chance to look at it."

"They're okay." Miles was indifferent. "He looks sort of fed up, but your mother is all smiles. So she should be. Arranging all this must have cost her a packet. At least it seems she's going to get some return on her investment."

Lani nodded, and then realizing Miles couldn't see her, she said, "Yes." She was wondering if her father had seen the pictures, and she started when Miles spoke again.

"So when do you think you'll have something to show me?" he asked, reverting to his original theme, and Lani gathered her thoughts with an effort.

"Give me until Monday," she said. "I promise I'll work over the weekend. I'll come into your office on Monday morning, and if you like what you see, you can take me out for lunch."

"Why not dinner on Saturday?" suggested Miles flatly. "Let's face it, you turned me down last week."

"And interrupt my working schedule?" she exclaimed, forcing a note of gaiety into her voice, and Miles sighed heavily before acceding to her arrangements.

With the phone call finished, Lani turned reluctantly toward the stairs, but then changing her mind again, she made her way along the corridor to the kitchen.

"Mrs. Evans, could I have a cup of coffee?" she asked appealingly, and the housekeeper turned from the pastry she was making to nod toward the percolator.

"Help yourself," she said, sprinkling flour over the scrubbed wooden board she was working on. "Just so long as you don't expect me to go washing my hands again, as I had to when the phone rang."

"I'm sorry, Mrs. Evans." Lani poured herself a mug of black coffee and cradled it between her palms. "I would have answered it, honestly, but—well, I was praying it wouldn't be Clare."

"And if it had been, do you think I'd have told her you were out?" inquired the housekeeper dryly. "Anyway, why shouldn't you want to speak to your mother? You went out with her last night, didn't you?"

"Yes." Lani sipped the strong aromatic liquid. "But that doesn't mean I like her calling me." She sighed. "As a matter of fact, I wish she'd never come back to London. I—we—daddy and I seem to get along a lot better when she's out of the country."

"Lani!" Mrs. Evans sounded shocked. "That's no way to speak of the woman who bore you!"

"Sometimes I find that difficult to believe," mumbled the girl into her cup. "Sometimes I think we have nothing in common."

"You've inherited her talent," declared the housekeeper staunchly. "Mrs. St. John always had a vivid imagination. I used to think that was why she went into opera. Because she enjoyed make-believe so much."

"You've known her a long time, haven't you, Mrs. Evans?"

"More than twenty years," agreed the old woman

reminiscently. "You were scarcely a month old when your daddy employed me. And your mother was already talking about her next role."

Lani sighed. "Do you think their marriage would have lasted as long as it did if they hadn't had me?"

"Who knows?" Mrs. Evans shrugged her bony shoulders. "They were both so different when they got married, and the years only served to widen the gulf between them. Maybe if your father had had more time for her in those early days—if your mother had had more patience with his work." She made a rueful face. "I'm afraid they were both too intent on their careers, and by the time your father realized what was happening, it was too late."

"He still loves her, you know." Lani finished her coffee and set down the mug. "He pretends he doesn't, but he does."

"Your father loves an illusion," responded Mrs. Evans sagely. "The woman he remembers never even existed. Now, run along with you, will you, and let me get on with my work."

Sitting at her drawing board again, Lani wondered if what Mrs. Evans had said was true. Her father did tend to cling to his memories of the good times they had had together. In all their conversations, he had never mentioned the rows that had punctuated their relationship, and the frigid hostile atmosphere Lani had learned to dread.

At twelve o'clock the phone rang again, and in spite of her reluctance to speak to her mother, Lani tossed her sketching pad aside and went to answer it. Besides,

Mrs. Evans might still be baking, and she had promised to take all calls.

Lifting the receiver, cautiously she said, "Hello," and the brief silence that greeted her made all the hairs on her arms and legs stand on end.

"Lani." The voice that said her name was unbelievably familiar, and her hand shook as she took the receiver away from her ear with the avowed intention of ringing off. But his "Lani! Lani, for God's sake, answer me!" tore aside her feeble veneer of indifference.

"What do you want?" she demanded unsteadily. "I thought it was my mother who was calling. Is—is she there with you? I expect she's quite ecstatic about your success. I hear you've got your picture in all the papers—"

"Lani, I want to see you." His flat unemotional words broke into her nervous flow of speech with the incision of a knife, and she broke off abruptly, shocked into silence. "I mean it," he added, his words falling into the breathless stillness around her. "I want to see you. Now, do we do this sensibly, or do we have to play the little charade we played before?"

Lani pressed her open palm against her jean-clad thigh, striving for control. "I really don't know what you mean, Mr. Pendragon," she hedged. "When you rang before, I was too busy to see you. I'm too busy now. Does my mother want to speak to me?"

"Your mother is not here," grated Jake harshly. "If you want to ring me back, you can reach me at the Gloucester Court Hotel. Now, do you want to do that, just to prove I'm not lying?"

"Why should I think you're lying?" she cried, but she was trembling nevertheless, and she was unable to keep the tremor out of her voice. "Really, Mr. Pendragon, isn't this rather melodramatic? How or where you live is no concern of mine."

"No, it's not," he agreed, without expression. "Even so, I'd like to get it out of the way if I can. Then perhaps we could get to the point of my call. That is— when are you prepared to see me?"

Lani's moist fingers slipped around the handset. "Does my mother know what you're doing?" she asked, keeping a tight rein on her emotions, and she heard the sudden intake of his breath.

"No," he said flatly. "She doesn't. Contrary to public opinion, Clare is not my keeper. I do not have to gain her permission to ask her daughter to have tea with me."

"*Tea?*"

Lani said the word with some surprise, and Jake confirmed it. "I can't get away before four o'clock," he stated bleakly. "But we could have tea here if you are prepared to trust me. As a matter of fact, it would suit me admirably if you would come here. I've got a lot of work to get through, and I don't have a lot of time."

Lani gasped. "You want me to come to your hotel!"

"Why not? It's perfectly reasonable. We won't be alone. I have a valet and a secretary within calling distance if you're afraid of my reputation."

"I—" Lani was speechless. "I can't come to your hotel! And in any case, if you're so busy, how have you found the time to make this call? Isn't it interrupting your concentration or something?"

"As a matter of fact, it is," replied Jake tautly. "Look, stop trying to score points, will you, and say what you think. After last night, I realize you must think me all kinds of a heel, but at least have the goodness to give me a chance to apologize."

"To apologize?"

"What else?" Jake was impatient. "Well? Will you come?"

"No." Lani made her refusal definite. "I can't. You shouldn't have asked me. I — I'd forgotten all about last night. Men who have been drinking aren't always responsible for their actions."

"Really?" She could tell by his tone that he was not pleased by her dismissal. "I see now you're more sophisticated than I thought. Okay. I'm glad to hear I didn't upset you. Goodbye, Lani. I'll see you around."

Not if I see you first, Lani told herself painfully, as she replaced the receiver. *The hypocrite,* she thought, stumping up the stairs to her studio. How dared he imagine he could get away with a simple apology! It would serve him right if she phoned her mother and told her what a bastard he was! The trouble was, she couldn't be certain Clare would believe her, and in this kind of situation, it was often the informer who came off worst.

Mrs. Evans brought her a sandwich and another cup of coffee at one o'clock, as she usually did when Lani was working, but although she thanked her, Lani had no appetite for the ham and cheese roll. With a feeling of desperation, she told the housekeeper she was going out, and ignoring Mrs. Evans's look of surprise, she pulled on a sheepskin jacket over her charcoal-smeared shirt and shabby jeans, and backed the Capri out of the garage.

The weather had improved considerably since her father left that morning, and now a watery sun was slanting through the bare branches of the trees in the square. Its brilliance gave more color to the lingering heads of chrysanthemums and caused her own spirits to lighten slightly at the prospect of getting some fresh air.

Accelerating rather less carefully than usual to the end of the cul-de-sac, she had to brake hard to avoid the vehicle that was just turning into Pelham Court. Shaken by the sudden emergency, Lani was groping irritably for the right gear when she realized that the car that had almost run into her was a dark green Porsche, and as she looked across the bonnet of her car into the interior of his, she recognized Jake's grim profile.

He recognized her in the same instant, but Lani had no intention of sticking around to find out why he had come. Almost without volition, her feet found the clutch and the accelerator, and jamming the car into bottom gear, she sent the Capri hurtling forward.

When the Porsche slotted in behind her on Glendower Street, she guessed he was not about to let her get away, and she sighed impatiently at the realization she could never outpace him on an open road. Her only chance of losing him lay in the mass of side roads and one-way streets that made up the heart of London, and turning right without warning, she allowed the Capri to speed her toward the first of a series of traffic lights.

A glance in her rearview mirror reminded her that Jake had a vehicle that could outmaneuver most other cars on the road, and she realized she would have to be much more sneaky if she wanted to escape him. Licking her lips, she switched on her left signal, turning right at the last moment, so that the Capri's tires squealed protestingly as she hauled the steering wheel around. To her intense annoyance, the Porsche merely waited until she had negotiated the corner before making any signal. She could almost hear the irate motorist, who was coming in the opposite direction and whose fender she almost scraped, saying, "Women drivers!" with every reason to feel aggrieved.

She guessed Jake was not exactly enjoying the detour even though he was obviously finding no difficulty in keeping up with her. On the contrary, there were times when he was evidently trying to overtake, and she had to swerve sideways to prevent his outwitting her. But for the most part the roads were too busy to allow for anything but the simple act of keeping going, and Lani's head was spinning by the time she had threaded her way in and out of the streets behind the Middlesex Hospital, only to find herself in another one-way street, with no alternative but to repeat the exercise.

Swinging the wheel, she turned out of Langham Gate into a street she had not seen before and then stood on her brakes as the blank wall of the nurses' home loomed up ahead of her. It was a dead end, a back entry she should have identified by the circular sign at its start, but she had been so intent on outwitting Jake she had not even noticed the unmistakable No Entry signs.

Hunching her shoulders, she looked into the rearview mirror, quite prepared to find Jake getting out of the Porsche behind her, but to her amazement the lane was deserted. There was no sign of the sleek green sports car that had tailed her all over the city, and she blinked her eyes disbelievingly, unable to accept that he had missed her diversion. But it must be so, she argued with herself impatiently. Somehow, she didn't quite know how, she had thrown him off the scent, and she expelled her breath almost deliriously at the thought of how angry he must be.

"*Out!*" The sudden command caught her unawares, and she gazed at Jake in amazement as he reached in and expertly extracted her keys. "I said out," he repeated, without a trace of warmth in his voice, and because she was so stunned, Lani found herself obeying him.

"I—I can't stay here. It's a No Entry," she protested, the logic of her argument causing him to quirk one dark brow.

"You should have thought of that before you turned in here," he remarked, putting her keys in his pocket. "I was waiting for you to make a mistake. The way you were driving, I'm amazed you're still in one piece."

"I'm a good driver," declared Lani sullenly, as surprise gave way to resentment. "And I don't sneak up on people when they're least expecting it. You could have given me a heart attack for the second time today."

"Only for the second time?" Jake was coldly sardonic. "You surprise me. I should have thought it was the third at least."

"You think you're so clever, don't you?"

"The stock response." He shrugged. "No, I don't think I'm particularly clever at all. If I were I would be back at the hotel practicing instead of following you on this crazy car chase all over London."

Lani sniffed. "No one asked you to follow me."

"No, that's true," he conceded. "However, it must have occurred to you that I hadn't driven all the way to Pelham Court just for the exercise, and as you childishly decided to play cops and robbers, I had no choice but to join in."

Lani glanced around. "So where's your car?"

"Parked in front of the hospital," he declared carelessly. "Unlike you, I do not ignore No Entry signs. The police are apt to get annoyed over things like that."

"Very funny." Lani made a face, but in fact it wasn't so funny after all. As it happened, she was beginning to feel depressed as well as foolish, and she looked up at him moodily, wondering what he was really thinking.

"So—" Jake expelled his breath heavily. "What now? Do we start all over, or as soon as I give you back your keys, are you going to make another run for it?"

"I won't do that," muttered Lani, holding out her hand. "Give me the keys. Like you, I'd prefer not to get a parking ticket."

Jake hesitated. "Will you follow me to my hotel?"

"No." Lani was definite. "I—I wanted some air. I was going to walk in the park. You can come with me, if you like. It's up to you."

Jake was suspicious. "What park?"

"Any park." Lani bent her head. "Regent's Park is not far from here. We could go there. Always supposing I can get out of here, of course."

"I'll help you," said Jake abruptly, dropping the keys

into her hand and walking toward the narrow exit. "You'd better reverse. I'll try and hold up the traffic so you can get out."

Once she was out and Jake was striding away to get his car, Lani pressed her lips together mutinously. He was so cool, she thought resentfully, so assured, so much in control of the situation. It wasn't her fault that he'd trailed her all over London. Nor could she be blamed for the time he had wasted. How much practicing did he have to do, for heaven's sake? He already played the piano like it was an extension of his fingers. Why couldn't he just leave her alone, instead of making her feel as if she was responsible for all of this?

She was lucky enough to find a parking space by the cricket ground, and she stood around impatiently, her hands thrust deep into the sheepskin's pockets, waiting for Jake to park. He reversed with enviable skill into a narrow space that Lani had rejected and then got out of the Porsche lithely, sliding his arms into the sleeves of a leather jacket.

"You waited," he remarked ironically, strolling toward her, adjusting the collar of his coat. "Shall we walk?"

"Where?" Lani scuffed her boot against the curb. "Along the canal? Into the zoo?"

"Let's just walk in the park," said Jake, inclining his head in the direction in which he wanted to go, and Lani shrugged indifferently as he fell into step beside her.

They skirted the canal and the zoological gardens and then left the paths to walk across the grass. It was damp but springy, and there were few people around to trouble them. Lani felt her guard relaxing as Jake spoke of the time of year and the weather and his own preference for warmer climes. Like her mother he was tanned, observed Lani, although with his dark skin it was not so noticeable, and she remembered bitterly that he had just spent three weeks in the Caribbean. Such thoughts did not make easy company, and when he spoke of the previous evening's recital, she had lost her mood of tolerance.

"What were you doing in Pelham Court?" she asked abruptly, anxious for him to get to the point. "You made your apologies quite adequately on the phone. Don't you think it was rather foolhardy coming to my father's house?"

"Probably." Jake's hands were pushed into the pockets of his pants, and he lifted his shoulders carelessly. "However, after some consideration, I knew I had to talk to you. I didn't want you to get the wrong impression of me."

"Could I do that?" Lani's tone was taut and challenging, and Jake's mouth tightened ominously. "As far as I'm concerned you can't excuse what happened, and I'm amazed at your temerity in believing I won't tell my mother."

Jake halted abruptly, his expression hard and angry. "Go ahead," he said curtly. "If that's what you want to do, tell her! I won't try to stop you. It's entirely your affair."

"Because you know my mother wouldn't believe me!" Lani burst out hotly, stopping beside him and gazing up at him through her long lashes. "She's so obsessed with you, she'd be bound to think I was making it up—that deep down inside I was jealous!"

"And aren't you?" he inquired harshly, regarding her through narrowed lids, and her resentment flared into action. Without really stopping to think what she was doing, she lifted her hand and slapped him full across his face, and then watched with a quivering sense of incredulity as the red weals her fingers had made rose lividly against his dark skin.

It was fortunate there was no one around to witness what had happened. Only a stalwart belt of trees looked on in silent recrimination, and Lani stepped back uncomfortably, half afraid he was about to return the compliment. But he didn't. He just stood there looking at her, waiting for her to make the next move, and she lifted her shoulders jerkily, feeling as if she was the guilty party. It didn't help that she was wearing no makeup, she thought helplessly, that her clothes were hardly elegant, and that such things were important when one was fighting a psychological battle. He had her at a disadvantage, as he had had from the beginning, not just because this meeting was unexpected, but because the sequence of events had left her feeling so vulnerable. And it certainly didn't help to know she would suffer in any physical comparison with Clare.

His fingers touching her chin, lifting her face to his, brought her out of her misery, but Lani's instinctive reaction was to get away from him. However, when she stepped back again, she came up against the bole of a tree behind her, and its coarse bark pricked the fabric of her jacket as her nervous feet trampled the grass at its base.

"I'm sorry." Jake's voice was now low and husky and unbelievably tender, disrupting her emotions as nothing else had ever done, and her heart palpitated wildly. "But when I'm with you, you make me feel so bloody selfish, and all I want to do is hurt you."

Lani put her hands down to her sides, gripping the bole of the tree as if for support. His words had not reassured her. On the contrary, she was very much afraid that if he continued to stroke her chin, she would not be able to resist the desire to turn her lips against his hand, and panic made her turn her head so that his fingers fell away.

But he didn't leave her to recover what little composure she had left. With a muffled oath, he moved toward her, and this time she had no choice but to look at him when he cradled her face in his hands.

"You're so—so—"

He broke off and she strove to find some word that might cause him to release her. "So silly? So childish? So lacking in sophistication?" she mumbled bitterly, and his gentleness gave way to sudden violence.

"You know that's not true," he muttered, his long fingers flexing against the slender column of her throat and then, with a groan of submission, he bent his head to hers.

His mouth touched hers tentatively at first, as if uncertain of its welcome, but when she did no more than restrain any resistance, his tongue darted between his lips to stroke the unyielding contours of hers. It was moist and seductive, a sensual, sensuous indication of what lovemaking could be, and Lani's head fell back against the tree's bark, its spikes tearing at her hair.

The persuasive kisses he was placing on her upper lip and on her lower one stirred the wanton emotions he had awakened the night before, and although she was trying to remain impassive, her head was swimming with the effort. He was an expert in the art of seduction, she thought despairingly, and when his tongue forced her lips to part, she felt a warm flood of sensation in her thighs.

With a little sigh, she gave up the unequal struggle, and the searching intimacy of his tongue in her mouth was a new and devastating violation. It was an irresistible reminder of the way he could tear aside her defenses, and its sexual possession brought her hands to clutch his sleeves.

As if he, too, was shaken by the hungry cohesion of their mouths, Jake's weight suddenly collapsed against her. With a murmured protest, his hands left her throat to open her coat and then grasped the burgeoning fullness of her breasts. Even through her shirt, she could feel her nipples cresting against his palms, and she knew an unholy impulse to tear her shirt aside and feel his touch upon her naked skin.

"*Lani,*" he said thickly, releasing her mouth to take a labored breath, and then with a supreme effort he put his hands against the bole of the tree and pushed himself away from her.

In the strained silence that followed his sudden withdrawal, Lani could do nothing. For a few numb moments, she was too shocked to move, and it was the errant wind needling at the fastening of her shirt that reminded her belatedly how cold she was. And it was not just an outer cold either. It was an inner one, too, crystallizing from the very core of her being, so that shame and guilt and indignation were all one, knotting like a painful growth inside her. With a feeling of self-disgust, she dragged her coat around her then, holding it in place with trembling arms, waiting, though she was not exactly aware of it, for the trite excuses he would offer.

"I did not mean this to happen," he said at last, and Lani lifted her shoulders, as if his words had confirmed her expectations. "I wanted to see you—but that was all. I did not intend to touch you. But you looked so indignant, and comforting you seemed such an inno-cent thing to do. *Innocent!*" He repeated the word savagely. "I must have been out of my mind!"

"Don't go on." Lani straightened away from the tree abruptly. "I've no doubt you believe everything you say." Her lips twisted. "That's what makes it so pathetic!"

"What do you mean?"

Jake, who had turned away to rake restless fingers through his hair, rounded on her with sudden hostility, but Lani refused to be dismayed. "Isn't this the mo-ment when you say we must never meet again?" she taunted coldly, her words belying the coil of pain that writhed inside her. "Forgive me, but weren't you about to say that you had wanted us to be friends, but how impossible that is now?"

"You little—"

Jake bit off an epithet, but Lani merely arched her brows. "What's wrong?" she asked. "Am I too out-spoken? Or was I too near the truth for your liking? What did you expect, Jake? More recriminations?"

He drew a savage breath. "Sometimes clichés can be true, you know," he snapped. "And as far as our never meeting again is concerned, you'd have to ask your mother about that, wouldn't you?"

Lani winced at the deliberate callousness of his words, but Jake ignored her sudden pallor. "Just to set the matter straight, I had intended to tell you, as gently as possible, that right now there's no place in my life for emotional complications," he added harshly. "But I see I was mistaken in considering your feelings. I suggest we go back before I say something I'll regret. You are still Clare's daughter, however unlikely that seems!"

They walked back in silence to where they had left the cars. Lani would have preferred to walk alone, but it seemed easier and infinitely more mature to maintain a facade of cold indifference. Although she was intensely conscious of his chilling presence beside her, she managed to look about her with every appearance of interest.

Once back at the parking area, however, her confidence deserted her, and she hurried to get into her car on legs that seemed suddenly unsure. The past few minutes had exhausted her remaining reserves of energy, and she tucked herself behind the wheel with a feeling of imminent collapse. She wasn't even convinced she had the will to drive herself back to Pelham Court, and she waited with some apprehension for Jake to leave first.

But he didn't. He drove the Porsche out of its space and then, leaving the engine running, he got out and walked back to where Lani was parked. He waited for her to wind down her window so that he could speak to her, but when she didn't, too choked up to face another confrontation with him, he gave a gesture of impatience and wrenched open her door.

"Just to put your mind at rest, I'll tell Clare I've seen you—" he declared coldly, pulling the door wide, and then broke off abruptly when he saw her tear-wet face. "For Christ's sake, Lani," he muttered, evidently stunned by her betraying breakdown. "Oh, for Christ's sake, what am I going to do with you?"

Lani didn't answer him. She couldn't. With tears running down her cheeks and into her mouth and her whole being gripped by the most agonizing kind of torment, she was incapable of defending herself and she knew it. He was to blame, she thought bitterly, looking up mistily into his startled eyes. If he had only left her alone, she might have come to terms with the way she was feeling. As it was, he had taken her world and turned it upside down.

Snatching the door from his unresisting fingers, she reached determinedly for the ignition. If he had driven away as any honorable man would have done, he would never have realized how he had hurt her, she sniffed miserably, and there was no point in prolonging her humiliation.

With trembling fingers, she fired the engine, and then cursed her own stupidity as it stalled at the first attempt. A second effort was more successful, and she finally got the car into gear and pulled away.

If she had expected Jake might try to stop her, she was mistaken. He simply stood there, his hands pushed deep into the pockets of his pants, waiting for her to leave. There was a curiously frustrated expression on his face, but she did not try to analyze it. No doubt he was cursing himself for ever getting involved with her. As she turned into Prince Albert Road, she saw him walking back to his car, and this time she had no illusions that he might decide to follow her.

CHAPTER SEVEN

FOR THE NEXT TWO WEEKS, Lani immersed herself in her work, refusing all invitations with the excuse that she simply did not have the time to spare. Even her consultations with Miles were kept on a business footing, and although he joked with her and said he had not intended she should become a recluse, Lani insisted it was the only way she could make any progress.

And to a certain extent she was right. By cutting herself off from all emotional relationships, she was able to concentrate totally on her work, and the satisfaction she gained from that helped to make up for the deficiencies in her life.

At first, it wasn't easy. The weekend after the scene with Jake, nothing seemed to go right for her, and Clare, calling to invite her to another party, became quite angry when she insisted she couldn't make it.

"Of course you can make it, Lani," she exclaimed tersely. "Having accepted you into my circle, the least you can do is show some gratitude for it. Besides, there'll be some interesting people for you to meet, people who might well be able to help you with your work."

Lani sighed. "I don't need any help, mother."

"My name is Clare, and everyone needs help," re-

torted her mother shortly. "In any case, I want you to
be there. Goodness knows, it's not so much to ask when
I shall be leaving for Paris in a couple of weeks."

"You're leaving?"

Lani's shocked reaction was evident, and Clare, mis-
understanding her daughter's feelings, quickly explained. "I shall be singing at La Scala in December,
and as Jake has visited France only briefly, I thought
we might spend a few days there before rehearsals
begin in Milan. Paris is such a beautiful city. I've
always felt it was my spiritual home. And I want Jake to
share that—as well as meet some people I know who
will be very useful to him."

Lani's lips compressed. "I see," she got out at last.
"Well, I'm sure you will enjoy yourselves. I—er—I suppose I may see you when you get back to England. Will
it be in January?"

"You mean you won't change your mind?"

Clare was incensed, but Lani was more determined
than ever now to avoid another meeting. "I'm afraid
not," she said. And unable to prevent herself, she added, "Unlike Mr. Pendragon, I find hard work the only
recipe for success."

As she had expected, Clare took exception to this,
and Lani had to listen while her mother informed her
with icy disdain that she couldn't possibly understand
how a *real* artist might feel. Just because she was
prepared to settle for the *mediocre* existence she had
chosen for herself did not mean everyone had to be so
provincial. There was more to the same vein, but Lani
closed her ears to the continuing stream of verbal
abuse, and when Clare rang off, she consoled herself

with the thought that she had probably burned her bridges so far as her mother was concerned.

During the second week of her enforced isolation, Roger St. John succumbed to a dose of influenza, and Lani's energies were divided between her studio and her father's bedroom. Roger seemed to pick up colds so much more easily now than he had before, and once again he developed the cough Lani had worried about the last time he was ill. She took the opportunity to mention her anxieties the next time the doctor called, and his advice was that her father needed a rest.

"He needs a holiday, Lani," he told her simply. "How long is it since you two got away together? Couldn't you persuade him to spend a few weeks in the sun? I believe Florida is very nice at this time of the year."

Lani sighed. "He won't go, Dr. Lawson. Do you think I haven't tried to persuade him? One of his colleagues offered him the use of his villa in the south of France in September, but he wouldn't take it. He just seems to live for his work, that's all, and if anyone threatens to take that away from him . . . ."

"I know what you mean." Dr. Lawson grimaced. "I have other patients with the same complaint. Okay, Lani—well, I'll just have to see what I can do."

In the event, Roger surprised both of them by submitting to Dr. Lawson's suggestion. "Christmas is coming," he said to Lani smoothly, after the physician had departed. "We could spend a few days in the West Indies, if you're agreeable. I know Mrs. Evans would like to visit her daughter in Reading, so there'd be no problem there."

"Oh, daddy!" Lani was so relieved she didn't know what to say. "But. . .where in the West Indies? Trinidad? Barbados? Oh, there are so many islands, and I'd like to visit them all."

"I thought—Antigua," said her father offhandedly, and Lani felt the first twinge of anxiety. "It seems to be the place most people want to go," he added. "And as we haven't been before, we ought to start somewhere."

Lani hesitated. "Then why not Barbados?"

"Because I want to go to Antigua," replied her father brusquely. "Good heavens, girl, I thought you didn't care where we went. Just so long as we got some sun, of course."

Lani sighed. "I don't. And. . .and if you want to go to Antigua, we'll go." But she couldn't help remembering that her father had said Clare had recently returned from a visit to Antigua, and her nerves were still too tense not to make the obvious connection.

With the completed sketches of Mogbat, Matilda's new apprentice, behind her, Lani began the slow process of plotting the first story. Her initial ideas took the form of a picture story, illustrating the narrative's development with a series of line drawings she would eventually transfer into actual paintings. She found the ideas for her stories developed themselves, and in spite of her fears about her father, she felt her enthusiasm returning as the butterfingered Matilda led her unsuspecting apprentice into a sequence of disastrous adventures that were both exciting and humorous. The world of make-believe was such an ideal world to escape to, and she resented the emotions that still intruded during her non-working hours.

One of her worst days occurred when she read in the morning newspaper that Clare had left for Paris the previous day. There was a picture of her at the airport, smiling as she was whisked through the departure lounge by a handful of security men, and although it was impossible to positively identify the dark-coated person accompanying her, Lani had little hesitation in deciding it was Jake. Clare Austin on her way to Milan, the caption under the photograph read, and after describing how she was to appear at the Milan opera house, the article concluded by confirming she would not be back in England again before the end of January.

It was only after Lani had snapped the points of several pencils that it occurred to her to wonder whether her father hadn't read something similar before his sudden acquiescence to their holiday. If he had learned that Clare was to spend Christmas out of the country, he might have assumed mistakenly she was returning to the Caribbean. After all, Clare had always liked the sun, and he had probably not known of her engagement in Milan. Still, Lani reflected dourly, once they got there he would soon learn the truth, and she was not going to tell him and jeopardize his health.

With Clare gone, Lani discovered a new sense of freedom. She no longer started every time the telephone rang, and when she drove out of Pelham Court, she was not continually watching for a certain dark green Porsche. She actually began to believe she had exaggerated the effect Jake's reappearance in her life had had on her, and only when she read some snippet of information about France or Italy did she feel the crippling depression that thinking of him evoked. But it was no use, she told herself, whenever she was feeling low. Even if Jake had not been the kind of man he was, he would never have been content to marry her. He was ruthless, he was selfish, and he was ambitious, and whatever it took to gain his own ends, he would do it.

Roger St. John returned to work at the beginning of December, and Lani, who had spent far too much time worrying over her father, was glad to get back to her book. The adventures of Matilda and Mogbat were reaching a critical stage, and she was eager to get the line drawings finished so she could start working in color. It was unlikely she would get that far before they were due to leave for Antigua, but she was eager to continue. Only in her studio did she truly feel alive, and she hoped the coming holiday would provide the adjustment she needed, too.

On the Wednesday afternoon of the week her father returned to work, Lani was working in her studio when the doorbell rang. She had been engrossed in the illustration of a jet-propelled broomstick Matilda had invented, but the unexpected sound disturbed her, and she sighed with some impatience at the realization that Mrs. Evans was out. Of course she could ignore the bell, she thought, tapping the end of her pencil against her teeth. But if it was someone like Sarah, who had recently been complaining that Lani was neglecting them, she would not take kindly to being left standing on the doorstep.

Taking a deep breath, Lani got up from her drawing board to walk to the door. As she did so, the bell pealed again, and she automatically quickened her step as she ran lightly down the stairs. A swift glance at her reflection in the hall mirror assured her she was reasonably presentable. Her hair, loosely secured with a piece of black velvet was untidy, but anyone who knew how often she ran her fingers through it while she was working, would not be surprised at that. And for once she was wearing quite a decent short-sleeved jumper, the hem of which actually overlapped her rather less presentable purple cords.

It had been a gloomy day, the misty veil of morning giving way only with reluctance to an overcast afternoon. Lani had had the light on over her drawing board for the past hour. Now as she opened the door to her visitor the shades of evening were already darkening the streets. She could hardly believe it was only three o'clock, and with this thought in her mind, she was totally unprepared for the man who stood outside.

Jake was propped against the concrete post that supported the canopy overhanging the doorstep, dressed in jeans and a brown leather jacket. He gave the appearance of having been there for some time, and Lani looked about her anxiously, wondering who else had seen him. He must be cold, she thought uneasily, noticing the lines of strain around his mouth. Then, more urgently she wondered, what was he doing here? Why wasn't he in Milan with Clare?

"Can I come in?" he asked at last, when it became obvious that Lani was too agitated to speak, and although she badly wanted to let him in, she shook her head.

"There's no one at home," she said jerkily. "I—our housekeeper has gone to her daughter's. My father's at work, and I'm in the house alone."

"That's what I thought," remarked Jake straightening and stepping onto the threshold. "Come on, Lani. Don't keep me hanging about. I didn't come all this way just to play verbal games."

Lani stepped aside, because if she hadn't he would have walked into her, but when he closed the door behind him, she reached nervously for the light switch. It was too dismal in the hall to see him properly, too claustrophobic there in the gloom to feel at ease, and while she was fumbling for the lamp, he stepped closer to her, and her words of protest were cut off by his mouth.

She fought herself free moments later, putting the width of the hall between them and turning on the main switch as she did so. The small chandelier lighted the hall and the stairs beyond, and she hovered on the bottom step, realizing she had to stay in control. She should not have let him in. As soon as she'd seen who it was, she should have slammed the door in his face. But seeing him there had aroused all the crazy emotions she had been trying so hard to suppress, and she had not had the will to turn him away.

Now Jake pushed his hands into the pockets of his jacket and looked about him with evident interest. As if attempting to reassure her, he made a wry inspection of his reflection in the hall mirror, and then his eyes alighted on the picture of the Brecon Beacons that Lani had painted and that her father had insisted on hanging in the hall.

"Yours?" he queried lightly, almost as if that urgent kiss had not taken place, and Lani nodded her head mutely, too unnerved to dissemble. "It's good," he commented, tilting his head to one side to read her signature. "Lani St. John. September 1980."

"What do you want?" Lani's fingers curved over the newel post. "Please—you can't stay here. If my father comes home and finds you, he'll . . . he'll . . . ."

"What will he do?" Jake's eyes were on a level with hers as she stood on the first step. "Throw me out?" He shrugged his shoulders. "He might try."

"You don't have to tell me you're stronger than my father," exclaimed Lani unsteadily. "But I'd rather you weren't obliged to prove it. He—he's not been well, and finding you here . . . it could be bad for him," she finished lamely.

Jake looked down at his booted feet and took a measured step toward her. "Okay," he said, looking up again. "If you promise to listen to what I have to say, I'll promise to be gone before your father gets home."

Lani moistened her dry lips. "Why do you keep doing this. Why can't you leave me alone? After—after what happened before, I thought you had had enough of me. You said yourself you had no time for—for complications."

"I said there was no place in my life for emotional complications," amended Jake, shortening the distance between them with each pantherlike tread. "Look—can't we talk somewhere else? I don't like to think our conversation is being observed."

"Observed?" Lani looked blank, and he explained.

"Outside," he said, gesturing beyond the fluted glass panels of the door. "There were two old ladies who seemed mightily interested in the fact that I was at your door. Do you think they might be curious as to why you invited me in, if you're not prepared to offer me a seat?"

Lani sighed. "I suppose you mean the Misses French," she exclaimed unhappily, recalling the spinster sisters who shared the house two doors away. Since Lani's college days, and even before that, they had shown an unhealthy interest in any young man who brought her home, and she could imagine what they were thinking now.

"Show me where you work," suggested Jake, reaching the foot of the stairs and placing one hand against the wall and the other over hers where it rested on the banister.

"I can't—"

"Why can't you?" he persisted softly. "I showed you where I worked all those years ago."

"That wasn't the same—"

"Why wasn't it?" His eyes narrowed. "I am interested, really. And—and if your father comes back, I promise I'll sneak out the back way."

Lani's heart quickened. "Jake—"

"Mmm?"

His eyes were on her mouth, and she could almost feel their touch. "Wh—where's Clare?" she breathed, introducing her mother's name deliberately, and he was not perturbed.

"In Milan, I guess," he responded huskily, pulling her hand free of his, she led the way upstairs.

Her studio had never looked more untidy, with crumpled paper on the floor and broken pencils littering her board. There were piles of sketch pads and notebooks, pots of ink and glue and solvent, and several half-squeezed tubes of paint tossed carelessly aside. Because she needed the space, there was little furniture: just her board and her desk and her easel, the cupboard where she kept supplies, the stool she sat on and an old chintzy sofa she sometimes used when she was checking her proofs. It was Spartan but functional, and Lani had always felt at ease there.

"So—this is Matilda's hideaway," remarked Jake, pausing for a moment in the doorway before following her into the room. His eyes moved in studied appraisal over the walls, hung with various paintings Lani had done over the years. "What are you working on at the moment? Or is that not for publication?"

"No, I—" Lani lifted her shoulders nervously, disconcerted by the fact that he had closed the door behind him. "I've... invented another character. Mogbat. He's—he's Matilda's new apprentice. Miles—that's my agent—he thought creating another character was a good idea."

"Is this Mogbat?" Jake queried, approaching her board and examining the drawing she had been working on, and Lani took her life in her hands and went to stand beside him.

"I—yes. Yes, that's him," she agreed, pointing at the little character, who was an endearing mix of cat and bat, and Jake turned his head and looked at her.

"You're trembling," he said, and she realized the hand she had extended had betrayed her. "Why are you trembling? You're not afraid of me, are you?"

Lani shook her head. "I expect I'm cold," she replied, with a remarkable degree of self-possession, considering how disturbed she felt inside. Just standing here beside him was taking every shred of self-control she had, and it didn't help when he turned fully toward her.

"I went to Paris," he said, and the unprincipled thought she had had that perhaps he had not accompanied her mother after all died.

"I know," she answered, refusing to look at him. "I saw Clare's picture in the paper. Did you enjoy the experience?"

"Paris was. . .interesting," he conceded, lifting one hand to take a strand of her hair between his fingers, and Lani knew she ought to move away from him. "I missed you," he added, taking the strand to his lips. "I kept wondering what you were doing and if you had forgiven me."

"Forgiven you?" Lani's breathing was constricted. "Why should you want my forgiveness? You seemed to blame me for what—for what happened that day."

"Did I?" He sounded surprised, but she refused to respond to the desire to see for herself. "Well, I can hardly blame you for this, can I? I flew back from Milan because I wanted to see you."

Lani steeled herself as his probing fingers stroked a line from her shoulder to her elbow. "And did you tell my mother why you were coming back?" she demanded tautly. "Or as she had served her purpose, did she no longer deserve your attention?"

"I told Clare I was coming back to England, yes," he responded harshly, his teasing fingers stilling their game and coming to rest inflexibly at the back of her neck. "I saw no point in hurting her by telling her I was coming to see you. But if you want that privilege, of course I can't prevent you."

Lani winced as he turned her to face him, and his grim expression softened slightly at her weakness. "Why do you persist in bringing up your mother's name every time we're together?" he demanded roughly. "I don't ask you about this man—Miles, or Paul Somers, or any of the other men in your life. Why do you insist on tormenting both of us?"

Lani hesitated. "But, you do. . .sleep with Clare, don't you?"

"I've slept with a lot of women," he replied flatly. "If that's what this charade is all about, then yes, I'm quite normal in that respect."

"That's not what I meant," said Lani unsteadily, but when he moved his hand to cup her nape she did not move away.

"I want you," Jake told her evenly, bending his head to brush his lips against the downy softness of her cheek. "I want to go to bed with you. Oh—not to sleep," he added as she quivered in his arms.

"You can't—we can't—" choked Lani, panicking as his lips reached the corner of her mouth and his hands drew her more firmly against him.

"I think we're going to have to," he stated, forcing his tongue between her teeth, and its sensual persuasion made all her limbs go weak.

But still she pushed against him, trying desperately to keep him away from her, and her senses swam as his lips sought the quivering curve of her jawline and the scented contours of her neck before returning to hers. It was only when he grasped her hands and pushed them down between them, and her fingers brushed the throbbing source of his manhood, that his name broke from her, and his hungry mouth possessed her with all its sexual skill.

"Yes," he said unsteadily. "Why else am I here? I need you, Lani. I can't eat or sleep or *work*! I can't do anything without thinking how much I want you, how much I want to feel you on me and under me — naked, together."

"Jake, this is crazy—"

"But good, hmm?" he breathed, his hands sliding beneath the skimpy jumper. "Take this off, can't you? I want to see your breasts."

"Jake—"

"Okay, okay," he muttered, releasing her for a moment to shrug off his jacket and let it fall to the floor. The silk shirt he was wearing under it rapidly followed, but when his hands went to the belt of his pants, Lani quickly turned away.

"Don't!" she protested, the blood rushing headlong through her veins, and suddenly she felt him close behind her.

"Why not?" he demanded, his mouth against her nape. "I'm not ashamed of you seeing my body." His hands probed the hem of her jumper to slide it up over her rib cage. "Let me undress you," he urged, his fingers closing possessively around her breasts, and her common-sense self deserted her as she yielded back against him.

The jumper was soon disposed of, and he released her hair from the scrap of velvet so that it fell in silken strands about her shoulders. Then, he turned her toward him, and although she desperately wanted to cover her nakedness, he wouldn't let her, and her eyes closed helplessly as he shamelessly looked his fill.

"Let's go to the couch," he said, capturing her hand in his, and she let him draw her after him to the chintz-covered sofa, shadowy in its corner. With a controlled kind of tenderness, he set her down on the couch, and then knelt beside her, covering her hands and wrists with urgent, emotive kisses that sent tingles up her arm.

When his mouth went to her breasts, she drew back from him, but she could not prevent what he was doing. She felt the exquisite sensuality of his tongue against her peaks, and his fingers went to mold their fullness as he took the whole areola between his teeth.

Somehow she was lying on the couch now, and he was beside her, his lips seeking hers again with increasing urgency. She knew he had unfastened the waistband of her jeans, and as his tongue plunged ever more deeply into her mouth, she felt the coolness of air against her stomach.

Once again, a sense of panic gripped her, but the sudden warmth of his thigh against hers made her realize he had shed his clothes too. One hard muscular leg imprisoned her, and the subtle fragrance of his skin was all around her. To her amazement, she found her hands reaching for him, drawing him down to her, and the smooth thickness of his hair felt deliciously virile between her fingers.

"You want me—say it!" he implored passionately, and with those tawny eyes burning with the fire of his emotions, Lani's hands moved down to caress the taut column of his throat.

"I want you," she repeated obediently, pulling his mouth back to hers, and Jake uttered a sigh of satisfaction as his body moved to cover hers.

This was a totally new experience to Lani. She had never shared with anyone else the kind of intimacies she was sharing with Jake, but she was distantly aware he did not know that. The feel of his skin against hers, the rough abrasion of his body hair, which curled upon his chest before arrowing down to his navel and beyond, the raw male scent of his body—these things had clouded her mind to the practical elements of the situation, and while she knew what he expected of her, when his leg moved to part hers, she found herself fighting a losing battle.

"*Yes*, Lani," he said harshly, evidently mistaking her withdrawal for a belated sense of conscience, and his hand between her thighs quickly disposed of her objections.

"I—no—you mustn't," she whispered brokenly, as his insistent touch brought her to a trembling submission, but he was no longer capable of listening to her. With a groan of urgency, his body sought the honeyed sheath of hers, and although there was a moment's hesitation when he met that unexpected obstacle, it was too late to prevent the inevitable from happening. Her gasp of pain was stifled against his shoulder as she felt that searing penetration, but Jake's hands in her hair forced her head back so that he could look at her.

"For Christ's sake, Lani!" he muttered half-savagely, but then, seeing the tears glistening in her eyes, he brought her close to him again and buried his face in the tangled curtain of red gold silk. "Lani, I can't stop now," he told her in a tortured voice, and she held her breath as he began to move.

To her immense surprise, he didn't hurt her. Unknowingly, her body had been prepared for him, and as her breathing quickened in tune with his, she found herself rising to meet the powerful thrust of his loins. Indeed, there was something incredibly satisfying in feeling him inside her, possessing her, filling her, and her mouth opened wide to the sensual flick of his tongue. With her teeth sinking into his skin as the sensations he was arousing brought her emotions to fever pitch, she could hardly believe the animallike moans she could hear issuing from her throat, and when the climax came, she cried out in wonder, her nails raking convulsively along the firm, smooth curve of his shoulder.

CHAPTER EIGHT

IT WAS SOME TIME LATER that Lani heard the sound of her father's Daimler turning into the drive. It could have been several minutes or several hours, she wasn't exactly sure. All she was sure of was that Jake was still stretched like a lazy panther beside her, his leg and his arm ensuring she could not escape without his notice.

"Hey," he protested sleepily, when she struggled into a sitting position. "Lani, don't go away. Not yet." His eyes caressed her. "We haven't finished—"

"I have," declared Lani frantically, scrambling off the couch. "Oh, please, you must hurry. Put your clothes on now! Can't you hear that engine? It's my father's car."

Jake shifted onto his back, folding his arms behind his head without shame. "So what?" he asked flatly. "What do you want me to do? Grab my clothes and climb down the drainpipe? Lani, *I* know you've never done this before." He grimaced. "Who better? But forget it. You can introduce me to your father. I doubt if he'll even remember me."

Lani expelled her breath in consternation. "You can't be serious!"

"Why not? It's the most sensible solution."

"Sensible!" Lani shook her head in raw frustration.

There was nothing sensible about introducing her father to Jake Pendragon, and remembering how Roger St. John had reacted to the young pianist, she knew a hopeless sense of impotence.

"Put your clothes on," she begged, hurrying into her cords and sweater, and with a gesture of indifference, Jake finally got off the couch.

"If you insist," he murmured, taking advantage of her fumbling efforts to fasten the button of her pants and depositing a lingering kiss at the corner of her lips. Lani trembled.

"Jake, please—" she whispered, when she could get her mouth free, and with a careless shrug, he reached for his clothes.

"If you don't like me the way I am, of course," he remarked with mocking insouciance, and Lani gazed at him helplessly, unable to tear her eyes away.

"I—it's not that," she protested breathlessly, as he zipped up his jeans, and Jake relented.

"I know," he assured her, his husky tone sending shivers of remembered ecstasy along her spine. "Do you think I'd be so obedient if I didn't think you cared?"

"Oh, *Jake!*"

Her limbs melted, and for a few more moments she watched him as he pulled on his shirt and fastened the buttons. There was an acute pleasure in sharing this intimacy with him, and her eyes moved over him possessively, delighting in the abandonment.

"I wouldn't advise you to look at me like that," he told her at last, picking up his jacket, and Lani's heart flipped at the naked hunger in his eyes. "Now, do I look presentable? Do you think your father will approve? I trust I don't look as if I've spent the last hour making passionate love to his daughter."

"You look good to me," murmured Lani unsteadily, trying to respond to his attempt to lighten the situation, and Jake's arm encircled her waist, drawing her against him.

"You know how I really feel, don't you?" he inquired, the hoarseness of emotion overlying his low attractive tones. "And we have things to talk about, don't we? So tell your father we're having dinner together, hmm? Tonight I want there to be no interruptions."

"Jake!" Lani looked up at him helplessly. "I—I can't do that."

"Why not? Do you want me to do it?" he asked evenly, but Lani quickly shook her head.

"I can't. . .introduce you to my father," she stated blankly, trying to ignore the sudden narrowing of those catlike eyes. "You—you did promise to leave if—if daddy came home. Please, let me handle this my way."

"If you insist." Jake lifted his shoulders in a curiously defeated gesture, and Lani was almost tempted to give in. But the memory of how her father had looked when he spoke of Jake Pendragon forced her to sustain her guard, and tentatively, she opened the studio door.

"I—I think my father's gone into his study," she said, after listening for a moment. "Come on. Let's go. You can leave without him even knowing you've been here."

"If that's what you want." Jake bent to turn out the lamp. "But remember, this was your idea, not mine."

Halfway down the stairs, Lani began to understand why Jake had been so unwilling to leave in this underhand way. His lovemaking—their being together—had been something sweet and beautiful. She was spoiling it. She was turning their meeting into something clandestine and tawdry, a sordid little affair, worthy only of concealment.

"Jake—"

She turned to him then, half persuaded that telling the truth could not be so bad. When she heard the sound of the study door, panic flared, raw and basic, and the need for subterfuge far outweighed that fleeting desire for confession. Without thought for anything but the need to protect herself and her father from any further pain, she caught Jake's hand and tugged him down the stairs, opening the door and propelling him outside with a careless disregard for his feelings.

"Wait!" Only as his fingers fastened around her wrist did she realize that he had permitted her reckless ejection when he could quite easily have resisted her. "Tonight," he said harshly. "You're having dinner with me tonight. Come to the hotel. I'll meet you in the lobby at seven o'clock."

"No!" Lani could hear her father coming along the hall and she blankly shook her head. "I can't," she said unsteadily. "I can't have dinner with you!" And pulling her wrist free, she closed the door abruptly, before he could protest.

"DADDY!"

Lani was appalled at her own duplicity as she turned to greet her father. With her back pressed firmly against the fluted panels of the door, as if by doing so she could prevent him from seeing the shadow of the man walking down the path, she gazed at him innocently, as if the idea that only minutes before she had been lying naked in a man's arms was nothing but foolish fantasy.

"Lani!" Her father looked at her in some surprise. "Have you just come in?"

"I—" The temptation to say she had was appealing, but he would hardly believe she had been out without a coat, and in any case, he was already having suspicions. "No."

"Someone's been here," he said perceptively, almost as if he could smell Jake's after-shave. "A man. It was a man, wasn't it, Lani? Who was it? Do I know him? And where were you when I got home?"

Lani expelled her breath a little unevenly. "I—we—we were in the studio," she said, controlling her color with difficulty. "He—well, it was a friend of Miles's, actually. John—John Brecon," she added as her eyes alighted on the painting Jake had noticed earlier.

"Really?" Roger St. John was looking distinctly skeptical now, and judging that Jake had had plenty of time to make his escape, Lani left the door to stroll with admirable casualness into the drawing room.

"Yes, really," she said, hoping her father would follow her, and breathing a sigh of relief when he did. "He—er—he's interested in my style of illustration. I've been showing him the sketches for the new book."

"So why was it necessary for him to leave with such despatch?" Roger inquired caustically. "I assume he's one of those long-haired youths I find so obnoxious. I can think of no other reason for you to behave like Mata Hari."

"I didn't behave like Mata Hari." Lani was stung by

his tone. Hostility was one thing, contempt was another. "He—he's quite nice actually. Now . . . did you have a good day? Would you like me to get you a drink?"

"I'll have a Scotch and soda," said her father tersely, seating himself by the fire Mrs. Evans had lighted earlier. "So if this young man was respectable, why was I not permitted to meet him?"

Lani sighed. "I didn't think you'd want to," she said, after a moment's pause. Then, with inspiration: "You don't usually have any time for my fellow artists."

"So the man's an artist, is he? I might have guessed." Roger's lips curled scornfully. "I'm not altogether sure I approve of young Rossiter sending him around here. After all, he knows you're here alone. The chap could have been an out-and-out bounder."

"I'm not a child," said Lani tensely, closing her eyes for a moment at the realization of how accurate her words had become. It hardly seemed credible that she had given herself to Jake so completely. With none of the shame she felt sure was yet to come. . . .

"I'm surprised you let him in," declared her father persistently, and she felt an immense sense of weariness.

"He—he phoned first," she said, walking toward the door.

"Who phoned?" Her father got to his feet to follow her.

"I—Miles, of course," exclaimed Lani unhappily, realizing how many lies she was having to tell to defend just one. "Honestly, daddy, it's no big deal. Forget it. He's gone now, for heaven's sake." She broke off a little tensely and then added steadily, "What would you like to eat? Mrs. Evans has left us a pork pie. Or I could cook you a steak, if you'd rather."

"Oh, the pie will do," said her father impatiently, not really giving the matter a lot of thought. He followed her into the kitchen. "What did you say the fellow's name was? Brecon? John Brecon? Should I have seen his work?"

"Oh, daddy!" Just for a moment, Lani's tenuously held control cracked, and her voice revealed its sudden weakness. But then, with an effort, she steeled herself again, and turning to the fridge, she said determinedly, "Does it really matter? You're not really interested in painting, are you? Now—would you like a salad with the pie, or shall I bake some potatoes?"

Roger sniffed. "You're not very forthcoming, are you, Lani? After all, I did come home while you were entertaining a young man upstairs in my house, didn't I? I don't think my anxiety is so unreasonable. You're still so...innocent in some ways."

Innocent! Lani's stomach contracted. Not any longer, she thought bitterly, as the import of her actions began to gnaw at her. Not since Jake had forced his way into her life, teaching her the subtle difference between persuasion and participation, seduction and submission.

The evening was a disaster in every way. The simple meal taken with her father was an uncomfortable affair, made the more so by her unwillingness to discuss the man he knew as John Brecon. She realized her attitude was probably not very sensible in the circumstances, but it was impossible for her to speak of Jake without experiencing a sense of guilt for what she had permitted to happen. She had always regarded herself as someone capable of controlling her emotions, and even that interlude in the park had not warned her of the real danger of his presence. This afternoon had been an illumination and a revelation, a mortifying discovery that she was as vulnerable as anyone else.

When the meal was over, a slightly disgruntled Roger St. John excused himself to work in his study, and Lani returned to her studio to try to recapture the mood of the afternoon. But it was impossible. The room was imbued with Jake's presence. She even fancied she could still smell his male scent, and the tumbled cushions on the couch bore their own witness. Dear God, she thought despairingly, she would never be able to work in here again! She would always see him here, looking over her shoulder at her drawing board, pulling her toward him, kissing her and caressing her and loving her....

No! Not love, she told herself severely. What he had done owed no allegiance to that much abused emotion. He had wanted her. He had told her so. He had made her want him. *And she had,* she remembered painfully. She had wanted him so badly, it had become a physical ache inside her. But the trouble was, her feelings had been so much less equivocal than his. In her mind, wanting and loving were one and the same thing, and the line drawn between the two had been obscured by his sexual expertise. She had no longer been in control of her mind or her body, and even now she could still recall the way he had made her feel. She had loved him then, she remembered, with a helpless

contempt for her body's betrayal. All her senses—
touch, taste, sight, smell, even the sound of his voice—
had seduced her to a state of eager surrender, and if
she despised herself now it was a little late to feel
remorse.

Seating herself at the drawing board, she gazed
unseeingly at the picture of Matilda and Mogbat. How
could *he*, she asked herself painfully. How could he use
her as he had and then return to Clare as if nothing
had happened? For she had few doubts that that was
what he would do. He had gone with Clare to Paris. He
had said so. He had taken advantage of the introductions she had arranged for him, and after escorting her
to Milan he had left. What reason had he given her
mother for returning to England? What reason would
he give for returning to Milan? Lani shook her head
confusedly, finding it suddenly too tortuous to be
borne, and putting her head down on her arm, she
gave way to the tears that had threatened for so long.

FOR SEVERAL DAYS the atmosphere between Lani and
her father remained strained. The subject of John
Brecon was never mentioned, but it was there in both
their minds, and Lani guessed her father was sulking
because she had been so uncommunicative. However,
as the time for their departure to Antigua approached,
other considerations became of more importance, and
although the idea of a holiday had never seemed less
appealing, Lani forced herself to behave as if she was
looking forward to it. There were clothes to be bought
and currency to be exchanged, and last-minute shopping expeditions for things like toothbrushes and sun-

tan cream. Her state of mind and the dissatisfaction she was experiencing with her work were temporarily numbed by these diversions. Even her father began to show some interest when the tickets and the hotel brochure arrived from the travel agent, and they spent several evenings discussing the final arrangements.

Even so, Lani still found herself getting up first in the morning so she could scan the daily paper for news of Jake before her father took it to the office. The columns had been full of articles about him just after his recital at the Royal Albert Hall, but now they were totally void of information. She could only assume that like her mother he was spending Christmas in Milan. She told herself she was doing this for her father, that her interest stemmed from a desire to protect him — but it wasn't really true. Despite her anguish, she desperately wanted to know where Jake was and what he was doing, and these weeks without that knowledge were tearing her in two.

The day before they were due to leave for Antigua, she did something that afterward she bitterly regretted; she telephoned the Gloucester Court Hotel and asked to speak to Mr. Pendragon.

The receptionist, a young woman with a decided opinion of herself, was not particularly friendly. "I'm not sure that Mr. Pendragon is in the hotel," she declared haughtily. "Who shall I tell his secretary is calling? Are you a relative, Miss — Miss — "

"He is staying there then?" said Lani, unwilling to give her name, and the receptionist cleared her throat.

"Mr. Pendragon has a suite at this hotel, yes," she affirmed crisply. "However, he does not take unsolicited calls, nor does he encourage fans to hang about the lobby—"

"I'm not a fan!" Lani interrupted indignantly, stung by the woman's contemptuous tone. "Oh, forget it," she added, putting down her receiver, and then sat for several minutes on the stairs with her head buried in her hands. She was no further forward. She still had no idea whether Jake had returned to Italy or not. And short of going to his hotel and keeping an watching vigil, there was nothing more she could do.

THE TEN DAYS she and her father spent in Antigua passed in a haze of blue skies, hot sunshine and blue green waters. The beaches of Antigua were almost white, coral sand bleached by the sun, and the waters that lapped about them were warm and soft and crystal clear.

Although Lani had started out with the distinct belief that she would not be able to relax, she did, and while she was not altogether sorry when it was time to return to England, she did get more from the holiday than she had expected.

To begin with, it was a relief to be away from London, from British newspapers and from the constant fear of coming upon Jake's image in one medium or another. It was a relief too to know that when the telephone rang it could not be for her, and even her father lost his look of consternation. If he had been disappointed that her mother was not staying on the island, he made no mention of it, and gradually they were both absorbed into the easy tempo of Caribbean life.

London, when they returned to it one gray January

day, was suffering the aftereffects of a snowstorm, which had brought down power lines in the West country and closed several rail routes into the city. Although Mrs. Evans had left the heating on in their absence and had lighted fires for their return, the house still felt decidedly chilly after their holiday in the sun. Lani, looking into her studio after depositing her cases in her room, shivered at the condensation on the windows and hurried down for afternoon tea, realizing she still had little enthusiasm for starting work again.

To her dismay, her father developed another cold only days after their return. The cold damp weather, combined with his determination to return to work whatever the temperature, had proved too much for his fragile constitution, and Dr. Lawson was worried as he confronted the girl in the sitting room.

"You really must persuade him to take more care of himself, Lani," he exclaimed. "I'm afraid it's pleurisy this time, and it could easily turn into pneumonia. Your father's a sick man. The good this holiday has done has all been wasted because of his obstinacy."

Lani bit her lip. "I'll see that he stays in bed, doctor. I'll do everything I can to help him get well."

"I know you will." Dr. Lawson viewed her anxious face sympathetically. "Don't worry. He'll be okay. Just don't let him get to his files until I say so."

It was an anxious few days until Roger St. John's temperature subsided and the pain he experienced every time he coughed disappeared. Lani seemed to spend all her time in the sickroom, and her legs ached from running up and down stairs with trays of soup and broth, scrambled eggs and savory beef jelly. Mrs. Evans did her share, but Lani could not allow her to trail up the stairs every time her employer needed a meal or his medicine. In consequence, the girl fell into bed most nights too exhausted to be prey to her nerves.

However, on the day the doctor pronounced her father fit enough to get up for the afternoon, Lani left the house for the first time since their return from Antigua. Dr. Lawson had advised her to go out and get some air. She was looking pale, he said, and he didn't want another invalid on his hands. So, wrapped up warmly against the chill of the icy wind, Lani reversed the Capri out of the garage, and drove to Regent's Park. She drove there deliberately, she knew, but she couldn't help it, and ignoring the painful twinge of memory, she set off across the frozen turf.

There were fewer people than on that afternoon she and Jake had walked there—only a few hardy animal lovers with their pets, and one or two children, accompanied by a parent or perhaps a nanny slipping and sliding resiliently across the ice on the pools. London in January, she thought, hunching her shoulders against the unwilling reminder. Clare had said she would be returning to London in January. Was that why she had come here? Because she had imagined Jake might come here too?

Her mood shattered, Lani turned back to her car. She was angry with herself for allowing thoughts of Jake to destroy her peace of mind, and she tossed her scarf and leather coat into the back of the car before slumping into her seat.

Once she was behind the wheel, however, her emotions would not so easily be controlled. Almost without her volition, it seemed, she turned right instead of left out of the parking area, her fingers flexing convulsively as she circled the park and followed the signs to Marble Arch. Gloucester Court Gate was only a stone's throw from Avenue Mews, and it was possible to drive past the Gloucester Court Hotel by taking a slight detour. Unerringly, she took the necessary diversions to bring her past the hotel, and gazed up at its windows rather recklessly as she drove by.

The hotel was a gray stone building fronting directly onto the street, pillars supporting its impressive facade. As she passed, she glimpsed the reception area beyond, with its subdued lighting, plush carpeting and straight-backed commissionaire who saluted all the guests. There was no way she could walk in there without drawing attention to herself, she thought dejectedly, slowing almost to a standstill, and then she started automatically when the driver behind sounded his horn. It had been a stupid idea anyway, she told herself severely, as she drove back to Pelham Court. But in spite of Jake's cruelty and his selfishness, she still wanted to see him.

Her father was sitting in the drawing room when she got back. He was still wearing his dressing gown, but he looked much better, settled in front of the open fire Mrs. Evans had lighted earlier. Lani saw at once that he had been working, but she couldn't blame him for that. It was more than a week since he had touched his briefcase, and in her present frame of mind, Lani thought she could understand his need for an occupation.

"I'll ask Mrs. Evans to bring us some tea," she said,

after depositing a cold kiss on his cheek, but Roger caught her arm as she would have drawn away.

"There was a call for you," he said, looking up into her startled face. "That young man—Brecon? I think it was him."

Lani straightened with an immense effort. After the time she had just spent thinking of Jake, it was as if her thoughts had conjured his phone call, and she gazed at her father blankly, unable to reply.

"Well?" Her father was waiting for her answer. "Are you going to ring him? I presume you have his number as he didn't leave a message."

"I—" Lani licked her dry lips. "Are you sure it was. . . him?"

"No, I'm not sure." Roger's response was somewhat irritable. "Mrs. Evans took the call. She said it was a man, and as he didn't give his name, I assumed it must be him. She said he had rung before."

"Before?" Lani blinked, knew a moment's wild euphoria, and then sobered. Of course. He had rung before. The afternoon he had accosted her in Glendower Street.

"What does this young man mean to you?" her father was asking now, his expression showing disapproval. "I thought—well, before we went away you allowed me to think your association was purely professional. Now, I'm not so sure."

"Oh, daddy. . . ."

"No, Lani. I insist that you tell me. I am your father, after all. I think I have a right to know."

Lani bent her head. "There's nothing to know," she mumbled unhappily.

"Yet Mrs. Evans says he has rung several times."

"Several times!" Lani's head jerked up. "Wh—when?"

"Perhaps you'd better ask her," Roger declared tersely, returning to the papers on his lap. "Obviously I've been wrong about you. You are your mother's daughter, after all."

Lani hesitated, staring frustratedly at her father's bent head, but when he didn't look up again, she couldn't restrain herself any longer. Whirling about, she went out of the room, covering the few yards to the kitchen in a matter of moments.

"Someone rang, Mrs. Evans?" she asked rather breathlessly, as the housekeeper turned at her entrance, and the older woman nodded.

"Some man," she agreed, wiping her hand on her apron. "Is your father wanting his tea? I've made some cheese scones. They'll be ready in a minute."

"He said—daddy said—this isn't the first time he's called."

Lani's grammar was suffering badly, and Mrs. Evans frowned. "I didn't hear him calling," she exclaimed, checking the contents of the tray. "I thought he'd likely wait until you got back—"

"Not daddy, Mrs. Evans." Lani was handling this badly, and she knew it. "The man—the man who rang; daddy said you said he had rung before."

"Oh, him." Mrs. Evans looked up, her eyes missing nothing on Lani's flushed face. "Yes, that's right, he did. I meant to tell you, but what with Mr. St. John being ill, and you run off your feet—"

"When, Mrs. Evans? When did he ring?" Lani had

to know, whatever the housekeeper might be thinking. "Please. I'd like to know."

"Well, let me see. . . ." Mrs. Evans cupped her chin with one hand. "I suppose the first time was the day you went away." She sighed. "Yes. I remember you'd left for the airport only minutes before, but of course I didn't tell him that."

Lani swallowed. "No?"

"No." Mrs. Evans was very definite. "I mean—I didn't know who he was, did I? He might have been up to no good. You don't go around telling people the house is going to be empty for ten days, now do you?"

"I suppose not." Lani tried to be patient. "So. . . he phoned again?"

"Yes." The housekeeper nodded. "On Christmas Eve, it was. He just caught me. I'd come up to make sure everything was okay, you know, and I got quite a shock when the phone rang."

Lani drew an uneven breath. "So what did you say?"

Mrs. Evans shrugged. "I told him you'd gone away for Christmas, didn't I? I didn't let on I was away too. Anyway, he said he'd ring after you got back and he has."

"Today."

"Well, he might have rung before," admitted Mrs. Evans unwillingly. "While your father was ill, I took the phone off the hook a time or two. Well—" this as Lani's eyes widened in dismay "—I knew there was nothing spoiling at that office of his, and you know what he's like when he thinks people are trying to get in touch with him."

It was a reasonable explanation, and remembering

how ill her father had been Lani could not fault Mrs. Evans's logic. But she couldn't help wondering how often Jake had rung, and what his reaction had been to the permanent busy signal.

"So...today," she prompted, as Mrs. Evans turned to take her baking out of the oven. "What—what did he say? Did you tell him I was out?"

"Yes." The housekeeper set the tray of golden brown scones on the ceramic hob. "Though whether he believed me, I don't know. I think he thought that excuse was wearing rather thin."

"But didn't you tell him daddy had been ill?" exclaimed Lani impatiently, and then colored anew at the housekeeper's raised eyebrows. "Well," she excused herself uncomfortably, "he must imagine I'm avoiding him. Didn't you say anything?"

"What else could I say?" exclaimed Mrs. Evans indignantly. "It was the truth, wasn't it? It seems to me there's something funny going on. Why doesn't he come to the house?"

Lani turned away. "Oh...it doesn't matter," she muttered, tucking her thumbs into the belt of her jeans. "I'm sorry if I was short with you. I guess...I guess I'm tired, that's all."

"Aren't we all?" grumbled Mrs. Evans dourly, and Lani left her buttering the scones with some aggression.

The doorbell rang when she was halfway up the stairs. Realizing the housekeeper was busy, Lani reluctantly ran back down to answer it. As on that other afternoon, it was almost dark outside, and she turned on the lights before opening the door.

As before, he was standing on the step, the Porsche parked at the gate for anyone to see. In black jeans and a black corded jacket, he blended into the darkness behind him, and only the unusual pallor of his face was plainly visible.

"So you are in," he said scathingly, the accusation—for that was what it was—accompanied by a contemptuous twisting of his mouth. Before Lani could make any response, he turned on his heel and walked away.

CHAPTER NINE

"WAIT!" WITHOUT GIVING HERSELF TIME to think, Lani went after him, almost losing her balance on the slippery path as she reached the gate. "Jake—Jake, wait a minute, please! You can't go away without telling me why you came."

He had reached the car and was unlocking it when she caught up with him, and he turned to her dispassionately in the fading light. "I came to prove to myself that I was wasting my time," he told her coldly. "The phone calls should have done it, but I had to be sure it was not some ploy of your father's."

"What?" she exclaimed helplessly. "What is daddy supposed to have done? I—Mrs. Evans has just told me about your phone calls. What with us being away and then my father being ill, I'm afraid she just forgot."

Jake expelled his breath on a disbelieving sigh. "Oh, come on," he said scornfully. "You don't really expect me to believe that, do you? You really didn't know I've been trying to reach you for more than three weeks?"

"No." Lani was trembling, but it was not the cold wind cutting through her skirt and sweater that was responsible. "It's true. Why should I lie to you? Since we got back from Antigua, my father's been in bed with pleurisy."

Jake's narrowed eyes scanned her anxious face. "Do you mean to tell me that until this afternoon you didn't know I'd been phoning you?"

"That's right."

"You've been in Antigua?"

"Over Christmas, yes. I—my father hasn't been well since the winter started, and the doctor recommended he get some sunshine."

"So you went to Antigua?" Jake's lips curled. "Why?"

Lani shrugged. "It was my father's choice." She bent her head. "I think perhaps he thought my mother might spend Christmas there."

"But she didn't."

Lani lifted her head and looked at him. "You'd know that better than I."

"Oh, yes." Jake's voice was flat. "Clare spent Christmas in Italy. She's due back this evening after a successful season in Milan."

"This evening!" Lani glanced half-apprehensively over her shoulder, as if afraid her father might have overheard. "Oh!" She cleared her throat convulsively. "And—and are you on your way to meet her?"

"Not right now, no." His tone was dry. "This is hardly en route to Heathrow, is it?" He raked back his hair with a weary hand. "No. As I said a few moments ago, I came to...well, to see you, I suppose." He let his breath out heavily. "Oh, *God*! Can we go some place and talk?"

Lani stared at him. "Now?"

"Yes now, for Christ's sake," he agreed harshly. "Or do you have something else to do? If so, just say the word and I'll—"

"Oh, Jake!" Her hands groped helplessly for his hand, closing round the supple texture of his palm, squeezing the cold fingers that curled about her own. "Jake," she said again, unsteadily, and uncaring that they were in full view of anyone who might care to look, he bent his head to hers with unerring accuracy.

His kiss was hard and searching, his hand at the nape of her neck almost cruelly possessive. Lani's lips parted involuntarily, her hands reaching out to grasp the lapels of his jacket, and the coldness inside her melted at the sensual invasion of his tongue.

"Get your coat," he said at last, lifting his head with evident reluctance, and Lani, her senses spinning back from that mindless precipice, gazed at him blankly.

"My coat?"

"You may need it later," he said huskily. "Don't be long. I'll wait in the car."

"I—I—my father. . . ."

"Tell him it's an emergency," said Jake roughly. "It is. Now, do you want me to do it?"

Lani shook her head and then turned rather dazedly toward the house. As she did so, the undrawn drawing-room curtains twitched ever so slightly, and she guessed, with a sinking heart, that her father had seen everything. She should have known, she thought, quickening her step; she should have guessed curiosity would get the better of him. She only hoped he had not identified her visitor in the streetlights. She could not face that now. Not now!

Roger St. John was standing at the drawing-room door when she entered the house, and she had to steel herself to face him after what he had seen. "I—I'm going out for a while," she said carefully, lifting her coat from the chest. "You don't mind, do you? I shan't be very long. I — Mrs. Evans is making the tea. I'll see you when I get back."

Her father's fist clenched on the lintel of the door. "You're going out with *him*?"

Lani glanced behind her. "Yes."

"That's John Brecon?"

Lani colored. "Yes."

"I thought you said you hardly knew him."

Lani sighed. "I'll tell you about it later, can I? I — he's waiting."

"Brecon?"

Lani moistened her lips. "Why do you keep saying that?"

"That *is* what you called him, isn't it?"

Lani draped her coat over her arm. "You know it is."

"Do I?" Her father's jaw hardened angrily. "You're a liar, Lani! A liar, do you hear me? My own daughter — the one person in the world I thought I could trust, and you've been lying to me!"

Lani blanched. "What do you mean?"

"That man —" her father lifted his arm and pointed "— that man is not John Brecon any more than I am. That name — it was meant to deceive me, wasn't it? You little liar! My God!" He clenched his fists. "I thought I knew you. I thought we cared about one another. And now I find you've been consorting with *him*, with your mother's lover! In heaven's name, have you taken leave of your senses? Are you going mad or am I? How can you? Your mother's latest fancy man! The parasite she's been sleeping with for the past six months!"

Lani was too shocked to defend herself. Although she already knew the things her father was saying, when they were spoken aloud they resounded through her brain like a death knell to any hopes she might be nurturing. Put into words, there seemed no possible justification for her behavior. Put into words, how could she even begin to imagine she and Jake might have a future together?

"You...don't...understand..." she began unsteadily, not sure herself how she was going to go on, when a sudden awareness silenced her. Someone was behind her, some other person's breathing had joined her own and her father's—some still, quiescent presence, attendant to her plea. Her head flew around immediately, her eyes widening when she found Jake standing right behind her, and her uncertainties were laid waste by the disturbing vulnerability of his gaze.

"Get out of my house!"

Roger St. John's incensed command gave substance to his feelings, but Jake showed no emotion at this unconventional introduction. His manner was calm as he looked at Lani, his voice cool as he asked, almost casually, "Are you ready?"

"No, she's not!" Roger stepped forward then, his breath coming shallowly as he labored for control. His hand shot out to imprison his daughter's arm, and facing Jake threateningly, he said again, "Get out of my house, do you hear? Lani is not going anywhere with *you!*"

"Don't you think we should allow Lani to decide that for herself?" Jake inquired quietly, and his youth and superior height made him an unequal adversary. "I'm sorry you feel this way, Mr. St. John, but I have no quarrel with you. I simply want to talk to Lani, and I intend to do so."

"Is that what you call it?" snapped Roger contemptuously. "*Talking!* I saw what you did to her just now, and there was very little in the way of conversation that I could see."

"Daddy, please—" Lani was troubled by the hectic color in her father's features and by the obvious fact that in any encounter Jake was bound to come out the victor. "Daddy, can't we go into the drawing room and talk about this like civilized people? The night air isn't good for you. You're only just out of bed!"

"That man is not coming into my house," declared her father vehemently. "Go on. Go! Get out of here before I call the police and have you thrown out. I don't know how you have the nerve to come here when you're living off my wife."

Jake's lean features hardened, and Lani's heart pumped anxiously. "Clare is not your wife, Mr. St. John," he stated succinctly. "Nor do I intend to defend our relationship to you. Please let go of your daughter's arm. I don't intend to leave here without her."

Lani groaned. The polite words, spoken so courteously, held an unmistakable trace of menace, and although she no longer knew what her feelings were, she could not allow this situation to deteriorate any further.

"Please, daddy," she said unsteadily, "you'd better let me go."

"With him?"

"Yes. With him." Lani glanced uneasily at Jake's taut face. "I'll be all right, honestly—"

"That was who you had here that day I came home and caught you, wasn't it?" her father was saying incredulously. "No wonder you sneaked out as soon as my back was turned, Pendragon. *Pendragon!*" He sneered. "What kind of a name is that?"

"My father's, sir," replied Jake flatly. "And I did not sneak out. Your daughter—"

"Oh, for heaven's sake, stop it! Both of you." Lani could see the mist wreathing round the lamp post outside the house, and the cold air drifting in through the open door was freezing. "You must get out of this draft, daddy. You're not well. You know what the doctor said."

"Clare's to blame for this," declared Roger St. John bitterly, shaking his head, and Lani realized he wasn't listening to her. "Corrupting her own daughter—"

"Clare has nothing to do with it," said Jake incisively. "Lani, are you coming or not?"

Lani moved her head helplessly, torn between love for her father and love for the man who he believed had betrayed him. Years of sharing and affection bound her to her father, but that gentle love could not be compared to the feelings she had for Jake. How could she choose between fondness and fascination, tenderness and passion, parent and lover? There was no choice to be made. No matter what her brain might dictate, her emotions would always prevail.

"I have to go with him, daddy," she said unsteadily now, gently but firmly removing her arm from his grasp. "Please, try to understand. I can't do anything else. I love him."

She knew a terrible compunction when her father

turned away. His face had contorted at her words, and he grasped the frame of the drawing-room door as he passed, as if needing that added support. It was a terrible moment, a moment when Lani felt as if she had suddenly gone beyond her depth into waters both uncharted and dangerous. Why was she doing this, she asked herself wildly. Why was she abandoning the man who had cared for her all these years for a relationship as nebulous as the mist that was invading the house? And then she turned to look at Jake, and all her questions were answered.

"Shall we go?" he suggested quietly, making no move to persuade her, and Lani hesitated only a second before nodding her head.

"Yes," she said tensely. "Yes, let's go," and preceded him out the door with tears smarting behind her eyes.

In the car Jake gave her a sideways glance. "Where do you want to go?" he asked, reaching for the ignition, and Lani lifted her shoulders.

"Anywhere," she said, avoiding his eyes. "Couldn't we—couldn't we have tea somewhere?"

Jake considered. "I guess so."

"But not at your hotel," she got out hastily. "I mean, I'd rather go to. . .to a café, or something."

"Okay." Jake made no comment on her qualification and without another word thrust the car into forward gear.

London was a hectic mass of people, lights and traffic. It was the rush hour, and everyone seemed bent on getting home in the shortest time possible. Pedestrians stepped carelessly into the road in front of the car; other vehicles squeezed together, fender to fender;

buses surged out ahead of them with a complete disregard for road courtesy, and the angry flashing of lights and honking of horns were a crazy accompaniment to the thumping in Lani's head.

"Christ!" muttered Jake succinctly when one particularly reckless individual almost came to grief beneath the wheels of the Porsche, and with a smothered oath, he pulled into a metered parking space. "This will have to do," he said, glancing briefly up and down the thoroughfare. "We can walk from here, if you have no objections. There's bound to be a snack bar somewhere."

"All right."

Lani groped blindly for her coat, but before she could open her door, Jake's hand closed over hers. "Are you?" he demanded huskily. "All right, I mean? Oh, hell, Lani, I didn't realize how your father felt."

"Didn't you?" Lani looked at him through lashes that were spikily damp. "How did you expect him to feel?"

"I don't know." Jake ran a frustrated hand around the back of his neck. "Clare said—oh, Christ! Clare said the divorce had been undefended. She said they were still friends. How the hell was I to know your father still harbored a grudge against her?"

Lani bent her head. "You must have realized that—that he wouldn't approve of...our relationship."

"Why not?" Jake's lean features were suddenly guarded. "Because of my association with your mother? That's a professional arrangement. Nothing more."

"How can you say that?" Lani lifted her head to stare

at him in the shadowy lights from the street outside. "Why, everyone knows that . . . that. . . ."

"That what?" he demanded harshly. "That your mother and I have been seen together on frequent occasions? That I've been her escort for numerous social engagements? That she likes everyone to think we're having an affair, because it's good for her image?"

Lani caught her breath. "Are—are you saying you've never slept with my mother?"

Jake's mouth hardened. "I'm saying you shouldn't believe everything you read in the newspapers." He thrust open his door. "Now, shall we get some tea?"

Lani got out of the car onto legs that were distinctly unsteady, and she was glad when Jake took her coat from her and held it so she could push her arms into the sleeves. His denial of everything she had believed about him had left her feeling weak and confused, and she no longer knew what she believed and what she didn't.

She knew she must look a mess, her eyes red and swollen from her tears, her mouth bare of any lipstick after Jake's passionate possession. It was unfair that he should look so darkly handsome and controlled, while her pale features mirrored every emotion.

A small café advertising cream buns turned out to be little more than a smoky dive, but Jake settled Lani at a corner table and went to fetch two mugs of treacly tea. Unlikely as it seemed, he was quite at home in this environment, and she reflected bitterly that he could adapt to any surroundings. She could quite believe in his playing piano in some sleazy nightclub in California, just as she could see him standing on the stage at the Royal Albert Hall, taking his final bow. It was one of the most attractive things about him, and looking around at the café's other occupants, she wondered how many would believe her if she told them who he was.

"So...." Jake straddled the chair opposite and viewed her over the shiny expanse of mottled Formica. "I'm sorry it's not more salubrious, but I guess what we have to say can be said as easily here as in the tearoom at the Ritz."

"Yes." Lani touched her cheek nervously. "In any case, I'm not really dressed for the Ritz, am I?"

"Do you want me to say you look good enough to me?" he asked dryly. "If it's compliments you want—"

"It's not!" Lani was indignant.

"Then stop worrying about your appearance. No one's looking at you but me. And I want you."

"Oh, Jake!" Lani would not meet his eyes, and growing impatient, he leaned across the table and captured one of her cold hands in both of his.

"I do. We both know it," he told her roughly. "I've not thought of anyone else since that afternoon we spent together."

Lani caught her breath. "Where—where did you spend Christmas?"

"Where do you think?" he demanded. "Here. In London. Trying to ring you."

Lani shook her head. "I can't believe this...."

"Why not? It's the truth. Ask your Mrs.—what did you call her?"

"Evans."

"Yes, Evans. She can verify I phoned on Christmas Eve. That was when she told me you had gone away. I didn't believe her."

Lani sighed. "This is crazy!"

"I agree." Jake squeezed her fingers between his. "I did not intend this to happen. As I told you before, I can't afford to get emotionally involved with anyone. There's too much at stake. Too many things that I've already sacrificed my self-respect for."

Lani stiffened. "Your self-respect?"

"Yes, my self-respect." Jake reached across to lift her chin and force her to look at him. "Do you think I like being known as Clare's protégé? Do you think I like the idea that without her help—without her financial assistance—I could never have got where I am now?"

"She supports you?" Lani's voice was constricted.

"She has." Jake lifted his shoulders. "I thought you knew that. I thought she told you."

Lani shook her head. "She didn't tell me."

"But you knew?" Jake could see the raw uncertainty in her eyes. "What did Clare tell you? What fabrication am I guilty of now?"

Lani hesitated a moment, and then when someone got up to play a record on the jukebox, she withdrew her hand and he didn't try to stop her. "She said," she murmured carefully, "she said she wanted us to be friends because... because we were the two people she cared most about."

"I see." Jake's lips twisted. "And that condemns me, of course."

"Isn't it true?" Lani gazed at him.

"That she cares about me?" Jake was deliberately obtuse.

"Yes. Yes." Lani's nerves were stretched to screaming pitch, and the throbbing in her head was like a hammer in her brain. "Why haven't you been honest with me? Why don't you admit that your relationship with my mother is not the — the business arrangement you say it is?"

"So, tell me what you want me to say," said Jake bleakly. "Will it alter the situation if I say I've been to bed with her? Will our need for one another be any less if I admit I've had — sex — with your mother?"

Lani gasped. "How can you ask that?" she choked.

"How can you?" he snapped in a low violent tone, and she was glad of the heavy beat of the music to drown his angry voice. "Oh, Christ, let's get out of here before I say something we'll both regret."

Outside the mist was thickening, and seeing the illuminated sign of a public house just across the road from where they were standing, Jake grasped Lani's wrist and dragged her after him toward the lighted entrance. "We can talk in here," he said, hustling her into a dimly lit bar and installing her in a corner booth before going to buy their drinks.

It was dark in the booth, but Lani was grateful for its enveloping anonymity. It was not the trendy sort of establishment frequented by a young professional crowd. It was just an ordinary pub, whose customers were mostly male and who showed very little interest in anything but the beer.

"Cozy, isn't it?" remarked Jake, depositing a martini in front of her. Then, sliding onto the banquette beside her, he smothered her response beneath the hungry pressure of his mouth.

It was almost nine o'clock when they emerged, and by then Lani was too bemused by Jake's lovemaking to voice any objections when he told her they were going to his hotel. The abortive caresses they had exchanged in the smoky atmosphere of the pub had left her feeling weak. She was no longer capable of denying she wanted him just as much as he wanted her.

The car was cold, but the engine started without effort, and Jake swung smoothly into the less hectic stream of traffic. Now there were few crazy pedestrians running the risk of being knocked down, and the encroaching gloom deterred anyone from driving recklessly.

It wasn't far from the pub to Gloucester Court Gate, and in a matter of minutes, Jake was easing the car into a parking space opposite the hotel, and coming around to help Lani out of her seat. "Are you having second thoughts?" he asked huskily as she got nervously to her feet, but although she knew she should, she quickly shook her head.

"Hurry," she said, wrapping her arms about herself protectively as he locked the car, and Jake swung his arm across her shoulders as they walked into the hotel.

"Good evening, Mr. Pendragon!"

The doorman had recognized him, and Lani's stomach plunged a little sickeningly as Jake returned his greeting. "Filthy night, isn't it?" he remarked, without any apparent trace of embarrassment, even though the doorman looked at her curiously, as if trying to decide who she was. Perhaps he thought she was some unusual type of call girl, she pondered uneasily, following Jake into the lift, but before this thought could crystallize, Jake drew her into his arms.

"Stop looking so worried," he ordered, his thumb

brushing her parted lips and probing the moistness within. "People come and go here all the time. Your reputation's quite intact, believe me."

Lani leaned against him, loving the feel of his hard body against hers. "Do you love me?" she breathed, and Jake's mouth descended on hers.

"What do you think?" he said against her lips, and it wasn't until later that she remembered he hadn't answered her.

Jake's suite was on the eighth floor. Lani emerged from the lift looking quite starry-eyed and totally unaware of how revealing her expression was. "You shouldn't look like that," said Jake somewhat thickly, "not before I make love to you."

Lani giggled. "I thought you'd been making love to me all evening," she countered as he fumbled for his key, and Jake regarded her possessively before seeking her mouth again.

"What we have been doing is not making love," he told her unsteadily. "If it were, I wouldn't be finding it so bloody difficult to put this key in the lock!"

Moments later he succeeded, and he pushed her forward into a room already lighted by half a dozen shaded lamps. Cream carpet, cream draperies, sofas upholstered in cream and purple velvet, even a grand piano standing squarely in the wide window embrasure—the room she was confronting bore all the hallmarks of gracious living. Only when she saw the high-heeled shoes, upended in the middle of the carpet, did her wonderment give way to a shocked awakening.

"What the hell—"

Jake's savage ejaculation was like an echo of her own

reaction, and she turned to look at him blankly as dismay gave way to condemnation. She had no need to be told whose shoes they were, nor indeed any desire to investigate the sounds of occupation coming through the open door of what she presumed to be a bedroom. Her mother was here. There was no other explanation, and her blood turned to ice at this awful humiliation.

Even so, she was not prepared for what happened next. As if on cue, Clare appeared in the open doorway, wearing nothing but a cream silk dressing gown, whose skirt flared wide to reveal her legs as she took the steps to bring her into the room.

"Darling," she began, and then, as if she had just become aware of her daughter's presence, she smiled before continuing, "Darling, how thoughtful of you to bring Lani to see me!"

Before Lani could say anything, however, before she could even begin to think what this tableau might mean, Jake's harsh voice intervened. "What are you doing here, Clare?" he demanded. "Just what bloody mischief are you hoping to incite now? You don't belong here. You know that. You're not welcome here. Now, do you go and put your clothes on or do I throw you out without them?"

"Oh, yes, that would make a pretty scene, wouldn't it?" cried Clare, her voice rising shrilly, and Lani, who had already faced one scene today with her father, did not think she could bear another.

"If—if you'll excuse me—" she was beginning, when Jake's fingers clamped about her arm, and once again she was made an unwilling witness to something she found totally distasteful.

"You're not going anywhere, Lani," he told her heavily. "For pity's sake, don't jump to conclusions here. It's not what you think."

"Isn't it? Isn't it?" Clare gazed at him tremulously. "How do you think she feels, seeing her own mother treated like this? Don't you think she has any shame? Doesn't she feel any compassion? Listen to him, Lani, listen to him! How do you like your prospective stepfather now?"

"I am not her prospective stepfather," snarled Jake savagely. "For Christ's sake, Clare, pull yourself together. I don't know what you think you're doing or why you're here, but—"

"I should have thought it was obvious!" exclaimed Clare, her voice shaking. "I came to see you, Jake. To *be* with you! Have you forgotten so soon what we meant to one another?"

"Clare—"

"*Mother*, please—"

They spoke simultaneously, Jake's anguished use of her name mingling with Lani's helpless plea. But it was to her daughter that Clare turned, her glittering eyes focusing suspiciously on the girl's pale face.

"Where have you been with him?" she demanded. "What have you been doing? Oh, don't bother to lie to me. I can see from your face what's been going on. You're quite the little viper, aren't you? Did you do this deliberately? I know you've always been jealous of me."

"That's not true."

Lani's denial was vehement, and Jake let go of her arm to approach the older woman. "Stop this, Clare, will you?" he said, grimly. "You know as well as I do, you and I don't have this kind of relationship."

"No, we don't, do we?" Lani blinked bewilderedly as Clare seemed to perform a volte-face. "We don't keep ourselves exclusively for one another, is that what you're saying? If either of us feels like a change we just go out and find someone else, hmm?"

Jake sighed wearily. "Clare, for God's sake, let me get you a cab. Get dressed, and I'll escort you downstairs."

"Oh, will you?" Clare came toward him on the balls of her feet. "How gallant! And will you take me home, too?"

"No."

Jake's response was final, and with a sudden movement Clare pressed herself against him, one arm arching around his neck with deliberate sensuality.

"No?" she breathed, her lips only inches from his, and Lani turned away from that blatant invitation.

"Go and put your clothes on, Clare."

The rejection was spoken through his teeth, and because she had her back to them, Lani did not see what happened. But evidently, taking advantage of her position, Clare had slipped her free hand into Jake's pocket, and now she brandished the Porsche keys with every appearance of triumph.

"I'll drive myself home then," she exclaimed, her voice taking on an hysterical pitch. "Who knows, I may find someone more to my liking," and before Jake could stop her, she had dipped under his outstretched arm and reached the door.

"Clare!" Jake's temper was getting the better of him

now, and Lani tried to catch her mother's arm in passing. But Clare was too quick for her, her arm lashing out wildly as she made good her escape, and Lani was left looking at Jake in helpless fascination.

"You've got to go after her," she said, spreading her hands wide. "She's got next to nothing on. She'll freeze."

"Do you think she doesn't know that?" demanded Jake violently, but shaking his head in resignation, he strode off down the hall.

Closing the door, Lani followed them. She didn't really want to go. She had the unwilling suspicion that this was all some wild gesture, that Clare had no more intention of driving herself home than she had. It was one of her mother's melodramas, one of her acting roles she was allowing to carry over into real life, a deliberate attempt to distract Jake and destroy whatever she believed was between him and Lani. Yet why was she here at the hotel? How had she known they were together? If what Jake said was true, she had had no reason to be there in his apartment. One of them was lying—but who?

She reached the lift as the gates were closing. Clare had evidently gone ahead of them, and Jake's face was tense as they waited for the elevator to reach the ground floor. It hardly seemed possible that only minutes before they had ascended in the lift so happily, and Lani looked up into Jake's eyes, as if seeking reassurance.

"It all comes down to who you believe, doesn't it?" he said flatly, making no move to touch her, and Lani's lips trembled as the lift doors slid apart.

There was no sign of Clare in the lobby, and looking about her, Lani wondered how she could have crossed this space without someone recognizing her. Or perhaps they had, she reflected. After all, if Clare had pulled her gown around her, it might conceivably have been taken for an evening dress. Opera stars were known to be temperamental and touchy. Who was likely to stop Clare Austin in full flight?

Half running after Jake's long stride, she followed him outside. The gray mist swirled and eddied in the lights from the hotel, and the cars parked opposite were scarcely distinguishable. But Clare's robe was distinguishable. It showed wraithlike through the gloom, and Lani saw with dismay that her mother had opened the Porsche and was getting inside.

"She's crazy!"

With an impatient oath, Jake started off the pavement toward the car, and as he did so Clare fired the engine. Lani, her palms pressed anxiously against her cold cheeks, had a grandstand view of her mother's expression as she slammed the Porsche into gear, but even so her cry of warning came too late. She doubted Jake believed her mother would actually go through with it—would actually drive at him with every intention of knocking him down. But she did. There was a horrified moment when Lani realized what Clare intended to do, when she started off the path, her arms reaching desperately for Jake as if to protect him from the blow—and then the sickening sound of impact as the car plowed into both of them.

CHAPTER TEN

LANI RECOVERED CONSCIOUSNESS in hospital, with a headache that made all her previous headaches seem paltry by comparison. Lifting her hand to her head, she discovered a bandage was covering her forehead, and even that small exertion left her feeling rather sick.

"Oh, you're awake."

The matter-of-fact tones of a nurse alerted her to the fact that she was lying in a narrow hospital bed, and as her aching brain began to function, panic flared inside her.

"Jake—" she cried, trying to lever herself up on her elbows, and her color ebbed alarmingly as pain engulfed her consciousness once again.

The next time she came around, Sarah was sitting by her bed. The unexpected sight of her cousin's wife brought awareness that much more quickly: Sarah was reading, and she didn't immediately notice Lani was awake, and remembering what had happened the last time she tried to sit up, Lani moistened her dry lips. "Jake," she said distinctly. "What happened to Jake?" Sarah thrust her book aside to gaze at her in evident relief.

"How do you feel?" she asked, leaning forward to take Lani's cold hand, which was lying on the coverlet.

"Oh, Lani, you gave us such a shock! Whatever possessed you to run into the road like that?"

Lani tried to move her head, but the effort was too great. Curling her fingers around the other woman's, she said, "Tell me, Sarah. I want to know. Where is Jake? Is—is he dead?"

"No. No, of course he's not dead." Sarah spoke almost impatiently, but the relief was so great that Lani's small store of strength deserted her. A little sigh escaped her as Sarah's face dissolved into blackness, and Sarah rang the bell urgently to summon the nurse.

When Lani next became aware of what was going on around her, it was dark beyond the windows of her room. A lamp was burning beside her bed, and there was a flickering light from a machine that seemed to be monitoring her progress, but she was alone. If she turned her head slightly, she could see a glass and a jug on the table beside her bed, and she longed to feel cool water on her parched tongue and lips.

"Don't even think of reaching for it."

The bright tones heralded the arrival of another nurse, and Lani licked her lips appealingly. "I'm. . . very thirsty," she said, her eyes turning toward the jug. "Do you think I could have a drink?"

"Oh, I should think so." The young nurse smiled encouragingly, and came around the bed to examine her medical chart. She poured liquid from the jug into the glass and leaned toward her. "Here—let me help you. Now, don't go overdoing it. You're still a long way from being well."

The tiny drop of water she was permitted was nectar, and Lani sank back willingly, aware that for the time being she was incapable of helping herself. "Thank you," she murmured, with a quavering breath. "That was delicious."

"Good." The nurse bent to examine her closely. "I think we might find you a little broth. Does the idea of food appeal to you?"

"Wh—what's wrong with me?" asked Lani huskily. "How long have I been here? Where...where is Jake? Can I see him?"

"Hey, now. One question at a time." The nurse straightened, plucking the bedclothes into place. "Doctor will tell you all about your injuries. As to how long you've been here—well, let's see, the better part of a week, I suppose."

"A week!" Lani was horrified, and the nurse made a soothing gesture.

"Now, calm yourself, Miss St. John," she said reprovingly. "If you go upsetting yourself, you'll never get well. You're making satisfactory progress. Isn't that enough for you? Now, settle down again, and I'll go and get that broth."

"Jake! Mr. Pendragon!" Lani's fingers curled into balls as she pleaded for information. "Please...please, you must tell me where he is. Is he in this hospital? I must know!"

The nurse was walking toward the door, but now she hesitated. "I presume you mean that man who was brought in with you," she said, and when Lani made a positive gesture, she added, "Then, no. I'm afraid he's not here anymore."

"Not...here?" Lani almost choked on the words. "You mean—you mean—"

"I mean he's been taken to St. Augustine's," said the nurse hastily. "The orthopedic hospital. He—well—it was decided he needed specialist treatment, and Mr. Holland is the best there is."

Lani quivered. "Orthopedics?" she said unsteadily. "What—what's that? I should know but—"

"I know. Your head feels like a suet pudding," the nurse sympathized, nodding. "Orthopedics is the branch of medicine associated with bones and muscles—"

"Giving our patient a lecture on practical diagnosis, Nurse Phillips?" The crisp tones of a senior nurse were not entirely friendly. "Ah—I see you are awake, Miss St. John. How are you feeling? Have you much pain?"

Lani moistened her dry lips again. "Just a faint throbbing," she admitted weakly. Then, as if to defend the young nurse, she added, "Nurse—Nurse Phillips was just explaining about the hospital where...where Mr. Pendragon has been taken. I wanted to know. I wanted to see him."

"I see." The senior nurse gave her junior a hostile glance. "I suggest you go and find Dr. Connor, Nurse Phillips. Ask him if he'd be kind enough to come and examine our patient."

Nurse Phillips beat a hasty retreat, and Lani met the head nurse's eyes with some degree of indignation. "I did ask her," she murmured, feeling obliged to offer a defense, but the older woman merely smiled as she bent to examine Lani's eyes.

"How long must I stay here?" Lani continued unevenly. "Nurse Phillips said I've been here almost a week already. Could you send a message to my father?

Could you let him know I've recovered consciousness?"

"All in good time, Miss St. John." Nurse McAllister—Lani read the name on her identity badge—lifted the medical chart. "Do you feel hungry? I think we might try a little soup, don't you?"

"Why not?" Lani was beginning to feel very tired again. Asking all these questions was wearing, particularly when she was getting no satisfactory answers, and she anticipated the doctor's arrival with something akin to despair.

When he came, he was younger than she expected, no more than forty or forty-five, with unruly brown hair, blue eyes that twinkled and a frank and forthright manner that completely negated Nurse McAllister's crisp formality. "I might have known you'd choose to wake up in the wee small hours," he declared, grimacing good-naturedly. "Don't you know we hardworking doctors need all the sleep we can get?"

"I'm sorry." Lani managed a faint smile in return, and he grinned irrepressibly.

"Ah well, as it's you I won't get angry," he declared, all the while carrying on a conversation in undertones with the head nurse. "So—are you feeling a little more human? Sure, you gave us all a worrying time for a while."

Lani drew a deep breath. "Why?" she asked. "Wh—what happened?"

"Don't you remember what happened?" Dr. Connor regarded her intently, and Lani tried to move her head in a positive gesture.

"I remember—I remember the car—" she said, and

broke off as Dr. Connor nodded vigorously, as if he understood.

"Well, you've got what we call a hairline fracture of your skull," he told her casually. "Nothing to get too steamed up about. It should knit together again without any problems."

"Is that all?"

"Sure, and isn't it enough?" He laughed, but Lani didn't join him, and he sighed. "Well, there are one or two bad bruises, and you may find it difficult to get around for a while, but you'll mend. You're young. You've been lucky."

He turned away to speak to the nurse again, but Lani put out a trembling hand. "Please—" she said, not quite knowing how to broach this. "My—my mother, she was driving the car; is—is she all right?"

The doctor and the nurse exchanged glances and then Dr. Connor smiled encouragingly. "Sure, she's fine," he said, depositing Lani's medical chart back on the end of the bed. "Now—we'll get you some food. You must be starving."

Lani closed her eyes for a moment and then opened them again. "Mr. Pendragon," she said, ignoring the nurse's sudden intake of breath. "I want to know about Mr. Pendragon. How. . . how badly hurt was he? When can I see him?"

Another exchange of glances, and then Dr. Connor came to regard her seriously. "Mr. Pendragon is going to be all right," he said firmly. "Nothing to worry about there. You just concentrate on getting well yourself. Then we'll talk about when you can see him."

Lani groaned. "Why won't you tell me?" she exclaimed. "Why do you persist in putting me off with feeble reassurances? Can't you see? I need to know the truth. If you won't tell me, then fetch my father here. He will."

"I can't do that, Miss St. John." Dr. Connor glanced around at the nurse. "Look, don't upset yourself like this. Don't you know you're not supposed to get excited?"

"Then stop exciting me," said Lani, breathing hard. "Is Jake alive? Is he really alive? Or is this tale about some other hospital just so much hot air?"

Dr. Connor sighed. "Of course he's alive, Miss St. John. I wouldn't lie to you about that. However, as you appear to know he has been taken to another hospital, I can say that his injuries were such that we couldn't treat them properly here. Besides, Mr. Holland operates at St. Augustine's. And. . . well, they have more facilities for private patients than we do."

Lani expelled her breath slowly. "Did—did the car go over him?"

"I can't answer that." Dr. Connor gazed at her steadily. "My dear, it was a terrible accident. It's not something either you or your mother should dwell upon too long."

Lani's lips parted. "An accident!" she echoed.

"An accident," said Dr. Connor flatly. "Sure, and no one in his right mind would believe anything else."

Lani closed her mouth again, her brain seething chaotically. *An accident,* she said to herself silently. *An accident!* It had been no accident. It had been a deliberate attempt to mow Jake down, and no one could believe otherwise.

Something in her eyes, something in her expression, must have warned the physician that she did not accept what he had said. Perhaps it was the way her fingers plucked agitatedly at the coverlet, or maybe it was the awful pallor of her skin. With a gesture of impatience Dr. Connor produced a hypodermic needle and Lani's anxieties drifted into the unwelcome rush of oblivion. . . .

She awakened to brightness, slats of watery sunshine shading the bed through half-drawn blinds. To her relief, the throbbing ache that had plagued her head the night before had eased to a bearable twinge, and she actually felt hungry for the first time since her accident.

Her accident!

The careless thought made her shift in sudden revulsion, and the nurse who had been seated by her bed, rose to her feet. "At last," she said gently. "We were beginning to think you didn't want to wake up. Now, just relax, Miss St. John, and I'll ask Nurse Henson to come in."

Deciding there was no point in distressing herself unnecessarily, Lani lay obediently while Nurse Henson examined her and then pronounced that she should have some lunch.

"Lunch?"

Lani blinked in surprise, and the nurse who had been there when she awakened smiled. "It's after one o'clock, Miss St. John," she said. "We should just have time to tidy you up before your visitors arrive."

It was easier to submit to Nurse Moray's ministrations than argue, Lani found. Besides, the idea of visitors was exciting. She was looking forward to seeing her father. She had been half surprised he had not been there when she first awakened, but she could only assume he had been and gone again while she was unconscious. After all, he was still a sick man himself, and it must have been a terrible shock when he discovered she was in hospital. Nevertheless, she anticipated his coming eagerly, firm in the belief that he would not prove so evasive on the subject of Jake Pendragon.

The mirror Nurse Moray produced at Lani's request was not so reassuring. Her narrow-boned features had never been plump, but they had never looked as pinched and drawn as they did now. Her cheeks had hollowed, there were caverns where bruised eyes gazed back at her reproachfully and the bones of her jawline stood out in stark relief. The bandage that disguised the injuries to her forehead was scarcely whiter than her skin, and she viewed her reflection with utter consternation.

"I look terrible!" she exclaimed. "Oh, heavens, do you have any makeup I could borrow?"

"Your cousin's wife brought your belongings when she came to see you," declared Nurse Moray comfortably, bending to extract Lani's makeup case from the locker beside her bed. "But don't go getting in a panic. You look perfectly all right to me. Be thankful they didn't have to shave your head. You would have had something to complain about then."

By the time Nurse Moray came to tell her her visitors had arrived, Lani thought she had repaired a little of the damage. At least her cheeks did not look quite so pale or her lips so colorless, and the young nursing officer had helped her to adjust her pillows so that her hair framed her taut features.

"Relax," said Nurse Moray, before leaving the room. "No one expects you to look glamorous. Believe me, they're only too relieved you're conscious."

Lani nodded. She knew the nurse was right. And after all, her father had cared for her through sickness and health for more than twenty years. It was foolish to worry about her appearance when Jake could be fighting for his life in some other hospital ward, and she tried to calm her nerves as footsteps sounded in the corridor outside.

But it was not her father who opened her door. It was Robin and Sarah who came into the room, carrying an enormous bouquet of roses and carnations, and although Lani was glad to see them, she couldn't prevent her eyes from moving past them, searching for that other face.

"Oh, love!" Sarah sniffed convulsively as she bent to kiss the other girl's cheek, and the dampness of her tears brought a new wave of anxiety sweeping over Lani. Where was her father? Why wasn't he here? Oh, surely her accident had not had more serious repercussions.

"Robin!" She reached desperately for his hand. "Oh, Robin, where's daddy?"

"Don't distress yourself, sweetheart." Robin sat down on the bed beside her, giving his wife a faintly impatient look. "Uncle Roger couldn't come, that's all. He's. . . not well. Nothing too serious," he added quickly to reassure her. "It's just. . . well, his cold got worse. You remember he had pleurisy, don't you? It deteriorated into pneumonia. He's been confined to his bed for the last four days."

"Oh—" Lani moved her head helplessly. "I knew this would happen, I knew it." She pressed her lips together. "He wouldn't listen to me. He persisted in standing in a draft, and I told him—"

"Yes, well... I guess that's how it happened." Robin exchanged a meaningful glance with his wife. "Anyway, he's recovering slowly, and I know he'll be delighted to learn you're looking so much better."

"Am I?" Lani's tone was faintly tearful, and Sarah, after blowing her nose, took the chair at the other side of the bed and pulled it closer.

"Of course you are, love," she exclaimed, forcing a bright smile. "You've no idea how worried we've been about you. You were unconscious for so long."

"I think Lani knows that," said Robin dryly, his finger removing a drop of moisture from his cousin's cheek. "It's good to see you awake again. It's not much fun visiting someone who just snores their way through your visit."

Lani's lips curved. "Did I do that?"

"Of course not." Sarah was indignant. "It's not you who snores, Lani, it's him. Like a pig!" She grimaced. "You've no idea what it's like. Sometimes I think I'll get the tape recorder and record the noise he makes so he can hear it for himself."

"She wouldn't dare," said Robin smugly. "She'd be too afraid I might record one of her interminable phone calls and replay it at one of her coffee mornings. I can just imagine how popular she'd be after that."

"Louse!" Sarah pulled a face.

"Gossip!" retorted Robin evenly, and Lani knew a sense of gratitude for their understanding.

"Do you know when you'll get out of here?" asked Sarah, after a moment. "Rob's going to have a word with the doctor when we leave here, but I wondered if they had said anything to you."

"No." Lani's tongue circled her upper lip. "Do. . .do you two know what happened?"

Robin sighed. "I don't think you should talk about the accident right now, Lani."

"Why not?"

"Well. . .well, because it's bound to be upsetting for you, and Nurse Moray said you were not to get excited."

Lani shook her head. "I'll only get excited if we don't talk about it," she declared unsteadily. "Please, Robin, do you know what happened?"

"Some of it." Robin took a deep breath. "Aunt Clare knocked you down, didn't she?"

"You know that?" Lani's voice trembled.

"Know it!" Sarah gasped. "It's been headlines in all the papers—"

"Shut up, Sarah, will you?" Robin spoke tersely, and his wife lapsed into an offended silence. "It was in the newspapers, Lani. How could it not be? Clare Austin's affairs are always news, and when she accidently runs down her latest boyfriend and her daughter, there's no way it could be kept a secret. Hell, I believe they've had some difficulty keeping reporters out of the hospital. You're a target, Lani. You might as well know it."

Lani gazed at him speechlessly, and lifting his shoulders Robin continued. "I mean—it is some story, isn't it? How the hell did it happen? The papers say she pressed the accelerator instead of the brake. It's easily done, I suppose, especially if you're driving a car you're not used to. But what were you doing, running into the road in front of her?"

Lani's eyes turned up to the ceiling. "Is that what Clare said? That she pressed the accelerator instead of the brake?"

"So it says."

"And...and Jake?" She had to ask. "Does it say how...how he is?"

Robin hesitated. "He's not here."

"I know that." Lani looked at him. "They told me he'd been taken to St. Augustine's. An orthopedic hospital. Do you know why?"

Robin shrugged. "I guess because of his injuries."

"But what were his injuries?" Lani stared at him tremulously. "I—I want to know, Robin."

"Well, I don't know, do I?" He shifted uncomfortably. "Why don't you ask your mother? She'll be coming to see you this evening, I expect."

"I don't want to see her."

Lani was vehement, and Robin exchanged another doubtful look with his wife. "Don't be silly, Lani," he began, but this time Sarah intervened.

"She doesn't have to see her if she doesn't want to," she declared staunchly. "And why don't you tell her about Jake Pendragon, too? She's got to know sooner or later."

"Sarah!"

Robin was furious, but Lani had heard enough to know that he was keeping something from her. "Tell me," she said, and the sharp edge to her voice warned Robin she was on the brink of hysteria.

"Oh, hell!" He leaned over her helplessly, almost as if he wanted to protect her from what was to come. And then, realizing he could delay no longer, he said, "They say he had a few cuts and bruises. Broken bones—you know the sort of thing. He was brought here to the Royal Memorial like you, but they decided he'd be better off with specialist treatment."

"Who decided?" Lani's voice quavered.

"Your mother, I guess," said Sarah flatly. "And it wasn't just a few broken bones, Lani. They say his hands were crushed."

"ARE YOU FEELING BETTER?"

Nurse Phillips was on duty again, and Lani looked up at her with lackluster eyes. "I suppose so," she said dully, unwilling to discuss it, and the young nurse lifted the two vases of flowers she had arranged from the bouquet.

"I'll just put these in the corridor for tonight," she said, burying her face in their fragrant perfume. "Hmm, aren't they beautiful? And such lovely colors, too."

Lani made no response, and when Nurse Phillips came back she looked down at her in mild frustration. "This won't do, you know," she said. "I agree your cousin shouldn't have blurted it out like that, about Mr. Pendragon, I mean, but your lying here fretting isn't going to help him or you, now is it?"

Lani shrugged, and warming to her theme, the nurse went on, "Refusing to see your mother wasn't very sensible either, was it? She's visited the hospital every day without fail since you've been here. She's been worried sick about you. How could you turn her away?"

"She came because it's expected of her," said Lani flatly, turning her face into the pillow. "Can you imagine what the papers would say if Clare didn't appear to be taking a proper interest in my recovery? Particularly when she's responsible!"

"Now, Miss St. John, that's no way to talk!"

Nurse Phillips was shocked, and Lani thought it typical that her mother should get all the sympathy. Clare had deliberately driven at Jake, she had knocked him down intentionally, and nothing she could say could erase Lani's memory of her mother's face as she drove the car forward. There had been no mistake, no accidental mix-up over the pedals. In those moments, Clare had wanted to kill Jake, and if her daughter had chosen to get involved, then that was her misfortune. "Oh, Jake," she whispered inwardly, feeling the desperation that helplessness can bring, and seeing the tears streaming down her patient's cheeks, Nurse Phillips quietly left the room.

Two days later, Lani was out of bed and sitting in a chair by the window when she had another visitor.

"Miles!" she exclaimed, when he came through the door, and he gathered her slim form into his arms with evident emotion.

"Oh, Lani!" he muttered at last, holding her at arm's length. "God, I've been so worried about you. And when Rob said you were feeling pretty low, I had to come and see you. I hope you don't mind."

"Mind? Why should I mind?" Lani was glad of the diversion. She had been unable to get any further information about Jake's condition, and her anxiety was hindering her recovery. She wanted to see him. She wanted to tell him that whatever happened, she would never stop loving him, and her confinement in the hospital was driving her to distraction.

"You're so thin!" Miles shook his head disbelievingly. "Don't they feed you in here? And why are you wearing that plaster? I thought the fracture was farther back."

"It is." Lani touched the plaster on her forehead indifferently. "This is just to cover a cut they put stitches in. Oh, the stitches are out now," she added, "but it's pretty ugly."

"Nothing about you is ugly," stated Miles forcefully, pulling a box of chocolates out of the pocket of his overcoat. "Here. I brought you these. I guessed you'd have plenty of flowers, and I was right. It's like a hothouse in here."

Lani glanced about her without interest. "I told them to put them in the wards," she said, "but there were too many. Clare sent most of them, of course. I wish she wouldn't."

Miles pulled up a chair and seated himself beside her. "You blame her," he said matter-of-factly. "I don't blame you. The woman must be an absolute fool. Imagine driving a car without knowing the accelerator from the brake."

Lani bent her head. "I'd rather not talk about it."

"No. No, of course not." Miles was trying to be tactful. "Anyway, you came out of it lightly, didn't you, compared to poor old Pendragon. They say he'll never play again, you know. The piano, I mean," he added, unaware of Lani's strained face. "These surgeon chaps are bloody marvelous, I know, but it takes more than mechanical skill to restore a talent like his."

Lani moaned, and realizing he had said something else to upset her, Miles was contrite. "Hey—Lani! What is it?" he exclaimed, his eyes widening at the horror in her face. "Come on, Lani, it wasn't your fault, love. How do you think your mother feels? She discovered him!"

Lani turned away, though she didn't draw her hands from his, and he squeezed them tightly. "Look—let's talk about something else, shall we?" he suggested. "I guess you've heard enough about Jake Pendragon to last you a lifetime."

"*No!*" Catching her breath, Lani forced herself to look at Miles again. "No, you don't understand," she said tremulously. "I do want to hear about Jake. Please—I'm afraid I'm just being silly."

"You're just feeling rather fragile at the moment, I know." To her relief, Miles accepted her explanation without question. "It's been quite an ordeal for you, hasn't it? What with your father being ill and all. Rob told me," he explained. "He seemed to think you were worrying about him, too."

"Daddy. Oh, yes." To her amazement, she had scarcely thought of her father since hearing about Jake, and her conscience smote her at the realization that his well-being had not come first. "I must write to him, now that I'm feeling so much better. I'm sure he'd like a letter from me."

"I'm sure he would," agreed Miles dryly. "However,

it has to be said, your condition has been more serious than his. Has he been in touch with you?"

Lani sighed. "You don't like my father, do you?"

"He doesn't like me," said Miles obliquely. "Anyway, I'm glad you're feeling better. Poor old Matilda is having to take a back seat."

Lani half smiled. "Matilda," she murmured, and then, returning to the subject uppermost in her thoughts, she said, "Tell me about... about Jake. Where did you hear about him not playing again?"

"On television," said Miles carelessly, not altogether pleased to be discussing something that seemed to have no bearing on their relationship. "When can you go home? Have the doctors reached a verdict?"

"At the end of the week, I think." Lani was not interested in talking about herself. "Tell me, is Jake still in hospital? Does my mother visit him?"

"How should I know?" Miles sighed. "Lani, what is this with Jake Pendragon? He's your mother's problem, not yours. Just because you were there when it happened—"

Lani took a deep breath. "Did the newspapers give any reason why I was there?" she asked tensely.

Miles frowned. "I understood you'd been having supper at the hotel with Pendragon and your mother. She had offered to drive you home, hadn't she?"

"That's what she said?"

"Your mother, yes." Miles looked at her impatiently. "Lani, why are you asking all these questions? Don't you remember what happened?"

"Oh, yes, I remember." Lani's tone was bitter, but she didn't pursue it any further. There was no point in involving Miles in something that was so intensely personal. Her only salvation lay with Jake himself.

Much to Miles's relief the rest of their conversation was limited to other things, like how soon Lani expected to be able to start work again, and if there was anything he could do she had only to say the word.

"There's nothing," she assured him gratefully. "Robin and Sarah have been wonderful. They've even suggested I spend a few days with them after I get out of hospital, but I'd rather go home. I want to reassure daddy I'm still in one piece."

"But will you be all right?" Miles was concerned. "I mean—a fractured skull can be very serious."

"I know." Lani smiled. "But I was lucky. The bone didn't splinter, and I've had no internal bleeding. Dr. Connor says it's because my head's so thick."

Miles looked doubtful. "Even so, you must take things easy."

"Oh, I will." Lani promised. "I've no intention of doing anything to prolong my stay in here."

In the event, Lani was spirited out of the hospital at the end of the week through a rear entrance. A handful of newsmen were still hanging around the front lobby, and suspecting Clare might use the opportunity to try to effect a reconciliation, Lani was anxious to avoid any publicity. Besides, she was still far from completely recovered, and even the short journey home in Robin's car left her feeling exhausted.

Mrs. Evans was at the door to greet her. The housekeeper had visited her once in the hospital, but it had not been a tremendously successful visit. She was evidently unhappy with her surroundings, and she had confessed to Lani that hospitals always made her nervous. They had spent most of the time discussing the different varieties of flowers Clare had sent and hardly mentioned her father's illness at all.

Now, however, Lani entered the house eagerly, and Mrs. Evans pointed toward the drawing room. "Your father's in there," she said, turning to invite Robin to come in, and Lani opened the door firmly and quickly stepped inside.

Roger St. John was sitting by the fire, and his head turned automatically at her entrance. She had the feeling he had seen Robin's car approach from the window, and his quickened breathing as she hurried across the room to kiss him seemed to confirm this. He was dressed, but only in the shabby tweed trousers and woolen cardigan he used about the house, and when she drew back to look at him, she saw he too had lost weight.

"Oh, daddy," she said, ridiculously overcome with tears, and he lifted his hand to cradle her cheek.

"It's so good to see you, my darling," he murmured, his own emotions thickening his voice. "What a terribly long time it has seemed. Can you ever forgive me?"

CHAPTER ELEVEN

"Forgive you?" Blinking back her tears, Lani pulled a chair close to his and seated herself beside him. "Oh, daddy, there's nothing to forgive. It wasn't your fault. Clare must have been out of her mind. She drove at Jake deliberately. I'll never forgive *her* — never!"

Roger St. John gazed at his daughter strangely. "You haven't seen Clare?"

"Not since the — not since what happened," said Lani vehemently. "Oh, she came to the hospital. I suppose you know about that. But I didn't want to see her, and they — the staff, that is — decided it was best if I didn't get upset."

Her father shook his head. "But that night—"

"The night it happened?" Lani's hands curled tightly together. "Oh, yes, I saw her that night. But we didn't exactly find time for conversation."

Roger lay back in his chair, staring at her. "What happened?"

"When? When Jake and I left here?" Lani winced at the memories this evoked. "I know you were furious, but you were wrong about Jake. He. . .well. . .he was not having an affair with. . .with my mother."

"You believe that?" Her father's lips twisted. "Lani, I realize you're infatuated with this fellow, but let's not pretend he's any saint. Clare—" He broke off abruptly, and then went on, "It's common knowledge, she'd been supporting him for almost a year!"

"I know that." Lani closed her eyes for a moment. "But that doesn't mean—" She sighed, realizing she was fighting a losing battle. "Anyway, that's over now. He loves me, daddy, and—and I love him. As soon as I can, I'm going to see him."

Roger's face was haggard. "You can't mean this."

"I do." Lani put her hand on his arm. "Oh, daddy, you don't know him, honestly. He's proud, but he's honest. He doesn't try to deny the things they say about him. He. . . he only lives for his music."

"No longer," said her father harshly. "Haven't you heard? His hands were injured in the accident. I doubt if he'll ever play the piano again."

"No!" Lani caught her breath.

As if regretting his cruelty, Roger said, "It may be the best thing that could happen—for you!"

"What do you mean?" Lani's voice was tremulous.

"Well—" Her father was bitter. "Clare has never associated herself with failure, has she?"

Mrs. Evans's appearance with a tray of tea prevented any further discussion of the matter, and Lani, still numbed by what her father had said, glanced around expectantly. "Where's Robin?"

"Oh—he left," said Mrs. Evans comfortably. "He guessed you and your father would have a lot to say to one another. He said he'd give you a ring this evening."

Lani sighed. "I never thanked him."

"I think he understood," the housekeeper assured

her. "Now, help yourselves to the sandwiches. I'll be back in a few minutes with some hot tea cakes."

Lani ate little, and as soon as tea was over, she excused herself.

"You're not. . . you're not going to see *him* tonight, are you?"

Her father's expression was tormented, and after a moment, Lani shook her head. "Not tonight," she agreed flatly. "I'm too weary. If you don't mind, I think I'll have an early night. It's been a long day."

"Of course. Of course."

Her father rose to his feet as if he intended to escort her, but Lani held up her hands, palms facing him. "I'll be okay, honestly," she said, backing toward the door, and with a helpless little gesture he subsided again.

In her room, Lani pressed her hot forehead against the cool glass of the window. She gazed down on the lamplit street, wondering how Jake was feeling tonight. She knew how desperate he must feel, knowing his future was hanging in the balance, and any compassion she felt could not be compared to the agony he must be suffering. It didn't help to suspect that however biased her father's words might have been, he was probably right. Without his ability to play, without that extraordinary talent that had shone so brilliantly in the concert hall, Jake could mean nothing to Clare. Although Lani was thankful for that, she had no conviction that their future would be any easier.

In the morning, things looked inexpressibly brighter. Jake was alive, that was the important thing, she told herself severely, making a determined effort to disguise the hollows in her cheeks. The last thing she wanted was for Jake to worry about her. He needed her strength to get better as well as his own.

Her father was still in bed when she came downstairs, and Mrs. Evans clicked her tongue reprovingly. "Now, I was going to fetch you breakfast in bed," she declared, when Lani entered the kitchen. "You're supposed to get plenty of rest, and here you are, up at eight o'clock."

"I wasn't tired," said Lani, without mentioning the fact that worrying about Jake had kept her awake half the night. "Just some toast and coffee for me, Mrs. Evans. I'm not really hungry either."

"So I noticed at teatime yesterday," retorted the housekeeper shortly. "Neither one of you ate more than a couple of sandwiches, and I might as well not have bothered to bake."

"I'm sorry." Lani slipped into a chair at the table. "I suppose it was the excitement of coming home. I was so looking forward to seeing daddy again. He's looking so old these days. I worry about him."

"Don't we all." Mrs. Evans was impatient. "I must say I was surprised he didn't go to see you in the hospital. He could have done, you know. Your cousin Robin offered to take him."

"Did he?" Lani tried not to feel hurt. "Oh, well—I suppose he didn't want to jeopardize his recovery a second time."

"Huh." Mrs. Evans snorted. "He brought it all upon himself, if you ask me," she declared. "A night like that. He ought to have had more sense."

Lani sighed. "Well, that's over now, isn't it? He is much better, and I'm grateful for that."

Mrs. Evans shook her head. "You're a good-hearted girl, Lani. I just hope this young man is worthy of you."

Lani colored. "You know about Jake?"

"I should do." Mrs. Evans grimaced as she poured coffee into an earthenware cup. "Your father's talked of nothing else since. . . well, since it happened."

Lani took the cup the housekeeper offered and studied its contents reflectively. "I suppose daddy told you he doesn't approve."

"I don't think your father is in any position to be objective," said Mrs. Evans candidly. "Now, you just take things easy. We don't want you having a relapse, do we?"

St. Augustine's Orthopedic Hospital was in Finsbury Park, not far from Old Street underground station. Having discovered this from a map of London she had found in her father's study, Lani had been tempted to take the train, but impatience and awareness of her weakness had persuaded her to take a cab, and she was glad afterward that she had.

Her father, coming into her bedroom earlier to find her applying her makeup, had quickly voiced his disapproval of what she was planning to do, and she had had to close her ears to his pleas. It was no use telling her she was a fool for going on with this, no use implying that if Jake was going to be crippled, she'd be better off without him. She loved her father, but she loved Jake more, and nothing could replace her need to be with him.

The taxi dropped her at the hospital gates, and after

paying the fare, Lani wrapped her cloak around her and walked slowly across the forecourt. It was a bitterly cold morning, and though the sun was shining, it gave off no heat. She felt quite exhausted by the time she reached the reception area.

"I'd like to see Mr. Pendragon," she told one of the uniformed men behind the glass partition. "My name is Miss St. John. Lani St. John. He does. . . know who I am."

There was a muffled conference between two of the men and a nurse, who was hovering by an inner door. Then the man Lani had addressed turned to her again.

"You'd be Miss Austin's daughter then?" he ventured, eyeing her doubtfully, and Lani expelled her breath wearily as she acknowledged that this was so.

"But I'm not here on behalf of my mother," she stated, supporting herself against the desk. "Please, do you think you could hurry it up? I'm not feeling very well myself."

The nurse, who had been listening to this exchange, now let herself out of the partitioned office and came toward her. "I'm afraid Mr. Pendragon isn't having any visitors, Miss St. John," she said apologetically. "He's most insistent upon it. I couldn't go against his wishes without his doctor's permission."

Lani's legs sagged. "Who is his doctor?"

"Mr. Holland."

Lani remembered she had heard that name before. "Then, could I see him, please?" she asked weakly. "I realize I don't have an appointment, but. . . but it is rather urgent."

The nurse sighed. "I'm afraid Mr. Holland isn't in

the hospital today, Miss St. John. He won't be available for consultation until Monday. Unless there's an emergency, of course."

Lani wanted to cry that this was an emergency, that she had to see Jake now, today, without any more delay. But she knew it would be useless. Consultant surgeons did not interrupt their schedules for emotional reasons.

"Monday," she said dully, wishing she could sit down, and the nurse nodded.

"I could make you an appointment for Monday morning," she said. "I believe—well, in the circumstances, I'm sure Mr. Holland would see you."

"Thank you." Lani took a deep breath. "But are you sure Mr. Pendragon won't see me anyway? I mean— couldn't you at least ask him? I'd be very grateful."

The nursing officer hesitated. "It really is most irregular, Miss St. John. I do have Mr. Holland's orders."

"But you did say it was Jake—I mean Mr. Pendragon, who said he didn't want to see anyone, didn't you?" Lani persisted faintly. "Oh, please, won't you try?"

She was sure the woman was going to refuse, and almost involuntarily she swayed toward her. It was not a deliberate plea for sympathy nor yet an attempt to draw her attention to her condition. But professional eyes took in her pallid face and strained expression, and relented.

"Here," she said, leading Lani to where a row of chairs had been supplied for visitors. "Sit down. I'll go and make some inquiries. I can't promise anything, of course, but I will find out."

"Oh, thank you." Lani's eyes were full of tears as she looked up at her, and the woman shook her head half-deprecatingly as she quickly walked away.

It seemed hours before she returned, and even before she spoke Lani could tell from her expression she was not bringing good news. "I'm sorry," she said, spreading her hands. "Mr. Pendragon won't see you. I did warn you he had refused all visitors, didn't I? I'm afraid you've had a wasted journey."

Lani blinked. "But why won't he see me?" She caught her breath and then went on raggedly, "I can understand him not wanting to see Clare, but why me? Why me?"

"I don't think you should upset yourself, Miss St. John." The nurse glanced quickly around the reception area to assure herself that their conversation was not being heard. "Patients...well, patients who have had some traumatic kind of shock often suffer withdrawal symptoms for a while. It's quite normal. Once he's accepted the situation—"

"What situation?" Lani struggled to her feet. "Is it true? Were his hands crushed? Won't he ever play again?"

"Oh, really—I can't make that kind of diagnosis, Miss St. John." The woman gazed at her compassionately. "Look, let me get you a cup of tea. You can drink it in my office. I'm sure you would prefer a few moment's privacy before you leave. We had a great deal of annoyance from reporters and so on, hanging around here earlier in the week, but thankfully, they seem to have left now."

Lani shook her head, her brief outburst having

drained what little strength she had left. "I think if you could just call me a taxi," she said, wrapping her cloak around her, "I'd rather go home. My father will worry."

Going home in the cab, she felt hopelessly inadequate. Weakness was responsible for the tears that ran unheeded down her cheeks, but it was a sense of impotence that made her feel so desperate. How could she achieve anything if Jake refused to speak to her? Did he blame her for what had happened? Did he blame her for her mother's fit of madness? Was she to bear the burden of guilt for creating the situation?

She shook her head, staring blindly through the cab window. If only he would speak to her, she fretted. If only she could be sure he did not hate her. Could it be that because of his injuries, he didn't want to see anyone, or had Clare been given an opportunity to influence him against her?

There was a car parked at the gate of Number 11, Pelham Court. Paying the taxi driver, Lani viewed it apprehensively. It was not a car she recognized, for it was sleek and black and luxurious, evidently belonging to someone to whom the demonstration of wealth was important. She knew of only one person who fitted that description.

How dare she come here, Lani asked herself incredulously, as she fumbled for her key. How dared she come here, upsetting her father and disrupting all their lives? Hadn't she done enough? Had she no shame? Hadn't the fact that she had seriously injured the two people she had said meant so much to her left no remorse? Was she so insensitive to their feelings that she believed she could behave as if the lies she had told the press were true?

Lani's hands were trembling as she threw off her cape and marched to the door of the drawing room. She could hear the low murmur of their voices, and her anger ran like a forceful stimulant through her veins. She forgot her illness and the appalling weakness she had felt in the taxi. She was filled with an artificial sensation of strength, as she charged to her father's defense.

The scene that met her eyes when she opened the drawing-room door, however, was somewhat different from what she had expected. To begin with, she had not expected to find her father and mother seated on opposite sides of the fireplace, giving every appearance of cordial normality. Nor had she expected the civilized tray of morning coffee, occupying the low table between them, with Clare dispensing cream and sugar as if this was her usual occupation. Her eyes, when they met her daughter's revealed nothing but guarded anticipation, and Lani turned to her father blankly, waiting for his explanation.

Roger St. John had risen at her entrance, and now he pointed to the chair in which he had been sitting and suggested she take it. "You look chilled to the bone, my dear," he exclaimed, urging her to join them. Lani stared at him aghast, her senses tilting.

"Yes, do sit down, Lani." Clare spoke at last, putting down her coffee cup and regarding her daughter coolly. "I'll ask Mrs. Evans to fetch another cup. You look as though—"

"Don't bother!" The words came stiffly from Lani's

lips, and she turned to her father in amazement. "What's going on here?" she asked. "Why is—why is *she* here? Did you invite her? Did you know she was coming?"

"Now, Lani—" began Roger awkwardly, only to have his words overridden by his ex-wife.

"He didn't know exactly when to expect me," Clare stated tersely, "but he knew I would come. After all, when you so childishly refused to see me in the hospital, I had to do something, didn't I?"

"I don't see why—"

"Oh, don't you?" Clare realized Lani was not about to sit down, and she rose abruptly to her feet. "Is it so unreasonable that I might want to assure myself that my daughter is making a satisfactory recovery? For heaven's sake," her voice broke with convincing sincerity, "I didn't mean to hurt *you*. You must know that for yourself."

"Just Jake, is that it?" Lani managed to sound a cynical note, and Clare's small hands clenched.

"I didn't mean to hurt anybody!" she exclaimed unsteadily. "I just wanted to get away—on my own. You...you had hurt me, Lani, you must know that, and I was desperate! Can't you try and understand my feelings? Jake—Jake and I had been so...close."

"You drove at Jake deliberately," said Lani, her voice shaking with emotion. "I saw you, Clare. I saw you! You may be able to deceive the press with stories of confusing the accelerator and the brake, but not me. You intended to hit him. I saw it in your face. I think you wanted to *kill* him! Instead of which, you've ruined his life, and I hope he sues you for every penny you've got!"

"And have you seen him?" demanded Clare tautly, apparently abandoning the attempt to defend her innocence. "Has Jake told you that's what he intends to do? Or has he confessed that he has no intention of bringing a suit against me, that contrary to your wild accusations, he doesn't blame me at all?"

"That's not true!" Lani stared at her.

"How do you know?" Clare lifted a scornful eyebrow. "Have you spoken to him?"

"I — why — no."

"You see. You don't know anything. Jake wouldn't bring a suit against me." Clare shook her head. "He owes me too much."

"I don't believe you." Lani was dogged. "He doesn't owe you anything. And he loves me. He . . . we . . . were going to get married. . . ."

Clare laughed then, a harsh condescending sound that was so much worse than anger. "Get married!" she echoed. "Oh, don't give me that, Lani. Jake may have been attracted to you, but believe me, marriage was never on the horizon — for either of us."

"But you said —"

"Yes? What did I say?" Clare had command of the situation now. "Did I say we were going to get married?"

Lani faltered. "But Elwyn Hughes said . . . it was in the newspapers. . . ."

"Elwyn Hughes is a gossip, and you've just proved you shouldn't believe all you read in the newspapers, Lani," retorted Clare crisply. "Now, if we've got that out of the way, can we start this conversation again like civilized people? Roger, ask Mrs. Evans to bring some fresh coffee. I'm sure this must be stone cold by now."

"I don't want any coffee." Lani could feel her self-control slipping away. She turned to her father desperately. She needed him now, she realized. She needed his support to prove to Clare they were united against her. He knew how she felt about Jake. He knew how Jake felt about her. It wasn't true that all Jake had wanted was an affair. As usual Clare believed only what she wanted to believe.

But she saw at once that something was wrong. Roger was rubbing his hands together anxiously, and the look he gave his daughter was not reassuring.

"Lani, I think you should listen to what your mother has to say," he said heavily. "Whatever you may think, she does care about you, you know."

"No!"

"Yes, she does." Roger sighed uneasily. "Lani, we're not just talking about the accident here, we're talking about your future."

"What do you mean?" Lani stared at him uncomprehendingly, and her father looked appealingly toward his ex-wife.

"What your father is trying to say, Lani, is that he doesn't think you should attempt to see Jake Pendragon again."

"No—"

"Yes." Clare was decisive. "We're only thinking of you. I don't know what you've read or heard, but I'm in a position to tell you, Jake is going to be a cripple for the rest of his life—"

"Oh, no!"

"Oh, yes. His injuries were more extensive than was at first imagined. He may never walk again, and his hands—"

"Stop it!" Lani pressed her palms against her cheeks and moved her head in a negating gesture, but Clare held her gaze implacably.

"I know it's hard for you to accept, Lani, but it is the truth. How do you think I feel? How do you think I can bear to look at him? He's got the best doctors that money can buy, treatment of the very first order, but to know that I'm indirectly responsible—"

"Indirectly!" Lani gasped, but Clare was adamant.

"Yes, indirectly," she said. "You don't really believe I'd have chosen this for him—"

"Yes. Yes, I do." Lani thrust away her father's detaining hand and stared at her mother with pure loathing. "This is exactly what you wanted, isn't it? You *bought* him! Oh, yes, I'll give you that. But when you saw us together, you realized how little that really meant. You drove at him on purpose. Nothing will change my mind about that. And if you think that by telling me Jake's going to be an invalid you can destroy our feelings for one another, then you know nothing about love!"

"You silly little bitch." Clare's mouth curled contemptuously. "I don't know why I came here. I don't know why I bothered. Why should I care if you choose to waste your life nurturing a thankless devotion for a man who'll never be able to return it? As your mother, I felt it was my duty to warn you, to try and make you see that you'd be better off forgetting him, but I see now I was wrong." She sneered. "You think Jake will be grateful because you're prepared to sacrifice yourself for him. Well, he won't. He won't thank you for complicating his existence. And remember, every time he looks at you he'll be reminded of what he's lost!"

Lani caught her breath. "You're vile—"

"No. Just practical." Clare snorted. "You're just like your father, do you know that? You think you've found a cause, don't you? Something to give your life meaning. Well, remember, pity is no substitute for passion!"

"Get—out—of—here!"

Lani was swaying with weakness, but Clare had one final thing to say. "Did your father confess what he said the night he came to my apartment? Did he tell you how he begged for us to get back together again? You were surprised to see me here, weren't you? Well, if your father had his way, all would be forgiven and I'd be living here for good."

Lani turned bewildered eyes to her father. "The... the night you went to her... apartment?" she said blankly. "What night? What does she mean?"

Clare let out a gulp of disbelief. "You mean he hasn't told you?" she exclaimed, and Lani saw her father blanch.

"What is she talking about, daddy," she asked shakily. "What is all this about? You didn't tell me you'd been to see her. When did you go? You've been ill."

"How about the night Jake was injured," said Clare, as Roger seemed to shrink within himself. "You remember? The night I arrived back from Milan, earlier than usual because of the fog, or I wouldn't have even been at the apartment when he called."

Lani moaned. "Oh, no—"

"Oh, yes." Clare was enjoying her moment of triumph. "Dear me, Roger, what a sly devil you are! Didn't you tell Lani how you taunted me that my— *lover* —had abandoned me for my daughter? Didn't you explain how you tried to use that information to your own advantage? That it was you who drove me to take such desperate measures to safeguard my investment!"

CHAPTER TWELVE

"ARE YOU SURE you want to go home?"

Sarah's voice was anxious as she viewed Lani's pale face, but Lani was definite. "Oh, yes," she said, bending to kiss the twins with some regret. "It's time I went back. I can't stay here indefinitely, and in any case, Jake should be getting out of hospital soon."

Sarah shook her head. "You don't know that. You're only guessing. It's only six weeks since the accident, you know."

"I know." Lani felt a constricting pain inside her. Six weeks! It seemed a lifetime.

"And how do you know he'll see you anyway?" Sarah persisted. "I don't know how many times you've rung the hospital, and always with the same result."

"It'll be different when he gets out," declared Lani, more confidently than she felt. "In any case, I have to try. Now that Clare has left for Los Angeles, I feel more optimistic."

"Lani, you don't know that your mother has been visiting him. Oh, I know what she told you, but you've said yourself, she has been known to...well, to exaggerate."

"Nevertheless, I have to do something." Lani drew herself up determinedly. "Sarah, I've got to get things straight between us. You and Robin have been very kind, but now I've got to stand on my own two feet."

"Ready?" Robin appeared at that moment, having brought his car out of the garage, and the two girls exchanged swift kisses.

"Ready," agreed Lani tremulously, picking up her shoulder bag, grateful that the twins started to argue over who was going to stand where to wave goodbye.

"We'd like to meet him one day," Sarah murmured as they followed Robin outside, and the younger girl forced a smile.

"You'll be the first," she promised, squeezing Sarah's hand, and then went to seat herself in the front of Robin's Sierra.

It was four weeks since she had seen her father, and as the miles disappeared, Lani could feel herself growing tense. She was not looking forward to seeing him again, remembering the way they had parted, but she had lived in Pelham Court all her life and she couldn't imagine striking out on her own.

"You could have stayed on, you know."

As if perceiving her thoughts, Robin ventured his own suggestion, and Lani gave him an affectionate smile. "Sarah said the same," she told him. "You two really have been marvelous! I don't know what I'd have done without you."

Robin shrugged. "You know you're always welcome in our house. Heavens, the twins think you're wonderful, and I know for a fact that Sarah takes advantage of your good nature."

"I like helping." Lani made a deprecating gesture. "Besides, I've not had much else to do, have I?"

"You've not done any work, you mean," Robin interjected. "Maybe being at Chalfont. . . ."

"No." Lani shook her head. "I haven't been able to concentrate on anything since. . .well, since it happened."

"You don't think—I mean—that blow on your head didn't—"

"I don't think so." Lani grimaced. "It's much more basic than that. If—*when*—I see Jake again, it'll be different then."

"And if he still refuses to see you?"

Robin was matter-of-fact, and Lani drew a deep breath. "He won't," she said determinedly. "I won't let him."

To her relief, her father was not at home when she arrived at Pelham Court. Mrs. Evans came bustling out to greet her, her lined face showing real pleasure that Lani was back. Robin left her to the housekeeper's ministrations with a knowing smile.

"I'm sure if your father had known you were coming back today, he wouldn't have gone to work," declared Mrs. Evans, helping her carry her things upstairs, and Lani reflected silently that this had been her belief, too.

"I've got some phone calls to make," she said, after declining the housekeeper's offer to help her unpack. "I'll get around to everything later, Mrs. Evans. What I'd like now is a nice cup of tea."

With Mrs. Evans busy in the kitchen, Lani went into her father's study to make her calls. Roger had had an extension put in there for business purposes, and it was much more private than the phone in the hall.

She rang the hospital first. It was three days since she

had last inquired about Jake's condition, and she was eager to assure herself he was still progressing satisfactorily. It had not been easy hiding her anxiety from Robin and Sarah; she was quite sure they thought she was making a fool of herself by calling so often. But the truth was, even that small link seemed to form a bond between her and Jake, and although he might not know it, Lani could delude herself that he did.

"I'm afraid Mr. Pendragon checked out several days ago." The receptionist shocked her out of her complacency, and Lani, who had been expecting the usual response, caught her breath.

"Checked out!" she echoed, realizing how ridiculous she must sound. "But I don't understand. Was his treatment finished?"

"Just a moment." The woman cut her off to make inquiries, but soon she was back with the polite reply that Mr. Pendragon had discharged himself on Tuesday. "I'm sorry," she added. "We have no further information."

"Thank you."

Lani responded automatically, the receiver clattering from her nerveless fingers. Jake had left the hospital, she told herself disbelievingly. He had discharged himself on the day Clare departed for Los Angeles.

She was still sitting staring at the phone when Mrs. Evans entered the room. "I thought you were here," she said, coming in without knocking. "Here's that cup of tea I promised you. Now, what would you like for your lunch?"

Lani looked up at her blankly, and the housekeeper

drew in her lips. "Now what's happened?" she exclaimed, tutting impatiently. "Is it Mrs. St. John again? That woman causes nothing but trouble!"

"Her name is *Miss* Austin," said Lani dully, pulling herself together with an effort. "And she left for Los Angeles three days ago."

"And good riddance." Mrs. Evans was unimpressed. "So what is it?"

"It's Jake," said Lani, shaking her head. "Jake Pendragon. You know. He. . . he's left the hospital, and I don't know where he's gone."

"I see." Mrs. Evans folded her arms. "And I suppose you think he's gone with your mother."

"No!" But Lani had to admit the thought had crossed her mind.

"Then why are you looking so glum? Have you tried Mr. Pendragon's hotel? The Gloucester Court, wasn't it?"

"As everybody knows," said Lani bitterly. "But no. No, I haven't tried there. Do you think I should?"

"Why not? If you want to know where he is. But I understood from your father that he had refused to see you."

Lani bent her head. "He had. He has. But I won't accept that. I have to see him, Mrs. Evans. I have to."

The housekeeper shrugged, and Lani hastily pulled out the telephone directory and found the number for the Gloucester Court Hotel. "It's here," she said, dialing the first three numbers, and Mrs. Evans made a tactful retreat.

"Mr. Pendragon vacated his suite a month ago."

The hotel receptionist flattened her faint hopes. "He didn't leave a forwarding address."

The hot sweet tea Mrs. Evans had provided restored Lani's sense of balance. There was no sense in panicking, she told herself severely, blinking back her tears. Just because three days ago she had believed she had weeks rather than days before Jake left hospital to devise some way of seeing him, was no reason to despair. What if he had left no clue to his whereabouts? Someone must know where he was. *But who,* a small voice inside her taunted hollowly, and she had no easy answer to give.

Perhaps he had gone with Clare, she thought fleetingly. But somehow she couldn't quite believe it. How could he have accompanied her mother? He still needed hospital treatment. Perhaps he had gone to another hospital. But where? *Where?*

During the afternoon, she sacrificed her pride and phoned some friends of her mother's. From the tones of their voices, she got the distinct impression that Jake's name was now taboo among Clare's inner circle, and she suspected they were only speaking to her on sufferance. No one, not even Maggie Pringle, who had been left behind to tie up her mother's affairs before joining her in California, was prepared to offer any information, and by the time Lani located Elwyn Hughes, she was at the end of her tether.

"Oh, Lani," he exclaimed, evidently as surprised as all the rest to hear from her. "How nice of you to call. What a pity I'm leaving for New York in the morning. We could have arranged to have lunch together one day."

Lani suffered his polite pleasantries in silence, and then asked flatly, "Did Jake go to Los Angeles with my mother, Mr. Hughes? I've tried to reach him at the hospital, you see, and they say he checked out the day Clare left for California."

There was silence for a moment, and she thought he was going to be as reticent as the rest, but then he said pointedly, "If he didn't tell you where he was going, Lani, he can't have wanted you to know."

Lani held her breath. "So he did go with Clare?"

"I didn't say that." Elwyn was evidently drawn two ways. "Lani, why have you come to me with this? Surely you must know I'm not entirely pleased with you for disrupting your mother's life."

"For disrupting *her* life!" There was a catch in Lani's voice. "How can you be so subjective? You know as well as I do that Clare's got off very lightly. She could have been convicted for reckless driving or even attempted murder!"

"Now, now, Lani, don't start making hysterical accusations. I was speaking personally, I admit it. But you have to remember your mother means a lot to me, and between you—you and Pendragon, that is—you could have destroyed her career."

Lani choked. "What about Jake? What about his career?"

"That was an unfortunate accident. No one—but no one—would wish it to have happened. But that doesn't alter the fact that that young man owes a lot to Clare, and I don't think he appreciated it."

"Oh, yes." Lani could hear the sob in her voice now. "He owes a lot to Clare all right. His injuries, his state of mind, the knowledge that he'll never play the piano again—"

Unable to continue, she slammed the receiver down, resting her face upon it and crying bitterly. Did no one care that Jake was the real victim here? Were they all so blind—or so prejudiced—they couldn't see the truth?

When the phone began to ring she was startled, raising her head in confusion and rubbing fiercely at her eyes. Then, taking a deep breath, she lifted the receiver, and was almost tempted to replace it again when she heard Elwyn's contrite tones.

"Don't hang up," he said at once. "I want to apologize. I guess that was pretty callous of me. Anyway, I just wanted to let you know that as far as I'm concerned, there's no hard feelings. Give me a call when I get back from the States. I really would like to try and make it up to you."

"Oh." Lani moved her shoulders wearily. "Forget it, Mr. Hughes. I guess I couldn't expect anything else. You did tell me once before how you felt about my mother. I should have realized you were unlikely to help me."

Elwyn sighed. "Lani, I would help you if I could, but I can't. Okay—Jake didn't go to Los Angeles, if that's of any use to you. How could he? Clare said he was still in traction. My guess is he's gone home to lick his wounds. Didn't I once hear something about Cornwall?"

Lani's lips parted. "Cornwall!" she breathed, in sudden anticipation. "Cornwall! Oh, of course." She shook her head helplessly, wondering why she hadn't thought of it before. Mrs. Worth! His grandmother. Obviously, he'd go there. It was his home. Hadn't he gone there once before to visit her, and arrived back so unexpectedly?

"I gather that means something to you."

Elwyn was waiting for her response, and realizing she had been staring into space for over half a minute, Lani gathered her wits. "Oh, yes. Yes," she said. "I—thank you, Mr. Hughes. I do appreciate it."

"Well, good luck." Elwyn spoke dryly now. "I gather you may need it. However, if you do see him, give him my regards. He really was a brilliant performer."

By the time her father arrived home from the office, Lani had carried the suitcase containing the clothes she had used at Robin and Sarah's downstairs again, and added various other items she thought she might need for a short stay. It was nearing the end of March, but it might still be cold in the West country, and she draped her leather coat and sheepskin jacket over her bag.

She was waiting in the drawing room when her father returned. She guessed he had seen her bag in the hall by the way he came bursting in on her.

"Lani! Oh, Lani!" he exclaimed emotionally, and she suffered his arms around her and his kiss on her cheek before stepping back from him. "You're home!" he said, gazing at her with moist eyes. "Oh, my dear, you don't know how happy this makes me."

Lani sighed. "I'm not staying," she said quietly, and she couldn't help the twinge of remorse she felt for his stunned bewilderment.

"Not staying?" he echoed faintly. "You mean... you're going back to Robin's?"

"No."

"Then what?" Her father blinked. "Oh, Lani, you're not leaving me, are you?"

Lani took a deep breath. "I'm going to Cornwall," she told him. "To Mount's Bay. You remember Mount's Bay, don't you? Where Mrs. Worth lives?"

"Yes, I remember Mount's Bay." Her father looked blank. "But why are you going there? To get away for a while? To be on your own?"

"No." Lani caught her lower lip between her teeth. "As a matter of fact, I expect I'll see Mrs. Worth."

"Mrs. Worth?" Roger sought the back of the sofa for support and stared at her uncomprehendingly. "For God's sake, Lani, what is this all about? What has Mrs. Worth to do with you?"

"You didn't recognize him, did you?" Lani's lips twisted. "The young man we met that day we went to see her. You do remember that?"

"Vaguely." Her father frowned. "There was a young man, yes. But I hardly spoke to him. Lani, what has this—"

"I spoke to him." She regarded him levelly. "I spent the morning with him, as a matter of fact. His name was Jake Pendragon."

"*No!*"

"Yes." Lani spoke without emphasis. "He's Mrs. Worth's grandson."

Roger shook his head. "You never told me."

"How could I?" Lani shrugged. "There was never an opportunity."

Roger put a hand to his head. "Are you saying that...that Pendragon is staying with his grandmother?"

"I believe so."

"But the fellow's in hospital."

"He was. He discharged himself earlier this week."

Roger made a helpless gesture. "I can't take this in...."

"You will." Lani bent and picked up her bag and her father stared at her in dismay.

"You can't mean—you don't intend to drive down there tonight!"

"I'm going to set out. How far I get will depend on how tired I am."

"But you can't." Roger spread his hands desperately. "Lani, you've only just got back. Can't we talk about this? Can't we spend some time together? Don't you want to hear what I have to say?"

"I think you've said enough, father," said Lani flatly, and the formal designation seemed to sever any lingering threads of the bond formed throughout her childhood.

Lani spent the night in Exeter. She had driven west along the M4, joining the M5 at Bristol and speeding south along the motorways. She surmised a more direct route would have taken her through Salisbury and Yeovil, but she had deliberately avoided roads that might cause some delay. Motorways at least gave her the impression that she was making good headway, and the uncrowded roads gave her time to think.

She spent the night at a motel adjoining the motorway and was up next morning in good time to get on her way. The fact that she had scarcely slept began to register around midmorning, but she pressed on regardless, arriving in Helston just before noon. She knew she ought to stop for something to eat, but the urge to get to her destination and find out if Jake was really there was too strong, and after refilling the petrol tank she drove on.

It took her almost an hour to find Tremorna Point. On that other occasion, when she had come with her father, she had paid little attention to her whereabouts, and the fact that they had driven from Penzance made a considerable difference. But at last she saw the crenellated turrets of the house she was looking for, standing out against the headland, and her hands trembled violently as she put the car into a lower gear and turned into the drive.

As she got out of the car, the wind took her breath away, and she staggered to regain her balance as the pounding roar of the surf came irresistibly to her ears. Although it was a brighter day than the previous occasion she had been here, it was still bitterly cold, and she hurriedly pulled out her leather coat and wrapped its warmth around her.

Her head was throbbing badly as she approached the pillared entrance, and it didn't help to look up and find the shuttered windows confronting her like so many closed eyes. Somebody had to be at home, she told herself determinedly. It had looked exactly the same when she had come with her father. She should not jump to conclusions, just because a few windows were blank.

An iron bellpull seemed the only method of attracting attention, and she tugged it firmly before thrusting her cold hands back into her pockets. The wind was wreaking havoc with her hair, and she hadn't brought a scarf, and she turned up her collar for protection.

To her immense relief, she heard someone coming as

she waited, and presently the door swung inward to expose a middle-aged woman dressed all in black. She was not Mrs. Worth, that much was obvious, but remembering that the old lady had had a housekeeper, Lani was not dismayed.

"I—I've come to see Mr. Pendragon," she said clearly. "Is. . . is he here?"

"Mr. Pendragon." The woman's voice had the soft mellow accent of the area. "You want to see Mr. Pendragon."

"Yes." Lani was trying to be patient, but anxiety and the throbbing in her head were putting an edge to her voice. "He is here, isn't he?"

"Who is it, Hannah?"

The harsh voice Lani had never expected to hear again echoed irritably down the stairs, and looking up, she saw the skinny figure of Mrs. Worth leaning over the balcony. In a nightgown and a flowing cashmere shawl, she seemed to have changed little since the last time Lani had seen her, except that now she was out of bed and the girl could see her bony outline.

"It's a young lady come to see Mr. Jake, Miss Amelia," said Hannah, giving Lani her first real throb of hope. "Shall I ask her in? It's a cold day outside."

"What does she want to see Jake for?"

Mrs. Worth's demanding tones were hardly polite, but Lani had come too far to be put off by the old woman's rudeness. "I want to talk to him, Mrs. Worth," she said staunchly. "My name is Lani St. John. I've come from London. If you'd just let him know I'm here—"

"St. John? St. John?" The old woman peered over the

balcony rail, staring at her. "I know someone called St. John. From London," she added. "My solicitor, Roger St. John. Did he send you?"

"No, Mrs. Worth." Lani controlled herself with difficulty. "I told you. I've come to see your grandson. Could you please...?"

"He's not here."

The words were chillingly final, and Lani stared up at her unbelievingly. It couldn't be true. Jake *had* to be here! The old woman was lying. She had to be.

"Are you sure?" With a pounding head Lani stood her ground, the wind whistling relentlessly about her ankles. "Please—it's very important that I speak with him. Don't you have any idea where he might be?"

"Why should I?" Mrs. Worth wrapped her shawl closer about her. "Jake Pendragon means nothing to me. Now, close the door, will you, Hannah. It's drafty."

Lani gasped. "Mrs. Worth—"

"I can't help you."

The old woman's voice faded away as she disappeared from the balcony, and Hannah regarded Lani compassionately as she made to close the door. "I'm sorry, miss," she said, evidently feeling some sympathy for the girl, and Lani shook her head bewilderedly as she began to turn away.

Then Hannah did a strange thing. With a surreptitious glance over her shoulder she quickly stepped outside, and touching Lani's sleeve she said, "He never lived here, you know. Didn't he tell you? He had... other arrangements. Do you know what I mean?"

Lani gazed at her incredulously. "The Sea House?" she breathed.

"I don't know."

Apparently, Hannah had decided she had said enough, and with an offhand lift of her shoulders, she slipped back inside the house. But Lani had heard enough to feel her spirits lifting, and with a rapidly increasing pulse, she hurried to the edge of the cliff.

The path was there as she remembered it, a little more overgrown perhaps, but accessible nonetheless. Slipping and sliding, trying to remember that if she tripped and fell her recklessness would be for nothing, she made her way down to the windswept veranda, her heart thundering in her ears like the mountainous thunder of the waves below her. It was all so familiar — amazingly familiar, considering she had only been there once before, and many years ago. This time there was no music to guide her, no lilting strains of a Chopin sonata to delight her ears, nothing but the sea and the wind as they battled for supremacy.

Lani refused to consider the possibility that he might not be there. As she struggled down the narrow cliff path, she refused to face the fact that any man who ought still to be in traction would find it virtually impossible to get down here. But he *had* to be here, she told herself desperately, and clambering up the wooden steps, she hammered loudly on the door.

No one answered, but then deep inside her she had not really expected anyone to. She had been crazy even to think Jake could be here. It was another dead end, another futile attempt to see him, and she lifted her head to the rugged slope she had just descended with sudden weakness. She couldn't climb that again, she thought despairingly. She simply didn't have the strength.

She fought her way against the wind around the veranda, looking for somewhere to sit and rest, and as she did so, she saw the shutters that protected the window had been opened. Stumbling, she grasped the window and, as on that other occasion, she peered inside. The room was exactly as she remembered it: the table, the chairs, the piano. There was even a fire glowing in the grate, and stretched on one of the sofas that faced each other across the hearth was a man. *Jake!* Lani's lips parted incredulously, and as she hovered there like some exposed voyeur he turned his head and saw her.

Ridiculously, Lani drew back out of sight. Seeing Jake like that had shocked her badly, and though he was the reason she had come, she found she couldn't face him. It was all very well telling herself back in London that if she could only see him, talk to him, everything would be all right between them, and quite another thing to accomplish the deed when faced with a man who was helpless. Of course, she thought faintly, that was why he hadn't answered the door. He wasn't able to. Somehow, someone must have carried him down here, on a stretcher perhaps. No doubt, someone was being paid to look after him. But right now, that someone was not at home. Jake was here alone.

Dragging herself away from the wall of the house, Lani turned back toward the door. This was the moment, she told herself vehemently, resisting the desire to run. Where moments before she had been incapable of the effort, now she felt as if she could climb the path in easy strides, anything, just to get away from here, and from the awful fear that Jake would reject her. Hope was a curious thing, she thought. For weeks she had kept herself going with the belief that sooner or later Jake would change his mind; she had even closed her thoughts to any other possibility. But now that she was faced with reality, now that she was actually here, and Jake was just on the other side of the wall, her hopes seemed as insubstantial as thistledown.

She had reached the door when it opened, and her breath caught momentarily in her throat. Jake was standing in the opening regarding her with unfriendly eyes, and she had a sense of déjà vu, as if all of this had happened before. But not quite as before, she acknowledged tensely, her eyes moving swiftly over the padded crutches tucked under his arms, his bandaged hands hanging loosely beside them. Nor was his haggard face so familiar, with a jagged scar running from his hairline to the dark curve of one eyebrow.

"Well?"

The single word epitomized the fear Lani had felt ever since she had peered through his window. There was no compassion in his voice, no liking either, and she gazed at him unsteadily, striving to remain composed.

"He—hello, Jake," she managed, twisting the strap of her shoulder bag between her fingers. "I . . . how are you?"

"What do you want, Lani?"

His voice held all the weary bitterness of weeks spent avoiding this very situation, and Lani felt her final defenses crumbling. She should not have come here, she thought miserably. She should have realized when he refused to see her that everything was over between them. How could she have been so conceited as to think she could succeed where everyone else had failed? He didn't want her. He never had. It had been a passing affair, as Clare had said, and now he only wanted to forget it.

"I—I—"

She found to her dismay that she couldn't go on. Her bitter disappointment, combined with the pain in her head and the fact that she had had next to nothing to eat since the previous day, were proving too much for her system. She must not have recovered yet from her spell in the hospital, she thought dizzily, as bright lights started to explode inside her head, and although she groped for the wall of the house, it was just beyond her reach....

CHAPTER THIRTEEN

WHEN LANI OPENED HER EYES, she found she was lying on a chintz-covered sofa. For a moment she didn't register where she was, and her gaze moved doubtfully over the logs burning in the grate and the solid stone mantel above it. The effort of trying to think brought a throbbing pain to her head, and she shifted restlessly on the soft cushions. As she did so, she glimpsed the booted feet stretched across the hearth beside her, and memory returned with shuddering intensity.

"Wh—what happened?"

"You fainted," said Jake flatly, seated on the edge of the sofa opposite, holding a glass of water between his bandaged fingers. "Here," he said. "Take these." Two capsules rested on his palm. "They won't do you any harm, and I can testify to their efficiency for treating pain."

Lani pulled herself up into a sitting position. "How—how do you know I'm in pain?"

"You mumbled something about a headache, before you collapsed at my feet," replied Jake briefly. "You look bloody awful. Are you sure you should be out?"

Lani took the capsules and the glass, her fingers flinching from the abrasive touch of the bandages. Swallowing the capsules obediently, she drank most of the water in the glass and then handed it back to him, taking care not to hurt him.

Jake's lips twisted at her rather obvious attempts to be discreet, and realizing she might not have much time before he threw her out again, Lani rushed into speech. "I thought—I mean—I hope I haven't been too much of a nuisance. I . . . how did you bring me in here?" She broke off in embarrassment. "I'm no lightweight."

"There's not that much of you," declared Jake carelessly, his eyes running guardedly over her slight figure. Even in the leather coat, which he must have unfastened, it was obvious she had lost a lot of weight, and Lani drew it around her protectively.

"But you—Cl—I mean—" It was difficult to find the right words. "Are . . . are you able to get about?"

"As you see," he responded, indicating the two crutches lying beside him. He hesitated and then added, "As soon as these are stronger—" he held out his hands dispassionately "—I should be able to manage on two sticks. Eventually I hope to abandon them also."

"Oh, but I thought—"

Lani broke off, and Jake arched his brows. "Yes? What did you think? That I was a cripple? That I'd be confined to a wheelchair?" He shrugged. "You know how people exaggerate. Particularly if it makes good copy."

Lani put her feet to the floor. "I didn't know you could walk. I didn't know anything about you." She paused. "If you'd let me come and see you—"

"I didn't want any visitors," said Jake harshly, swinging the crutches under his arms and getting abruptly to his feet. "And now, if you're feeling better, I suggest you leave. The wind's getting stronger and I shouldn't like to be responsible for you falling off the cliff."

Lani looked up at him tremulously. "At least tell me how you are? How you're managing? Who is looking after you?"

"Nobody is looking after me," retorted Jake shortly. "I don't need any looking after. I'm not entirely helpless, as you've just pointed out."

"But you can't mean you go up and down the cliff path every time you need—"

"No." He broke into her shocked protest with the flat syllable. And then, when she was evidently waiting for him to explain, he added, "Hannah brings me everything I need."

"Ah." Lani nodded, feeling the pain in her head receding at last. "But...shouldn't you be having therapy? I mean...they told me you discharged yourself from the hospital, and there are your bandages to change."

"I manage."

Jake was abrupt, and she got unsteadily to her feet. "Even so...."

"For God's sake!" He swore savagely, and then looking into her eyes with unmistakable hostility he demanded, "Why did you come here, Lani? I should have thought I made my feelings perfectly clear. I didn't want to see you when I was in London, and I don't want to see you now. How could you think I would?" He lifted his bandaged hands with ironic emphasis. "What did you expect me to do? Greet the cause of my disability with open arms?" He shook his head scornfully. "You know very little about human nature!"

Lani's breath caught in her throat. "You... *blame*...me?"

"Why not?" Jake stared at her coldly. "I knew from the start I couldn't afford the luxury of an emotional entanglement, and I was right. I should have quit while I was ahead. As soon as I'd made it with you, I should have got the hell out of that situation."

His words were so contemptuous, so cruel, that for a moment Lani forgot the crash and his injuries and the fact that he was probably still suffering a considerable amount of pain. All she could see were his scornful eyes and mocking lips, and without hesitation she pushed him aside and stumbled toward the door. She had had enough, she thought despairingly. She couldn't take any more. Clare was right. He didn't want her, and she was only hurting herself by staying.

She didn't immediately realize that the force of her action had knocked him off his feet. The first thing she heard was the sound of wood hitting wood as his crutches fell to the floor, and then the sickening thud of his body as it met the hard wood. Turning in horror, she saw what she had done, and she let out a gasp of dismay. Abandoning her intention to walk out on him, she ran back to his side, dropping to her knees beside him and cradling his head in her arms.

"Jake!" Her fingers fluttered anxiously over his chest and arms. "Oh, Jake—*darling*! Are you all right?" She rested her cheek against his temple. "I'm sorry, I'm sorry. Please, please, tell me you're not hurt."

"I'm all right."

His voice was curiously strained, and drawing back, Lani looked down into his dark face. She was so close she could see the brittle line of skin that edged his scar and the pulse that beat at his temple with erratic palpitation. His lips were parted, his forced breath rising up to her, cool and sweet, and her eyes met his in helpless supplication.

"Damn you, Lani," he said very distinctly, and with more strength than she had given him credit for, he forced her back from him and rolled over so that he was looking down at her. "Damn you," he said once more, his eyes smoldering with emotion, and then his mouth covered hers and she was lost.

His whole weight was upon her, imprisoning her against the hard floor, but Lani hardly felt the discomfort. Her lips opened wide to his, her arms sliding around his neck, her fingers tangling eagerly in the hair at his nape. For fully a minute, Jake held her in that suffocating embrace, his bandaged hands cupping her neck, his hungry mouth seeking and finding a matching urgency. His tongue slipped between her lips and hers encircled it, feeling him, tasting him, and wanting his possession.

But then, when there was no mistaking the hardening muscle throbbing against her stomach, Jake abruptly rolled away from her. Fumbling for his crutches, he jammed them beneath his arms and got to his feet, staggering as he did so but managing to keep his balance. For a few moments he stood still, breathing deeply, and Lani scrambled up onto her knees to face him. In spite of what had happened, she sensed his raw frustration, and her nerves twisted uneasily when she met his thwarted gaze.

"Get up," he said, leaning heavily on the crutches as he made his way toward the door. "I want you to get out of here—*now!* And don't come back."

Lani hesitated and then got obediently to her feet. But she didn't follow him toward the door. Instead she shed her leather coat onto the arm of one of the sofas and moved on slightly shaky legs to warm her hands at the fire.

She had her back to him, so she couldn't see the scowl that contorted his face at her insubordination. But she could feel the anger emanating from him, and his voice was harsh when he exclaimed, "What the hell do you think you're doing?"

Realizing the gamble she was taking, Lani schooled her features and turned toward him. "I'm staying," she said, taking her life into her hands, and his reaction was not unexpected.

"Like hell you are!" he swore violently. "You're leaving now. This minute. For Christ's sake, get out of here before I break your bloody neck!"

"No." Lani stood her ground, even though her knees felt like jelly. "You can't make me. I want to stay."

"Well, I don't want you to stay." Jake dragged himself back across the room. "Are you crazy or something? You can't stay here if I don't want you. Lani, for pity's sake, stop all this nonsense."

"It's not nonsense." Lani drew a deep breath. "You need someone here to look after you—to care about you—"

"No—"

"—and I want to do it." She shook her head at the look of fury in his face, and hurried on. "I care about you, Jake. I—I love you, you know that, and you love me—"

"*No!*" Jake overrode her ruthlessly. "No, I don't love you, Lani. I thought I'd made that plain." He lifted his eyes heavenward for a moment and then continued vehemently. "You've got it wrong. Love never came into it. I wanted you, yes, I wanted your body. But that's all. I never said I loved you, did I? Can you honestly tell me that I did?"

Lani quivered, tempted even now to give up and go home, but something, some inner core of conviction, forced her to go on. "It doesn't matter," she said doggedly. "All right. So you don't love me. But you still want me—"

"Because of what happened just now?" he snarled. "Because I had a perfectly natural reaction to a woman's body? God, Lani, these injuries don't mean I'm impotent. Hopefully, I'm still normal in that respect. But it's been a long time since I had a woman's softness under me, and I can't help it if I can't disguise my sex!"

Lani bent her head. "I'm staying."

"What do you mean, you're staying? Where do you think you're going to stay?"

"Here." She hesitated. "I presume there are bedrooms. Don't worry. I can look after myself."

"This is *crazy!*"

Still glaring at her, Jake lowered himself onto the arm of the sofa nearest to him. Evidently, weakness was getting the better of valor, and lines of strain were etched beside his nose and mouth. But he continued to look at her with bitter loathing, and Lani could not deny she had set herself a daunting task.

"Are you saying you're staying here with or without my permission?" he asked tautly, and Lani nodded. "What makes you think I'll let you?"

Lani hesitated for a moment. Then she spread her hands. "How can you stop me?" she asked, her logic as cruel as his had been, and she winced at the pain she saw in his face.

"I assume you mean because of these?" he responded at last, displaying his hands, and Lani lifted her shoulders.

"If you say so."

"And what happens when they get stronger, when I'm not so dependent on these?" he muttered, thrusting the crutches aside.

Lani shrugged. "I'll face that when it happens," she said, amazed at her temerity. "Now, could I have something to eat? I didn't stop for lunch, and I'm starving!"

A pulse in Jake's jaw throbbed revealingly. "Why ask me?" he demanded, staring down at his hands, and Lani had to steel herself to walk past him. "By the way—" as she reached the door, which she remembered led into the kitchen, his voice arrested her "—there are no...*bedrooms*," he told her, emphasizing the plural. "There is one bedroom—mine; and a boxroom, full of old music and manuscripts. There's only one bed, too. Mine again, and I have no intention of shifting out of it for you."

"I wouldn't expect you to." Lani's tongue appeared to moisten her dry lips. "We could...share it."

"No!"

This time his anger brought him half off the sofa, but the obvious pain this caused him drove him back again. And Lani knew that in this he would have his way. Her staying here against his will was one thing; forcing herself into his bed was quite another, and she lifted her shoulders as she opened the door.

"I can sleep down here," she said, refusing to be deterred by his frustration, and before he could say anything more, she closed the door behind her.

She found herself in a narrow passage at the back of the house, with two doors leading off it. It was lucky one of these was open, for the passage was unlit, and stepping through the doorway, she saw she was in the kitchen.

It was a surprisingly modern kitchen, considering the apparent age of the house, and in spite of his enforced disability, it was remarkably clean and neat. Hannah again, she suspected, relieved that the housekeeper had not abandoned him even if his grandmother had. At least he wouldn't starve with her to tend to his needs, and Lani felt an immense amount of gratitude for the woman who had helped her, too.

After plugging in the electric kettle, she surveyed her surroundings. An examination of the cupboards that flanked the sink and draining area revealed pans and cleaning materials, while the wall cupboards above the fridge and washing machine contained china and glassware. She found tins and jars of food, as well as cereal and such staples as flour and sugar, in yet another cupboard, and the fridge was amply stocked too.

Lani was whipping up some eggs to make omelets when she became aware that someone was watching her. Looking up, she found Jake had come to stand at the kitchen door, supporting himself with one shoulder against the jamb.

"You don't have to do this, you know," he said harshly, and Lani sighed. "There are plenty of decent restaurants in Helston or Penzance. Why don't you go and buy yourself some lunch? Why this desire to play house, all of a sudden?"

"I like cooking," she said quietly. "As a matter of fact, it was one of the few things I enjoyed at the finishing school daddy sent me to. And I'm quite good at it, too. As you'll find out."

"Will I?" His mouth hardened. "I'm quite capable of opening a tin. I have an electric opener, if you haven't noticed."

"You can't live out of tins and prepacked foods," retorted Lani flatly. "Just because you're—well, just because you're—"

"Crippled?" he supplied. "Was that what you were going to accuse me of? Beware what you say, Lani. I won't always be as helpless as I am now."

Lani turned away to put the frying pan on the stove. Then, ignoring his scowling face, she asked, "Have you eaten today?"

Jake's mouth compressed. "You can't really mean to go through with this."

"Through with what?" She was deliberately obtuse.

"You know." He breathed heavily. "Staying here!"

"Why not?"

"Because you can't." His eyes burned with his frustration. "For Christ's sake, Lani, don't you care what people think?"

"Not particularly."

"Not even your father?"

"Especially not him," she responded tautly. "Now, do you want something to eat or don't you?"

"I'm not hungry," he muttered savagely. Then: "Lani, come to your senses! If you stay here, people will assume we're living together."

"We will be."

"You know what I mean." He shook his head. "Don't you care about your reputation?"

"My reputation?" Lani caught her breath. "Oh, Jake, since when have you cared about my reputation?"

"All right, then, mine," he snapped angrily. "I don't want everybody to think you're my mistress!"

"No?" Lani smarted at the deliberate insult, but she didn't show it. "Oh, well," she said lightly, "that's just too bad, isn't it? Because I'm not about to walk out."

Jake was regarding her broodingly now, and ignoring his malevolent gaze, she poured half the beaten eggs into the pan. She had grated some cheese, and this quickly followed them, producing an aroma that was both savory and mouth-watering.

"Very well." She thought for a moment Jake had finally accepted that she was to stay, but his next words were like a physical blow. "I don't want Clare to come back and find you here," he stated, his eyes holding hers without compassion. "As soon as I can get these fingers working again, I'm going to get back to my music, and this time there'll be no distractions, except ones I can handle!"

Lani weathered this verbal slap in the face with amazing resilience, considering there was always the possibility that he meant it. But somehow she knew she had gone beyond the point of no return, and nothing he said now could change that.

"So why did you leave the hospital?" she inquired reasonably, managing to go on with her work as if she were not fighting for her survival. "I mean," she added, "why didn't you let them put you on a course of therapy? As I remember, that is the usual treat—"

"Shut up!"

His anguished voice silenced her, and in the pregnant hush that followed, she knew an almost irresistible urge to go and comfort him. He looked so defeated suddenly, so alone. If only she could help him, she thought. If only he would let her.

None of this showed in her face, of course. She knew only too well that Jake would interpret her concern as pity, and he would not thank her for it. Instead, she had to stand by helplessly as he abruptly turned away, and pretend to be intent on dishing up the omelet as he dragged himself out of her sight.

Determined not to let his despair get to her, Lani put the omelet to keep warm while she made the second. While it was frying, she opened a tin of tomatoes, as there were no fresh ones, and made a spicy sauce to serve with the eggs. It was a makeshift meal, she reflected, after setting plates and cutlery on a tray, but at least it was colorful, and it smelled quite delicious as she carried the tray through to the living room.

Jake was slumped on the sofa again, not even glancing up at her entrance. He looked as if the events of the past hour had drained every drop of strength from him, and Lani's heart contracted. Was she doing the right thing, she fretted, forcing him to let her stay here? As he so obviously wanted her to leave, oughtn't she to comply with his wishes? But then she remembered the minutes she had spent in his arms, minutes when she could have sworn he was hungry for her love, and her doubts receded. She couldn't leave him, not without giving them both a chance. If by staying she became his whipping boy, then so be it. Better that than nothing at all.

She spread the linen tablecloth she had found in a kitchen drawer over the gateleg table. Setting out plates and cutlery, she was not displeased with her efforts and she turned determinedly to Jake, who was now feeding logs onto the fire.

"I've made us a meal," she said, coloring in spite of herself. "Please, will you come to the table? Or I can bring it over there, if you'd rather."

Jake turned to look at her, and his eyes were as cold as marble. "I told you," he declared harshly, "I'm not hungry. When I want something to eat I'll get it. Now, go away, will you? I'm busy."

Lani's jaw quivered briefly, but then it hardened. "You don't want anything from me, is that it?"

"That's about it," he agreed, lolling back against the sofa and looking up at her. "If you insist on staying here...well, as you say, there's not a lot I can do about that right now. But that doesn't mean I have to collaborate with you, does it?"

"You—you bastard!"

"Very probably." His mouth thinned. "I've been

called many things in my lifetime. However, one thing I don't have to do is argue my legitimacy with you. Why don't you go and eat up your food like a good girl."

"There's too much for one," said Lani stiffly, refusing to give up, and Jake gave a savage thrust at the sputtering logs with his boot. It must have hurt him to do so, for he went quite white and collapsed weakly against the cushions. But his eyes were still scathing as they met her anxious gaze.

"Go away," he told her tightly. "I don't care if you've overdone the cordon bleu bit. Eat it yourself. You look as though you need it. You're as skinny as a beanpole!"

Most of the eggs went into the dustbin. Lani's appetite had been negligible for weeks, and although she had felt quite hungry while she was preparing the meal, Jake's attitude had destroyed any enjoyment she might have taken in it.

Deciding there was no point in trying to reason with him in this mood, she washed the dishes and put them away and then decided to explore the rest of the house. After all, if she was going to stay here, she had to be conversant with the layout of the place.

A soft green carpet flowed up the stairs, and after only a momentary hesitation, Lani climbed to the upper floor. She switched on the light on the landing, which was similar in situation to the hall below and then surveyed the two doors that confronted her, wondering which, if either, was the bathroom.

The first room she peered into was definitely not the bathroom. It was, as Jake had said, a boxroom, filled with piles of music scores and dusty manuscripts, and evidently unused since his return. The wallpaper was quite pretty, and she supposed that a duster and polish would soon put a shine on the windows, but there was no bed, as he had also said, and she couldn't see herself sleeping on the floor.

The other room was not the bathroom either, but Lani stepped inside nevertheless. This was Jake's room, obviously, and she gazed about her curiously, eager to learn anything that might help her understand him. It was a huge room, as big as or perhaps even bigger than the room below, with a carpet patterned in shades of brown and cream, and long velour curtains at the windows.

The view from the windows was spectacular, and Lani guessed that on summer nights it must be lovely to open the casement and listen to the murmur of the sea on the rocks below. Right now, the thunderous roar was not inviting, and she turned her eyes to the room again.

It was furnished Spartanly, with a heavy oak wardrobe and matching chest of drawers, and a massive four-poster bed. Despite its evident age, the bed was equipped with a modern mattress, and its valance and down-filled quilt fitted perfectly with their surroundings. There were bookshelves beside the bed and a heavy bedside cabinet, and incongruously enough there stood a solid mahogany desk in the window embrasure. Perhaps Jake used to work here sometimes, she reflected, lingering longer than she should. It made her realize how little she knew about him and his life, beyond what Elwyn Hughes had told her.

She eventually discovered the bathroom was opposite the kitchen downstairs. After attending to her needs, she returned to the living room. She half expected Jake to make some comment on her prolonged absence—he must have known where she was and what she was doing—but he didn't. He was still sitting by the fire, gazing darkly into the flames, and he only allowed her a brooding appraisal when she came to join him.

The afternoon had slipped away, and Lani wondered rather anxiously when Jake intended to make his evening meal. She was uncomfortably aware that her suitcase and the rest of her things were still resting in her car, and she wasn't at all convinced Jake would not lock her out if she went to get them.

Seating herself on the sofa opposite him, she tried not to stare too obviously at him. But his lean dark face and hollow features were irresistibly appealing, and after so many weeks without seeing him, she was hungry for any intimacy.

"Don't do that," he said at last, revealing he was not indifferent to her eyes upon him, and Lani's spirits lifted at this evidence of his awareness.

"Don't do what?" she asked innocently, and he turned his head on the cushions until he could see her.

"The wind's getting stronger," he remarked. "I shouldn't like to be out on the cliff road tonight." He glanced at his watch. "I guess you've got a little over an hour before it gets dark."

Lani shrugged. "I'm not going anywhere."

Jake suppressed the oath that twisted his lips and bent to massage his thigh, as if his emotional condition was having some effect on his physical one. "You really mean to stay?" he demanded heavily. "You're out of your mind."

"I don't think so."

Jake regarded her frustratingly for a few seconds, and then, adopting a different tone of voice, he said: "Look, I realize you think you're on some crusade here, but it wouldn't work, believe me!"

"Why wouldn't it?"

He sighed. "Well, because you'd be wasting your time. You have a job—a career. You can't afford this kind of commitment."

"Surely I'm the best judge of that."

"No!" His denial was as violent as before, and abandoning his brief attempt at persuasion, his mouth set in a thin line. "What do I have to do to get you out of here?" he snarled. "Are you so thick-skinned that nothing I say can touch you?"

"It seems like it, doesn't it?" she remarked, leaning back and crossing her legs, and the thoughtless action exposed the slender line of her thigh. With her skirt riding up above her knees, the whole length of her legs was outlined in sharp relief, and although she would never have thought of using her body against him, his sudden intake of breath was plainly audible. His eyes were on her legs, on the shapely curve of bone and muscle he had once caressed with such pleasure, and Lani's response was purely instinctive. Without hesitation, her hands moved to stroke their lissome beauty, and the sensuality of her trailing fingers was not lost on Jake. She was not consciously arousing him, she was doing something that seemed to come naturally to her, and the man opposite could not tear his eyes away.

Only when her hands probed the buttons of her shirt did he seem to come to his senses. With a constricted groan, he grasped his crutches and hauled himself to his feet. Without looking at her again, he dragged himself to the door that led into the hall, and levering it open, he disappeared through it. Moments later, she heard the thumping sound as he mounted the stairs and crossed the landing, and then silence.

Without realizing it, she had been holding her breath, and now she expelled it on a shuddering sigh. Pulling her skirt down over her knees again, she got unsteadily to her feet, and as she did so she realized her shameless behavior had given her the opportunity she needed. She could get her things from the car now. Jake was unlikely to come downstairs again immediately, and if she intended to go through with this, she had to have a change of clothes.

Pulling on her leather coat, she tied the belt around her securely before letting herself out of the house. As Jake had said, the wind was increasing in force, and it was an effort to fight her way up the cliff path.

The Capri was still parked where she had left it, and deciding it would be safer in a less exposed position, she drove it around the side of the house and parked it beside a row of outbuildings. Then, gathering her belongings together, she struggled back to the path. No one accosted her. No one knew she was here, except Hannah, and she was unlikely to tell.

With the wind buffeting her unsteady progress, Lani at last reached the foot of the steps, and setting down her suitcase, she paused a moment to recover her breath. Having negotiated the path twice in one day, she was positively incredulous that Jake should have made it at all in his condition, and she thought it was a measure of the man himself that he had refused to be deterred. He was stubborn, that much was obvious, but how stubborn Lani had yet to find out.

With a somewhat weary shrug of her shoulders, she picked up her suitcase again and climbed the steps. Although she had still entertained some doubts as to whether Jake might attempt to bar her from the house, the door opened effortlessly to her touch, the wind taking it out of her fingers and slamming it noisily against the wall inside. Turning slightly to accommodate the suitcase and the rest of her belongings, Lani stepped thankfully in out of the wind, and then froze at the sound of Jake's crutches as he came hurriedly down the stairs. He must have thought she was just leaving, she speculated apprehensively, and closed the door behind her with nerveless fingers.

He came into the living room with amazing speed, only to stop in his tracks at the sight of Lani, laden down with her coat, her case and the rug from the car, which she thought she might need. Her lips had parted to deliver the taut rejoinder that he was wasting his time, that she had already been up to the car and got her things, and that if he had intended to lock the door, he was too late, but the words were never spoken. The look of palpable relief that crossed Jake's face as he realized she had not walked out on him was breathtaking, and for a heart-stopping moment she was bereft of speech.

But then, as if realizing how revealing his expression must be, Jake turned his head away and took several steadying breaths. His reckless progress down the stairs had taken what little strength he had, and Lani ached to go to him as he struggled to the sofa.

"Did you think I'd gone?" she ventured at last, dropping her bags to the floor and unfastening her coat, and he regarded her defeatedly.

"Yes," he said, without prevarication. "Yes, I thought you'd gone. It would be better for both of us if you had."

CHAPTER FOURTEEN

SLEEPING ON A SOFA was not the same as sleeping in a bed, Lani found. To begin with, it wasn't long enough, and she had spent most of the night curled up into a ball. And in addition, the cushions were not the same as a mattress, and no matter how she tried, she could not avoid the discomforting crevice where one cushion joined another.

It had been a wild night, too, the wind whistling eerily around the eaves of the Sea House, making Lani wonder how securely its foundations had been set. It seemed so precarious, set out on its ledge, and alone in the dark, she had been sure she felt it move.

However, in the morning the wind had dropped somewhat and the sun was shining, and sliding out from beneath her quilt, Lani tiptoed across to the windows. Drawing the curtains aside, she had her first glimpse of a friendly ocean, blue seas stretching as far as the horizon, glistening like a jewel beneath the sun's rays.

She did not linger long at the window. The fire had gone out in the night and the grate was cold. She was cold, too, even in her beige silk pajamas, and the polished floor was cold to her bare feet, with only a rug on the hearth to protect them.

Rummaging in her case, which she had not been

able to unpack the night before, she found her mules and pushed her feet into them. Then, rubbing her arms briskly, she hurried into the kitchen, plugging in the kettle before searching for some firewood.

She discovered a pile of sticks just outside the back door, stacked beside a load of logs. She didn't have to look any further for fuel, and scurrying back inside, she quickly raked out the grate and relighted the fire.

By the time the logs were crackling merrily the kettle had boiled and Lani made tea. Setting out two cups and saucers, she added both milk and sugar to Jake's, surmising that like most men he liked his tea sweet.

It was only as she was climbing the stairs that it crossed her mind that her attire was hardly respectable. Having lived with only her father and Mrs. Evans all these years, she had grown used to flitting about the house half dressed, and it hadn't occurred to her to stop and put some clothes on before taking Jake his tea.

Besides, she reflected ruefully, there was no guarantee that he would let her into his room. Last night, he had avoided every overture she made, and eventually he had taken himself off to the kitchen. It was some time later that she discovered he had opened a tin of ravioli, and that and a can of Coke were all he had had since her arrival.

He had provided a quilt for her to use, however. She had found that in the living room when she returned from the bathroom before settling down for the night. And as she snuggled under its soft feathers, she had recalled with a glimmer of hope that moment when she had returned from her trip to the car. No matter that it might have been his unadmitted need for company that had brought that look of relief to his face. In an obscure way, he needed her companionship, and for the present that was enough.

A board creaked at the top of the stairs as she crossed the landing, and she started at the unexpected sound. Then, reaching his door she tapped on the panels, waiting with some trepidation for his reaction. When there was none, she opened the door anyway, stepping inside with more daring than confidence.

It was still comparatively early, barely half-past seven, but Jake was awake. He was lying on his back in the middle of the huge bed, his arms resting against the pillows above his head, his chest bare above the quilt. He had heard her, and his head turned toward the door as she came into the room. His eyes narrowed as he took in her attire, but Lani ignored his expression. Feeling a little flame of excitement inside her at the realization he was briefly at her mercy, she approached the bed and looked down at him with carefully assumed nonchalance.

"I've brought you some tea," she said, when he made no move to sit up. "Would you like me to help you? I could prop up your pillows, if you'd like."

"I don't need any assistance," he responded tautly. "As you've brought the tea, you might as well put it down. I may drink it later."

"And I may just pour it over your head," exclaimed Lani, with a grimace. "Couldn't you at least say thank you?"

Jake shrugged. "All right. Thank you."

Lani sighed. "Did you sleep well?"

"Very well." He paused. "Did you?"

She lifted her shoulders. "Reasonably."

He frowned. "What was wrong?"

"Nothing."

"Lani—"

"Oh, well, my legs are too long, I guess," she mumbled. "It's a lovely morning. The sun is shining."

"You did open the couch out, didn't you?" he queried, and Lani looked blank.

"Open it out?"

"They convert to double beds," Jake explained levelly. "I'm sorry. I should have told you."

Lani gasped. "You mean—"

"I'm afraid so."

She shook her head. "And I spent the night curled up like a ball!"

"You did insist on staying," he reminded her dryly, and she had no answer for that.

"Anyway," she said, setting his cup down on the bedside cabinet, "now that we've stopped shouting at each other, isn't it time we talked? Really talked, I mean?"

"Lani—"

"No, listen to me, please." With cautious optimism, she seated herself on the side of his bed, and taking comfort from the fact that he didn't move away from her, she said: "I know you didn't ask me to come here, and maybe I am being presumptuous in staying, but I do want to help you. *I do!*" She sighed. "And we can't go on living together in a state of armed conflict. It just isn't sensible. How can I help you to get better if you won't even speak to me?"

"No one can help me to get better," retorted Jake

flatly, but he made no attempt to dislodge her. "I've got to do this myself. It's the only way. That's why I discharged myself from the hospital."

Lani caught her lower lip between her teeth. "But—wasn't that rather precipitate? I mean, they wouldn't have expected you to stay there if you hadn't needed treatment."

"What treatment?" Jake was harsh suddenly. "Holland knows one of my legs will never be completely cured. And my hands—" he surveyed them with undisguised dislike "—what they need is exercise, the kind of exercise they can't ever give them."

Lani hesitated for a moment, and then purposefully she reached for one of his hands and held it between both of hers. She half expected him to pull away, but he didn't, and with her tongue between her teeth, she started to unwind the bandage.

"What do you think you're doing?" Jake would have drawn away then, but she wouldn't let him, and after a charged look had passed between them, he let her have her way. "It's not very pretty," he said, as the last of the bandages came off, and Lani visibly paled at his careless understatement. "You see now why I keep the bandages on," he remarked bitterly. "I avoid looking at them as much as possible."

Lani shook her head. "How did it happen?"

"They tell me it was the glass from the headlights," he replied with a grimace. "They also tell me I've been very lucky. Years ago, I should probably have lost the use of one or both of them."

"And you haven't?"

Jake shook his head, flexing his fingers without too

much effort, turning them so that they curled with disturbing firmness around her palm. "They're weak," he said dispassionately. "So many of the bones were broken, and in places they had protruded through the muscle. But they've sewn me together quite adequately, and they get stronger every day."

"I read. . . that your hands were crushed."

"I suppose they must have been," he replied flatly. "But fortunately only one of the tendons was actually severed. It was the nerves they were concerned about, but they've done a good job."

Lani shook her head, and then, unable to prevent herself, she lifted his hand to her face, pressing her lips to its scarred and battered exterior. "Oh, Jake," she breathed, and he could feel her tears against his skin. "You don't have to hide them. . . ."

He withdrew his hand abruptly, and she was left to wipe her tears away. "I told you. I find them repulsive," he declared, reaching for the bandage. "Now, do you want to help me do this, or must I replace it myself?"

Lani hung back, loath to pander to his stubbornness, but then, realizing he would do it with or without her assistance, she took the bandage from him and deftly rewound it.

"Thanks." He examined her efforts with approval. "That's the neatest it's looked since I left St. Augustine's."

"You mean they encouraged you?"

"I told them I wanted to disguise them until I got home," he admitted carelessly. "What does it matter? I'll never play again."

Lani stared at him. "But you said—"

"That was yesterday." Jake sighed and shifted to a more comfortable position. "This morning, lying here, I realized how foolish it was for me to lie about something so obvious. Sooner or later, you were bound to find out anyway." His lips twisted. "When the quotes brilliant young concert pianist close quotes didn't return to the platform," he added mockingly.

"Oh, Jake!"

"Stop saying, 'oh, Jake,' and be thankful it wasn't you. I was told your only serious injury was a fractured skull. I gather that has mended now."

Lani bent her head. "I think so."

"Good."

Jake's unbandaged fingertips brushed the hem of her jacket, and on impulse, she exclaimed, "You don't mean that about not playing again, do you? Don't you think—don't you think you owe it to yourself—to everybody who has had faith in you—"

Jake's expression hardened. "And don't you think I've paid my debt to society?" he demanded roughly. "Or are you talking in financial terms?"

Lani bent her head. "It's nothing to do with me."

"No, it's not," he agreed harshly. "And we've talked long enough. Go and put some clothes on. You're shivering."

"Jake—"

"Not now, Lani." His tone was forced, a muscle jerking at his jawline. "Hannah will be coming shortly, and I don't want her to find you up here."

"I'm sorry."

Lani got abruptly to her feet, and as if regretting his

harsh tone, Jake rolled onto his side facing her. "Look, I will drink the tea, I promise," he told her evenly. "It was kind of you to bring it up. I do appreciate it, honestly."

"Do you?"

Her response was deliberately provocative, but the tears glinting on her lashes were not assumed. "Yes," he said roughly, and then, looking away from her, he added, "It isn't easy going up and down stairs on these!" He gestured toward his legs. "I usually wait until Hannah puts in an appearance."

Lani moistened her lips. "You didn't tell me about your legs. Were they very badly injured?"

"Not desperately." He sighed. "One of them is fairly good now, and the other—" He broke off, but after a moment he continued "My knee was damaged. It's had to have surgery. For the present, it's still pretty useless."

"Can I see?"

"Lani!"

"Well, can I?"

"I think not." He drew a labored breath. "Unlike you, I don't wear pajamas, and—"

"I don't mind." Lani's eyes moved over his limbs outlined beneath the quilt. "I have...seen you that way before."

"I know."

All of a sudden, the atmosphere was charged with emotion, and just as suddenly, Lani's confidence deserted her. She felt as if she had been prodding a sleeping tiger and it had abruptly turned to confront her. All her preconceived notions were swept away by the look in Jake's eyes, and a wave of shame engulfed her at the realization of what she had done. This wasn't how she had meant it to be. She didn't want Jake to take her because he was starved of female companionship and she had made herself available. If he touched her now, it would be the result of her wanton offer, she realized sickly, and that thought alone was enough to cool her blood.

"Lani," he said, and the rawness of his tone sent her scuttling toward the door.

"Some other time perhaps," she murmured lamely, and was out the door and down the stairs before he could respond.

SHE WAS WASHED AND dressed in honey-colored corded pants and a matching skinny-rib sweater when the housekeeper arrived. Hannah evidently had her own key, and Lani was doing her hair in the bathroom when she heard its abortive rattle in the lock. No doubt Jake generally removed his key before going to bed, she speculated, hurrying to let the woman in, and Hannah confirmed this as she put her key away.

"Miss...St. John, isn't it?" she said, not looking especially surprised to see her, and the girl nodded.

"Actually, my name's Lani," she volunteered, as Hannah came into the room and started to remove her coat. "I...thank you for letting me know Jake was here. I didn't know where to look next."

Hannah's homely face registered a quiet satisfaction. "I'm sure you'd have thought of it yourself sooner or later," she demurred, folding her coat over the back of a chair. "I gather he was pleased to see you, seeing as you spent the night."

"Oh—" Lani looked down at the quilt, crumpled as she had left it, and bent to gather it up into her arms. "I—er—would you like some tea...or coffee? I haven't had time to prepare any breakfast yet."

"Bless you, you don't have to wait on me, miss," Hannah exclaimed, lifting one end of the quilt and helping Lani to fold it. "I generally come down about this time to make Jake a meal and to do whatever needs to be done. Miss Amelia doesn't wake until later, you see."

"You mean Mrs. Worth," said Lani, with a grimace. "Doesn't she care about her grandson at all? When I spoke to her yesterday, she acted as if he was a...a virtual stranger."

"Ah, well," Hannah took the quilt from Lani and showed her where to stow it away in the cavity beneath the sofa. "You shouldn't pay too much attention to what Mrs. Worth says. She and Jake have always had a kind of love-hate relationship."

"Love-hate?"

Lani sounded skeptical, but Hannah's expression was convincing. "Of course," she said, leading the way into the kitchen. "It's always been that way. They're too alike, I suppose, too stubborn. In any event, don't you run away with the idea that Miss Amelia doesn't care about her grandson. It just isn't true."

"But she was so objectionable!"

"Yes, well...." Hannah looked Lani up and down briefly. "You're lucky she didn't realize who you were. If she'd suspected you were that woman's daughter, she'd have had the police throw you off the property."

Lani caught her breath. "But—you know."

"Yes." Hannah opened up the percolator and after emptying out the grains, spooned some fresh coffee into the strainer. "But I was prepared to give you the benefit of the doubt. I thought Jake would get rid of you soon enough if that was what he wanted."

Lani glanced apprehensively toward the open door and the stairs beyond and then shook her head. "I don't know what to say. I suppose you've read about the. . . the accident in the papers."

"If it was an accident," remarked Hannah sagely, setting the coffee to perk. "It seems to me it should be your mother down here visiting, if she cares about him as much as the papers say. Instead of which, you turn up, all pale-cheeked and heavy-eyed, and he doesn't turn you away."

Lani sighed. "It's not quite that simple—"

"Nothing ever is." Hannah looked at her steadily. "Anyway, it's none of my business. Just so long as you know what you're doing."

"Oh, I know." Lani made an involuntary gesture. "And thanks. For your confidence."

Hannah shrugged. "He needs someone. I can't be here all the time, and this is a lonely place."

"He could stay up at the house, couldn't he?"

"He could." Hannah grimaced. "But he won't. Oh, it's all history now, but I suppose he still bears a grudge against his grandmother for the way she behaved toward his father."

"His father?" Lani frowned, and then as casually as she could, she pushed the door almost closed, so the funnel of the stairs was not so widely visible. "What about his father?"

Hannah took a packet of bacon from the fridge and began to open it. "I suppose there's no harm in telling you," she said. "Well, Miss Elizabeth—that was Jake's mother, you understand—she was the apple of her parents' eye. They only had the one child, you see, and she was thoroughly spoiled. Oh, she was a beautiful girl, I'll give you that. But they gave her too much of her own way, and when she fell in love with Jake's father, she wouldn't listen to reason. I mean, John Pendragon was a traveling man. It was obvious he wouldn't settle down in any one place for long. But Miss Elizabeth wouldn't have it, and she married him against her parents' wishes."

Lani nodded. "Jake once told me that."

"About his father?"

"Well, about his mother marrying against her mother's wishes."

"Ah." Hannah nodded. "Miss Amelia took it hard, she did. An unforgiving person she can be, if she feels she's been slighted."

Lani frowned. "What about Elizabeth's father?"

"Jake's grandfather?" Hannah pursed her lips. "He died. Soon after Miss Elizabeth left home. It was he who left her this house. Everything else went to Miss Amelia."

"I see." Lani nodded. "And what is...a traveling man?"

"A tinker! A Gypsy!" declared Jake's ironic tones behind her. "Filling her in on the family history, Hannah? I hope you haven't forgotten the bit about my grandfather jumping off the cliff."

Hannah did not look too perturbed. "Your grandfather did not jump off the cliff, Jake, as well you know. It was an accident, a terrible accident. Your grandmother just chose to blame your mother for it."

Jake used his crutches to ease himself into a more comfortable position against the door frame. "And why should I complain?" he inquired sardonically. "Without the old man's death, the Sea House might never have been mine."

Hannah gave him a reproving look, and then, turning on the grill, she began spreading slices of bacon across the pan. "So how are you feeling this morning?" she asked, evidently deciding not to get into an argument with him, and Jake lifted one shoulder in a careless gesture.

"As well as can be expected," he remarked. "Isn't that what they say?" He paused and cast a mocking glance in Lani's direction. "You've met my unexpected houseguest?"

"We introduced ourselves," said Hannah dryly. "She came to the house yesterday afternoon looking for you."

"And you told her where I was, of course," put in Jake caustically. "I wondered about that."

"I would have remembered," exclaimed Lani defensively. "I just thought—that is—your grandmother—"

"You thought the old lady might be caring for me, is that right?" Jake's lips curled scornfully. "Oh, Hannah, she doesn't know old Amelia very well, does she?"

Hannah set the bacon to grill and began putting bread into the toaster. "Where will you have this?" she asked, with a certain amount of impatience. "In here as usual, or shall I set the table in the other room?"

Jake arched his brows at Lani, and she looked abruptly away from his mocking gaze. "Oh, in here, please," she said, going to the drawer where she knew the knives and forks were kept. "And just toast for me. I'm not very hungry."

"Nor am I," said Jake, leaving the door to make his way to a chair at the table. "Don't bother with the eggs, Hannah. I'll just have a bacon sandwich."

"You should have a proper breakfast," protested the woman, setting some cornflakes and a jug of creamy Cornish milk on the table. But Jake merely poured himself a glass of orange juice from a carton Hannah had also provided, and Lani saw the woman's expression mirror her concern.

"How long is Miss St. John staying?" Hannah asked, when the coffee was ready and she could set the percolator on the table, and Jake lifted one dark eyebrow.

"You'd better ask her," he remarked, helping himself to some of the strong aromatic liquid. "I didn't invite her."

Lani colored. "I . . . a few days," she answered awkwardly, avoiding his provoking glance. "If there's anything I can do while I'm here, please tell me. I don't want to be a nuisance."

"Hah!"

Jake's sardonic ejaculation was indicative of his reaction to this, but Hannah ignored it. "I'm sure we'll work something out," she replied comfortably. "Now, I'll go and make the bed and tidy around. If there's anything else you want, just give me a call."

With Hannah's departure, Lani was intensely aware of Jake's eyes upon her, and steeling her features, she turned to look at him. "She's nice," she said, deliberately bringing Hannah's name into the conversation. "Does she have any children of her own?"

"No." Jake's response was clipped. "She's not married. And while that might not mean a lot today, it used to when she was young."

Lani nodded. "Has. . .has she worked for your grandmother for long?"

"Thirty years, I guess." Jake shrugged. "She came first as maid to my mother and stayed on to become my grandmother's housekeeper."

"I see." Lani cradled her coffee cup between her palms and cast about desperately for something else to say. "I suppose that's how she knows the family so well."

"The family history, you mean," corrected Jake dryly. "Are you satisfied now you know the whole story?"

Lani sighed. "Do you mind my knowing?"

"Why should I mind?" Jake regarded her broodingly. "Maybe discovering I'm the son of a Gypsy will convince you you're wasting your time here."

Lani bent her head. "We can't help who our fathers are." She shrugged, not wanting to think about her own father, and added, "I always thought there was something romantic about living in a caravan and traveling from place to place."

Jake groaned. "Well, I hate to disappoint you, but there's not. It wasn't like that." He paused, and then went on. "My father worked for a traveling circus and fair. There's nothing romantic about that. Mostly, I remember being hauled out of bed to help pull down the tent late at night, and my fingers feeling like chips of ice and my breath frosting in the air. I remember us always being short of food and money and being squashed together in one small caravan—my mother, my father, his mother and me."

Lani gazed at him. "How old were you when you came to live here?"

Jake gave her a considering look. "Ten. Why?"

"I just wondered." She hesitated. "Did your father come too?"

"No." Jake shook his head. "Just my mother and me."

Lani bit her lip. "But—she's dead now."

"She died when I was seventeen," said Jake dispassionately. "I don't think she ever got over losing my father. He threw her out, you see. There was another woman involved." His lips twisted. "I remember once seeing them together. I didn't understand what was going on, but I remember my mother crying, and I remember her losing the baby she was carrying."

"She was pregnant?"

"For the umpteenth time," agreed Jake flatly. "Fortunately, I was the only child she carried to full term. Although if there had been others, my father might not have behaved as he did."

"Or maybe he would." Lani pressed her lips together. "So your mother came home."

"Not home, no. Here," said Jake, glancing about him. "This was our home for seven years, until her health failed, and the doctors discovered she should never have attempted to have more children. She had a blood deficiency, you see, and pregnancy aggravated the condition. She was only thirty-nine when she died."

"I'm sorry."

"Yes. So was I." Jake shrugged. "I guess I felt responsible."

"But it wasn't your fault. What happened was inevitable." She paused. "Did you see your father again?"

"No." Jake shook his head. "My grandmother—my father's mother, that is—sent word that he had been killed when one of the metal props collapsed when they were erecting the tent, but I didn't hear about it until I got back to England three months ago." He gazed unseeingly across the room. "I didn't even feel anything. It had been too long. I would have gone to his funeral if I had known, but—" He shrugged his shoulders. "It was too late."

Lani found there was nothing she could say, and they were still sitting there in silence when Hannah returned. As if sensing the atmosphere between them, she quickly cleared the table and washed the dishes, and Lani got up at once to help her dry them.

"I—er—I'm going in to Helston this afternoon," Hannah remarked when she was finished, looking expectantly at Jake. "Was there anything special you wanted?"

"I don't think so," he said, hooking his crutches beneath his arms and getting to his feet. "I'll see you tomorrow, Hannah. The usual time."

Hannah hesitated. "You did say something about some...liniment, when I was here yesterday," she ventured, and Lani heard Jake's impatient intake of breath.

"It doesn't matter," he answered, his voice full of meaning and Hannah gave a resigned shrug of her shoulders as she went to get her coat.

Lani looked after her and then turned back to Jake. "Get it," she said. "Don't let my being here stop you. I'll even help you use it, if you'll let me—"

"Forget it!" Jake cut her off and followed Hannah through to the living room, and Lani shook her head unhappily as she went after them.

Hannah hesitated when she reached the outer door. "There's plenty of food," she said, "and I'll fetch some fresh bread in the morning. She paused, looking at Jake again. "Do you want me to tell your grandmother Miss St. John is staying here?"

"I don't want you to tell my grandmother anything," Jake replied tersely, reaching past her to open the door. "Goodbye, Hannah. Take care."

CHAPTER FIFTEEN

LANI WAS KNEELING on the window seat, looking out over the vast expanse of ocean, when Jake closed the door and came slowly back to the hearth. But she couldn't resist turning to look at him, aware of the raw uncertainty of his mood.

"You realize Hannah will talk, don't you?" he said, halting in the middle of the floor. "Did you tell her where you slept?"

"I imagine she saw for herself," said Lani levelly, nodding to where her suitcase was propped behind the sofa. "She even helped me fold the quilt and showed me where to stow it away."

Jake shook his head, and with a gesture of impatience, he lowered himself onto one of the sofas. "And what do you propose to do while you're here?" he exclaimed. "You'll be bored out of your mind."

"Are you?"

He sighed. "I sleep a lot."

"I'll sleep a lot, too."

He rested his head against the back of the sofa. "Lani—"

"Don't." She caught her upper lip between her teeth. "Please. I won't get in your way, I promise."

"And when your father finds out where you are?"

"My father knows where I am," said Lani unevenly. "I — er — I'll make some more coffee. You relax. I won't be long."

But when she came back he was asleep, and her heart turned in her breast at his unexpected vulnerability. With trembling fingers, she gathered up the rug she had brought from her car and draped it over him, taking care not to disturb him. Then, tiptoeing out again, she drank her coffee alone in the kitchen.

Jake was still sleeping when she went back to check on him later. On impulse she slipped on her boots and sheepskin jacket and left the house by the back door to get some air. The sun was warm on her shoulders, and the salt-laden atmosphere was invigorating. The cries of the sea gulls wheeling overhead and the muted roar of the surf added to her mood of sudden optimism, and holding on to the iron structure, she slowly descended the cliff face.

She discovered a steep path, evidently used at one time to reach the cove below, and although she was not normally so impetuous, she managed to scramble down it. Holding on to clumps of weed growing out of the rock to slow her progress, she eventually reached the graveled base of the cliff and realized with some surprise that in summer one could probably swim from here. From above, the tiny shelf of land cut into the cliff base was hidden, and only the rocks were visible, harsh and menacing.

She glanced up at the Sea House, rearing above her. Had Jake used this path as a boy, she wondered. Had he clambered down the cliff looking for birds' eggs, or swum from this cove in hot weather? She could imagine him as a boy, thin and dark and suntanned, springing over the rocks with surefooted grace, stripping off his clothes to swim in the wild ocean and emerging again to lie here in the sun.

She was still standing there lost in thought when she heard a cry. At first she thought it was another gull, but the sound seemed too human for that, and when it was repeated, she turned to look up the cliff path.

"Lani!"

The voice came to her indistinctly on the wind, and her breath caught in her throat at the sight of Jake, holding on to one of the iron supports high above her.

"*Lani!*"

He called her name again, and realizing he hadn't seen her, she quickly scrambled up the path again toward him. Unlike her, he was not wearing a coat, only a shirt and the corded pants and waistcoat he had worn in the house, and although the air was mild, it was by no means warm enough to be out without adequate protection.

"I'm here," she called, amazed at the speed with which she negotiated the path. "What are you doing out here? You'll get frozen."

Jake's mouth tightened. "And what the hell are you doing?" he snapped, as she reached him. "Climbing the cliffs like a mountain goat! God—I thought you'd fallen!"

"You cared?" she asked, unable to resist the taunt, and he turned away.

"Only to the extent that I don't want another death on my conscience," he retorted harshly. "Damn!" he cried as he jarred his injured knee. "I should have realized I'd have been useless to help anyway."

Lani sighed, hurrying to take his arm, but he shrugged her away. "I can manage," he declared, hauling himself up with the aid of the iron supports and preceding her into the kitchen where his crutches were propped by the door.

Lani followed him inside, and after closing the door she offered an apologetic glance. "I'm sorry," she said. "I thought you were asleep."

Jake lowered himself onto one of the kitchen chairs. "I should have warned you," he said dourly. "That path is dangerous. It's years since anyone used it."

Lani shrugged. "I took care."

"If there'd been any subsidence, it wouldn't have mattered how much care you took," retorted Jake grimly. "As soon as I realized where you'd gone, I came after you. Not very effectively, as it turned out."

Lani unfastened her coat. "I'm grateful, anyway."

"Why? For proving once again how helpless I am?" His lips twisted. "Let's face it, if you had been lying unconscious at the foot of the cliff, there was nothing I could do about it."

Lani sighed. "But I wasn't. Nothing happened." She tossed her coat onto a chair. "It's lunchtime. What would you like to eat?"

"Beans on toast," said Jake at once, pulling himself to his feet. "And I can make it. You go and . . . take it easy. Opening a tin should not prove too arduous."

Lani shook her head, but there was nothing she could do to change his mind. Despite the fact that after his laborious traverse of the cliff he looked exhausted, his will was inviolable. Finally, she left him to his task.

In fact, the simple meal was tasty. When Jake summoned Lani to the table, she found she enjoyed her lunch. Perhaps the breath of sea air had given her an appetite. Whatever it was, she ate more enthusiastically than she had done for weeks.

Afterward, they retired to the living room, and deciding she was not going to allow Jake to lapse into a sullen silence, Lani approached the piano. It was the one thing she could think of likely to evoke strong reaction, and she was not disappointed when Jake said harshly, "What are you doing?"

"I'm just looking," Lani replied casually, opening the lid and running her fingers over the keys. In spite of its neglect, the notes did not sound too badly out of tune, and she thought what a pity it was that Jake was making no attempt to play again. After all, he had said his hands were gaining strength, and remembering how he had dragged himself outside after her without his crutches, she was convinced he could do it.

"Leave it!" he said now, his jaw hardening at her unsubtle invitation, and Lani seated herself upon the stool and cupped her chin in her hand.

"Why?" she asked. "Why shouldn't I look at it? You won't."

"No, that's right, I won't," he agreed flatly. "And your amateur psychology won't work, either. If you imagine that by staying here you'll somehow convince me that I'll play again, you're mistaken. It's a simple fact of life that muscles need constant exercise to sustain their elasticity."

"I realize that." Lani was defensive. "I'm not saying

you could sit down and play a Chopin sonata right off. But with time and exercise—"

"No!"

"Why not?"

"I've just explained to you."

"You've explained nothing. Other people who... who have accidents start again—"

"Concert pianists?" he inquired skeptically, and she flushed.

"I don't believe you can't play. Your hands were strong enough to hold on to the metal support out there."

"Oh, Lani! It's not a question of strength."

"Then what is it a question of?"

Jake sighed. "I used to practice for hours every day—"

"How many hours?"

"Eight, mostly."

"Eight!" She was astonished.

"Lani, playing the piano is not like—well, not like being a boxer, or an athlete. It's not just a question of getting back into condition. My hands—" he looked down at them half-angrily "—my hands don't feel the same. They're...clumsy, stiff! God, I doubt if I could play Chopsticks the way they feel right now."

"But surely that's why you should start using them."

"No."

"What do you mean, no?"

"I mean, I don't want to play the piano anymore."

"That's not true—"

"All right." His mouth tightened. "I'll rephrase that. I don't want to play the kind of piano I'm going to be capable of playing."

"Oh, Jake! How do you know what you're capable of?"

His eyes smoldered angrily. "I know!"

Lani shook her head. "I never thought you were a defeatist."

"*A defeatist!*" He gazed at her in shocked disbelief, and Lani shifted a little uncomfortably beneath that burning appraisal.

"Well, a coward, then," she mumbled, the one no better than the other, and with a muffled imprecation, Jake hauled himself to his feet. Ignoring his crutches, he dragged himself across the floor to her side, and she stumbled awkwardly out of the way as he flung himself down at the piano.

The notes that echoed around the quiet room were like a death knell to her hopes. It was a cacophony of sound bearing little resemblance to the prelude she vaguely recognized it to be, and she held her breath when Jake brought his bandaged hands down heavily on the keyboard, before slamming the lid shut.

"Satisfied?" he asked, looking sideways at her, and she couldn't think of anything to say. "So," he added, dragging himself back to the sofa, "if that's the reason you've been hanging on here, to get me to prove that I really am washed up, your mission is accomplished. You can go back to daddy and tell him he has nothing more to fear from Jake Pendragon."

LANI WAS IN THE KITCHEN, trying to decide what to prepare for the evening meal, when she heard voices from the other room. One was Jake's—she would recognize his deep tones anywhere—but the other was feminine, and unable to deny her curiosity, she peeped into the living room. A girl was seated on the sofa opposite Jake, a pretty girl of about eighteen Lani guessed, and her stomach contracted painfully at the realization that Jake was talking quite amicably to her. In fact, as Lani looked into the room they both laughed, and she felt a sudden pang as she acknowledged he had not relaxed so fully with her.

The girl saw her at once, and she sobered abruptly, getting to her feet again and pushing her hands into the pockets of her tweed jacket. Her action caused Jake to glance around also, and his expression grew instantly guarded.

"Oh, Lani," he said, and she was obliged to come right into the room. "You don't know Susan, do you? She's Hannah's niece. She just came to see how I was."

"Hello."

Lani endeavored to be polite, but judging from Susan's response she needn't have bothered. The younger girl was barely civil, and turning back to Jake, she made her farewells. "I'll probably see you next week," she said, with a conspiratorial smile. "When you're not so... tied up."

"Fine." Jake made to get up, but Susan wouldn't let him.

"You rest easy," she said, making for the door. "We don't want you overdoing things, do we? G'bye."

Jake nodded, and the girl slipped out the door with scarcely a glance in Lani's direction.

Her departure left a hollow silence, and realizing the younger girl was probably jealous, Lani tried to be charitable. "What a pretty girl," she said, walking around the sofa so Jake could not avoid looking at her. "How old is she?"

"Seventeen, I guess." Jake was offhand, and Lani could have shaken him for his indifference.

"She's Hannah's niece?"

"I said so." He looked up at her in cool inquiry. "Did you like her?"

Lani shrugged. "I don't think she liked me."

"Why shouldn't she?"

Lani sighed. "You're not that naive."

"You think she's jealous?"

"Even though she has no reason to be," agreed Lani wearily, and unable to withstand his deliberate baiting, she walked swiftly toward the door.

"Doesn't she?"

The quiet question was barely audible, but she heard it, and halting, she glanced back at him. "What do you mean?"

Jake, who had turned to look at her, now presented her his back. "Nothing," he said, and she did not have the nerve to confront him again.

She decided to make a steak-and-kidney pie for dinner, using a tin of meat she had found in the cupboard. It didn't take long to make the pastry, and after the pie was in the oven, she went back into the living room to set the table. Jake was not there, and she looked about her in surprise. Then, deciding he had probably gone to the bathroom, she did what she had come for and returned to the kitchen to check on her baking.

Crossing the narrow hall, however, she heard a sound from upstairs, and she paused in sudden alarm. It had sounded suspiciously like a groan, and remembering Jake's exertions earlier, she didn't hesitate before going to investigate.

Jake was in his bedroom, sitting on the side of the bed, and he looked up half-angrily when Lani appeared. He had removed his jeans and the bandages on his hands, and was engrossed in the process of massaging some liniment into his knee, and Lani gazed at him helplessly, unable to withdraw.

"What are you doing?" she exclaimed, looking at the bottle in his hand. "Did Hannah come back? Or—no, it was the girl, wasn't it? Susan. She brought the embrocation Hannah mentioned, didn't she?"

"And if she did?" Jake expelled his breath resignedly. "Okay. So Hannah got the stuff without my permission. I thought I might as well give it a try. Even if it is just an old wives' remedy."

Lani left the door and came toward him. "Can I help you?" she asked awkwardly. "I mean...I have had some experience with my father. I'm sure you'd find it easier."

"I'm sure I would too." Jake hesitated a moment and then held the bottle out toward her. "Why not? Since you insist on acting the martyr."

Lani took the bottle and knelt down before him, trying to concentrate on the task in hand. Now that she was closer, she could see the scars where the surgeon had operated on his knee, and the other visible scars the crash had left. Compared to the brownness of his skin, they stood out in harsh relief, and she could imagine the pain he must have suffered before the bones knitted together.

The liniment did not have an unpleasant smell, and

Lani poured a little into her palm before applying it to his leg. Then, working rhythmically, she massaged the liquid into his knee, taking care not to bear down too heavily and cause him more pain than was necessary. After a while the tautness beneath her fingers grew less, and he relaxed back on his hands, allowing her to continue unsupervised. Indeed when Lani glanced up at him she saw he had closed his eyes, and she felt an overwhelming sense of pride that he should have confidence in her.

Almost involuntarily, her hands slowed, smoothing the skin over the bones with unknowing sensitivity. As her eyes moved up over the strong sinews of his thighs to the flat muscles of his stomach, her feelings took over, and without her being aware of it, her fingers betrayed the turbulent emotions stirring inside her.

Immediately Jake's eyes flicked open, and she drew back at once, her face coloring at the guilty remembrance of her thoughts. She hoped he couldn't read her mind as she quickly screwed the cap back on the bottle and wiped her hands on a tissue. After what had happened that morning, she had no intention of inciting his unwilling passion, and licking her dry lips, she got unsteadily to her feet.

"Does that feel better?" she asked, trying to behave naturally, and Jake sat up.

"I think it does," he said, after a moment. "Thanks. I'm grateful. You did a good job."

"It was nothing." Lani shrugged her shoulders. "I—er—I've made a pie for dinner. You will have some, won't you?"

"How could I refuse?" Jake looked up at her with a

faintly mocking expression. "If you'll just give me time to put my pants on—"

"Do you—oh, no." She flushed anew. "You can manage, can't you?"

"I think I'm going to have to," replied Jake ruefully. "Go serve your pie. I'll be down in a little while."

Dinner was quite a pleasant meal. Jake seemed to put himself out to be polite, and the flaky pie and its accompanying vegetables came in for some compliments. Lani welcomed his lack of aggression, but she couldn't help wishing it was not just because of the massage, and she suspected that by the next morning he'd have resumed hostilities.

During the evening, they played Scrabble, Jake surprising her by producing the board from the cabinet in the corner. "My mother and I used to play years ago," he confessed, managing to draw the heavy curtains across the windows by supporting himself against the window seat. He came back to sit opposite her. "Isn't this cozy?" His lips twisted. "Who could ask for anything more?"

Apart from the occasional comment of this kind, it was an enjoyable evening. Taken at its face value, Jake's attitude was one of casual amiability, and although Lani found him looking at her oddly sometimes, on the whole he behaved faultlessly toward her. He was an amusing companion, but she had known that already, and she couldn't help the occasional pang when she reflected on what they had lost.

About ten o'clock, Jake said he was going to bed, and Lani watched him leave the room with some regret. Although it had been a long day, and she was tired, she had not wanted the evening to end, and she got undressed with a feeling of anticlimax.

Jake had shown her how to pull out the sofa so that it uncoiled into a double bed, and she found Hannah had put out fresh sheets and pillowcases to complement the quilt she had used the night before. Indeed, the bed was remarkably comfortable once she was snuggled beneath the covers, and certainly an improvement on the previous night's arrangement.

She fell asleep immediately, lulled by the flickering light of the dying fire, and awakened to find herself standing on the cliff path outside. It was morning, and an icy wind was blowing, howling about the exposed eaves of the Sea House and chilling her to the core. She was wearing only her pajamas, she saw with dismay, and they offered no protection from the elements. She was cold and she was frightened, disoriented by her surroundings and totally incapable of working out why she was there.

Turning back, she tried to enter the house by the door she had used the previous morning, but it was locked, and the key was turned against her. When she groped her way to the window and looked into the kitchen, she saw Jake and Hannah's niece, Susan, sitting at the table, laughing together. They looked up and saw her at the window, but although she waved and knocked at the glass, they made no attempt to open the door. They didn't seem to care that she was locked outside and freezing to death. They just talked and laughed together, completely ignoring her.

Realizing she had to get indoors somehow, Lani scrambled around the side of the building. But there was no way of reaching the other door without climbing down the cliff, and her hands were already sore and bleeding.

Gasping for breath, she clutched at the iron support nearest to her, and began the precarious climb down the cliff. Her feet, in the fluffy mules, offered no purchase on the slippery slope, and her cold hands were losing their grip. Sobbing desperately, she made one last attempt to save herself, but already she could see the caldron of water far below her and the jagged pointed rocks, just waiting for their victim. Like a leaf from a tree she was falling, falling, and although she called Jake's name, she had no hope of rescue. . . .

"Lani! Lani, wake up! It's all right, do you hear me? You're safe. Safe! Lani, come on — I'm here. Beside you. Don't fight me."

She awakened to a room lighted by one softly shaded lamp, to the awareness of moistness at the nape of her neck and a comforting hand pushed into the tumbled softness of her hair. She was cradled against a warm chest, where fine whorls of hair, freed by the opening of silk lapels, invaded her nose and mouth, and her panic gave way to weak exhaustion as she looked up into Jake's anxious face.

"I — I —"

"You were dreaming," he said, interrupting her stammered attempt at speech. "I heard you cry out. Are you all right now?"

"I . . . think so." Lani moved her head in a gesture of acknowledgment. "I remember now, I was outside on the cliff path. I — I slipped."

"That's what comes of going in for these dangerous expeditions," remarked Jake softly, smoothing damp strands of hair back from her forehead, and she realized he was not wearing the bandages. "What happened? Did I push you off the cliff? The way you were fighting me just now, you'd have thought I was the devil incarnate!"

Lani's lips parted. "I'm sorry. Did I hurt you?"

"I'll survive," he responded dryly. "I guess that game of Scrabble was too stimulating for you. The excitement, you know. It can do strange things to people."

Lani offered a tremulous smile. "You're very good at this sort of thing, aren't you?" she murmured. "Have you had a lot of experience?"

"In comforting damsels in distress?" He grinned wryly. "Not nearly as much as I'd like. We Knights of the Bar Sinister aren't called upon quite so often."

"You're not a Knight of the Bar Sinister," she protested, and much to her regret, he lowered her back against the pillows.

"I might as well be," he retorted, permitting his fingers to trail down her cheek. "Now, settle down like a good girl. It's time you were asleep."

Lani pressed her lips together. "Did...did I wake you up?"

"No." Jake's response was clipped, and he drew the lapels of his gold silk robe closer around him before reaching for his crutches. "I was reading," he said, dashing her hopes that thoughts of her might have kept him awake. "It's only a little after midnight. A long time until morning."

"Yes."

Lani propped herself up on her elbows, trying to appear as composed as he was, but it was difficult with his thigh wedged firmly against hers, even though the thickness of the bedclothes separated them, and the warmth of his body still lingered on her skin.

"Good night then," he said, grasping the sides of the bed to lever himself upward, but before he did so, he leaned toward her. "Sleep well," he said, brushing her mouth with his, and Lani, too bemused to resist felt her lips part in eager submission.

Jake drew back, but not far, his eyes darkening with sudden emotion. For a moment he scanned the tremulous invitation of wide green eyes and a softly curving mouth, and then his control snapped. With a groan, he turned to her, gathering her up into his arms with an urgency born of long denial, and his lips swooped down on hers with hungry possession.

Lani's senses swirled in a dizzying vortex as his hands slid into her hair. His mouth moved over hers searchingly, sending ripples of fire through her blood, his tongue tasting the moist sweetness hidden within. His kisses were deep, breathtaking, robbing her of all resistance creating a melting heat that threatened to consume her.

When his lips left hers, it was only to seek the delicate curve of her cheek, his teeth tugging sensuously at her earlobe, evoking shivers of delight. His hand slid down from her nape to invade the neckline of her pajama jacket, disposing of its fastening and exposing one rose-tipped breast. He caught his breath as he bent to its pointed crest, and Lani moaned as he drew the covers from her and revealed her lissome form to his hungry gaze.

"Beautiful," he groaned, moving onto the bed beside her, and sliding the jacket from her shoulders. When her arms were freed, her fingers went to the cord of his robe, and he did not stop her when she tugged it loose. His lean brown body was so achingly familiar, and her fingers stroked his shoulders eagerly, delighting in his response. Her spine arched toward him, instinctively inviting his caress, and Jake's smoldering gaze swept over her before he captured her mouth again.

When his lips trailed a burning path from her breast to the elastic waistband of her pajama trousers, she quivered beneath his touch, and she trembled uncontrollably when he tugged the offending scrap of beige silk down over her hips. His lips followed the progress of his hands, seeking and finding her most sensitive places, and a cry of protest broke from her lips at this most intimate invasion.

"Let me," he said, lifting his eyes to look at her, and in their burning depths she found no will to resist. Her legs parted involuntarily, easing his exploration, and he probed her honeyed sweetness, bringing her to the brink of ecstasy.

"Oh, Jake," she groaned, when he sought her mouth once more, her hands moving over the hair-roughened skin of his chest to the growth that arrowed down below his navel, and he shuddered.

"Touch me," he said, his mouth against her neck, and she felt his teeth lightly graze her skin as her unsteady fingers found his swollen manhood. "God, I want you," he muttered, unable to deny himself any longer, and Lani arched toward him with equal fervor.

This time there was no pain, only pleasure, a steadily

increasing storm that surged and seethed inside her, as Jake penetrated the very heart of her being. She moved with him, inciting him, bringing them both to a high peak of rapture that finally exploded and shattered into lingering fragments of enchantment. She didn't want to let him go. Even when he slumped against her, lazily sated and replete, she nestled closer to him, and he wrapped his arms and legs around her and sank into a deep slumber.

CHAPTER SIXTEEN

IT WAS THE SOUND OF VOICES that disturbed Lani next morning.

She came back to consciousness unwillingly, gripped by the belief that the delicious weakness she was experiencing would dissipate as soon as she opened her eyes. But to her delight, the languorous feeling did not disappear. On the contrary, as she shifted in the bed and discovered her nakedness, the memory of what had happened the night before swept over her, and with it a mindless rapture she was not imagining. Even her skin felt sensitized, the linen sheet an abrasion to flesh left bruised by Jake's lovemaking. But it was a sensuous abrasion. Almost experimentally her palms touched the hardening peaks of her breasts, left tender from the probing caress of Jake's tongue, and as they did so, she felt a corresponding ache between her thighs.

"—into the kitchen—"

The softly uttered words caused Lani to abandon her innocent exploration, and rolling into a ball, she twisted around in the bed. Jake, dressed now in black jeans and a matching silk shirt, was conducting a conversation with Hannah in undertones, and the woman was nodding her head in agreement to his suggestion that they should go into the other room.

However, Hannah had noticed Lani's sudden movement, and drawing Jake's attention to it, she said, "I'm
sorry. Did we wake you?"

"It's all right." Lani endeavored to keep beneath the
covers, her eyes darting irresistibly to Jake's dark face.
"I — er — I should have been up anyway. I must have
overslept."

"It's the sea air," said Hannah comfortably, bustling
over to the hearth and starting to rake out the ashes.
"My, it's not very warm in here, is it? Never mind, I'll
soon get the fire going and then I'll make some tea."

She disappeared out to the kitchen with the tray of
ashes she had taken from the grate, and Lani struggled
into a sitting position, tucking the sheet securely
beneath her arms. She was overpoweringly conscious of
Jake's tawny eyes upon her, and she wondered what he
was thinking and how long he had been up.

"Is — er — is it a fine morning?" she asked, glancing
toward the windows where someone had half drawn the
curtains, and Jake nodded.

"It's not raining, if that's what you mean," he offered shortly, using his crutches to move across the
floor. She saw to her surprise he had not replaced the
bandages. His hands, the hands that had given her so
much pleasure the night before, now gripped the lower
bars of the crutches, and although he put very little
weight upon them, he no longer tried to hide them.

"Jake—" she began, putting out her hand toward
him, but he quickly shook his head.

"Not now, Lani," he said crisply, moving toward the
door. "I — er — I've put your suitcase up in the bedroom. As soon as you like, you can get dressed up

there. And there's room in the wardrobe, if you want to unpack your things."

Lani gazed at him tremulously. "You mean—I'm to sleep upstairs in future?"

"And I'll sleep down here," agreed Jake flatly, pulling open the door, and she was left to her uneasy thoughts as he went to find Hannah.

Unable to talk to Jake to discover exactly what he had meant by his remarks, Lani sprang hastily out of bed. Then, wrapping the quilt around her, sarong-fashion, she hurried to the door, only to fall back awkwardly when Hannah came bursting through.

"Oh, I'm sorry, miss," she exclaimed, exhibiting her sooty hands. "I didn't realize you'd be getting up yet. I was going to bring you a nice cup of tea."

"That's all right, Hannah." Lani forced a faint smile. "I—er—I didn't bring a dressing gown. I'm just going to put my clothes on."

Hannah frowned. "You've got nothing on, have you, miss?" she exclaimed. "Good heavens, you must be freezing on this cold floor. I thought I saw a nice pair of pajamas yesterday. I assumed they belonged to you."

"They did. They do!" Lani glanced back guiltily towards the bed. "I—er—I was hot in the night. I took them off."

"Really?" Hannah's response was even, but unable to sustain any more of this conversation, Lani offered another apologetic smile and made good her escape.

By the time she had washed and brushed her teeth, and then scuttled upstairs to put on the corded pants and sweater she had worn the day before, Lani felt a little less vulnerable. Jake's strange behavior and

Hannah's questions had left her feeling distinctly raw, and she deliberately unpacked her case and put her things away before going back downstairs.

The huge wardrobe easily accommodated her coats and dresses, and the skirts and pants she had brought. Her underwear slotted into a shirt rack, set at one side of the hanging rail, and her suitcase slid under the bed. The room looked exactly as she had found it, except that now her makeup case resided beside Jake's brushes on the dressing table.

Picking up one of the brushes, she held it against her cheek for a moment. The wholesome scent it emitted owed nothing to any oil or hair cream. Jake's hair was free of any conditioner and lay thick and smooth against his head. Unlike the hair on the other parts of his body, she reflected, with a suddenly quickening pulse.

"Tea's ready!"

Hannah's call startled her, and quickly putting the brush back on the dressing table, she went downstairs again. Jake was in the kitchen too, seated at the pine table, but he barely glanced up as she took the seat beside him and accepted the steaming beverage Hannah proffered. He seemed deep in thought, his attention drawn to the circling patterns in his cup, and Lani reflected that Hannah probably saw no change in his attitude toward her.

When breakfast was over, Jake disappeared into the other room, and Lani, helping Hannah to clear the table, found the woman's eyes upon her. "Tell me," Hannah said, "do you know if Jake used that embrocation I sent him? Susan said she gave it to him, but he's not mentioned it."

"Oh, yes." Lani put the plate aside and made a point of folding the tea towel to give herself time to think. "I—er—he put some on before dinner last night. I don't know if it's done him any good."

"It will. If he uses it regularly," declared Hannah firmly. "My old granny used to swear by it for easing her arthritis, and if he won't have the proper treatment, he's got to do something to keep the muscles from seizing up."

Lani caught her lower lip between her teeth. "Why do you think he abandoned the proper treatment?" she asked, unable to prevent the question. "I mean . . . well, I know he doesn't have much faith in what they can do for him, but why did he discharge himself from the hospital?"

Hannah hesitated. "I thought you might know that."

"Me?"

"Yes." The woman paused. "I thought at first it was because your mother had walked out on him, but now I'm not so sure."

"What do you mean?"

"Well—" Hannah shrugged "—those pictures they put in the papers, they didn't tell the whole story, did they? You know, I never really believed Jake could have fallen for a woman like her. And when you came here asking for him, I knew I was right."

Lani flushed. "I'd never walk out on him."

"I know that now." Hannah nodded. "But he might not believe it."

"Why?"

Hannah dried her hands thoughtfully. "Well, it's obvious his injuries are going to take some time to mend.

It said in the papers he'd never play the piano again, and I know he's not touched that one in there since he came back. I dust it, and it's never been used."

"He did...touch it yesterday." Lani bent her head. "Oh, not willingly," she added, as Hannah looked expectantly at her. "I...made him do it. I think he hated me afterward."

Hannah shook her head. "I don't think he hates you, miss."

"Don't you?" Lani knew a momentary lift of her spirits.

"No." Hannah was definite. "I've seen the way he looks at you. He doesn't hate you. At least, not in the way you mean."

"Is there more than one way to hate someone?"

"I think so." Hannah considered. "The hate you're talking about is the one most people encounter—the kind of hate you feel for someone you dislike or despise. I'm talking about something else, something more akin to frustration—the desperation you feel when the thing you want most is out of reach."

"But I'm not out of reach," exclaimed Lani impulsively, and Hannah's lips drew down.

"Perhaps he thinks you are," she said, coloring slightly. And then, giving a faintly embarrassed laugh, she added, "Heavens, what am I saying? You'll think I'm a real old busybody, won't you? It's really none of my business. I only meant to say...well, you could hurt him, and I don't want that to happen."

"I don't want that to happen either," protested Lani. "I—I love him."

"Do you?" Hannah studied the girl's troubled features sympathetically for a moment. "Well, you'll have to convince him of that, won't you? Because it was you he ran away from, wasn't it? Not Clare Austin."

IT WAS SOMETHING Lani had not even suspected, and although she didn't have complete faith in Hannah's interpretation of Jake's behavior she couldn't entirely dismiss it from her mind. It might explain why Jake had refused to see her, but dared she suppose he had been thinking of her and not himself? After all, he had said his attraction to her was purely physical. How could she believe he would deny his feelings, when she had been so candid about hers? She needed to talk to him, but until Hannah's departure she was unable to do so. Instead, she paced restlessly around the kitchen, trying to compose the words she was going to use.

Yet after Hannah had put on her coat and departed, Lani still lingered in the kitchen. Her initial excitement had given way to a state of uncertainty, and the idea that Jake might be hiding his real feelings had no conviction. It was far more likely that his bitter disappointment at his present disabilities had driven him to escape from the hounding of the gutter press. He obviously needed time to rest and recuperate. Hannah was a romantic. She didn't see things the way they really were. Jake had no love for Lani. He had no love for anyone. Just a driving ambition, which had temporarily been quenched.

"What are you doing out here?"

Jake's impatient voice broke into her fretful thoughts, and she turned abruptly from the window to gaze unhappily at him. "I—oh, I was just thinking, that's all," she offered, pushing her hands into the back pockets of her jeans. "Did—er—did you want some more coffee? I think there's some in the percolator. Hannah made quite—"

"I don't want any coffee," Jake interrupted her harshly. "Believe it or not, but it isn't the panacea for all ills. Now, I asked you what you were doing. Do I get a straight answer, or are you going to fob me off with more lies?"

"I was not lying." Lani flushed. "I was thinking, honestly. I do have a brain, you know."

"Oh, I know." Jake propped his crutches against the table and managed to half sit, half lean against the edge. "You're a very clever young woman. I'd be the first to admit it."

"I'm not clever—"

"Talented, then."

Lani sighed. "I was not thinking about myself."

"Weren't you?" Jake's tawny eyes narrowed. "Then let me guess: you were thinking about me."

Lani bent her head. "We have to talk."

"What about?" He paused. "Last night?"

"Among other things." Lani glanced up at him. "Why did you say you were going to sleep downstairs in future?"

"Because I am," he declared shortly. "If you persist in staying here after last night, the least I can do is offer you a proper bed."

Lani shook her head. "Do you regret what happened last night?"

"What do you think?" Jake heaved a sigh. "Lani, don't be naive. You know why it happened. You're a very desirable lady. I'd have had to be made of ice not to appreciate that."

"Then—"

"But it won't happen again," he overrode her forcefully. "Not because you're any less desirable today than you were yesterday, but simply because I need to keep my self-respect, if nothing else."

"Your...self-respect?"

"Yes." He massaged the back of his neck with evident impatience. "Look, I don't know how to put this, but it wouldn't be fair to—to use you. And that's what I would be doing—using you to satisfy my own needs, my own lusts—"

"No—"

"Yes." He was adamant. "I'm feeling pretty low right now, and I can't deny it's a temptation to take advantage of your...your generosity."

"It's not generosity!" Lani brought her hands out of her pockets to ball in frustration at her sides. "I love you, Jake, you know I do. Why won't you accept my feelings for what they are?"

"Because you don't know what you're saying," he snapped savagely. "You've got some romantic notion of what our relationship could be, and you won't listen to reason!"

"What's reasonable about what you're saying?" Lani gazed at him tremulously. "I don't believe—I don't believe you could do what you did last night, without—without there being any feeling on your side."

"You're wrong." Jake shook his head, his jaw hard and uncompromising. "For Christ's sake, Lani, a man doesn't need to feel anything for a woman to have sex with her!"

"And that's all it was?" Lani's voice shook.

"As far as I'm concerned, yes."

"I don't believe you."

"You're going to have to."

Lani shook her head. "I won't. I won't!"

"Then you're going to get hurt."

Lani sniffed, the prick of tears making her eyes smart. "Before. . . before the crash. . . ."

Jake closed his eyes. "I don't want to talk about before the crash."

"Why not?"

"Because it's not relevant." He opened his eyes again. "It's now that matters. Here and now. And I don't intend to jeopardize my immortal soul by taking advantage of a silly little virgin I shouldn't have violated in the first place!"

Lani caught her breath. "You—you brute!"

"Exactly. That's what I am. After all, it's not as if there aren't plenty of available women around to satisfy my baser instincts should the need arise."

"Like Hannah's niece, I suppose," cried Lani bitterly, and Jake inclined his head.

"At least Susan would know the score," he essayed cruelly, and Lani knew she couldn't take any more. If she stayed here a moment longer, she would burst into tears and humiliate herself completely, and clamping her teeth together, she started toward the door.

She didn't reach it. As she brushed past Jake, with her head down and her breath coming in shallow gasps, his own constraint snapped, and with an an-

guished sound, he caught her forearm, staying her
blind progress.

"It's not true," he said between his teeth as she made
a frantic effort to free herself. "God help me, I can't go
on pretending I don't care. I was lying. I wanted to
make love to you. I want to make love to you now. But
that doesn't mean I'll do it. It simply means I'm not the
bastard I wanted you to think."

"Jake—"

Lani stopped struggling and stared at him with tear-
wet eyes, and his lips twisted mockingly as he met her
tremulous gaze. "Ironic isn't it?" he said, arching one
dark brow. "I thought I knew all the answers. It seems
like I was wrong."

Lani's forehead furrowed. "You mean . . . you *do* love
me?" she breathed softly, touching his cheek, but he
flinched away from her gentle caress.

"Love!" he said tautly. "What is love? I don't think I
know the meaning of the word. I only know how you
make me feel, how you twist my emotions, so that hurting you hurts me more." He groaned, and pulled her
between his legs, turning his mouth against her neck.
"But that's the problem, isn't it? Knowing I should
send you away, and finding a way to do it."

Lani caught her breath, drawing back to look at him
incredulously. "What do you mean? I don't want to go
away."

"Not now," said Jake steadily. "Not today. Not this
week. Maybe not even this month. But sooner or later
you will, and that's why this can't go on."

"Jake—"

"No, listen to me." He drew an uneven breath.

"What we have is good, I know, but that doesn't mean you can't have the same with someone else—"

"No!"

"Yes." Jake sighed. "Lani, I don't want to hurt you, I don't want to hurt either of us, but it would be easier for both of us if we ended it now."

Lani held up her head. "You don't want me then."

"For Christ's sake!" Jake stared at her frustratedly for a moment, and then he grasped a handful of her hair, forcing her head to his. His lips ground into hers with savage intensity, the taut strength of his body imprinted on hers as he made no attempt to hide his arousal. His tongue forced its way between her teeth, exploring the parted sweetness of her mouth, and Lani's bones melted beneath his passionate assault. His hands caressed her urgently, so that her breasts surged against the thin wool of her sweater, and when his fingers probed the inner curve of her thigh, her limbs grew weak and trembly.

"Does that answer your question?" he demanded at length, thrusting her away from him, and her eyes lowered irresistibly to the taut cloth of his pants. "Yes. I want you. But it won't work. I have no career, no job, no prospects! Go find yourself some wealthy businessman, Lani. Someone who isn't crippled! Someone you can respect!"

He left her then, dragging himself out of the room on his crutches, and presently she heard him mounting the stairs. She knew he was disturbed and angry, as much with himself for his lack of control as with her for causing it, and she wanted to go after him and make him take back his words. But she couldn't. He was determined to drive a wedge between them, to create a situation where she would be compelled to leave him, to force her to the conclusion that he was simply not worth her efforts.

Fifteen minutes later she was seated in the Capri, fishing in her handbag for the car keys. It had been an impulsive decision to leave the house for a while, to get completely away on her own, to try to come to terms with Jake's state of mind. She needed time to calm her own churning emotions, to think objectively and to determine what she was going to do.

Emotively, there was no decision to be made. She loved Jake and she wanted to stay with him. She didn't care what he did or where they lived, so long as they were together. But in practical terms it was not so simple.

She could not go on living here, being a drain on his resources, without contributing anything. Yet she could hardly offer to pay board and lodging when Jake wanted her to leave. Effectively, he was limiting the length of time she could stay at the Sea House, and her thoughts were in a turmoil as she drove away from Tremorna Point.

She took the road that led inland away from the sea, seeking the quiet stretches of moorland that offered the peace and tranquillity she needed. With only the birds for company, she drove over the downs and parked for a while in a lonely spot overlooking a natural sanctuary. There was something soothing about watching the ducks and wild geese that flew in to feed, and her own problems receded as her brain ceased to race. Something would turn up, she told herself fiercely. Somehow, some way, Jake must be made to believe in himself again. And until that happened, she had to see it through.

When she finally turned back toward Helston, it was late afternoon. She had lingered longer than she'd intended, and she realized with a pang she had had nothing to eat or drink since early that morning. She wondered if Jake had missed her and whether he understood what had driven her away. Or had he been relieved that she had gone out for a few hours, to escape her disrupting presence?

A dampness was invading the air as she drove up Mrs. Worth's drive and circled the house to park where she had parked before. Getting out of the car and locking it, she reflected that it could probably be more comfortably accommodated in one of the garages that flanked the stable block, but that would mean contacting Jake's grandmother, and she had no desire to do that.

However, as she turned the corner of the house, she came up short at the sight of Hannah, hovering on the porch. The housekeeper waved her arm agitatedly, bidding the girl to approach, and Lani looped the strap of her bag over her shoulder and thrust her hands into her pockets as she made the necessary detour.

"Is something wrong?" she asked, when she was close enough for Hannah to hear her, and the sudden apprehension that gripped her made her glance half-fearfully toward the cliff.

But Hannah merely shook her head, her accompanying gesture soothing any fears Lani might be harboring about Jake, and said conspiratorially: "Mrs. Worth wants to see you."

"Me?" Lani gazed at Hannah blankly. "But why? How? I didn't know she knew I was here."

"She saw you. This morning," said Hannah, grimacing. "I suppose she heard your car. She can be quite perceptive, if she's a mind for it. Anyway, you'd better come in. She doesn't like to be kept waiting."

"I'll bet she doesn't," said Lani dryly, and then with a shrug, she complied. "Do you know why she wants to see me? I mean—it's not as if I know the woman. Apart from two encounters, which were hardly polite."

Hannah closed the door behind them, and bade Lani follow her up the stairs. "I shouldn't expect too much of this visit either," she advised in an undertone. "Mrs. Worth is not known for her philanthropy. I suspect what she really wants to do is find out who you are and why you're here."

Lani sighed. "Do I have to tell her?"

"Well, I've had to admit that you're staying with Jake," said Hannah uncomfortably. "I shouldn't let her worry you. She does have Jake's interests at heart."

Lani was shown into the same bedroom she had visited years before with her father. Indeed, the room even looked the same, with its collection of tables and chairs and bric-a-brac, and there was the same scent of decay in the air.

However, this time Mrs. Worth was not in the huge bed. She was seated on a low sofa, though she was still wearing her high-necked nightgown, with a man's velvet-trimmed dressing gown wrapped around her scrawny form. What hair she had was almost obscured by a frilly cotton bonnet, but wisps stuck out here and there, almost as white as the bonnet itself.

"Miss St. John, Mrs. Worth," said Hannah, ushering the girl into the room, and Lani advanced reluctantly to stand before that imperious little figure.

"You may leave us, Hannah," declared the old lady dismissingly, when the housekeeper seemed disposed to linger, and the door closed behind her with a decided click. "Sit down, miss, sit down," she said, gesturing toward an upright chair opposite, which had a faded Regency stripe, and Lani subsided cautiously, determined not to be intimidated.

"So," Mrs. Worth said consideringly, surveying the girl with a practiced eye, "you're living with my grandson, are you?"

Lani moistened her dry lips. "I'm . . . staying with him," she amended evenly.

"You're not his mistress then?"

Lani gasped. "I don't see that that's any concern of yours, Mrs. Worth."

"Don't you?" The old woman arched her eyebrows. "Hoity-toity, are we? Well, let me tell you, anything to do with my grandson is my business!"

"I'd never have guessed." Lani made the retort without consideration and then bent her head impatiently. The old woman was trying to rile her, and she was falling for the bait. She had to keep her temper if she wanted to keep her self-respect.

"You think I neglect him, don't you?" Mrs. Worth suggested crisply. "Oh, don't bother to answer that, I can see you do. But don't imagine that because he takes you to his bed, you automatically gain the right to criticize his family."

Lani took a deep breath. "I never thought any such thing."

"No? But you don't like me, do you, Miss St. John? You needn't deny it. I'm very good at reading characters."

Lani shook her head. "I'm sure you didn't bring me here to discuss my opinion of you, Mrs. Worth."

"No." Mrs. Worth paused. "No, you're right. I didn't. But it helps to know where one stands, doesn't it? It's obvious you're harboring resentment."

Lani expelled her breath disbelievingly. "Mrs. Worth, the only two occasions we have spoken together, you have been...well, less than polite. I don't see how you can blame me for my attitude, when you deliberately misled me about Jake's whereabouts."

"*Two* occasions?"

"I told you. I came here once before with my father."

"Oh, yes. Yes, I remember. Your father is my solicitor, isn't he? Well, you couldn't expect me to discuss my private affairs in the company of a child."

"It wasn't what you said, it was the way you said it," said Lani flatly. "Anyway, that's not important now. Why did you ask to see me?"

"Presently, presently." Mrs. Worth refused to be hurried. "There's no special rush, is there? You're not going anywhere, are you?"

Lani compressed her lips. "That depends."

"Depends? Depends on what?"

"That's between Jake and me, Mrs. Worth."

The old woman's brows drew together. "You're not planning on walking out on him, are you?"

"No." Lani gazed at her indignantly. "I wouldn't do that. I wouldn't hurt anyone I—I said I loved."

"Unlike your mother, one presumes," remarked Mrs. Worth tartly, disposing once and for all of the myth that she did not know Lani's real identity. "I suppose Jake has told you of my daughter's misfortunes?"

"He told me. Yes."

"And did he also tell you that when Elizabeth died, I offered him a home here—in this house—and he rejected it?"

"No. But it doesn't surprise me that he rejected it," said Lani quietly. "Mrs. Worth—"

"Have you never made a mistake, Miss St. John? Have you never done something you've lived to regret? I admit, I did treat my daughter badly, but she treated us badly too, and my husband did not get over it. He fell from the cliffs, you know. Oh, some people said he jumped, but it wasn't so. There was a postmortem, you see, and it was discovered he had had a stroke just before he fell. I'm afraid I did blame Elizabeth then."

Lani shifted a little uncomfortably. "I really don't think this has anything to do with me, Mrs. Worth."

"If you're in love with Jake, it should." The old woman leaned toward her. "Tell me about him. Tell me about my grandson. How is he managing? He's such a frustrating man. He won't accept my help."

"Have you offered it?" Lani stared at her in surprise.

"I shouldn't have to," retorted Mrs. Worth irritably. "I'm his grandmother, aren't I? He should know he has only to come to me—"

"And you should know he'll never do that," said Lani forcefully. "Whatever happens, however he fares, he'll never ask you for assistance."

Mrs. Worth drew back. "Why not?"

"Would you?" Lani tilted her head. "Would you ask him for help?"

"It's different for me. I'm an old woman—"

"He's your grandson, Mrs. Worth. Regrettably, there are resemblances."

The old woman caught her breath. "You don't care what you say to me, do you?"

Lani bent her head. "I'm only telling the truth."

"And you do care about my grandson?"

"I've said so."

"Does he care about you?"

Lani looked up. "I think so."

"You're not sure?"

Lani shook her head. "It's not the same for him. . . ."

"What do you mean?"

"Oh. . . ." Lani turned her head away. "He thinks I'm too young to know my own mind. He thinks I should find someone else, someone with. . .prospects."

"Prospects?" Mrs. Worth snorted. "Jake has prospects. He's my heir. When I die, he'll be a wealthy man."

"I don't think those are the kind of prospects that matter to him," said Lani carefully. "He sees himself as. . .as a failure. He won't listen to reason. He knows he shouldn't have left the hospital, that he should be having therapy, but—"

"Wait!" Mrs. Worth interrupted her. "Are you saying Jake discharged himself from the hospital in London?"

Lani nodded. "Didn't you know?"

"How could I?" exclaimed Mrs. Worth tersely. "I haven't seen him. He doesn't confide in me."

Lani shrugged, somewhat amazed to find herself discussing Jake with this arrogant old woman. To her astonishment, she was actually beginning to feel some sympathy for the old lady, and realizing she had said more than enough, she got to her feet.

"I think I'd better be going."

"Must you?" Mrs. Worth looked up at her with real regret. "But you'll come and see me again? You'll keep me informed of Jake's condition?"

"I don't know whether I can do that, Mrs. Worth," Lani replied honestly. "Perhaps it's something you should find out for yourself."

Outside again, Lani felt a growing sense of incredulity at what had happened. Half an hour ago, she had regarded Mrs. Worth as little more than a selfish old woman, using her money to manipulate her own ends. But suddenly, she was just another human being, a lonely human being, whose actions had denied her the one thing she craved—the love of her grandson.

Realizing abruptly how late it was, Lani put all thoughts of Jake's grandmother aside, and hurriedly made her descent of the cliff path. It was after six, and by now Jake might be wondering where she was. Unless

Hannah had informed him what was going on, and somehow she doubted the housekeeper would do that.

Slipping on the moist earth, she reached the veranda steps and climbed them swiftly. Now that she was here again, her heart was beating rapidly, and her fingers trembled as she reached for the handle of the door.

If she had expected some positive reaction to her lateness, she was disappointed. When she entered the living room, she found Jake sprawled on the sofa reading a magazine, and his faintly drawn expression could have been accounted for in half a dozen different ways. She did not flatter herself that he had missed her, only that he might have wondered where she had gone.

"I'm sorry I'm late," she said, closing the door behind her, and his eyebrows arched dismissingly. "I . . . went for a drive. I needed time to think."

Jake put the magazine aside and swung his feet to the floor. "And have you?" he asked tautly. "Thought, I mean? I assume you've considered leaving. What is your decision?"

Lani sighed. "I want to stay."

"I see." Jake's cheeks hollowed for a moment, and then, reaching for one crutch, he hauled himself to his feet. "Well, I've been thinking, too."

Lani quivered. "Oh, yes?"

"Yes." Jake straightened, his expression somber. "I've decided to let you stay, too." He paused, as her eyes widened in surprise, and then went on. "I've decided I'd be a fool to let you go. This afternoon I realized I'd grown used to having you around. I don't want to be alone again."

Lani gulped. "You mean—"

"I mean I'm selfish enough to accept your offer of . . . friendship, companionship, call it what you will."

Lani gazed at him. "For how long?"

"I don't know." Jake flexed his fingers instinctively. "That's up to you, I suppose. You can work here. The desk upstairs should prove suitable for conversion, and I won't trouble you unless I have to."

"Oh, Jake!"

Lani would have gone to him then, but he quickly turned away, dragging himself toward the kitchen with determined steps. "I suggest we have some food," he said, jerking open the door, and Lani was left to wonder exactly what he meant.

CHAPTER SEVENTEEN

BY THE FOLLOWING MORNING, Lani had learned what Jake's compromise meant. After spending a lonely night in the comfortable bed upstairs and coming down to find Jake already dressed and ready for the day, she quickly realized his intention was to stifle all feeling between them. He had agreed to let her stay but it was not an emotive victory. It was more in the nature of an armistice. Hostilities would cease, but there was no question of a reconciliation.

It was not an easy draught to swallow, but short of creating further conflict between them, Lani had to accept it. She was still here, she told herself fiercely; he had not completely rejected her. It was up to her to prove her staying power, to show him she meant what she said.

"I—er—I'll have to go back to London to collect all my paints and drawing equipment," she ventured over the breakfast Hannah had prepared, and Jake cast a brooding glance in her direction.

"How long will that take?" he queried, arching one dark brow, and Lani licked her lips nervously before giving her reply.

"If—if I left later on this morning, I could be back by tomorrow night," she murmured, aware of his suspicious gaze. "I couldn't do it all in one day. I really ought to see Miles and explain."

"Miles?"

"Miles Rossiter. You remember? He's my agent. He's probably beginning to wonder when I'm coming back."

"I see." Jake pushed his coffee cup aside. "And will Rossiter try to persuade you to stay?"

"He may try," said Lani honestly. "But he won't succeed. I'll be back tomorrow night. I promise."

"You don't have to promise that to me," declared Jake harshly, suddenly thrusting back his chair and getting to his feet. "I shall survive, no doubt. I always have. Give my regards to your father. Tell him I half wish I had taken his advice."

Driving along the A30, Lani forced herself to accept the fact that she would have to get used to Jake's occasional spurts of cruelty. It was his escape valve; his way of releasing the pent-up frustration that was threatening to destroy him. He didn't mean it, she told herself, not very convincingly. He was only letting off steam. But it hurt nevertheless, and she wished they could have parted on more amicable terms.

She reached London in the late afternoon and drove immediately to Pelham Court, arriving there before her father got home from the office.

"Why, Lani, my dear," exclaimed Mrs. Evans, hearing her in the hall and bustling through from the kitchen. "You're a sight for sore eyes and no mistake. Oh, your father will be pleased. He's missed you, you know."

Lani's smile was faint, but she removed her coat and

laid it over the chest before pushing open the drawing-room door. "It's good to see you, Mrs. Evans," she responded, surveying the familiar room with troubled eyes. "Do you think I could have a sandwich? I haven't eaten a thing since this morning."

"Of course." Mrs. Evans was understanding. "You fetch your cases out of the car, and by the time you've put them upstairs, I'll have a nice cup of tea ready for you."

"I—don't have any cases, Mrs. Evans." Lani lifted her shoulders in a gesture of regret. "I'm not staying. At least, only tonight. I just came for some more of my things."

Mrs. Evans's lips parted. "You mean you're going back to Cornwall?"

"That's right."

Mrs. Evans shook her head. "Well, I don't know, I'm sure. Your father won't like it, Lani."

"I'm sorry." Lani turned away. "But my father has only himself to blame."

While Mrs. Evans was preparing her tea, Lani phoned Miles. "Lani!" he exclaimed, with evident relief. "Hell, I was beginning to think I'd have to hire a private detective to find you. What with your father denying all knowledge of your whereabouts and the publishers hounding me for the new book—" He broke off impatiently. "Anyway, you're back now, thank goodness. When can we meet?"

"It's not that simple, Miles." Lani gave a rueful sigh. "Look, all right, I'll see you this evening. But please, don't expect too much."

"You mean you haven't been working," said Miles

flatly. "Well, don't worry. I guess I can hold them off for a few weeks longer. Where shall we eat? My apartment? You have some explaining to do, young lady, and it might be easier done in private."

Lani hesitated. "I can't have dinner with you, Miles. I've got to talk to my father, too. I'll come round after we've eaten. Say about nine o'clock?"

"All right." Miles was obviously amazed that she had agreed to come to his apartment after holding off for so long. "I'll see you about nine. Don't keep me waiting."

Lani was in the bath when her father got home. She heard his car in the drive, and she was irresistibly reminded of that other occasion when his arrival home had aroused such panic inside her. It didn't panic her now, but it did stir feelings that were best forgotten. Feelings like anger and resentment and the bitter taste of betrayal that would never quite disperse.

Mrs. Evans must have told him she was home, for she was drying herself when her father knocked at her bedroom door. "Can I come in, Lani?" he called, his voice low and anxious, and Lani wrapped a robe around her before allowing him to enter.

"Hello, father," she greeted him politely, retreating behind a chair when he would have embraced her. "How are you? You look well. I imagine the warmer weather is more to your liking."

"Lani, Lani. . . ." Roger St. John spread his hands appealingly. "Must we go on with this? We're not strangers. We're father and daughter. You're treating me as if — well, as if we hardly knew one another."

"I'm sorry." Lani picked up her hairbrush from the dressing table and began stroking the bristles through her hair. "I thought it would be easier if we behaved as strangers. Anything else is likely to create unpleasantness."

"For mercy's sake, child, haven't you forgiven me yet?" Roger raised his eyes heavenward, as if seeking divine guidance. "Can't you understand? I did what I did out of jealousy. I wanted to see Clare squirm, I admit it. How was I to know how she would react?"

Lani found her hand was trembling, and replaced the brush on the tray. "It doesn't matter," she said unsteadily. "It's over now, and nothing you say can change the situation. I'd really rather not talk about it. That's not why I came home."

"At least you still regard this as your home," he exclaimed bitterly. "Though not for long, I hear. Mrs. Evans says you're returning to Cornwall. Is it true? Are you living with that man?"

Lani expelled her breath slowly. "I'm living in his house," she replied, letting him make what he liked of that. "I came back to get my work. I want to finish the book, and I've arranged to see Miles later this evening to explain the situation to him."

"I understood you couldn't work," said her father tersely. "Robin said—"

"I think I can now," Lani interrupted swiftly, realizing as she did so how amazing that was. "I'm going to try, anyway."

Her father sighed. "You've spoken to Rossiter, I suppose."

"On the phone this afternoon, yes."

"Did he tell you he's been pestering me here, trying to find out where you were?"

"But you wouldn't tell him."

"No." Her father clasped his hands together. "Do you think I'm proud of the fact that my daughter is cohabitating with the man my wife has discarded?" he demanded contemptuously. "For God's sake, Lani, come home for good. Jake Pendragon can be nothing but trouble for you."

MILES'S APARTMENT was just as sophisticated and modern as she had expected. He met her as she was parking her car in India Mews and escorted her inside the building with his hand beneath her elbow.

"You can't be too careful," he remarked as they entered the lift. "At this time of the night there can be some dubious characters around, and I shouldn't like to spoil our evening."

Lani managed a faint smile, but she detached herself from his lingering fingers as she did so, putting the width of the lift between them.

The apartment Miles unlocked was all chrome and teak and plate glass. Even the carpet, which was a shade off white, added to the impression of space-age living, and although Lani found it interesting, she preferred more traditional furnishings.

Accepting the offer of a drink, she seated herself on a cream leather couch, tensing a little as it sank toward the floor. With her eyes drawn to a cubist painting, she endeavored to make herself comfortable, wishing she'd chosen one of the tubular armchairs when Miles stretched his length beside her.

"So," he said, handing her the martini she had requested, "where have you been? I've rung around to all your friends and not even Robin had an inkling."

Lani sipped her martini slowly, and then said, "Did. . .did Robin tell you anything?"

"Should he have done?" Miles shrugged. "Only that you were finding it hard to settle down to writing again. Is that what you mean?"

Lani hesitated. "Did he mention Jake Pendragon?"

"Jake Pendragon?" Miles frowned. "You mean your mother's protégé? No. Why would he? Unless you've heard how he is since the accident?"

Lani sighed. "Yes. I've heard." She paused and then hurried on before she could change her mind. "That's where I've been, Miles. With Jake Pendragon."

Miles, who had been relaxing beside her on the low couch, now jerked upright. "You've been with Jake Pendragon?" he echoed incredulously. "Why, for heaven's sake? It wasn't your fault he was hurt. No, don't tell me your mother's got you playing nursemaid until she gets back! Lani, you can't—"

"It's nothing like that." Now Lani pushed herself up, too, getting to her feet and pacing restlessly around the room. "You don't understand, Miles. I ought to have told you before—when you came to visit me in the hospital. You asked why I was interested in Jake, and I should have explained."

"Explained? Explained what?" Miles gazed at her in dawning comprehension. "You can't mean. . .you're not. . .involved with him?"

Lani bent her head. "I'm in love with him, yes."

Miles uttered an oath. "You're not serious!"

"I am." Lani took a deep breath. "That's why I wanted to see you, to talk to you. I wanted to explain

where I'll be from now on, how you can get in touch
with me—"

"You mean you're living with him?"

Lani sighed. "Yes."

"Where? Not in London."

"In Cornwall, actually." Lani moistened her lips.
"His grandmother has a house midway between Helston and Penzance. You can leave a message for me
there."

Miles shook his head. "You're not living with his
grandmother then?"

"No." Lani hesitated, and then she admitted, "Jake
owns some property close by. He doesn't have a
phone."

"His grandmother's name's Pendragon, too?"

"Oh, no." Lani shook her head. "Her name is
Worth. Mrs. Worth. Tremorna Point. I don't know the
number, but I expect you can get it from directory inquiries."

Miles came to his feet looking slightly staggered. "I
can't believe this, you know," he muttered heavily.
"For pity's sake, Lani, whatever possessed you to get involved with him? He's—he's a cripple!"

"Don't ever use that word again," exclaimed Lani
fiercely, setting down her glass and reaching for the
coat she had discarded. "Jake's not a cripple. He's par-
tially disabled, that's all. And. . . and given time—"

"—he'll recover, I know," muttered Miles skeptically. "If you believed that, you wouldn't get so angry with
me for saying it."

Lani faced him squarely. "I don't really care," she
said, disrupting his scornful demeanor. "Whether Jake

recovers or not, I mean. Oh, I care because it's what he wants, but for myself, I'm quite happy as things are."

Miles pursed his lips. "Don't you mean that so long as Pendragon is crippled, you don't have any competition?" he suggested harshly, and Lani winced.

"No—"

"I don't believe you." Miles gazed at her impatiently. "Oh, Lani, what will you do if your mother comes back? If she takes it into her head that she wants him after all? What will he do if he has to choose between you and his career?"

IT WAS SIX O'CLOCK the following evening when Lani arrived back at Tremorna Point. Parking the car in its usual place, she hoped Mrs. Worth would not detain her today, and unpacked her things with a speed born of anxiety.

However, no one appeared to delay her, and draping the bag containing her sketching pad and painting materials over one shoulder, she tucked the portable drawing board under her arm. She had brought another suitcase of clothes, too, but she decided she would have to make two journeys. Tackling the cliff path was going to be arduous enough, and she was glad it was not as windy as it had been before.

Even so, she found the greatest difficulty coping with the easel and the heavy canvas holdall. She realized she should have brought the suitcase and the holdall together and gone back for the easel, but it was too late to turn back now. Once or twice the wooden struts of the drawing board caught in tussocks of grass, almost unbalancing her, and just when she thought she had safely made it, the legs went between the bars of the wooden handrail that led up to the veranda, and she was catapulted backward onto the rough earth.

Her cry of pain and frustration was instinctive, and she struggled to her feet again with real discomfort. She was glad she was wearing cords to protect her knees from the scrubby slope, but her spine felt bruised and she ached all over.

Hauling the offending article onto the veranda, she collected the holdall and thrust open the door. "It's me," she called in a small voice, somewhat chastened to think that Jake had not even troubled to come and see if she was hurt. But when she entered the room, she found it was empty.

"Jake!"

With a gesture of resignation, she managed to get her belongings inside the door and went in search of her quarry. She assumed he must be in the kitchen preparing something to eat, and that was why he had not heard her, but she found the kitchen was unoccupied also.

"Jake!"

Refusing to give in to a sense of apprehension, Lani ran up the stairs to the bedroom, pushing open the door without hesitation. But like the living room and the kitchen, the bedroom was deserted also, and panic gripped her as she came back down the stairs. Where was he? Where could he be, she asked herself frantically. Surely he couldn't be so cruel as to disappear without leaving any word.

"Oh, Jake. . ." she breathed miserably, sinking down onto the bottom step and burying her face in her hands, and as she did so she heard the sound of running water. Lifting her head, she realized someone was in the bathroom, and without giving any thought to the proprieties, she jumped up and opened the bathroom door.

"Who the hell — *Lani*!"

Jake's furious protest ended with the impatient use of her name, but Lani hovered in the doorway helplessly, too relieved to see him to pay any attention to his opposition. The realization that he was there before her, not miles away as she had suspected, was too emotional a revelation to dismiss, and the fact that his only article of attire was the cream towel around his hips was simply an added incentive to stand and stare.

"For Christ's sake, Lani, get out of here!" he ordered, reaching for the brown toweling robe he had discarded before bathing. But she forestalled him, snatching up the robe and holding it out for him.

Although he glared at her frustratedly, he had little choice but to do as she intended. Favoring his unscarred leg, he managed to turn so that she could slide the robe up over his shoulders, and her fingers tingled where they touched his smooth brown skin. She ached to put her lips against his flesh, to stroke her tongue along the fine, sun-bleached hairs that etched his spine and caress the muscled narrow line of his hips — but she didn't. She helped him on with the robe and then stepped back abruptly, saying in a low voice, "I didn't know where you were. I was worried."

"What do you mean?"

He turned again to face her, and Lani retreated to the open doorway. "Didn't you hear me calling you?"

she asked defensively. "I've even been upstairs looking for you. I—I fell off the veranda steps. If you're interested, that is."

Jake was hooking a crutch under his arm as she spoke, but her words brought his head up. "You fell off the steps?" he echoed tersely. "How the hell did you do that?"

"I was carrying my easel," said Lani, with a sniff. "You might ask if I hurt myself. Instead of looking so angry."

"I assume it was nothing too serious since you've been up and down the stairs," he responded bleakly. "But yes. As a matter of fact, I did hear you. That was when I decided to get out of the bath."

Lani hunched her shoulders. "You could have answered."

"Yes." Jake regarded her dourly. "However, as I didn't feel like greeting you in the manner to which you're no doubt accustomed, I decided to let you wait."

Lani pressed her lips together. "I gather you haven't missed me."

"Oh, you're wrong." But Jake's tawny eyes were not glittering with pleasurable anticipation. "This morning I desperately wished your neck was within reach of my hands, but of course it wasn't."

Lani blinked. "I don't understand."

"My grandmother came to see me," explained Jake harshly. "Now get out of here, will you? I would like to get dressed."

Lani gazed at him disbelievingly. "Your grandmother came to see you!" she exclaimed. "Mrs. Worth came here!"

"She's not an invalid, you know," said Jake grimly.
"She just likes to act like one. Close the door after you.
I'm getting cold."

Lani went out and closed the door half-bemusedly,
the realization that Jake's grandmother had taken the
trouble to come down here to see him overriding all
else. Mrs. Worth had actually walked down the cliff
path to see her grandson, and what was more amazing,
she had walked up it again. But why? Why now? Lani
trembled as she crossed the living-room floor to the
windows. Had her conversation with the old lady had
anything to do with it? And more important, had Mrs.
Worth told Jake they had talked together?

She was still standing there when Jake appeared,
dressed now in close-fitting fine wool pants and a dark
suede shirt with lacings at the neck. She noticed he
seemed to be managing quite adequately with only one
crutch now, and he had not replaced the bandages
on his hands since the night he had come to her bed.
In consequence, his hands were losing the pallor
that being denied the air had caused, and he had never
looked more disturbing or more dangerously vulnerable.

Miles's words came back to her with unwilling penetration, and she wondered what Jake would do if Clare
chose to interfere in his life again. If her mother
thought he was improving, she might just take another
chance, and whatever Jake's own feelings, Lani had no
doubts that Clare's interest was not wholly mercenary.
She had wanted Jake—the man and his music—and
given time and incentive, he might just forget....

"Why are you still wearing your coat?" he asked now,

and Lani looked down at her sheepskin jacket rather blankly.

"Oh, I've left the suitcase I brought in the car," she murmured uneasily. "I'll get it later. Shall I make some tea?"

"Not yet," said Jake flatly, propping himself on the arm of one of the couches. "Why didn't you tell me you'd seen the old lady? Were you afraid I'd throw you out if I thought you were fraternizing with the enemy?"

"She's not your enemy."

"Don't you believe it." Jake's lips twisted. "She wants to take me over—control me. Total command—isn't that the strategic word for it?"

Lani sighed. "She cares about you. She wants to help you."

"She wants to *own* me!"

"She came to see you."

"Because you shamed her into it," he retorted harshly.

"That's not true." Lani twisted her hands together. "She . . . she just wanted a reason. She's a very sad old woman."

"I can see she's got an ally in you."

"That's not true." Lani shook her head. "I didn't let her intimidate me, that's all."

"No?" Jake's short laugh had no humor in it. "Yet you managed to tell her everything about me. Even to my discharging myself from the hospital."

Lani's shoulders sagged. "I didn't intend to."

"Exactly. But my grandmother managed to worm the truth from you just the same."

Lani met his stormy gaze unwillingly. "What—what did she want?"

"To talk to me." Jake's mouth compressed.

"What about?"

Lani couldn't prevent the question, and Jake's eyes perceptibly narrowed. "Why should I tell you? You didn't confide in me."

"I would have, but—"

"—but you knew how I'd react," Jake finished for her caustically. "What's the matter? Did she ask you about our relationship?"

Lani bent her head. "Perhaps."

"You told her you were Clare's daughter, anyway."

"I didn't." Lani was indignant. "She already knew. In any case, what does it matter?"

Jake shook his head. "She thinks I should marry you," he remarked offhandedly, and Lani's face suffused with color. "Did you know that?"

"No." Lani resisted the impulse to turn away.

"I wonder what you said to make her change her mind about you," he added consideringly.

"Why ask me?" Lani retorted, with some difficulty. His careless words were more painful than he knew. "Is that the only reason she came to see you?"

"Not the only one, no." Jake's tone was flat now. "She came to assure herself that you had not walked out on me." He hesitated. "And to suggest that I avail myself of the services of the physiotherapist at the hospital in Penzance."

Lani held her breath. "And did you agree?"

"No."

"Oh."

She couldn't hide her disappointment, and the emotional strain of this conversation was becoming too much for her. For a moment she thought she had done some good, but obviously Jake's feelings toward his grandmother had not changed, and aware of his brooding gaze upon her, she shifted from one foot to the other.

"You give up easily, don't you?" he remarked suddenly, and her eyes darted to meet his. "The old lady doesn't," he added, his mouth twisting derisively. "This afternoon a physiotherapist arrived to see me. Summoned from Plymouth at my grandmother's request. She knew, as you evidently didn't, that I wouldn't turn the woman away."

Lani blinked. "A woman?"

"A Miss Shelley. By the time she'd finished with me, I felt worse than I did immediately after the car hit me."

Lani nodded. "So that was why—"

"—I was taking a bath at this hour of the day, yes," he finished for her. "To try and ease my aching muscles!"

Lani tried to smile. "She must have done some good then."

"Because I was in agony?" Jake was sardonic.

"No." Lani sighed. "But it may help."

"Save me the platitudes." Jake shook his head. "Enough to say that once again the old lady has got her own way."

"She means well."

"I imagine the same could have been said of Pandora, before she opened the box." Jake's eyes held hers. "But I am tempted to call her bluff."

"What do you mean?"

"I mean—perhaps I should marry you," he remarked dispassionately, and Lani's knees trembled beneath her.

"M—marry me?" she breathed, hardly daring to believe he was serious, and Jake nodded.

"Why not?" he asked bleakly. "What a surprise the old lady will have when she discovers Clare Austin's daughter can be just as two-faced as her mother!"

"Must you be so callous?"

Lani shivered in revulsion, and now she did turn away, her breast heaving as she fought to govern the anguish his bitterness had evoked. He had said some harsh things to her in the past, but this was by far the cruellest, and her nails dug into her palms as she tried to control her feelings.

"Well?"

His taunting request for an answer forced her to turn her head, and mastering the ball of misery in her throat, she managed to say scornfully: "You don't really expect me to take your proposal seriously, do you?"

"Don't I?"

His unblinking stare was almost her undoing, but although Lani desperately wanted to accept, she knew there would be no future for her on his terms. "We can all have second thoughts, you know," she said, over her shoulder. "You shouldn't—"

"What kind of second thoughts?" Jake pushed himself up from the arm of the sofa, his irony disappearing beneath a sudden surge of hostility. Grasping her shoulder, he swung her around to face him, and although his torment wrung her heart, she knew she must not give in. "I thought it was what you wanted," he added harshly. "Or has living here with me already begun to pall?"

"I . . . perhaps it has." Lani moistened her dry lips with a tentative tongue. "Or perhaps I need more time to consider your offer."

"Well, forget it!" Jake's catlike eyes spat fire. "The offer's withdrawn. It should never have been made in the first place. You're right. We all have second thoughts. And mine are more inflexible than yours."

Lani's nerve cracked. "Jake . . . ."

But he was not listening to her. With aggressive speed, he was propelling himself across the floor, and only when he reached the door did he pause. "I expect you'll be leaving," he said coldly. "Perhaps you'd let Hannah know, so she doesn't bring more food than I can stomach!"

CHAPTER EIGHTEEN

THE REGENCY ROOM of the Bentynck Hotel was crowded with people, and Lani, sipping her third glass of champagne, endeavored to look as if she was enjoying herself. After all, this reception was being held on her behalf, and she owed it to her publishers to behave as if she was flattered by their enthusiasm for the new book. It was amazing that the story of Matilda and Mogbat had appeared at all, completed as it had been in the least auspicious circumstances. But at last the proofs had been checked and the artwork approved, and *Matilda's New Apprentice* was ready to meet its readers.

The trouble was, Lani was always uneasy when she was away from the Sea House. Leaving Jake alone was something she seldom did, and although she knew he would not thank her for it, she never stayed in London longer than was necessary.

Not that she flattered herself he missed her. On the contrary, since Mrs. Worth had insisted that Hannah divided her time equally between her house and that of her grandson, Jake was never alone for long, and the housekeeper's presence had helped to alleviate the strained situation between him and Lani. In addition, Judith Shelley, his physiotherapist, visited almost every day, and while she was working with her patient, Lani tended to keep out of the way.

The past three months had not been easy. It had taken a great deal of determination to stay on after that disastrous scene with Jake, particularly when she knew she had brought the present situation on herself. But Jake's proposal had taken her completely by surprise, and although she had desperately wanted to accept, his reasons for making it had robbed her of that right. She knew Jake had expected her to leave—and indeed there were times when she wondered exactly why she stayed—but something, some lingering hope that all could not be lost, kept her at the Sea House, the brunt of Jake's sarcasm and his anger.

The fact that Mrs. Worth had become her ally was of little comfort to her. Lani could not help but blame Jake's grandmother for the deterioration in their relationship. Besides, Jake blamed Lani for encouraging his grandmother's interference in his affairs, and the fact that he was getting better, that his muscles were becoming supple and his manipulative powers stronger, seemed no consolation.

The night he had come to her bed and comforted her—the night he had made love to her—seemed very far away now. Such contact as they had was chiefly confined to impersonal matters except on those occasions when Jake chose to aim his caustic wit in her direction. They were not frequent occasions, and Lani suspected the level of whiskey in the decanter that Hannah kept filled had much to do with it. Nevertheless, she dreaded those nights when he chose to sit and stare at her across the firelit width of the hearth, his tawny eyes appraising her and belittling her attempts to remain composed. His words were always insolent, the manner of their delivery sardonic, and Lani was left in little doubt of his contempt for her.

Yet, still she stayed, weathering his humiliation and his contempt, convincing herself, not very successfully, that eventually things would improve. She realized that if someone had told her two people could live together as she and Jake were doing, sharing the same house, yet living apart, she would not have believed them. But it could happen. She had ample proof of that. And only the fact that Jake had not actually thrown her out left her any room for hope.

It hurt badly, particularly when she knew he was not so uncommunicative with Hannah or with Judith Shelley. Sometimes, when Lani was working upstairs, she heard him laughing with the physiotherapist, and on those occasions she had to set her jaw against the bitter pangs of jealousy. Not that Judith encouraged her fears. On the contrary, although she was an expert at her job, she was no femme fatale, and she and Lani often shared a cup of coffee together after Jake had gone to take his shower. Even so, she could not help resenting the hours they spent together, hours that she and Jake might have shared. . . .

"Having a good time?"

Miles's affectionate voice in her ear and his arm slipping lightly around her waist brought Lani out of her reverie. She turned to look at him ruefully. "Not very," she confessed, lifting the heat-dampened weight of her hair from her neck. "It's very warm in here. How soon do you think I can leave?"

"Well. . . ." Miles glanced around. "The speeches are over and the champagne's almost gone. I should think we could leave quite soon, if that's what you'd like. You are going to have dinner with me, aren't you? I know a delightful little pub on the river where they serve the most delicious scampi you've ever tasted."

Lani hesitated. "Well. . . "

"Lani, you promised!"

"I know I did." She sighed. "Oh, all right. But I mustn't be late back. I want to leave for Cornwall first thing in the morning."

Miles shook his head. "So soon!"

Lani shrugged. "Of course. Why not?"

"Oh, I don't know." Miles expelled his breath resignedly. "I suppose I'm wondering how long this situation is going to last."

Lani arched one quizzical brow. "What situation?"

"Don't be coy." Miles grimaced. "Your commuting between here and Cornwall, of course. I mean, it's not as if you're married to him or anything."

Lani bent her head. "That's my affair."

"It's mine too," Miles contradicted earnestly. "I care about you, Lani, you know I do. Why, I'd even hoped—" He broke off then, but she knew what he had been about to say. "I just don't like Pendragon taking advantage of you like this," he went on. "I know it's not really my place to say so, but dammit, Lani, I can't pretend to approve of your relationship."

Lani lifted her shoulders. "You don't know what our relationship is, Miles."

"I know you're living together," he retorted roughly. "I'm not a complete fool. Jake Pendragon's not the kind of man to...well, to waste his opportunities."

Lani forced a tight smile. "I'd never have expected prudishness from you, Miles."

"It's not prudishness," he retorted. "I just don't want you to get hurt, that's all. And Pendragon will hurt you. I know it."

Lani turned her head away. "I'd rather not talk about it."

Miles sighed. "All right. All right. So how is he, anyway? Has he heard from your mother?"

"Why do you keep bringing my mother's name into this?" Lani pressed her annoyingly unsteady lips together. "I've told you, Clare is still in the United States. She's not interested in Jake anymore — in either of us!"

Miles shrugged. "If you say so."

"I do say so." Lani walked jerkily toward the door. "Are you coming? Or shall I take a taxi home?"

Lani spent the night at Pelham Court as usual, but she was awake at first light and packing her case into the boot of the Capri when Roger St. John came downstairs. Her relationship with her father was still extremely fragile, and he made no comment when she said she wasn't stopping for breakfast.

"Drive carefully, darling," was his only concession to his anxieties, and Lani offered her cheek for his kiss with more warmth than of late.

"Look after yourself," she murmured, relieved to see that the warmer weather had routed the unhealthy pallor of his illness. "Tell Mrs. Evans goodbye, will you? And thank her for pressing my shirts."

"I will." Her father lifted his hand in farewell. "See you soon."

Lani's journey was completed in record time. In spite of the fact that the holiday season had begun, the roads on this midweek morning were not crowded, and her early start had given her an advantage. The weather, too, was favorable. An early morning mist gave way to a shimmering heat, and the chimneys and spires of villages glimpsed at the side of the motorway wavered in the haze. For the first time, she felt an unfamiliar, and not altogether welcome, sense of homecoming, as the orderly acres of Wiltshire and Somerset gave way to the wilder reaches of the West country. She knew this road so well now, and with the sun casting its brilliance over moors and streams, and the distant elusive luster of the sea, she couldn't help a feeling of identity.

She hoped Mrs. Worth was not watching out for her as she turned between the gates of the house on Tremorna Point. Since her unexpected visit to the Sea House, Jake's grandmother seemed to have acquired a new lease on life, and she no longer spent all her days closeted in her bedroom. According to Hannah, she insisted on getting dressed most mornings, and instead of issuing her instructions from her bed, she issued them from the chaise longue in the drawing room.

As Lani drove around the house now, she thought how much better it looked without the concealing bars of the shutters. Although it would never be a handsome dwelling, in the afternoon sunlight it did have a certain elegance. Like me, thought Lani ruefully, viewing her thin arms without pleasure. Somehow, these days, she seldom had any appetite, and although she ate enough to live on, she took little enjoyment from it. Always at the back of her mind was the troublesome anxiety of wondering what the future might hold, and even today, with the sea like a benediction, sucking softly against the rocks below her, she knew the familiar sense of apprehension she invariably felt after being away from the Sea House for any length of time.

Mrs. Worth had not sent Hannah to intercept her, and she started down the cliff path with some relief. It was always difficult to be civil when she was obsessed with how Jake was and what mood he might be in, and her pulse quickened automatically when she saw the roof of the house below her.

She paused to take a breath, sweeping back the red gold curtain of hair, which had grown so much longer lately since she had given up going to the hairdresser's. She would braid it tonight, she thought, and looking forward to the coolness of a glass of iced water, and as she bent to pick up her case again, then she heard the sound she had heard once before. Softly on the still afternoon air she heard the unmistakable notes of a piano, and her heart pounded in her chest as she stumbled forward.

She didn't know why, but her footsteps slowed as she neared the steps leading up to the veranda. The music—for it *was* music, tuneful lyrical music— was much louder here, and although she told herself it must be the radio, or a record player on the stereo, she was loath to intrude. To her knowledge, Jake had never shown any interest in any form of music since his incapacitation, and even the thought that he might have changed his mind was enough to hold her motionless. That it might actually be Jake playing was too much to hope; it was beyond her capabilities, and she didn't even know if she wanted to find out. The fact that he was doing whatever it was he was doing in her absence was a potent deterrent, and she stood there transfixed as the melody washed over her. It was not a piece she had heard before, she realized, but somehow she felt sure she would hear it again. It had that certain indefinable appeal that made it stand out from the ordinary, and with this thought came another that caused her to tighten her lips impatiently: it was not Jake's kind of music!

It was not Brahms or Beethoven, it was not Chopin or Rachmaninoff; it was not classical music at all. She was standing there worrying over whether she should interrupt his listening, when all the time it was probably Hannah, or that niece of hers, Susan, tuned in to the top twenty on the radio.

Abandoning her hesitancy, Lani climbed the steps and swung across the slats of the veranda to the door. She was not best pleased at the thought that Jake might be entertaining Susan in her absence, and she swung open the door with a distinct lack of discretion.

The music stopped immediately and Lani, halfway into the room, halted disconcertedly. Although Jake was not now playing, he had evidently been doing so, and the speed with which she had made her entrance had prevented him from putting the necessary distance between himself and the piano. Instead, he sat there motionless at the keys. Lani's mouth and throat dried up at the realization of what she had done. She would have given anything to have been able to turn around and walk out again, without his having seen her, but it was too late, she had to make the best of it, and she shook her head bewilderedly as he reached for his walking stick.

"You're early," he said, taking the onus from her and getting to his feet. Lately, he had been able to abandon the use of the crutches altogether, and although she knew he still had a lot of pain with his knee, he was no longer incapable of walking unaided.

"I—yes," she answered, dropping her suitcase to the floor and closing the door behind her. "Umm...I'm sorry."

Jake disregarded her apology as he made his way to the table, where a jug of iced lemon juice stood on a tray. Pouring some into a glass, he surprised her still further by bringing the glass back to her and offering it. "Take it," he said, as she made a hesitant gesture. "You look as if you need it."

Lani took the glass gratefully and swallowed at least a third of its contents immediately. "Thank you," she said, aware of him watching her. "I was terribly thirsty. How did you know?"

Jake's lips twisted. "I didn't. You just looked as if you were about to pass out. You'd better sit down. I guess the heat's getting to you."

"It's not the heat."

The defensive words spilled helplessly from Lani's lips, but then, realizing he was unlikely to confide in her, she walked on somewhat unsteady legs to the sofa and sat down. He was right. She did feel decidedly shaken, and she didn't know how to handle the confused turmoil of her thoughts. What did it mean, she asked herself incredulously. How long had this been going on? And more important, why had he been playing in secret, when he must know how much it would mean to her?

Jake circled the sofa to take the seat opposite, lean and disturbing in an open-necked collarless T-shirt and tight-fitting cotton pants. His feet were encased in rubber-soled track shoes, and they extended into Lani's line of vision as he stretched his legs across the hearth between them.

"Why are you looking like that?" he inquired brusquely, and Lani permitted herself a swift glance up at him. But she didn't say anything, and massaging his thigh, he added, "What do you expect me to do? Apologize?"

"Oh, no." Lani spoke accusingly. "No, I wouldn't expect that from you." She had recovered herself somewhat now, and resentment was taking the place of consternation. "Just tell me honestly, it was you playing, wasn't it? Evidently your improvement has been greater than I thought."

Jake expelled his breath impatiently. "Don't be a fool! I was...playing around, that's all. It was nothing demanding, believe me. Just a piece I wrote several years ago, when I believed my only future was in composition."

Lani met his brooding gaze. "You wrote...that piece?"

"For my sins, yes. Why? Was it so bad?"

"No." Lani was as vehemently honest as before.

"No. No, it was terrific, really! I—I loved it. I thought it was a pop tune."

"Oh, great!" Jake grimaced, but somehow she didn't think he was angry with her.

"It's true." Lani was enthusiastic. "Did you ever try to get it published?"

"No." Jake regarded her tolerantly. "It's not that easy, believe me."

"But it's good!" Lani protested. "Have you written any others?"

Jake's mouth turned down at the corners. "Not recently, no."

Lani flushed. "I don't mean recently."

Jake shrugged. "Some, I guess. Before I went to seek my fortune in the States." He was ironic.

Lani ignored his sarcasm. "Well, I think you should let someone see them—hear them."

"Do you?" Jake tipped his head back against the upholstery. "You think I might be nurturing another talent?" He was mocking. "Forget it, Lani. I'm finished with music."

Lani sighed. "But you can play the piano...."

"I can strum the keys," he corrected her flatly. "That's not playing."

"It's better than you did before," she reminded him fiercely, but Jake shook his head.

"I was...teasing," he said carefully. "That day I made that cacophony of sound, I was only trying to show you how futile it was."

Lani stared at him. "You mean—" She glanced toward the piano. "You mean, you could always play like that?"

"Well...." Jake pulled a wry face. "Not quite as well, perhaps. I have had some practice."

Lani's jaw quivered. "Without telling me!"

"When you were not here," he amended.

"What a rotten thing to do!"

"As you say." His mouth tightened. "However, I intended telling you eventually."

"I don't believe you."

"Please yourself." His brief mood of amicability was dispersing, and Lani could see the familiar signs of hostility creeping back into his expression. But she couldn't remain silent.

"I suppose Hannah knows all about it," she flared. "And Judith! I suppose she feels it's all down to her!"

"Judith recommended I use my hands as much as possible, yes," he conceded, infuriating her still further, and Lani sprang up from the sofa.

"You—you're despicable," she exclaimed fiercely, her breast heaving with the force of her emotions. "You knew how much this would mean to me, and yet you deliberately hid it from me!"

"And you wonder why?" he countered harshly, rising to face her. "I knew this would happen. I knew how you'd react. For God's sake, Lani, stop dramatizing the situation!"

"Dramatizing the situation!" she echoed disbelievingly. "You tell me you've been playing the piano behind my back, and because I'm hurt that you didn't confide in me, you accuse me of overreacting!"

Jake expelled his breath wearily. "I didn't want you to build up your hopes unnecessarily," he retorted.

"Oh, really?" Lani gazed at him scornfully. "Or

were you secretly hoping to resume your career without telling me!"

"Don't be ridiculous!"

"What's so ridiculous?" Miles's words came back to her with unwanted clarity. "Has my mother been in touch with you? Is that what it is? Has she told you she's prepared to give you another chance, so long as you promise to be a good boy this time?"

Jake's face contorted. "You're crazy!"

"Am I? I wonder."

With a stifled sob, Lani whirled about, unwilling to let him see how he had upset her. She ought to walk out of here right now, she told herself bitterly. He was a liar and a cheat, and she was simply destroying herself by remaining.

"Lani—"

His frustrated use of her name was like an abrasive caress, and just when she was deciding she needed some time to think this out, his tortured breath seared the exposed curve of her neck. He was so close she could feel the heat of his body even through the cotton overalls she had worn for traveling, and her lungs constricted when his hands gripped her waist. Unable to resist, she was drawn back against the hard length of his body, and as her heart fluttered uncontrollably his tongue brushed the sensitive skin of her neck. It was warm and moist and unbearably sensuous, and she felt herself yielding against him, inviting him to go on.

With a groan, his teeth ground into the soft flesh below her ear, hurting her and exciting her all at once, making her twist sinuously against his body, inciting his desire. It was so long since he had touched her, so long since he had held her and kissed her and let her feel the effect she was having on him. He turned her around to face him, and she felt his pulsating tautness pressing against her stomach.

"If only I didn't want you so much," he grated, cradling her face between his two hands and gazing down at her with smoldering eyes. Then, when her lips parted in protest, he lowered his head and the hungry pressure of his mouth moved over hers.

It was a violent, passionate invasion of her innermost feelings. His kiss left her weak and helpless, incapable of preventing the intimate exploration of her body that accompanied it. His hands moved knowingly from her breasts to her thighs, sliding inside the overalls to seek beneath the hem of the short-sleeved cotton shirt she wore with them. Her breasts swelled, the nipples hardening instinctively, and his tongue plunged deeply into her mouth as he molded their aching fullness.

Lani's senses swam, her loins throbbing in expectation of his touch. She wanted him to touch her, everywhere, but more than that she wanted the possession of his body, invading her, filling her. . . .

Automatically her hands reached for him, pushing his shirt aside so she could bury her face in the fine hair that arrowed down over his flat stomach. She wanted to touch him and taste him, to take him into her and possess him as his fingers were possessing her. Her hands moved down over his chest to the revealing tautness of his pants, finding his zip and propelling it downward. She could feel the throbbing urgency of his desire beneath her fingers, and he shuddered convulsively at that intimate caress.

"Christ, Lani—" he choked against her lips, and then they both froze at the sound of footsteps mounting to the veranda.

All at once she was free, and as she hurried to restore her clothes to some semblance of order, Jake composed himself. By the time Judith Shelley—for it was the physiotherapist—knocked at the door, his expression was quite impassive, and only Lani was aware of the smoldering passion in his eyes and the pulse beating erratically at his temple.

"You're back," were Judith's first words when Lani opened the door to her, and the younger woman nodded unnecessarily and stepped awkwardly aside.

"Earlier than expected," she agreed, exchanging an oblique look with Jake, and his mouth twitched at the silent communication before he moved to greet his guest.

Judith entered the room without hesitation, obviously unaware of any undercurrents between them. She was approximately the same height as Lani but of a heavier build, and obviously in fine physical condition. She was a pleasant girl, and extremely feminine in her attitudes, sharing with Lani a love of casual clothes and French perfume and the poems of the great romantics.

"Well," she said, when she saw Jake moving without the aid of his stick. "You're evidently feeling much better than when I last saw you." She turned to Lani. "Two days ago when I came, he was as grumpy as a bear. And distinctly uncooperative."

"Was he?"

Lani's eyes had widened at this unexpected piece of information, but although she looked to Jake for confirmation, he was not responsive. "I don't think Lani wants to hear about that, Judith," he declared, glancing behind him for the stick he had apparently decided he needed after all. "Where do you want me? Here or on the veranda?"

"What an offer!" gurgled Judith delightedly, but Jake was in no mood to respond to her teasing.

"Can we get on with it?" he demanded, challenging Lani's probing gaze. Judith shrugged at Lani behind his back, before agreeing that outdoors might be best.

"It's so warm, isn't it?" she murmured to Lani, as Jake preceded her outside, and Lani nodded absently, too wrapped up in her own thoughts to pay Judith a lot of attention. The information that Jake had been objectionable earlier in the week was too disturbing to ignore. She had left for London on Monday morning. Jake must have missed her after all, and his resentment was due to the time she spent away from the Sea House—and him!

It was such a tantalizing conclusion that the time Judith spent giving Jake his treatment passed in a daze. Although Lani went out to the kitchen and prepared a fresh jug of iced fruit juice, she was hardly conscious of what she was doing, and she was most surprised when she returned to the living room to find that the physiotherapist had left. Only Jake was on the veranda, stretched out on the cushioned divan that Judith made use of for his massage.

When Lani emerged from the house, he regarded

her through narrowed eyes. He had shed his shirt and pants and was lying there with a towel draped across his hips. He looked lean and brown and healthy, and Lani's nails curled into her palms as she anticipated what must happen next.

"You look relaxed," she murmured, tucking her hands inside the bib of the overalls to hide their trembling. But Jake had noticed. With a lithe movement he swung his feet to the floor, and wrapping the towel securely around him, he rose to his feet.

"I'll go and take a shower," he said, moving purposefully toward the door, and Lani stepped into his path.

"Not yet," she breathed, putting out her hand to touch him, but he neatly sidestepped her fingers.

"I think I must," he retorted smoothly, reaching the corner of the building. "Sit down. Take it easy. I won't be long." He paused. "You and I have things to talk about."

Lani pressed her lips together. "Can't we talk about them now?" she pleaded, taking a step toward him, but Jake shook his head.

"I'm not decent," he declared, looking down at the towel, and Lani shook her head.

"You are to me."

"No, Lani," he said harshly. "No, I'm not." And without a backward glance, he turned the corner of the veranda, disappearing into the building with unaccustomed speed.

By the time he returned, Lani was feeling decidedly dejected. She had seated herself on the divan with her back propped against the wall of the house, but although the sun was still shining, she was far from contented. Something was wrong, she told herself fiercely. She knew it. Judith's inopportune arrival had done more than postpone their lovemaking. It had destroyed whatever it was that had brought them together, and Lani's heart was heavy as Jake emerged from the house.

"Do you want a drink?" he inquired, indicating the glass in his hand, but Lani shook her head and concentrated on the sun spots dancing on the water below her. She was miserably close to tears, and she was no longer convinced she could go on as before, if that was what Jake expected.

Jake considered the contents of his glass and then set it down on the windowsill behind the divan. He seemed withdrawn and ill at ease, and Lani wondered bitterly what had happened to change his mood.

When she didn't look up again, he moved to the rail of the veranda and propped his back against it. Then, folding his arms, he said quietly, "I want you to leave, Lani. Today. Tonight. As soon as possible. I can't trust myself with you anymore, and I want you to go."

Lani looked up then, her breath catching in her throat. "You . . . expect me to go?"

"Yes." He was adamant.

"But I don't want to go." Faced with the alternatives, Lani knew she would rather do anything than leave him. "Before Judith came, we—"

"Before Judith came I lost my head," he declared bitterly. "I'm sorry, but you asked for it. What happened? Did your London boyfriend let you down or something?"

Lani gasped. "I don't have a London boyfriend."

"No?"

"No. You know I don't. Jake, what is this all about?"

Jake's lips curled. "That man—Rossiter; he seems very attentive."

"Miles is my agent!"

"I know he's always sending messages. Via Hannah, of course."

Lani couldn't believe this. "Jake, they were business messages. He was concerned about the new book."

"Was he?" Jake considered her broodingly.

"Yes." Lani pushed herself to her feet. "Jake, are you jealous?"

"Why should I be?" His tone was bleak. "I have no exclusive rights to your company."

Lani shook her head bewilderedly. "I don't understand any of this."

"Don't you?" Jake looked skeptical. "And I suppose throwing your mother's name into the conversation earlier was just accidental, wasn't it?"

Lani sighed. "My mother has nothing to do with it."

"Hasn't she?"

"No." Lani took a deep breath. "Jake, can't we talk about this civilly? We've lived together too long—"

"We have not *lived* together," he contradicted her harshly. "We have shared the same house, that's all. Oh, I realize now I was crazy to let you stay here, but as long as I kept my hands off you, you were no real threat. Then this afternoon—well, I guess you proved the need was still there. That I hadn't destroyed it, only subdued it for a while. And I can't live with that."

Lani stared at him incredulously. "Why?"

"Because I don't want that kind of arrangement."

"I don't believe you."

"You're going to have to."

"Jake, you said you cared about me!"

Jake regarded her coldly. "Things were different then."

"How different?"

"I was still living with the delusion that you cared about me."

"But I do." Lani spread her hands. "You know I do."

"I'm not talking about pity, Lani."

"Nor am I!"

"But you didn't feel strongly enough to accept a permanent relationship!" he stated grimly.

"A permanent relationship!" Lani was confused. "I don't know what you mean."

"Of course you do," he grated angrily. "The afternoon I told you the old lady had been here. I seem to remember offering you a partnership you turned down."

Lani's lips parted. "You mean . . . your *proposal*?"

"You remember." He was coldly sardonic.

Lani gulped. "But you weren't serious."

"Wasn't I?"

"You said you'd call your grandmother's bluff."

"I may have said something of the kind."

"You know you did." Lani gazed at him in dismay. "You knew I would refuse on those terms. You *wanted* me to refuse."

"Did I?"

"Stop baiting me, Jake. You can't really believe I'd refuse to marry you." Her knees shook. "Why otherwise would I have stayed?"

"I've asked myself that question many times."

"And?"

"I've found no satisfactory answer until today."

"Oh, *Jake*!"

The tears she had been fighting back for almost an hour suddenly overflowed, and turning away she fumbled desperately for a tissue. It was all too much for her: the sense of betrayal she had felt when she had found him playing the piano, the emotional storm that had followed it, the terrible sense of anticlimax when Jake left her on the veranda, and now the unbelievable agony of his sending her away. She sobbed as if her heart would break, and the man leaning on the veranda rail gazed at her averted head in grim frustration.

"God, Lani—" he began, leaving the rail to approach her, but she pressed herself against the wall of the house and would not look at him.

It was then that she saw it, the corner of a white envelope lying on the slats of the veranda, almost hidden beneath the divan. Half wild with grief, half blind with tears, she nevertheless bent to retrieve it, and turning it over, she gazed at it through a haze of tears. The significance of its postmark might not have alerted her to the identity of the sender, but the handwriting was too distinctive to be ignored. The letter was from her mother, addressed to Jake.

Jake had stopped when she picked up the letter, now, when she raised her drowned green eyes to him, waiting—although she was not consciously aware of it—for his explanation, he shrugged.

"Read it," he said flatly, making no attempt to offer a defense, but Lani threw the envelope onto the divan, as if by touching it she was contaminating herself.

"I don't need to read it," she choked. "I can guess what it says. Somehow, I don't know how, Clare's poisoned your mind against me, hasn't she? After all this time, you'd still sooner believe her than me."

"I don't know what to believe anymore." Jake's mouth compressed. "I thought I could trust you—"

"And now you don't?" Lani quivered. "Why? What has she said? That it wasn't her driving the car after all? That it was me?"

"Don't be foolish—"

"What's so foolish? I thought I could trust *you*, and now I find you've been corresponding with my mother behind my back."

"I have not been corresponding with your mother." His tone was harsh. "What do you think I am?"

"I'm beginning to wonder."

"What do you mean?"

"Well—" Lani spoke recklessly, not stopping to choose her words. "It does seem strange that she should write to you now, doesn't it? Just when you're beginning to recover. If I wasn't so gullible, I might think you had written to her. Asking her to lend a helping hand!"

"You think that?" His voice was taut.

"Why not?" Lani spoke tremulously. "She helped you once before. Why not again?"

Jake's face was set and cold. "What are you imply-ing?"

Lani shrugged, bent on a course of self-destruction. "How do I know why she made you her protégé? I've only your word that it was a business arrangement. Perhaps it wasn't. Perhaps the terms were rather more personal. Is that why she's written? To check on her investment?"

The draft of Jake's passing hand chilled her cheek, but he did not strike her. At the last moment, he drew back, and his fingers passed harmlessly in front of her face. But the reason for his anger did not go away. It remained between them like an impenetrable barrier, and Lani knew there was nothing more she could say.

"Get out of my sight!" he said distinctly, and the quiet words were more terrifying than the heat of his anger. Now there was no emotion, only cold deter-mination, and with a helpless sob, she ran into the house.

CHAPTER NINETEEN

"THIS IS NICE." Miles walked around the living room of the apartment, nodding his approval. "You've got good taste. I always knew it. But are you sure you're going to be happy living here alone?"

"Oh, I think so." Lani swung away so that he should not see her face. Just occasionally, questions like that still had the power to distress her, but gradually she was learning to live with herself again. In less than a moment she was turning to offer Miles a drink. "Scotch or sherry," she said. "I'm afraid you don't have a great deal of choice. But the whisky is a malt one. My father sent it as a kind of apartment-warming gift."

Miles accepted the Scotch and lounged onto the couch, surveying the room again with admiring eyes. "I must say you've worked wonders with the woodwork. It was quite a sickly shade of green, if I remember correctly."

"It was only paint, put on over the original grain," explained Lani, handing him his drink. "I simply stripped the wood back to its natural color and stained it myself."

"You make it sound easy," exclaimed Miles impatiently. "You must have spent hours on it."

"Well, yes, I did." Lani curled her legs beneath her on the cushioned rocker she had bought in the saleroom, remembering with some gratitude how thankful she had been to be able to work herself to physical exhaustion after her return from Cornwall. "But I enjoyed it. And you must admit, I did have good materials to work with."

"Well, yes." Miles was honest. "But I can't deny I wouldn't have preferred you to be working on another book instead of playing around at do-it-yourself."

"I wasn't playing around." Lani looked about her with real satisfaction. "This is my home, Miles. I'm going to live here for a long time. I wanted it to be as I had designed it, not someone else."

Miles shrugged. "Oh, well, you've finished now, haven't you? How long is it since you moved in? Three weeks, four weeks?"

"It's six weeks actually," said Lani, sipping the sherry she had poured for herself. "Would you like another Scotch? Or are you hurrying off somewhere?"

Miles grimaced. "Is that a polite way of saying you don't want my company for dinner?"

Lani gave a rueful smile. "Well, I was planning on having an early night."

"All right. I can take the hint. But I will have another Scotch, thank you. Before I take myself off to my lonely bachelor pad."

Lani uncoiled herself and went to pour him another drink, but this time when she held the glass out for him to take, he took hold of her wrist instead. "How long?" he asked, his eyebrows lifting in interrogation. "How long before you thaw out, ice maiden? It's been nearly two months. You can't go on like this. Sooner or later, you've got to crack."

"Let go of my wrist, Miles." Lani freed herself with determination, and after setting down his glass on the low table beside the couch, she retreated to her chair. "That wasn't fair," she said, after she was seated again. "I don't interfere in your life, and you shouldn't interfere in mine. The Lani you see is the only Lani there is. Now, can we please talk about something else?"

Miles regarded her impatiently. "Why won't you talk to me?"

"I thought that's what we were doing. Talking."

"You know what I mean." Miles looked at her over the rim of his glass. "Have you seen your mother yet? You must know she's back in London."

Lani sighed. "Miles, I've just asked you—"

"—to mind my own business, yes, I know. But you are my business, Lani, and you're just burning yourself up."

"Me?" Lani forced a short laugh. "You just said I hadn't done any work."

"That's not what I mean and you know it." Miles shook his head. "Since you came back from Cornwall you've been all tied up inside yourself, and unless you let yourself unwind, you're going to have a nervous breakdown."

"Oh, thanks." Lani tilted her head back against the chair. "That's all I needed to know."

"Lani, stop it." Miles swallowed the remainder of his drink and got to his feet to gaze down at her. "I've bitten my tongue for the past two months, but I'm damned if I'm going to stand by and watch you tear yourself to pieces without even trying to stop you."

"Oh, really, Miles. . . ." Lani adopted a bored tone, but he was not deceived.

"I mean it," he said. "I'm not leaving here until you tell me what happened in Cornwall. For God's sake, Lani, what did Pendragon do?"

Lani swung her feet to the floor. "It's very sweet of you, Miles, but really, you're dramatizing the situation. My. . .relationship with—with Jake. . .is over. I told you. We agreed to part."

"Just like that?"

"Just like that."

"I don't believe you."

"That's your prerogative."

"Lani, stop it!" Miles stood his empty glass on the table. "I've known you too long not to be able to tell when something is wrong. And as your father's not doing anything about it, I intend to."

"Shall we leave my father out of this?" Lani drew a steadying breath and rose to face him. "Miles, I know you mean well, but I don't need your help, honestly. If—if I've been a little. . . withdrawn lately, well, I suppose that's because I've been working so hard to get the apartment straight. Once I get back to work. . . ." She forced a smile. "Give me time."

"The story of my life," muttered Miles bitterly, and when she arched an inquiring brow, he grimaced. "Giving you time," he explained. "Time to see your mother—time to spend with your father—time to get over Pendragon's accident—time to kill yourself, perhaps?"

Lani flushed. "Don't be silly."

"It's not silly to try and stop someone from hurting themselves, is it?"

"Miles, I'm not hurting myself!"

"No." He regarded her dourly. "I should imagine Pendragon's done a pretty good job in that direction."

"Oh, Miles!"

"Isn't it true?"

Lani bend her head. "I think you'd better go."

"Why? Because I'm getting near the truth?"

"Yes! No! I mean—oh, Miles, stop badgering me!" She looked at him wearily. "Can't you see I don't want to talk about it?"

"And can't you see that you must?" he countered fiercely. "And there is no one else, is there? Except Robin, and somehow I doubt you'd burden him with your troubles."

Lani closed her eyes for a moment and then opened them again. "What do you want me to tell you?" she asked. "You know what happened. Jake and I had a row. I left. End of story."

"Is it?" Miles expelled his breath impatiently. "Are you going to tell me you don't love him anymore? That there's hope for me yet?"

Lani moved her head from side to side. "I don't want to talk about my feelings."

"Why not? If they're so clean-cut?"

"They're not." Lani uttered a little groan and sank down into the rocking chair again. "All right, all right. My feelings for Jake haven't changed, but... well, I found out my mother had been writing to him."

"Clare?"

"Yes." Lani lay back tiredly. "Don't ask me why, because I don't know. I only know Jake was prepared to take her word before mine, and—and I lost my temper and said some things I shouldn't have."

Miles frowned. "And you walked out?"

"He asked me to leave."

"He *asked* you to?"

"All right. He threw me out!" Lani was ironic. "I didn't even stop to collect my belongings. He sent them on later."

"And that was the last you heard from him?"

"Apart from the piece of music he sent me, yes."

Miles blinked. "A piece of music! What piece of music?"

"Oh—" Lani was weary. "It was a piece he had written. I—I had admired it. I thought he might get it published. He didn't think it was any good."

"And he sent it to you? Why?"

"I don't know. Perhaps because he thought I wasn't any good either."

"Didn't you ask him?"

"No." Lani pressed her lips together. "He didn't expect me to. He sent no letter or anything. Just the piece of manuscript, in an envelope, on its own."

Miles shook his head. "How strange!"

"Yes." Lani nodded. She had thought so too when she'd opened it, until time and lack of confidence had convinced her he did not expect any response.

"So. . .where is it?"

Lani looked up at him. "Why?"

"I'd like to see it."

Lani made a sound of impatience. "Why?"

"Because I would. You say it's good. I have a friend in the business who might know."

"It's not classical music."

"My friend doesn't deal in classical music."

Lani hesitated. "I'm not sure I should."

"Why not? He sent it to you. It's yours. And you thought it was good enough to be published."

"I know I did, but—"

"But what?"

"Well, I may be no judge."

Miles gave her an old-fashioned look. "What's the matter? Does it have sentimental value?"

Lani sighed. "What if it does?" She considered a moment and then got to her feet. "Just a minute."

The scored sheet of manuscript looked quite ordinary when she gave it to Miles, but he handled it with unexpected reverence. "Concerto," he said, nodding toward the word Jake had scribbled in the top left corner of the page. "What does that mean? You said it wasn't classical."

"It's not." Lani shrugged, looking over his shoulder. "Perhaps that was his title for it."

"Hmm." Miles looked reflective. "Well, it might just prove suitable, after all, Concerto! It has a certain appeal."

Lani drew back. "You won't lose it, will you?"

"No." Miles rolled the sheet into a tube and tapped it significantly. "I'll photocopy this at the office and let you have it back. I'll give Danny the copy."

"Danny?"

"This chap I know in the music business. Leave it

with me, Lani. Even if nothing comes of it, you can't lose anything, can you?"

Two DAYS LATER, Lani was in the makeshift studio she had designed for herself, arranging her books and artistic equipment, when her doorbell rang. It was noon, and she had been just about to make herself a cup of coffee and a sandwich, she hoped her visitor, whoever it was, wouldn't stay too long. She planned to make a real effort to get down to work this afternoon, and a prolonged interruption would disrupt her schedule.

The apartment was quite spacious, one of the reasons why Lani had taken it in the first place, and the doorbell rang again as she was crossing the living room. Beyond the tall bay windows, Kilburn Avenue was bathed in the warmth of an unusually mild September, but already the leaves were turning yellow on the trees, and here and there a bare branch bore witness to the storms that had lashed the south coast for the past week.

"Mother!"

Lani's instinctive reaction to the elegantly-clad woman waiting outside was more revealing than she knew. Clare regarded her impatiently before stepping across the threshold. "I won't wait for you to invite me in, darling," she said, ignoring her daughter's shocked face. "So this is your little hideaway. How quaint!"

Lani gathered her senses, and rather than expose their conversation to careless ears, she closed the door. "What do you want, mother?" she asked, supporting herself against the panels. "Did father send you here? He had no right to give you my address."

"Oh, don't be silly, darling." Clare sauntered casually across the dark blue carpet, surveying her surroundings with negligent interest. "We are related, albeit unwillingly. And I wanted to see you. It's not so unusual. I care about you."

"Don't let's pretend, mother." Lani pushed herself away from the door, running the palms of her hands down the seams of her pants. In a paint-daubed smock and worn jeans, she was painfully aware of how her appearance compared with Clare's sophisticated elegance, and even the attractive furnishings of the living room suffered beneath her mother's critical appraisal. "Why have you come here? We have nothing to say to one another."

"I disagree." Clare dropped the soft jacket she was carrying onto the couch and looked around. "May I sit down?"

Lani hesitated, but she knew she couldn't really refuse, and with a resigned gesture, she nodded. "If you must. I was just about to have some coffee. Do you want some?"

"Oh, nothing for me, darling." Clare shuddered, as if the thought of food or drink was anathema to her. "But you have something by all means. You look as if you need it. You're so thin!"

Lani came around the couch, but she didn't sit beside her mother. Instead she perched on the arm, regarding her tensely, waiting with a sense of apprehension for Clare to go on.

"Your father tells me you've been living here for

almost two months," she remarked at last, and Lani inclined her head. "Since you came back from Cornwall, wasn't it?" Clare added. "Why didn't you go home?"

"I didn't want to live at home," replied Lani stiffly. "I thought it was time I had my own place. I realize this may not seem very fashionable to you, but I like it."

"Well, it's hardly the Ritz, is it, darling?" Clare's lips curled. "But I suppose it does have a bohemian charm, if you like that kind of thing."

"I do."

"Good." Clare crossed her silk-clad legs and relaxed against the cushions. "I'm glad you're happy." She paused. "I knew that infatuation you had for Jake wouldn't last."

"Did you?" Lani swallowed the constriction in her throat. "And I suppose you had nothing to do with that, either."

"Me!" Clare looked dismayed. "I'm sure you can't blame me for the mess you've made of your life. Be thankful you've come out of it unscathed. It could have proved awkward."

"Awkward?"

"Well, yes." Clare spread her hands. "I mean, what you did was foolhardy, wasn't it? Forcing yourself on him. Oh, yes—" this as Lani's jaw sagged "—he told me what happened. How you insisted on staying, even though you knew there was no future in it. I did warn you, Lani. Jake's not the marrying kind. And what would you have done if you'd become pregnant?"

Lani opened her mouth to contradict her, and then

closed it again. Clare would learn nothing from her, she told herself fiercely. If Jake chose to tell her how they had lived for the three months she was at the Sea House, that was his affair. Evidently he hadn't done so yet, or Clare would not be here, probing her daughter's feelings.

"Is that all?" she asked now, and Clare gave an impatient gesture.

"No, it's not all," she declared. "I wanted you to be the first to know that I've offered to take Jake under my wing again. His hands have recovered dexterity beyond anyone's belief, and although it may be months—years—before he can play professionally again, I firmly believe that can happen. There's an osteopath in Switzerland who has had considerable success in the treatment of athletes. You may remember the long jumper who broke his leg, Martin Adler? Well, Dr. Heinrich has treated him, and now they're saying he'll be joining the next Olympic team. He's very clever. Heinrich, I mean. And of course Jake will have plenty of time for practice. I shall take a house there, so he doesn't have to live in a hotel, and of course I shall join him whenever my commitments permit me."

Lani had sat silent throughout her mother's speech, her taut features registering little emotion, and now Clare's mouth took on a petulant slant. "Well?" she exclaimed. "Don't you have anything to say? I thought you might have found it in your heart to be grateful to me. After all, I am restoring what was taken away."

"What you took away, mother." Lani's face was

naturally pale, so that the blood draining out of her cheeks was hardly noticeable, and Clare was unaware of the strain it had been for Lani to speak at all.

"Oh, really!" she exclaimed irritably. "What happened... happened. It was an accident, an appalling accident. I drove recklessly, I've admitted it. But I was almost out of my mind with grief—"

"With jealousy," insisted Lani doggedly. "You knew Jake and I had been together. You hated that!"

"All right." Clare gave up trying to humor her. "All right, I was jealous. Why not? Jake belonged to me, not you."

"People don't *belong* to anybody, mother!"

"That's a naive interpretation. Jake and I were lovers."

"No!"

"Of course we were." Clare regarded her pityingly. "Did he tell you we weren't? Well, I might have expected it. You were always such a prudish creature, weren't you?"

Lani rose to her feet and pointed toward the door with a shaking finger. "I want you to leave, mother. Now. This minute. I don't have to listen to your lies in my own home."

"Lies?" Clare arched her painted brows. "If you really believed I was lying, you wouldn't be throwing me out."

Lani's hand fell to her side. "You don't care about anyone but yourself, do you?"

"Nonsense. I care about lots of things."

"Do you care about Jake?"

"Of course I do. Or I shouldn't be going to so much expense for him, should I?"

"I don't know." Lani's head was throbbing, and she knew she would get no work done today. Then, despising herself for the question, she asked, "Just tell me what you wrote to Jake in that letter. What lies did you tell him about me?"

"What a fetish you have about lies, Lani. I didn't tell Jake any lies. I simply told him the truth, that's all. Something you had evidently omitted to do."

"The truth?" Lani looked blank. "What truth?"

"About your father, of course. Oh, it took me some time to think of it, but eventually I guessed you had been protecting Roger. It's like you."

"Protecting him? How?"

"By not telling Jake it was Roger who drove me to take such desperate measures."

Lani stared at her. "But I assumed Jake knew. I was sure you had told him."

"I'm afraid not." Gathering her jacket and handbag, Clare rose smoothly to her feet to face her daughter. "I believe it came as quite a shock to him— Jake, I mean—particularly when I explained you had felt—what shall I say—responsible for what happened."

Lani's lips trembled, and she pressed them together to hide her emotion before articulating tightly, "You mean you let Jake think I was hiding it from him?"

"Well, weren't you?"

"No!"

"Oh, well...." Clare shrugged and walked delicately to the door. "It doesn't matter now, does it? In the circumstances, it's probably the best thing that could have happened. Your...affair wasn't getting anywhere, was it? You did the right thing by walking out. You've saved yourself a lot of heartache."

Lani shook her head. "Why did you involve me in your life? Why didn't you just forget I ever existed?"

"Oh!" Clare opened the door and then turned to look at her. "That was Elwyn's idea, not mine. You know how he sentimentalizes family relationships. He thought it would be good publicity for us to be seen together."

Lani caught her breath. "And that was all it was?"

"What else? I was never the maternal type. But of course, you know that, don't you, darling?"

CHAPTER TWENTY

BY THE TIME MILES SHOWED UP some days later, Lani had managed to push her mother's intrusion into her life to the back of her mind. She hadn't forgotten it, she hadn't even tried to do so. But she had succeeded in convincing herself nothing good could come from brooding over it, and she had herself in control again.

Nevertheless, the memory of the things Clare had said had given her some sleepless nights, and the dark circles around her eyes only accentuated her pallor. She was taut and brittle, like a finely drawn piece of glass, although she told herself she would feel better once she started working again, the urge to create was proving elusive.

Miles's first reaction was one of concern for her appearance. "What the hell have you been doing with yourself?" was his way of putting it, and Lani quickly turned away to ask why he had come.

"Do I have to have a reason?" he demanded, closing the door behind him. "If you refuse to answer your telephone, what else am I to do?"

Lani flushed. "Was that you who rang? I was afraid it might be mother. She came here a few days ago, and I'd rather not speak to her again."

"Like that, was it?" Miles grimaced. "Why doesn't

she leave you alone? Can't she see she's only wasting her time?"

Lani didn't want to talk about Clare, and subsiding onto the couch, she looked up at him with determined brightness. "Well," she said, "I can't believe you've nothing better to do than visit me in the middle of the afternoon. What's the matter? Don't tell me the publishers are screaming for another manuscript!"

"Well, I've no doubt they would, if they thought there was one in the offing," remarked Miles, seating himself on the chair opposite and pulling a roll of paper out of his pocket. "But actually, this is why I came." He handed the roll of paper to her. "To return this manuscript."

"Oh," Lani was relieved. "The music! What happened? Did Danny—that was his name, wasn't it—did he like it?"

Miles lay back in his chair and crossed one ankle over his knee. "Yes," he said smugly. "Yes, as a matter of fact he liked it very much. As a matter of fact he wants to know if Pendragon has written anything else."

Lani stiffened. "Why are you asking me?"

"Well, it did cross my mind that you might know."

Lani shook her head. "You'll have to ask him," she said tautly. "It's nothing to do with me."

"All right." Miles lifted an appeasing hand. "I told Danny I didn't think you'd want to get involved. Not with anything else, anyway."

"What do you mean?"

"That," said Miles, pointing at the paper in her

hand. "Danny thinks he might know a band who'd record it."

"A band!" Lani stared at him. "You mean—electric organs, guitars, that sort of thing?"

"You've got it. Of course, it won't sound exactly like it did when Pendragon played it, but Danny thinks we could have a winner."

Lani shook her head. "I can't believe it. It's not that easy."

"Lani, in all things, luck plays the predominant part. Don't let anyone tell you otherwise. And," he shrugged, "let's face it, it isn't always what you know, but *who*! I'm lucky. Danny Apollo is a friend of mine. This little concerto went straight to the man!"

Lani blinked. "Danny Apollo!" Even she had heard of Apollo Records.

"I knew you'd be pleased." Miles uncrossed his legs and leaned toward her, his elbows resting on his knees. "So what do you say? Are you going to give him the go-ahead?"

"Me?" Lani shrank back in alarm. "Miles, this is nothing to do with me. It's. . . it's Jake's composition, not mine."

"But he sent it to you."

"I know."

"You mean you're going to refuse?"

Lani pressed the piece of manuscript to her chest. "I—I can't make that decision."

Miles gave an impatient snort. "All right. Then we'll just have to contact Pendragon himself, won't we? As you say, it is his composition. I'm sure he won't be as reluctant as you are." He shook his head incredulously. "Do you have any idea how much this could gross? If it makes the top ten—"

"Don't, Miles." Lani shuddered convulsively. "I don't think you understand. I—Clare—Clare came to tell me that—that Jake is going to work with her again. She's found a specialist in Switzerland, someone who is willing to work with Jake and help him recover his piano-playing abilities. In a matter of months, maybe a year or so, he's hoping to return to the concert platform. I don't think he'll be interested in writing...this kind of music, do you?"

Miles pressed his hands down on his knees and got to his feet. "You mean, even after what happened—"

"Yes, yes." Lani was sick of thinking about it. "So you see—"

"He must be crazy!"

"Or ambitious," said Lani quietly. "Now, please, can we talk about something else?"

KILBURN HIGH STREET WAS BUSY on Saturday afternoon, and Lani usually managed to avoid it. But for the past few weeks she had been finding it very hard to coordinate her thoughts with her actions, and at three o'clock that afternoon, she had realized she hadn't a scrap of food in the apartment. With the prospect of the weekend ahead, she knew she had to make some kind of effort, particularly as Robin and Sarah had promised to call on Sunday.

In consequence, she had pulled on a shabby sleeveless waistcoat over her shirt and jeans, and securing her hair with a leather thong, she had hurried down to the supermarket. She seldom used the car for these expeditions. It was so much easier to walk and avoid the frustration of searching for somewhere to park, and unless she had a lot to carry, she generally enjoyed the exercise.

Walking back along Kilburn Avenue, she reflected that she was not particularly looking forward to Robin's and Sarah's visit the following day. Sarah's eyes were far too sharp, and lately she spent much of the time they were together scolding Lani for not looking after herself better. Lani knew her admonishments were well meant, but the connotations were still too painful. She was dreading the possibility that her cousin and his wife might have learned of Clare's intentions from the media. Lani herself had avoided reading newspapers since Clare's visit. She did not want to read about her mother's new crusade.

She was walking along with her head down, and had almost reached her gate before she saw the car parked at the curb outside. It was a dark green car, sleek and low slung, and with quickening heartbeats, she saw the man propped against it.

Her instinctive reaction was to turn and run, but that was quickly stifled. She had nothing to fear from him, after all, she thought, her lips tightening indignantly. He had no right to come here. No right at all. And she would swiftly tell him so.

"Lani."

His greeting was accompanied by his pushing himself up and away from the car, and she couldn't help observing how much more easily he moved now. Without any previous knowledge, she would never have guessed that six months ago he had been incapable of dragging himself around without the aid of crutches, when now he looked so fit and well. Unlike herself, she reflected bitterly, comparing her hollow-eyed frailty to his muscled strength. In narrow-fitting black cords and a black silk shirt, he looked as attractive as he had the first time she saw him, and only the lines etched beside his mouth and nose revealed that perhaps he still found walking painful.

"Jake." Her use of his name was clipped and off-hand. "What are you doing here?"

Jake's mouth compressed. "Oh, I think you'll be able to work that out for yourself," he remarked dryly. "This is where you live, isn't it?" He looked up at the windows of the house. "Which floor do you occupy?"

"The first," Lani replied stiffly. "The house is divided into eight apartments. Two in the basement, two on the ground floor, two on the first floor, and—"

"I get the picture." Jake moved toward the gate. "Shall we go in?"

"No." Lani stood her ground, even though her bag was heavy and her arm was aching. "I don't know why you've come here, Jake, but I'd rather you didn't come in. We have nothing left to say to one another, and quite honestly—"

"Lani!" He expelled his breath heavily. "You don't really think I'm going to take that from you, do you? Now, you came to my house and I let you in. Don't you think you owe me the same privilege?"

"That was different." Lani's lips quivered. "I collapsed on your doorstep. You had no choice."

"And would you like me to do that?" Jake's tawny

eyes challenged hers. "I could quite easily. Driving up to London wasn't as easy as I thought it would be, and quite honestly, my leg is aching pretty badly."

"Jake!" Lani cast a helpless look about her and then turned to him again. "Jake, why are you doing this? Why do you want to see me? I—Clare's already told me what you're going to do. If you think explanations are necessary, forget it. It—it's over. I . . . I'm glad it's turned out so well for you. . . ."

"Can we go inside?" Jake spoke doggedly, but there was weariness in his tone now, and Lani gazed at him despairingly.

"Oh, all right," she conceded, despising herself for giving in to him, and pulling her keys out of her pocket, she preceded him up the path to the front door of the house.

Inside, the cloisterlike gloom of the hall enveloped them, and reminded of other occasions, Lani refused his offer to carry her bag and ran hurriedly up the stairs. By the time he reached the first floor, she had unlocked her door, and she hastened across the living room to the kitchen to deposit her shopping bag.

Although she tried to compose herself, she was still in a state of some agitation when she returned to the living room, and it didn't help to find Jake had made himself at home in her absence. He was now comfortably ensconced on her couch, and she hovered nervously in the doorway unsure whether or not to offer him refreshment.

"Would you like a drink?" she asked at last, glancing awkwardly over her shoulder. "I only have sherry, I'm afraid, or coffee."

"I don't want anything," replied Jake quietly. "Come and sit down." He patted the couch beside him. "I want to talk to you."

Lani moistened her dry lips. "Look, Jake—"

"I said come and sit down," he repeated with solemn insistence. "You look as if you need it. Now, I realize I may be responsible for the way you look, but I'm trying to make amends—"

"*What?*" Lani gazed at him in horror. "What did you say? That...that you may be responsible for the way I look?" She caught her breath. "Who told you that? My mother?" She shook her head. "My God! You've got a bloody nerve—"

"Cool it, Lani!" Reluctantly, Jake got to his feet again and started toward her. "Look, I'm doing this badly—"

"Yes, you are!" Lani was trembling with a mixture of anger and despair—anger, that he should think he could come here and appease her with a few words of apology, and despair for the fleeting, but unquenchable, hope she had had that perhaps Clare had been lying after all. "I think you'd better go. Your...your mistress has explained the situation very satisfactorily, and—"

"She's *not* my mistress!" Overcoming without difficulty Lani's frantic efforts to keep him at bay, Jake lunged toward her, grasping her arms and jerking her toward him. "For Christ's sake, Lani, we don't have to go through all that again, do we?" One hand encircled her throat, forcing her face up to his. "I wanted to do this properly, I wanted to tell you how it really is before we got this far, but you leave me no choice!" and taking advantage of her openmouthed frustration, he lowered his head to hers.

Fighting him desperately, Lani's teeth closed on his lips until she could taste his blood in her mouth, but still he would not let her go. With grim persistence, his mouth possessed and ravaged hers, his tongue making its own exploration, until weakness and her inherent need of him turned panic into passion. Her nails, which had been raking his shoulders through the fine silk of his shirt, now dug helplessly into his taut flesh, and her legs crumpled as she yielded against him.

As if sensing her submission, his lips softened, and now his probing tongue was frankly sensuous. His hands slid over her shoulders to her waist, sliding beneath the loose waistcoat and separating her shirt from her pants so that his hands could spread against the quivering skin of her spine. With infinite gentleness, his mouth moved against hers, depositing kisses on the upper lip and the lower and at each corner, before returning to possess its parted sweetness. With unquestionable expertise, he was seducing her to a state of total surrender, and Lani's senses stirred in latent desperation.

"You—you bastard!" she moaned, dragging her mouth from his and turning her head away. But Jake was not prepared to let her escape so easily.

"Why am I a bastard?" he demanded, gripping her nape with one hand and controlling her flailing fists with the other. "Wasn't it you who scorned *me* for believing Clare's lies? Yet you seem incredibly eager to believe her now!"

"Stop trying to change the subject!" she cried, twisting desperately against him. "What do you want from me, Jake? What kind of a man are you? You don't want me. You sent me away. Why have you come back now when you must know that anything between us is finished?"

"You don't believe that, any more than I do," he retorted harshly. "If you'd only give me a chance to explain—"

"Explain?" she interrupted him tremulously. "Explain what? Why you've decided to accept Clare's offer? Why you're going to go and live in Switzerland—"

"I am not going to live in Switzerland!" he grated, but Lani was not listening to him.

"What's the matter, Jake? Is your conscience pricking you? Well, don't let it. I should have realized all along I was only second best!"

Her freedom came as a complete surprise to her, and she swayed unsteadily when he suddenly gave up the struggle to let her go. One minute she was fighting to keep him away from her and the next he had turned his back on her and was walking wearily toward the couch. She noticed almost inconsequently that he favored one leg more than the other, and when he reached the cushioned seat, he lowered himself onto it with a weariness that was almost her undoing.

"What are you doing?" she exclaimed, aware that unless she sustained the momentum of her anger, she was in real danger of giving in to him yet again. "You can't stay here. I . . . I have work to do. Oh, Jake, why are you tormenting me like this? What do you want me to say? What do you want me to do?"

Jake looked up at her steadily. "Marry me," he said, without emphasis, and she clutched the back of the rocking chair for its support.

"Wh—what did you say?" she echoed faintly, unable to believe what she had heard, and Jake repeated his startling suggestion.

"Marry me," he said, still sitting on the edge of the couch, his legs parted, his hands hanging loosely between, almost as if they were discussing the weather, and Lani moved her head incredulously from side to side.

"It—it's cruel to tease people," she got out at last. "I think you'd better go. If this is some clever scheme you've dreamed up with my mother . . . ."

"For God's sake, forget about your mother!" snarled Jake, showing some emotion at last. "You asked me what I wanted of you, and I've told you. Now, I'd advise you to consider your answer carefully because, goddammit, I may never have the nerve to ask you again!"

"The nerve?" Lani found she couldn't sustain his stare. "Jake, please—"

"Oh, *Lani*!" He pushed himself to his feet again. "Okay, I'll say it once more: I want to marry you. There, is that convincing enough for you? If not, I don't know how else I can say it. I've tried to show you how I feel, but you won't let me touch you!"

Lani gulped. "But I don't understand. What about Clare?"

"What about Clare?" he demanded flatly.

"But—you know. She told me she's going to help

you return to your career. She told me there's some doctor in Switzerland who can help you. Isn't that true?"

"That there's a doctor in Switzerland who can possibly help me? Maybe." Jake shrugged, but as Lani's mouth drew down he hastened on. "But if you'd been listening to me, you'd know that I have no intention of going to Switzerland."

Lani quivered. "But Clare said. . . ."

"I can imagine," he put in forcefully. "I'm sure she said a lot of things, most of which were pure fabrication."

Lani wouldn't let herself believe this. "You mean. . . she hasn't been to see you?"

"Oh, yes." Jake inclined his head. "Oh, yes, she came to see me. At my invitation, I might add."

"At your invitation?" Lani looked troubled.

"Yes." Jake sighed. "Do you want to hear this? Or am I merely wasting my time and yours?"

Lani lifted her shoulders uncertainly. "I . . . want to hear."

"Okay." Jake nodded to the couch behind him. "Do you want to sit down?"

"There?"

"Why not?" His lips twisted. "Or do you still not trust me?"

Lani hesitated. "No, I—oh, all right. Why not?" She circled the rocking chair and came to take a seat on the couch, being sure to put some distance between where she was sitting and where he was standing. However, Jake moved along the couch before sitting down, and when he did so, she could not prevent her thigh from brushing his.

"All right?" he said, turning to look at her, and she drew back against the flowered upholstery, overwhelmingly conscious of the effect he was having on her.

"All right," she agreed breathily, and half turning toward her, he began.

"You remember the letter you saw?" he asked, and Lani wondered if she would ever forget it. "Well, I guess Clare has told you what was in it." Lani nodded, and he continued: "So try to imagine how I felt reading it. It wasn't easy being told that the only reason you'd come to Cornwall was that your mother had begged you to do it."

"What?" Lani was aghast, and Jake sighed.

"You said you knew what was in the letter," he reminded her quietly, but Lani only went on shaking her head.

"You don't understand," she exclaimed. "Clare didn't tell me that. She...she said you were mad because she'd confessed that my father had driven her to...to do what she did."

"Your father?"

"Yes. Oh...." Lani made a helpless gesture. "You might as well know, my father went to see my mother that night, after she arrived back from Milan. He... he told her we were together. He was trying to persuade her that she was wasting her time with you."

Jake frowned. "You're talking about the night we were injured?"

"Yes." Lani nodded.

"But I know that." Jake looked perplexed. "I— Clare told me about your father a couple of days after the accident, when she forced her way into my room at the hospital. I was in no state to stop her, and the staff were taken in by her tears and her undoubted remorse. I'm sure she regretted what she'd done the minute it was over, but it was too late then."

Lani blinked. "Then . . . then what . . . ?"

"I'm trying to tell you," he stated, unable to resist the temptation to finger an errant strand of hair bobbing by her ear. "Lani, did you or did you not come down to Cornwall because Clare asked you to?"

"I did not!" Lani was vehement. "As a matter of fact, she told me not to go. She said I was wasting my time."

"That figures." Jake's mouth took on a sensual slant. "So why did you come?"

"You know why." Lani looked away from him. "Jake, if this is—"

"Stop jumping to conclusions," he stopped her huskily, and the fingers that had previously been toying with her hair now lightly brushed her cheek. "Let me tell you how it was, hmm?"

Lani licked her lips. "If you must."

"Oh, I must," he told her gently. "Even though what I really want to do is something much more satisfying."

"Jake!"

She turned to look at him then, half in trembling, half in protest, and unable to prevent himself, he ran his fingers over her mouth, stroking her lips apart and probing the moistness within.

"Okay," he said, when at last she summoned the courage to push his fingers away. "Well, you know how it was when you first came to the Sea House. I wanted you, you know that, but it didn't seem fair to put that upon you. I mean—I was little more than an invalid, and I was pretty sure, even then, that you were motivated by pity—"

"No!"

Lani could not let him say that, and his hand closed possessively over her knee as he acknowledged her protest. "I think I know that now," he said huskily. "But right then I was feeling pretty sorry for myself, and I guess it was easier to believe that than take the responsibility for someone else's feelings."

"But you didn't throw me out," Lani murmured unwillingly, and he gave her a wry smile.

"How could I? I was sick with jealousy every time you came up to London to see that chap, Rossiter."

"So you tried to drive me away?"

"Well. . . ." He paused. "I guess I thought if you got sick of me I could always console myself with the thought that you didn't really care about me after all."

Lani shook her head. "I can't take this in. . . ."

"Why not? Don't you believe me? Can you think of any other reason why I'd let you stay there? Particularly after you let my grandmother interfere?"

Lani shook her head. "But the physiotherapy has helped you!"

"I know that now." Jake sighed. "Honey, try to put yourself in my position, will you? There was I, a physical wreck with no foreseeable chance of rehabilitation, and there was this beautiful girl I was crazy about, throwing her future away on a cripple!"

He groaned. "I was pigheaded, I know that, but right after the crash, I didn't believe in miracles anymore."

"Oh, Jake!"

"It's true." He looked rueful. "Look, when your mother found me in that nightclub in California, I started to believe there were such things as fairy godmothers, after all. But we all know how that turned out, and I guess I wasn't in the market for more self-destruction."

"I thought you blamed me. . . I thought you hated me."

"Hated you?" Jake raised his eyes heavenward for a moment. "Oh, love, you have no idea how hard it was for me to keep away from you."

Lani shivered. "And the letter?"

"Ah, yes. The letter." Jake grimaced. "That was perfect timing on Clare's part, had she but known it."

"It was?"

"Yes." Jake sighed. "I'd almost decided to confide my feelings to you—hell, if Judith hadn't arrived when she did, I'd have thrown caution to the winds and taken my chances. You'd already discovered I was playing around on the piano again. Given time, I was pretty sure I could improve that ability, and I desperately wanted to share that with you. But you know what happened. Clare's letter arrived, and I guess I was still too suspicious of anyone's motives to consider it reasonably. I just blew my top, like the fool I am, and you walked out."

"You ordered me to leave!" Lani protested, and Jake gave her a wry look.

"Not for the first time," he reminded her gently. "Why did you obey me then and not before?"

Lani uttered a husky laugh. "I suppose. . . I suppose because it was Clare who had written to you," she confessed, and he nodded. "But why did you ask her to come and see you?"

"Because I knew I had to convince her once and for all that our association was over."

"But she came to see me. . . ."

"Afterward?" Jake nodded. "I guessed she would. She's a vindictive lady, your mother. Having failed with me, I suppose she had to make one last attempt with you."

"But. . . ." Lani hesitated. "Did you tell her I stayed in Cornwall against your will?"

"Yes." Jake frowned. "As I recall it, she made this thing about persuading you to come and look after me, and I explained that if that was the only reason you had come, you'd been pretty slow in accepting my dismissal."

"Oh!" Lani breathed more easily. "And then?"

"She left." Jake sighed. "Oh, there were threats and recriminations, but we both knew they had no substance. Our relationship was never an emotional one. Whatever she may have told you."

"I believe it." And Lani knew she did. "But why did you wait so long?"

"To come here?" Jake's fingers caressed her thigh with disturbing insistence. "Well, I had to prove something to myself, you see. I sent you that piece of music so you might begin to understand, but when you didn't reply. . . ."

"Did you expect me to?"

"I hoped," he conceded honestly. "But anyway, perhaps it was as well you didn't. That way, I wasn't diverted. I was obliged to go ahead with an idea you had given me."

"Me?"

"Yes, you." He regarded her possessively. "The music? Remember?"

Lani stared at him. "You mean—you sent it to a publisher?"

"Well, not the piece I sent you," he told her softly. "But others, yes."

Lani gasped. "And?"

"It helps to have friends in the business," he admitted modestly.

Lani shook her head. "Not—Danny Apollo!"

"No. Cliff Collins." Jake paused. "I met him while I was in the States. He came to the club one night, just after I'd met Clare, and heard me playing something of my own. He said if ever I...well, if ever I wanted to move into that side of the business, I should contact him." He shrugged. "But you know how it is. People say things. And I guess I didn't really hold out much hope, but—" He gave her a rueful smile. "He liked the two songs I sent him, and what do you know? He's going to record one of them himself."

"Oh, Jake!" Lani caught her breath. Cliff Collins was one of the most popular New Wave singers in America.

"I know. Good, isn't it?" he conceded, and she saw the faint surge of color that darkened his cheeks.

"So...what do you say? Can you forgive me for...
well, for everything?"

"Oh, Jake, you've always known I loved you!"

"*Loved?*" His features sobered. "Past tense?"

"Past tense, present tense, future tense," said Lani
with a little shiver, and unable to resist the caressing
touch of his fingers any longer, she looped her arm
around his neck and drew him toward her. "Kiss me,
Jake," she breathed. "Kiss me, please! I promise I
won't stop you this time...."

"So THIS IS YOUR BEDROOM," murmured Jake, some
time later, turning onto his back to survey the high
molded ceiling. "Very nice." He turned his head on
the pillow to look at her. "You'll forgive my earlier
negligence, I'm sure. But a little while ago, I was in
no fit state to admire the decor—only its occupant."

Lani gave a tremulous smile, still scarcely able to
believe this was happening, and as if sensing her
bemusement, Jake rolled onto his side again and drew
her close to him.

"Good, hmm?" he murmured, pushing back the
damp strands of hair from her temple. "But so pale!
We must do something about that. How does Tahiti
sound to you? I thought we might spend part of our
honeymoon there. And then we've an invitation to
visit Cliff in California, if the idea appeals to you."

"Oh, Jake!" Lani turned her lips against his smooth
brown shoulder, her tongue loving the taste of his
heated skin. "Anywhere with you, I don't mind. So
long as we're together."

"My sentiments exactly," he agreed, nuzzling her

throat with his lips. "But relieve my jealousy, will you? Who is Danny Apollo?"

Lani's lips parted. "You've heard of Apollo Records, haven't you?"

"That Apollo?"

"Hmm."

Jake frowned. "So how do you know him?"

"Don't scowl like that." Lani's eyes danced. "Miles talked to me about him. He's a friend of his. He took that piece of music you sent me to show him." She paused. "He wanted to produce it."

"And?"

Lani's hand slipped from his chest down over the taut curve of his hip. "I wouldn't let him."

Jake shuddered at the intimacy of her caress, but he murmured, "Why not?" as he moved to control her, and she shrugged.

"It's yours, not mine. I said Miles would have to speak to you."

"I gave it to you," replied Jake softly, propping himself up on one elbow so he could look down at her. "I thought its title might have persuaded you to come back."

"Its title?" Lani's tongue circled her lips. "Concerto?"

"A piece of music in three movements," he murmured, bending his head to caress her breasts with his lips. "We had shared the first two. I wanted us to share the third."

"Oh, Jake!" She shook her head helplessly, and when she arched toward him, the silken strands brushed his mouth. "Love me," she breathed, her movements a sinuous invitation Jake had no power to resist. . . .

It was six months before they returned to England, months when Lani learned what it was to be both happy and content. By then Jake's child was growing inside her, and she had never looked more beautiful. The angular lines had all been erased by a lissome covering of flesh, and Jake's love had given her a self-confidence that even her writing had never produced.

The dinner party they gave at Lani's apartment soon after their return was by way of a belated celebration of their wedding—a wedding that had taken place only days after Jake's arrival at the apartment that memorable Saturday afternoon six months before. The only guests then had been Robin, Sarah and Lani's father, but the dinner party now was rather more elaborate. Jake's grandmother was invited, and Miles, and to everyone's surprise, Clare and Elwyn Hughes arrived soon after they had all sat down to eat.

"It wouldn't be Clare if she didn't make an entrance," murmured Jake to his wife, squeezing her shoulder as he went to greet the new arrivals, and watching her husband with her mother, Lani had to admit no one would ever have guessed the acrimony with which their marriage had been received.

But it was later, after their guests had departed, that Lani was most content, curled up on Jake's knee on the rocking chair, his lips gently nibbling her ear.

"I think it all went very well, don't you?" she murmured, drawing back to look at him, and Jake gave a lazy nod.

"Very well," he agreed, fingering a strand of her hair, which had grown even longer since their honeymoon in Tahiti. "We can settle down to married life now, knowing we've settled all our differences."

"Clare was very nice, wasn't she?" ventured Lani generously. "She really seemed pleased about the baby."

Jake grinned. "Do you think that's why she's accepted Elwyn's proposal after all these years? Because she's afraid that becoming a grandmother will explode the myth of her remaining eternally youthful?"

Lani buried her face in his neck. "That's cynical."

"But not unlikely, I daresay," remarked Jake wryly. "Anyway, at least your father seems to have accepted their separation at last."

"Yes. Poor daddy." For the first time since Jake was injured, Lani was learning to forgive her father for what he had done. "He says he's looking forward to becoming a grandparent. I think he wants to show us he really is sorry for what happened."

"Well, that's all in the past now," murmured Jake, parting the lapels of her smock dress and inhaling her fragrance. "Just so long as you don't regret anything, Mrs. Pendragon. That's all that matters to me."

"Regret anything?" Lani looked puzzled. "What could I regret?"

"This?" Jake watched her intently as his hand moved possessively over the swollen mound of her belly. "Was it selfish of me to allow this to happen?"

"It does take two," pointed out Lani mischievously, her eyes dancing. "Oh, Jake, don't be silly. I can think of nothing more satisfying than feeling your child kicking inside me—well," she amended, dimpling, "perhaps *one* thing!"

Jake's eyes darkened with emotion. "You know I adore you, don't you? Being married to you has only made it harder for me to accept you have a life of your own. But I don't want you to think I'm trying to stop you from writing or painting."

"Darling," Lani shook her head, "with one successful writer in the family, I can afford to be lazy. Besides, I'll have plenty of time for writing when I'm telling our children stories. Right now, I'm quite content to share your limelight. Believe me, I have everything I want."

"You're sure?"

The baby kicked beneath his hand, and Lani laughed softly. "Quite sure," she told him. "And your son seems to agree with me."

Harlequin Photo
~ Calendar ~

Turn Your Favorite Photo into a Calendar.

The Browns

Uniquely yours, this 10x17½" calendar features your favorite photograph, with any name you wish in attractive lettering at the bottom. A delightfully personal and practical idea!

Send us your favorite color print, black-and-white print, negative, or slide, any size (we'll return it), along with **3** proofs of purchase (coupon below) from a June or July release of Harlequin Romance, Harlequin Presents, Harlequin Superromance, Harlequin American Romance or Harlequin Temptation, plus $5.75 (includes shipping and handling).

Harlequin Photo Calendar Offer
(PROOF OF PURCHASE)